COUNSELOR

COUNSELOR
First Edition

Copyright © 2016 by Victor Giannini
All rights reserved

This book is a work of fiction. All characters and events portrayed in it
are fictitious, except where specific historical events are mentioned or
cited in context. Any resemblance to real people or events is
coincidental.

Printed in the United States of America

Published by Silverthought Press
www.silverthought.com

Front cover art: "Tim's Curse"
Copyright © 2015 by Victor Giannini
www.victorsinvisible.com

Back cover art: "Kitsune"
Illustration: "Tracy's Ghost"
Copyright © 2015 by Mia Berg
www.miaberg.com

ISBN: 978-0-9970103-0-5

COUNSELOR

— a novel by —
Victor Giannini

[silverthought]
PHILADELPHIA | NEW YORK

Dedicated To:

2005

TABLE OF CONTENTS

BOOK THREE: The Doom Generation

BOOK ONE:
The Barren Sea

The Curse

Every villain thinks they're a hero.

But last night I learned that some of us… can be both.

It was a brutal lesson, one that came at great cost. Being forced into another impossible choice. Knowing that every answer is the wrong one. Who do you abandon this time, and why? Someone will die, and no one will truly win… but at least you still get a vote! That's the worst part, really.

So I made a choice. Beneath the gaze of indifferent, undead gods, the laughter of gunfire and silent screams, the lament of waves and smoke. And here I stand, stranded, strange, and stupid.

Look, I'm sure you could have done better.

Let's not even argue that.

But we were forced to act and this time I did not run away. Yet when dawn broke across our island, I already knew that all of the madness, pain, and chaos hadn't gone away. Just changed. It's still smothering me like a living fog, blurring that already hazy line between good and evil, into more philosophical bullshit.

So if Barry is actually right… then I should just chill the hell out. Because human morality is ultimately subjective. Guilt and regret, those bastard twins born of good and evil's secret affair, have no true power. If that argument really shielded Barry against all I still endure, then… I'm happy for him. Still… Subjective morality makes me laugh. Not much else does these days.

I believe Barry gets the joke. But I don't. However, standing alone on this beach, waiting for my friend and accepting last night's war, I can assure you of this: No matter our intentions, the consequences of our actions are still quite real. I can't keep pretending that good intentions equal innocence. Nobody is innocent in the end. What's done can't be undone. The dead stay dead. This Curse taught me that much, if nothing else.

No matter how you cut it, I'm not a hero.

Don't mistake this for an excuse.

Just an explanation. It's a new day and I'm still nothing more than another member in a gang of orphans. Stubborn survivors, too broken to live, but too angry to die. And so we did awful things to awful people, but for good reasons. Barry says we're heroes for that... and good people, in general. But if he stood beside me now, staring down that angry setting sun, even he'd realize why I've lost faith in our confirmation bias.

So what if most of us survived? What does that even prove? That we really are the good guys? Fine, I'll take that, so far as the police are concerned. But on the cosmic scale, it's far more likely that we were just the better guys.

Suppose there is some solace in that...

And it's true that right here and now, I can finally embrace my past without shame. No more secrets, no more lies. Finally free to be grateful for my past, for those few years with Tracy defined solely by love without sorrow. So I'll take that.

But was it worth it?

Honestly, I'm not sure...

But trust me, that's still an improvement.

Still, I wish I was wrong. About everything. I wish there was a right answer, even if I got it wrong. I wish the Curse would just take me and spare those I love. I wish that I could turn to you and simply say:

Hello! My name is Timothy Dune. And I'm completely, totally, fucked.

But no, I'm not that lucky. The truth remains:

My name is Timothy Dune, and I am Cursed to poison everyone I love, to watch them die. And still completely, totally, fucked.

The Curse is no joke.

It was cast long ago.

When I was five.

That's right, just a little boy. Sure, I wasn't a saint, but what kid is? I'd assault slugs just because, and melt bugs. Throw worms at girls. Even steal candy, then lie when caught. My birth banished any hopes my parents had of peaceful sleep. But no devil is wicked enough to claim I was a monster. I've met those rare freaks... even fought beside one. They didn't seem to suffer beneath any curse, or anything at all. So why damn an innocent child before their life really started?

You could make a decent case against me if the Curse was judgment for last night. But no, that would make too much sense! This unearthly logic is all twisted, backwards. Unshackled by time, monstrously beyond human logic.

That's why I'm still terrified.

The Curse spits on the very concept of cause and effect. I'll admit I'm no expert on time, but nobody deserves damnation based on some future, vague crimes.

Right?

No, it can't work like that. My life must be a mistake. An aberration in an otherwise just and orderly universe. So if that's the case, then I can accept that life is cruel... but then it must also be fair. And in the name of fairness:

Hello! My name is Tim. I'm hung-over, angry, and Cursed. Why? Well, now I hereby confess my unforgivable crime:

Picture the Bahamas. You're barely five. A family vacation in paradise. Since your parents love you, they immediately send you away. They brought you kicking and screaming into the world, so they can be allowed to Jet Ski, make love under palm trees, and sip weird pink drinks all day (but Mom still saves those little neon umbrellas for you). So of course you're sent to a day camp for annoying kids.

You're in awe of the pearl white sand, playing in a roped off section of that perfectly blue, crystal ocean. The camp counselors watch wordless, like totems, as you swim with shrimp, manta and stingrays, all manner of strange fish and candy colored coral. They even give you a minnow to feed these docile, clownish fish.

It takes a few tries, but you grab hold. Gently bring it to shore. It's a baby ray, one you've watched in snorkeled awe. When it swam below, it was so sleek, so black, so beautiful. Now, in your hands, it's smooth, soft, somewhat limp.

You turn it over, only to find hidden slits and gasping, pulsing gills. Like a fat wet bug. The pale, milky underside of that thing... It seemed so elegant and pure before. Now its true face is revealed, wrinkly, white, alien.

You drop it in the sand.

You raise your foot. And...

Your fate is sealed.

Game over. Better luck next life, kid!

Believe me, I did not stomp on that ray. No harm came to it. I paused, and then a camp counselor slapped me down. As I lay stunned, he cradled that deceptive creature back to the sea. The sun cast his silhouette into a colossus, clad in board shorts and clamshells. I expected him to return and finish me off. But he merely pointed down as if his finger could kill. His gaze was paralyzing. Those eyes burning with disgust. Judging me. Such distain that I couldn't even speak. Time seemed to die. Nobody helped. Not even the minnow, useless in the sand beside me. The words couldn't break free. I'm innocent! I didn't do it, you saw! Everyone saw!

But when he finally broke the silence, time crawled forward once again. And although clearly furious, he spoke so soft, slow, and almost... sad?

My parents put me here. They trusted him to protect me. But this man no longer spoke for the resort. Now he spoke for some nameless, primal god. I couldn't fight back, just sat there, scared and stupid.

Thus, he invoked the Curse:

You have violated an innocent creature of the Mother Ocean. And so you are now cursed to keep violating. To poison all that you love, and watch them die. To forever swim the barren seas alone.

Asshole.

As I grew up, I didn't believe in his Curse, or his god, or any gods at all. Each year brought the random highs and lows that we all endure. Nobody dying from poison voodoo. Life was life. My family struggled but we survived. And I wasn't alone. I'd made good friends, better than I deserved. And even fell in love.

But then they started to die. At first it was normal, in all the worst ways. But then they kept dying. One by one, with less time to mourn before the next. It was all so fast... although it's always too fast.

Now I believe.

Fucking hell, do I believe.

This Curse has taken everything from me. Piece by piece. Just slow enough to make me watch. Even my past isn't safe. The memories I take to bed, the proof I wasn't always alone... they fade like photos left in the sun. Now all that's left is a deep longing for things that can never be mine. Things that can never want me back, like oceans, and ghosts.

The Idiot King

Twenty-two years after the Bahamas horror, I sit on this sunset shore, trying to accept all of last night. Covered in dirt, blood, and bile, exhausted beyond any natural form, thinking of ghosts, and gangsters, docks, sharks, drugs and scaled beasts. And my friends. The best of them are now either dead, insane, or destined for jail. Soon. And unless Julio pulls another miracle, I'll be joining them to waste my new life behind bars instead of in them.

Why? I did my best. Didn't give up, plus I kept my word... so why did everything go wrong yet again? And why do I feel an acidic disgust that isn't entirely uncomfortable? Even somewhat invigorating. Fueled by hate. Just like ... no, I'm not like *him*.

My head knows the path, the facts tracing a path from her death years ago right up to last night's losses. A few hours ago, when the final steel door slammed shut on the past and left me in this moment. But my heart refuses it. Stuck in a strange dissonance. Not quite denial, not quite hell. Well, at least that much hasn't changed. Everything else is up for grabs. I should be used to life changing in a breath, but I don't think that's possible without completely fading away. I can't become that. She'd hate me—that much I know for sure.

All I can do is stare at the ocean. It's a flat day. No waves. No breeze. Doesn't feel like summer. Nothing feels quite right. Maybe this is shock? I could make up a silent prayer to Konshu and just wait for Bernard, my roommate, to return with coffee. Be right back. He promised. Wants to know what he missed. Every fucked up detail... Of course he does. He deserves to know, after all. But he's taking his sweet damned time.

My eyes are raw, as red as the horizon, where the endless ocean meets the burning sun. They merely pretend to touch.

Almost made it to thirty...

But the sad part is, I'm actually happy.

For the first time since Tracy Cameron died, I'm actually happy.

That's what this strange feeling is! I flop back into the sand. Wiggle myself in, relishing the coarse grains in my hair. Love picking it out of the tangles. What a night... strange and terrible deeds, mutant mercy and justice. I ran with devils through the dead shark fields, challenged our island's cyclopean lord, faced the Savage Boss, and the final fox's trial. I'd even seen Hell, wounded its king, and still managed to limp away. Not bad, not too bad at all. But then I blew it when he...

God damn it, what's taking Bernard so long? We live fifty feet away!

He must like leaving me at the mercy of my own rabid thoughts. Wonder what he thinks of it all? I've known Burn for so long, as long as Barry and the rest. He's been my friend since the start. And played his role last night. And I guess last night started a long time ago, as all these things do. Cause and effect. The cause being my first mistake, fearing that stupid stingray. But my worst mistake... loving the wrong girl. Being stupid enough to think I'm special. That curses aren't real, monsters don't exist, and that I'm a good person.

It's getting darker now. I stare up at the sky and salute it with one finger. Despite an unfortunate life in an unfortunate world, Tracy kept me going. Kept me alive, naïve, and hopeful. Even strong. So I loved the wrong girl? Yeah, I guess. But the perfect girl? Absolutely.

Perfect girl, wrong world, stupid boy.

But she wanted me.

And of course I wanted her. Enough to risk... anything. Everything. Not just The Curse, but the standard human curse. To love for the sake of loss. And all that's happened since. But no arcane wizard could've predicted the chain of events caused by our affair. Maybe Tracy started it, but... she didn't see the end of it.

Was it really an overdose?

Or a suicide?

They never did decide. Just one more secret Tracy took to the grave. Certainly not our only secret, but... they'll never know what I lost. We lost. We. Must not forget that Barry lost his sister while I secretly mourned my lover. Yet I told myself it was worth it. It was. Every day, for three years since she died. Over one-thousand-one-hundred-and-three days of silent screaming out for her, telling myself she was worth it.

I still do.

Because now I can remember. That part of my diseased brain hasn't broken, it never could, but now I'm free of guilt and shame. Or could be...

Burn can take his time, because right now I can still see her, see us that first night. The memory is more vivid than last night. As clear as I the whitewash crashing at my feet, and those clouds all shot up by the sun. It's not quite evening yet, but the crescent moon does not care, rising above the sun like a scythe to slice across all those shining gods we call stars.

Seeing the sun beside the moon will always be weird.

Damn it, Bernard! Where are you? I really need that coffee and I don't want to be alone, I'm starting to lose it again. I might fall...

My eyes close. I am falling.

Promised I'd let her go.

But what if my memories do burn up? Use it or lose it, right? Just one more time. Fall back into the past. One last fix and then I'll let you go. Don't care if I sound like a junkie. It's just a dream but I still go back to another summer night, six years and another lifetime ago. Back to the fire pit hidden in the woods behind her... behind *their*, house.

Yes, the inside of my eyelids are a screen, and I can see her, can smell wood burn and taste salt and sweat. More than a memory. Madness? I can't afford to care. I'm already there. The beach is gone, Burn is gone, the coffee and the pain, all gone. Can almost hear her now. Hear us having *that* talk, word for word. Hear the insects spying, and her breath, confident and calm, but still afraid.

They'll never know how crazy it really was. When she broke me, freed me, then pieced us both back together. Before it all came crashing down, and she left me drowning in blood, betrayal, and madness.

No.

I sit up and scan the empty beach. Still no sign of him. Must stay awake. Must stay here. I owe it to both of them. To everyone. After all we accomplished, what was the point if everything changed, but I refuse to accept it this time? No, I promised...

I promise too much.

Something taunts my hubris. Laughs at the cycle. Yes, go ahead, Tim. You really are stupid. Bernard clearly abandoned you! As usual. You're alone and miss her and time is dying even faster. See, nothing's changed! So hide from tomorrow and the oncoming storms. Go back to the old, dead days. You promised to let her go? So what? Risk poisoning the past to relive it. Just one more time. Lay back down and curl up, go live in the past and waste it all. Coward. Crazy. Keep clinging to denial.

They're right. Your friends aren't joking. You're crazy. When are you going to admit it? Can you finally let it go, Timmy? Or are you going to let them find you crying again?

Oh, fuck this.

I have no tears left.

Tracy told me that we never really die, until the very last person to speak our name does. I can just close my eyes and say her name. Sink into rapidly cooling sand, while the ocean roars and the sun sinks, and avoid facing last night. So you promised them many things. And failed. At least you tried. No one can say you never tried. Go relive it, mourn it all. You'd be crazy not to! Cling to the best night in your selfish, shitty, little life. You've earned it.

Right on cue, here he comes to ruin it!

The sand is echoing his sandals slapping toward me. Unbelievable timing. He must plan this shit. He's close, I can smell him, like chicken soup and surfboard wax... and fresh, delicious coffee. A Moroccan blend, most likely, perhaps some hair of the dog, as well. Definitely steaming hot, full of false life fuel. He didn't abandon you, idiot. Just wait...

No. Now it's his turn to wait.

Stay still, Tim. Snore if you must. Your nervous system is shot, mind is in shreds, you've lost blood, there's toxins clogging your whole system, heart's probably failing... it's just a quick nap.

A little dream before the story ends.

"Tim? Yo, are you okay? You look pale as fuck."

Keep calm and don't look. She's waiting for you, somewhere in the records of your foolish mind. He'll be here when you come back.

"Get up, man! Drink this. Come on, it's fresh! What the hell are you doing? Dude, I totally know you're awake. I just heard you talking to yourself. Bro, come on, don't pull this shit! I waited here all day for you to return! This isn't funny, you promised to tell me what happened! Tell me what Barry... Yo, for real, don't make me pour this on you! Seriously, tell me what... Open your eyes or I'll pour this on you. I'll burn your face right off, bro."

I'll call his bluff.

Perhaps if I did bother to open my eyes, I'd feel better, cloaked beneath Burn's shadow. Maybe just one sip and I'll be okay...

But it's too late. I'm already gone, slipping back six years. Back to

Tracy, my little fire cat. To the flames dancing beside us, face to face on our log, and me frozen in shock. That awkward, perfect moment when all of this began. When she doomed us with that first kiss...

"No. No, Tracy, please don't."

I'm pulling away from her lips, just as slowly as she'd kissed mine. Is this terror or ecstasy? I stare at her mouth, lips still parted as if waiting, not daring to look in her eyes.

"Don't?"

"Tracy, we can't do this."

"We can't?" Tracy sounds as confused as I am. Not hurt, exactly. Nor angry. I hope. The fire pit casts dancing shadows across her face, but I'm still staring at her mouth. She flicks my cheek. Hard. "Hey! What do you mean we can't do this? Why not?"

Yeah, Tim, why not? How many nights have you wanted to die instead of sleep, dreaming about this little sin to fill the hole in your life? And to ruin it. But you could never cross that line, no matter how many burning fantasies made it seem okay.

But this is real, and she kissed you.

It's really not that weird, is it? You're what's weird. Not her. She's everything to you, and look, life actually is fair, this is... just too good to be true. What will everyone think when they hear? Betraying a lifetime of trust with lust. No, love. And lust. Just chill out, Tracy's not fifteen. She's eighteen, and I'm only twenty-two! That's not so much a gap as when we were kids. No, avoid that word... Kids. Yuck. But for Hell's sake, anyone who knows use would argue she's 'older' than me, right? More mature, for sure, but...

No, it's not even that. That's not my true fear. You know better. Dreams don't come true. You're cursed, aren't you? You don't get the girl. Not the one you love. You're a loser, a coward, a kid in a man's body. Not even that! But look at her. So I do. And she's... being quite patient.

Is this possible? She secretly... My love isn't futile? Or wrong?

Tracy, little Tracy Cameron, actually wants *me*. But she's not little, she's smart and strong, Kevlar lingerie and the promise of life, and grown up a long time ago. Fast. Too fast, because she had to.

"Tim, where are you?" She snaps her fingers but I don't blink. She hasn't leaned away. So close. So ready, so in charge.

No, Tracy is just confused, mistaking affection for love. Hell, we've been bonded for most of my life, and for all of hers. That's the little girl you took care of. You protect her, the victim of abuse and neglect. You, and her older brother. Your best friend. You've been her shield for so long, so of course she'd... Stop!

Tracy isn't a victim, she isn't a little girl anymore. Tracy's a young woman, very likely a genius, and now wields her own sword in the darkness. A survivor, a warrior who leaves her peers jealous, enthralled, or filled with lust. And leaves me in awe. She's become so... admirable, really. And yes, hot. We never planned on that ever happening, years ago when it became clear her mom and dad would fail their children.

Plus, *she* brought *me* out here. Except that's normal, we chill out at this fire all the time. You've had a hundred nights like this. But not like this. No, this isn't normal, her making a move on her surrogate older brother. That's all I am to her. Always on call, ready to drop everything for her. To talk, to read, to comfort, to listen, drive, cope, party, laugh, vent, to understand. I'm just a shoulder. That's all everyone thinks I should be.

But then she kissed me.

"Tim, what the fuck? Are you okay? You look like I just punched you in the face." She's laughing. But not at me. "Dude, say something. Blink. I'll do it again if—"

"You kissed me."

"Yes, I did," she says as if humoring a child. "I'm going to again. You get a do over, not that this first was bad. Ready?"

"No, this is wrong." I shake my head before finally looking her in the eye. "We're practically family. This must be illegal. Somewhere."

"Illegal? Ha! Give me a break. As if legality has ever concerned you before. That joint wasn't legal." She points to the burnt out roach at our feet. And the beer. "Or maybe you just fake it? Been lying for years, trying to impress Julio and show up Barry?" She teases me. But that's a genuine smile, eyes creased, pretty as all hell. But now that smile's fading. She glances down the hidden trails, making sure we're still alone. Looks at the fire, then the dirt and broken bottles, then back to me. No smile. "Shit, Tim. I thought you... Don't you run away from me. Not now."

As if I could... She's nearly glowing under this full moon. Perfect, even though nothing's really changed, although everything has. But right now Tracy's dressed as always, at least these days. Black, torn jeans, leather jacket with useless zippers, chains, pins for cool things I barely recognize. Belt studded with bullets and spikes on her wrist. Leather boots. Then there's her army of piercings, way more than one for each ear, a small nose ring, and my favorite, that one eyebrow ring on the right. Perhaps more... And despite her naturally red hair, she's dyed it the color of flame. All this armor, hiding a brilliant, shining soul. Braver, smarter, more beautiful and inspiring than anyone I've ever known. And I've know everyone in Thornwood. All the patterns, all the archetypes, and maybe she's one, but still the only one I've ever known. Trusted. Loved.

Anyone in their right mind would want her, and she could have anyone, for better or worse. You've seen it be for the worst, when she was just a kid. But you're not anyone, you're sick, some fucked up freak. Wanting her in the darkest most private thoughts you've been carrying for over a year, hoping she'd say or do something to break the spell for you. Well, she just did something, moron. Say something. Even the wrong thing, just say anything!

"Look, Trace, the problem is… ha, man, it is not you. Believe me, it's absolutely, positively, fucking-aces, definitely not you."

And as I lean away, she slides across the log to kill the gap. Right at the edge now. The fire crackles, whips and lashes at the sky, frames us along with thick black branches under a pearl white moon. We're too far from the beach, but I can smell the sand, the sea, the salt and freedom in her hair, sweat drying on her skin.

"Well, come on then, you loser. What is it? Is it my brother? Do not tell me you're afraid of him!"

"Afraid of Barry? Come on now, be serious." I turn away, wringing my hands. "Remember, I know karate. Plus I have my sword. I'm deadly."

"Right, right, how could anyone forget?" She rolls her eyes. But despite her grin, they're becoming too shiny. "That's not what I meant. Are you afraid he'll hate us?"

A spider creeps out of the log.

"Us? No. Hate me," I say, staring at the spider. Won't touch it. Too big. Barry would have to hate me. It's a rule. A matter of honor. Isn't it? Could my blood-brother actually *not* hate me for loving his younger sister? How couldn't he, and how couldn't she realize that? The spider creeps between our hands, blocking us. Forget the spider. "Well, think about it. I mean, wouldn't you?"

"Wouldn't I hate you, if you dated Barry? Wow, well when you put it that way—"

"Look, even if this, this..." I can't stop thinking about that kiss. As expected as a meteor bursting out of my car. The taste of cigarettes and strawberries. Soft yet strong. Exactly like I imagined. "Whatever this is, just keep in mind I didn't do anything. *You* kissed *me*. You started it. Plus, I figured you had better taste in men." Fake a laugh as I flick the spider into the grass. "Do you really think Barry would hate me?"

Tracy and Barry Cameron are the closest thing to siblings I've got. Family since forever. Sure, my parents love me, but their mom certainly doesn't. And their father... truly doesn't matter, you idiot! Still, I'm scared. I hate this, but I love it, but I'm scared. We all grew up together. Yes, even Barry could hate a traitor. If I'm half the good-guy I ever believed, then I must derail this! They'll flay you alive, you moron. But somehow don't lose her. I have nothing in my head to handle this situation. Nothing to fall back on, for this is dreamt of, yet impossible territory. She's being impulsive. There is no alternate reality where I'm good enough for her, let alone one where we can avoid destroying everyone around us by indulging this taboo.

But then her lips brush my cheek, and every muscle tenses, and I feel the same in her. Swallow, don't move, yet somehow I can speak. "So anyway, um... hey, have you read any of those books yet?"

"Yes..." She hasn't pulled away. The words are right in my ear. "All of them. Relax, I'll give them back. Don't change the subject."

"Wait, you read all of them? Already?" The surprise twists me around, almost into a kiss. Somehow I'm surprised, as if anything else is shocking now. She doesn't flinch, though. And either way, she feels... more than me? Half my height but somehow bigger. Last couple years she's been growing, exponentially. Wiser. Stronger. Sees backstage, doesn't take shit. Even now, no matter how awkward I am, doesn't she see I'm trying to save us from... what?

"Tim, I love the books and all that, but—"

Books, right. Fall back on the books, nature's best hiding spot for the strange and unusual.

"No, I'm seriously impressed. Most of that stuff is pretty esoteric. It's tough to digest occult based ontology. Look, I'm not saying you're lying, just that it takes more than one reading to grasp every—"

"Yeah, I get it, dude. But I did. And if I didn't, I did enough. It just… took a while. So I didn't get around to any schoolwork again."

"Tracy, what the hell? No more of this! You're going to fail high school at this rate! What's wrong with you? You could've aced senior year, easy. You shouldn't be held back, let alone in summer school! You're too brilliant. No, don't argue with me. We both know it. So, what's really going on with you?"

No answer. She stares into the fire pit.

"Trace?"

Is she changing her mind? Realizing what line we crossed? One that still felt so god-damned good? A fat little beetle scampers out of our log. The fire makes it look like perfect, smooth, like living onyx. She picks it up, turning it over, examining its little wiggling legs.

She flicks it into the fire.

"Fuck all that. Look at me. What's your problem? I thought… I really thought you felt the same. I mean, you're pretty bad at hiding it."

Bad? Seven hells, I hope she's wrong or everyone we know is going to come crashing down on me in a shockwave of hate and disgust. Thinking I'm some kind of monster, preying on her 'innocence and youth'. Instead of realizing that, I just pray for her to survive this youth. I crack my neck and just ask. "Aren't you my… Don't you feel like my little sister?"

"Not anymore. Not for a long time."

"But I've known you since you were born! You were just a little kid, I've watched you grow up! I think me and Barry looked after you more than… What exactly is a long time? And if this your way of asking how I feel, then yes, of course I love you. Trace, I'm not going anywhere. I won't ever abandon you. Neither will your brother. But I love you like a… Well, maybe I feel kind of strange about things, but I can't just forget…" My rambling voice is gradually fading in time with our fire.

"Oh, come on, that's all? I already have a brother, you just said so. And you're right. I've grown up. With you. The only stable people, the only… Ha, you know what? *You* sound like the kid here. People grow up, Tim. Granted, you're doing it a little slower than average, but don't judge yourself by your peers." She's biting that smile again. Goes from sincere right back to brave. Fun. Sincere fun.

"Very funny. Look, I know you're no kid, believe me, I know. Uh, wait, don't take the wrong way. I meant, I respect you, and this isn't about age. Not really. I'm afraid of how our families will react. Seriously, think about it, Tracy. This is some form of pseudo-incest. Isn't it?"

"Tim. Shut up. You want this." She leans in again. "And I want you. Not for tonight, not for a week. I want you. And you want me, and we both know it. I knew this would be a *little* awkward, but you're acting… man, you're acting like a coward. That's not the Tim I know. Not the real one."

She's right. She's always right. I've spent two shameful years losing sleep over this queer desire. Dreams I didn't want, yet never stopped. But she wasn't the aggressor in any of those. Just figured I'm the one who's awful and weird. "No, I mean yes, but… Damn it. It's just fucking weird!"

"True, it's kinda weird. And you're right. About us. That's my point. We really have known each other forever. Like no one else. And everyone else… they just suck. They lie, and use us, and leave us. They ignore you, because they're either boring, or afraid, or hateful, and insecure. It's always the same pattern, ignorantly judging anything unknown. But for them. Right? I mean, why is this even a debate? I'm not shocked that you're a bit surprised, just that you're so afraid. Don't you remember all the bullshit we've been through? Doesn't that mean anything? Don't you trust me?"

I do. It does. I bite my lip, remembering holding her without a hint of lust, just pure need to protect her. Keep one innocent person in this world from being ruined. Hiding her from violence, holding her hand to face real-life nightmares. Abusive… boyfriends. Men. Parents. Cruel, absent drug addicts hiding under titles like "Mom" and "Dad". And far worse… But she doesn't know that it's a two way street, this kind of teamwork. What we've been through. My growing isolation, both of our families' disintegrations. Just stupid pain. I bite down even harder, and then she brushes the hair out of my eyes.

"Plus you know this ain't incest, you dork." Her smile came back. Just like a fox in the grass. Always hiding there, waiting to sneak up and bite.

"But I used to babysit you. That doesn't weird you out?" I ask only because I have to ask. But her hand is still on my shoulder. No, you idiot. Of course it doesn't bother her. Keep it up, Tim. You're going to blow it. Do you *want* to? And yet, I still weasel around it. "And either way, college starts soon. I'm finally leaving, too. You actually pushed for it."

"Tim, I'm glad. You need to. Seriously, you finally decided to go and live up to your potential, instead of rotting here. You'd want the same for me. You aren't shy about constantly annoying the fuck out of me over it! Although most people your age have already graduated." She laughs at me. "At least you can overlap with Barry before he does."

People your age.

I can't help being a late bloomer. Can't help being chained to this place. Hard to escape small towns, small minds, big problems. But she could be an undergrad, too. I could call her a hypocrite. Challenge whatever she's challenging. That's right, Tim, keep pushing. But she's still smiling. So patient. Tracy gets what she wants, and holy shit, she really, truly, wants me. I try to light a cigarette that isn't even there. She doesn't comment, or even light one of hers. She always tries not to smoke around me.

"Nice try, by the way, but you're running out of arguments, Mr. Dune. After all, you're studying local. So you'll just have to suck it up and come visit me every weekend. That, or I'll have to keep skipping school and come to you." She's not pleading anymore. Sounds as sure of herself as ever, even those rare times she's wrong. "We'll only be about, what, an hour apart? That's even closer than the hospital is! No big deal, right? And then I'll... I'll just get my stupid diploma and enroll, too, or something."

"Yes, please! You're brilliant, see? I don't get it. It's just, what if we...? How...?" My words slip away right as I freeze. Just realized she's not touching me. When exactly did we lose contact? That way she's looking at me. Oh man, I know that look. It's always been there. Fuck the gods, she doesn't just want me. She's not talking about a fling, and I haven't been listening at all this whole fucking time, she's actually in—

"Tim. Please. Stop. It doesn't matter." Tracy shakes the hair out of her face before forcing one last smile for me. She looks tired. "You'll come back. I know it. You always come back."

My hands drop. My jaw hangs open like as ass, but I don't care. She's gripping the log strong, but she's trembling. Confidence flows over, but I can see it, that faint tremor in her fingers. This whole time I've been looking for the cosmic joke on me, not realizing she's also afraid. Wow, Tim, you neurotic shit-brained worm.

You actually convinced Tracy you'd reject her.

Even after she's shed all her armor for me. Again. It's my turn.

My hands close around my face. Why am I so afraid to be happy? I'm so lucky. She believes in me. She's brave enough to just go and kiss me mid-sentence. To do this. How can I be anything less for her? I plant my hand down on our log and look at this amazing young woman, framed by white night and blue fire.

Everything makes sense again.

She lifts her head, sits up, her eyes ask for the last time. I smile for her. For real. "Tracy, you're right. I'm sorry. Of course I'll come back. Every single chance I get. Hell, I can—"

I kiss her. The damage is done. We don't stop.

Her fingers dance slowly across my knee, tremor free, and mine find the small of her back.

We stop.

She looks back at the fire.

The beetle pops.

It's okay. Breathe. Namu amida butsu... Oh shit, shit, my best friend's little sister is in love with me and I want this. I really, really want this. I want to wipe away her tears and hold her and fuck her and kiss her and fall asleep with her head on my chest.

It's my fault that I've been alone. I didn't dare ask. She did. So that has to make it okay. Right? But no one can ever know, not yet, not now, anyway. Because... No. Stop it, you idiot king! No more thinking, no more fear. It's time for heart, for flesh, and blood.

I kiss her again, on the cheek. Where her jaw line slopes down to her neck. She twists into me, chest to chest. We press foreheads. A strand of her hair sticks on my lip. Her cheek slides against my temple, and then she arches up across me, tracing my face with hers. Her mouth is just beneath mine.

"I'm sorry, you just don't know how bad I've wanted this," I whisper. "But what if they find out? Barry could come walking through that trail any minute. They'll never understand. They won't let us—"

"Tim. Babe." She puts her finger on my lips. Her eyelashes brush me. "Shut up. I don't give a shit. I really don't. We can keep this secret if it'll make you just shut up."

Her knee slides over my leg, her head nestles against my neck. I shut up.

"And for real, you're too paranoid. Silly. I get it, you think we're being... scandalous or something. I'm not stupid. Just chill out, okay?

We don't have to go around town, shouting about our undying, star-struck love. Listen. Look at me. Barry's always trusted you to protect me. Even my mom does. She hates you, but she still trusts you. Only you. Think about that. They've always trusted to protect me. From bad dreams. Ghosts. Criminals. Monsters, and..."

Her father.

"Barry and Jay got rid of him. I just hid upstairs with you."

She bursts into an odd laugh, sudden tears shining in the fire. She spits into the dirt before hugging me.

"Of course you were with me. You're a better medic than a warrior. But... I still trust your fearsome karate."

Already, smile wrinkles are pushing the tears away. We stare into each other, and both realize this is really happening. Her eyes. Her strange eyes, green around the pupils, then ringed in hazel, encircled by a thin strip of blue. And they want my dark, dull, shit-brown eyes. And at that very moment, when I should feel more desire and love than ever... I can't shake this fear.

I scan the woods. We're safely hidden, but my mind still sees a wicked totem hiding amongst the trees. I can hear words echoing across time, see that man's veiny neck twisting sideways, his burnt lips bared back as he cursed me. To poison all I love. To swim barren seas. Alone. Never really believed it, even if those words are stitched into my soul. But now, now it seems almost...

It's bullshit.

Tracy's arms tighten around me, her face on my chest, hair smelling like some pretty flower I'll never know the name of. Yes. Even if that Curse exists, it was still unjust. I never hurt that stupid stingray. And injustice can be fought. Especially with her at my side. I kiss her hair. It's easy. Every heartbeat screams that things have changed. Forever. Even as we pretend they're not. "Uh, so... so the books were good? Because I dumped a lot of the weirdest alien shit on you."

"Yeah, but I'm ready for more." She runs her hand through my hair. "Just promise you'll never drop actual shit on me, okay, babe? Next time, I want your best. The rare ones you brag about. The stuff about anti-gods and unborn dimensions. Invisible societies. I want your underground comics and dusty books full of anti-worlds, ancient devils, and god-eaters."

"Speaking of, I learned about a new god we could use the blessing of right about now. An Egyptian one called Konshu."

"Mmm, I know that one," she says, resting on me, speaking into me. "It was in that story about... I forget. It's a moon deity, right?"

"Defender of the night travelers. Yeah. Wonder what it looks like?"

"Armored in bones, I'd say," she says, still and soft and warm. "You know Konshu also means 'One Who Lives on Hearts', right? Creepy. Ha. But it's all good, I want to keep diving. Deeper. Right into all that fun, crazy shit you always ramble about. It's cool. You're cool."

"Yeah. Ha. Well, you're cool, too. Whatever. It's all... Everything's cool," I whisper. This can't be undone. She could have anyone and she chose me. I brush her hair back, tucking it behind her ear. The four rings running up it balance against her hot skin. "You're too cool for a guy who's never had a real girlfriend."

"No shit." She beams up at me, and I realize that for the first time in my pathetic life, I do have a girlfriend.

"So I'm, like, your boyfriend now. Right?"

She snuggles in tighter, nearly knocking me off the log. "That's the idea. My weird, sexy, secret boyfriend."

Wow. This means we're probably going to have sex. I wonder when. I could wonder a lot of things, but really, right now, I'm perfectly happy. I wrap my lanky arms around my girlfriend. "Don't worry, Trace. We'll dive."

"Good. And you don't worry either, babe. This is going to be fun. And weird." She somehow nuzzles in deeper. "Just keep protecting me. Even I need help sometimes."

I take a deep breath, then cup her chin to lift her face. Kiss her forehead.

"I will. I swear to god, Tracy. I will always protect you."

"Ha!"

"What's so funny?"

"Tim, you don't believe in god."

My eyelids peel open, I blink, and six years pass. The memory fades. The sun is nearly done creeping below the sea. Bernard is gone. There's a cold cup of coffee knocked over beside me. How long was I dreaming? Small waves start crashing in. I'm rubbing sand through my hair. Don't hear any sirens. No shotguns cocking in the dunes, no ambulances. But last night still happened. It's still real. What would Tracy think of it all?

Could she still somehow be proud of me?

Too many questions. Too tired.

So for now I'll just stay on our beach, just a few miles from that fire pit I once felt was a shrine. It's alright now. Because it's almost over. There's no one left to fail. It's about time for the Curse to come and take me, too. Save the least for last, and all that crap. It's oddly comforting. I'm at peace with it. With what I am. At least the truth is finally clear. No doubt about it. Funny, because now I know the truth. I actually do deserve it.

But somehow even that's not enough. This acceptance won't erase that one question. My first, and my last. The one I thought could be answered.

That kiss... what if I had just walked away?

If I had the courage to break both our hearts, would she still be alive?

Karate Never Works

I admit it.

I'm afraid of the city.

For one, I never know where to park my car. And the subway knows no mercy, itself an infinite labyrinth of tomb-like tunnels, endlessly serving false serpents, who themselves never cease consuming and expelling weary humans. As for them... only in the concrete chaos of this free-reign prison could millions of people form a hive-mind that still births the purest isolation. Even the darkness is wrong. Cities are never truly dark. Just a limp twilight. Shades of purple and gray, squirming in the gutters. A reminder that although the darkness can't consume all, the light is surely gone. A city is a cyst. The country is a lie. The islands are alone, embraced and thrashed at random by an indifferent, manic ocean.

Yet Barry Cameron is here now, somewhere in Brooklyn. Truth is, I'll bitch about it till my tongue rots, but Barry needs me. Pain in the ass or not, I can't bear denying him anything. Not with our history. Not with the secrets his sister took to the grave.

But I didn't bother asking his address, figuring he knows his new neighborhood as well as the home he abandoned. Were I to go hunting for him, I'd surely get lost in this false jungle. Not to mention finding a safe haven to park... So I watch and wait in the safety of a headache-bright diner, hoping his crazy bitch mother actually told him the right place to come meet me.

It's only been four hours, counting the drive across Sponge Island, but I'm burning to grab the ginger bastard by the short hairs, throw him in my trunk, and haul ass back to Thornwood. Back to our own private island-hell, with pitch-black nights, and our own shames, crimes, and ghosts. The city knows the dark, the evil that sifts through night. But an island night is truly dark. Never hidden by light pollution in the hue of a ripe gutter piss.

No matter, this night is dark enough on its own. Tonight is an evil anniversary, and the catalyst for all the horror and hubris to come. The sun stole away long ago, and outside the graffiti splatters across the landscape like a gunshot wound, glowing under street lights. Most of it screams the night's theme: 'muerto'. Morte. Guasto, maro, Aivaki, vdeka.

Have to distract myself, so I study the night roads, pretending the diner window can guard me from them. But I've been staring at this same street for a long time, seeing nothing but dirt and pain. Restless hunger and burning eyes. Cellophane dreams. Pipes. Even in here, I can smell the faint stench of faithless monks rotting in the sewers below, with rats' nests, and stingrays swarming through their bones.

Damn it, Tim. Seven hells and a cat's tits, is it all really that bad? Or has the Curse poisoned your perception now, too? It's true, I come from no paradise. Most of Sponge Island sucks for stupid reasons, and despite its resort town veneer, my hometown, Thornwood, is a ghost world nine months a year. And everywhere is just as cold, hungry, and cruel as any city. But it's home. Cradled by water on all sides. Thornwood's been my whole life. All my friends, my family, my love…

But Barry left us after Tracy died, choosing to cram himself into this brick honeycomb. And he really needs to get his ass in gear and get over here before I sober up and leave without him. Getting twitchy, hints of fear. But he's out there, another soul added to the city's undead millions. They say this place survives by day. Below its highways, in slums, parks, and bars, prisons and skyscrapers. But at night, in this sleepless city, her citizens wander the Kingdom of Bones like all other men. Getting lost in the Toothless Gardens, hiding in Fields of Human Hair, where every step is pain and another memory lost. Yes, we're all subjects within the Deadland's realm. Its borders are intangible, a thin veil we call 'sleep'.

Sleep…

So tired, maybe I really will sleep tonight. Even Bernard's legendary snoring won't keep me awake. So what is taking him so long? Could have driven here less frantically, had I predicted he'd keep me waiting this long. The diner will expel me eventually; even I can't hide here forever. The only waitress on duty said that if I won't leave, it's time to order something more than my cheeseburger and coffee. It has been a long time, so I concurred.

"I haven't finished eating, but I'll have more water."

She crossed her arms.

"I'll have another water… please? And butter? I'll pay for it."

She just stood there staring at me, chewing her gum like a cow, while I kept my eyes on the window. SNAP! Her gum was like a thunderclap.

I slowly returned her stare. Gentlemen must pick and choose their battles.

"Okay… more coffee, too. Fresh, this time. The expensive kind, please," I said. She doesn't know I tip well, and was nearly gone before I could shout the rest. "And the water! I still want the ice water. With ice!"

Thank you. Barry better fucking get here before I lose what's left of my mind. I can almost hear Tracy mocking me, telling me to suck it up and help her older bro. Of course I will, Trace.

I take another bite from my cheeseburger. Watch humans shuffling outside, hungry, angry, afraid. My weariness amazes me. Nursing stale coffee and half a cheeseburger, I wait for Barry to finally show up, so I can fulfill this obligation and return to my busy schedule of beer and naps. This favor his mother thrust on me puts me way behind schedule. Have a lot of drinking alone in the dark to finish before dawn.

I lay my head on my arms. The lone cook is shouting at a kitchen TV before snapping it off. The only other customer is an old man, snoring beside a cold bowl of soup and grilled cheese. Not even a radio on. Then a fiery shadow slips past the window.

It's him.

I keep my back to the door as it opens. Sit up straighter. Feeling oddly nervous now. But it's only Barry. No reason to feel…

"Tim?"

I turn around, deliberately slow. Cool. Leaning my arm over the booth, giving a short, sharp wave. As he walks toward me, I just can't keep up the act. I find myself walking towards him, reaching out to grasp his hand, but falling into a hug instead. My body tenses, then I return it. Hard to remember the last time I actually touched another human being.

Barry held me at arm's length. "It's good to see you, Tim. Ha, look at you. Man, you haven't changed at all! Still wearing that creepy Hawaiian shirt."

"It looked good all through high school and college. Still does." I pull away and return to the booth. I talk over my shoulder, trying to fake the cool-cat act again. "It's good to see you, too."

It really is.

"Brother, what a night." He sat down across from me, a mix of concern and intrigue in his eyes. The crappy fluorescent lighting made his red hair orange. I stared back, noticing his tired smile, the bags under his eyes. The window reflects my contrast to him: shaggy brown hair, thin face, bags under my eyes as well. We're too young to look this old.

"How are you holding up?" he asked.

"I think I'm still drunk."

"What?" Barry lowered his voice, as if we'd get in trouble with some unseen authority who gives a damn. "You drove all the way from Thornwood drunk?"

"I was already a few rums deep when your mom showed up. No choice, really. Duty called. Trust me, I did my best to dissuade her, but you know how your mom is when she's wasted. So here I am."

"Shit," he said. He stared out the window, then smiled at me. "Well, I really appreciate this. Even if Thornwood had a working train station, it's still way too late. What a night for my car to break down, huh? It's almost fate."

What a night indeed.

Three years to the day we found his sister Tracy lying in bed, a statue of concrete and silk. Three years that have passed minute by minute, by minute.

"Anything for you, hermano," I said. "Can't leave you stranded. Not even your mom should be alone tonight."

"You two still not getting along, huh?" he laughed, staring at the laminated menu.

"Oh no, not at all. After a mere twenty-eight years, I've accepted that she's never gonna be my biggest fan. Except when duty calls. Is she willing to put her son's life in my hands? Put her parental responsibility on my shoulders indefinitely? Of course! Show me a bit of respect? Ha."

"Ha, yes, I'm well aware. I'll never understand that." He smiled for my sake, examining the ceiling rather than facing me. "But you practically grew up in my house. How *could* she possibly resist Timothy Dune's legendary charm?"

"She must have better judgment than you."

"Well, you said it. Whatever her reasons, she's treated you like blood. Maybe that's why she's so comfortable… dropping her fake pleasantries for you?"

Such an honor. I shrugged. As usual, Ms. Cameron was barely coherent when she knocked at my door. A cab idling in the street behind her, so zonked on pills and booze that she could barely curse me for having no phone. Thought that would save me from this kind of crap.

And money.

But I'm not truly helping her, of course. Barry's happy, but why does he think I'm here? For him? Or have the years finally made him smell my guilt? Could he fake the need for a ride, even fake our friendship, if he knew the truth about Tracy and me? About his best buddy, Tim the Traitor, running around with his baby sister behind his back? Tim the Cursed Killer? No, not that. I'm not... her death... it can't be because of me. No. No. It. Was. Not.

"What was not?"

"What?"

"You just mumbled to yourself about... something. Barely coherent. Are you sure you're okay, Tim?"

"I'm, uh... You know I'm a little drunk. Relax."

"Seriously, if you're drunk, then I have to drive," Barry said. He placed the menu down and leaned over his crossed arms.

"No chance!" I stabbed a finger at him. "Your mom summoned me, broke my peace. Fine, but I'm no servant. I'm in control now, buddy."

"Let's at least get you sober before we take off, okay? It's going to be dawn before we get back."

"Not a bad idea."

The waitress came over, chewing her gum deliberately. SNAP. She got her pad out.

"Coffee and a milkshake, please," Barry said.

"What kind?" she asked, her eyes glazing off to nowhere. She's another redhead, too. Statistically odd. They've surrounded me all my life, shadowing me like a living circle of fire.

"Strawberry."

I looked away and concentrated on the diner. Like the both of us, it was long, awkward, and thin. Built into an alley, a desperate attempt to capitalize on every inch of precious space. It's likely that many people were raped and shot on this hallowed ground, before it was sold to serve a higher commercial purpose.

"I'll have the same," I said.

She didn't even nod, let alone bring my previous order. I watched her ass fade into the distance. "She kinda looks like Tracy. Maybe it's just her hair and the eyebrow ring. Come to think of it, her cheeks are too sharp, she's a bit too tall..."

"She doesn't have an eyebrow ring," Barry said, staring me down as

I stared at her.

"Yes, she did."

"The waitress, Tim. She doesn't have an eyebrow ring."

Oh. I bit my lip. Abort! Derail him.

"Your car is a piece of shit," I said. "How can you afford a studio apartment but not a reliable ride? Oh, and by the way, pal, you're picking up the check."

"Deal. Who needs a reliable car when you got reliable friends?" He clapped me on the shoulder.

My laughter is strange. Sounds like a foreign tongue, barely retained. That is… not good.

"Sure it is. It's good to have friends like you. The older we get, the more we feel like brothers, you know?"

What?

"To be honest," he continued, taking a sip of my water, "I'm actually glad my car burned out. It's really good to see you again, whatever the… occasion. It's been too long."

"Yeah sure. It's been, what? Three whole months? I know I'm relentlessly magnetic, but you—"

"Uh, Tim, I've been living here almost a year."

A year? Not possible. Math has never been my ally, but I can't be *that* off. "Whatever, Barry. It's your own fault I lost track of you. You're the one who left us. What the hell made you move to Brooklyn anyway? If you're going to leave, then really leave. Man, I hate this fucking city. Come on, let's go."

"I don't. And I'd feel a lot better if you had some more coffee first. New York is fun when you get the hang of it. There's so much opportunity everywhere."

Our order came. I made sure not to stare at her this time.

"Barry, why'd you really go?"

"To get away." He put his coffee down and stared out the window.

"Nobody gets away."

"You're wrong."

I tried to imagine Barry's veins pulled from his skin, stretching out across Brooklyn and down Sponge Island, all the way to his nice house in the woods. A tangled web of heart and blood, forever chaining him to his past.

"Besides, I'm finally getting my work published in the right places.

35

And I never would have done that without the contacts I made, just hanging around bars and going to readings. And it's not just one story, I mean, it's my best so far, but it's—"

"Oh, right. Your story. Congrats. This glass is filthy." I stared down at my milkshake. "I ordered strawberry. Is this chocolate?"

"Ah, it's just a dirty glass," Barry said. "Drink up! And it's not just a story. It's the next piece in my collection."

"The one with no title, agent, or publisher?"

We sipped our milkshakes and coffee, our eyes anywhere but on each other.

"What time is it?"

Barry pulled his cell phone out. "A little after two. You're not driving yet, dude. Are you gonna be okay for work tomorrow?"

"Christ, it really will be dawn. It doesn't matter. Not an issue," I said, waving my hand. "Fuck Burger Don. I'm never going back there. Getting paid ten bucks an hour to be a miserable all day? I can do that for free."

"So you got fired?"

I grinned, trying to retain my rebel veneer, rather than acknowledge he's right.

"Of course I'm right. So how are you going to pay your bills? Eat? Get beer?"

"I'm going to starve to death on the beach. Should take about two weeks, tops. Assuming no one bothers me. Maybe two days, without water. Got a nice spot behind my place all staked out."

Barry shrugged. "Speaking of home, how's good old Thornwood doing?"

"It ain't the resort paradise we grew up in," I said. "Those greedy fucks drove rent so high not one local store remains. Housing market crashed with the economy again. Remember how many 'for sale' signs were stuck in everyone's front lawn a couple years ago? Well, most didn't get sold, but the families are gone. Now most of those houses have nice, wholesome squatters in them now."

"No shit?"

"No shit. The fishermen are starving because the goddamn ocean is a pool of puke and cancer, the middle class are poor, the poor are dead, we're all on drugs, and the only tourists left are the psycho-rich. Like, you can't even cater for those bastards unless *you* make six figures. I'm talking gold helicopters, boiled giraffe and lemur entrees. Amazon sex slaves and pools of liquid heroin."

"You've got to be kidding me! You always make everything sound so extreme."

"Like you would know. You'll see. Tomorrow. Our economy is basically built on the drug trade now. Remember Savage Jefe? He pretty much openly operates out of Tomahok now. Drugs are the only thing keeping people flipping burgers and mopping mansion floors. So if the cops make too many busts, they kill the local cash flow, and then their pay gets cut."

"Right. Sounds quite apocalyptic. Seems I got out just in time. Are Julio and Bernard still around?"

"Of course. Burn's still crashing at my place and Julio's still stalking the streets, pushing his wares. But enough of that. We have more than enough to be depressed about." I glared down at my milkshake, trying to make it die. "Are you okay?"

"Well… sort of. I still miss her more than anything. It still feels so unreal. But tonight's not… it's not as bad as it was last year."

Lucky bastard. Or selfish. Note to self, being selfish might make luck. "That's a good sign. It means you'll be fine."

"I'll be fine," he repeated.

"Not me, though. I'm still fucked!" I slapped his arm, trying to make him look back up. "Cursed, as you know. But I'm sure you'll be fine. Someday. I'm happy for you."

That felt like a lie, but I meant it. I swear.

"You? Happy? Ha, that's refreshing. Tim, you'll be fine, too. And you're not cursed, you crazy bastard." He gripped his coffee, double handed. He glanced out the window again. "You know who's fucked? Claude."

"Claude? Claude. Hmm… High School Claude?"

"Yeah, that Claude. I heard he went down to Florida last week and… he killed himself."

"Claude snuffed himself? I always knew he was a smart one." I slowly sucked at my dirty milkshake. "How'd he do it?"

"Heard it was a gunshot, on the porch. Right in his temple. Horrible thing. Suicide."

True. I don't bother reminding him that we don't know for sure if Tracy killed herself. All that booze and pills scattered about her, it could have been… it could have been a lot of things. A mistake, an attempt at aborting… No. Stop. All roads, all those disgusting 'what-if' paths, they just lead to the same end.

"People die for strange reasons," I said. "Who knows why Claude shot himself? Haven't even thought about him in over ten years. His life could have been pure torture, for all we know."

"Still, why would anyone…" He trailed off. We both know he's not really thinking about Claude.

"Tragic, but dull. Me, I'd have cut my wrists on the beach and just strolled into the sea."

"How poetic. Sometimes I forget that you really are a sick bastard."

"Thank you," I said, raising my glass. Almost made him laugh.

"And Lucas Boil. He's fucked. As much as we might hate him, he's over in Iraq right now. Poor guy."

"Good. I hope he gets his vicious head blown off."

"Jesus, Tim! The guy is a prick, but still, have some respect."

"For what? He's a beast. A bully and a cat butcher. Or did you forget our childhood already? The hell with that meat-bag." I slapped my hand on the table. Then sighed, leaning back. "Sorry. Look man, it's just the night, you know. This is a bad night. My nerves are raw. You look good, but… I'm sure you feel it, too."

"Worse than you know. But it's weird." Barry clasped his hands around his empty cup again, peering down as if some answer lay pooled at the bottom. "Every time I think about Tracy, my chest gets cold. But once in a while I notice it's just a little bit less than before. And then I can't help but remember that I'm getting published soon. My career is picking up steam, and I can finally start living off my writing. I'm living on my own, escaped home. And I feel good. Then that makes me feel even worse."

"Like I said, you're healing, man. It's only been three years," I said. He wouldn't look at me. "Barry, it's okay to stop hurting someday." I bit my lip and thought about that very special dead girl. I hate those words together. Dead. Girl. Powerful words. Bad combo. Dead, girl, fire, sea, beetle, pop, save, ray, graves…

"What's this now, spoken word?" Barry asked. The friendly concern in his eyes frightens me. He can tell something's off, but still too polite to ask. Soft bastard. Bless him.

"I told you. I'm drunk. It's just… babbling." I suddenly lurched over the table, grabbed his shoulders, and shook him. "Listen to me, you fool.

Don't feel bad about feeling good." I let him go. "Believe me, it won't last."

"Right."

"For now, you can beat yourself up over writing cheap sci-fi crap. And you're still ugly. And only getting older. Are you starting to bald?"

He's smiling again. Good. Sometimes that's all I can do for the Camerons. Their personal mutant chauffeur, babysitter, brother, clown. Calm them down. And stab them in the back. Bad, Tim. Get back on track. "So how the hell do you hide in Brooklyn, but still keep up with local gossip? I haven't heard jack shit from anyone in years."

"It's your own fault. You don't have a computer, any sort of phone, and I'm guessing you barely go out on the town anymore. Right? And when was the last time you even visited Julio? You're lucky Bernard still lives with you or you'd be totally alone. Buy a cell phone, for Christ's sake. You need keep up with life, you damned Luddite."

"I can neither tolerate nor afford that kind of luxury. Nerd. Besides, cell phones are just one more step toward tracking implants in the back of our skulls."

"Look who's getting sci-fi now," he said. He shut his eyes. "You used to love all that stuff. Tracy, too. Sci-fi, horror, pseudo-psychological magical fiction."

"Yeah, well... Things change."

Can't tell him that I buried my collection of books, oddities, and tomes beneath my porch while I wasn't with him to bury her. Barry waves politely to the waitress, and if she even noticed, she's pretending she didn't. Too busy texting behind the counter.

"Hmmm. I was thinking on the subway," Barry continued.

"Congratulations."

Oh damn it. I know what this means. Here comes another brilliant idea to sit and nod through. As if reading the stories every single time isn't enough. And I do read them all. I swear. I glance around the diner, looking for something to ruin this. The waitress went into the back with the chef. The old man snores.

"I want to write this story about America just totally caving in on itself," he said. "One day the weight of all this greed and hypocrisy pushes the whole damn country straight into the Earth's core. Like a sinkhole to Hell. Cool, right? Imagine all the oceans pouring into this huge hole, waterfalls the size of our continent filling the American sinkhole. Of course, the world's sea level would get insanely low, right? There'd be all this new land for the first time in since, well, Pangaea."

Why does he do this? The world's ugly enough without his flourishes.

"And I'd write about how the world, everyone, tries moving in on it. Resources, space, it'd be local, political, personal chaos. Countries at war on paper and in the fields of dead oceans. Common man turning to gangs and violence. Just your cup of tea, now that I think of it."

Hmmm. True. Sip some coffee. "So you've created this dead world hundreds of miles below our current one. A lifeless, dried out, seabed, full of whale carcasses and rotting sharks. Mountains of suffocated fish. The whole thing smelling of grime and scales. Could be like the ruins of an alien planet..."

"Yeah, exactly! Cool, huh? I'll call it—Nightmerica," he said, waving his hands out. "Maybe that's how I can get my first collection together."

"Christ, that's terrible," I said, slowly tilting my head down, locked onto his face. I know my eyes are creepy now. I practice this in the mirror. "Tell me again, just how exactly do you keep managing to get published?"

Barry sighed and leaned back in the booth, resting his elbows on the top. Spreading his great literary wings for my poor, directionless ass. Yes, he's moved on. Yes, he has a life. Yes, he as a future. Hooray for—

"Tim!" Barry grabbed my arm, his face paler than possible, and his grip clamped on my arm like a vice. Never heard someone whisper so loudly. "Tim! Look! Someone's here... He looks like bad news."

Didn't even hear this 'bad news' enter, and wish my creative-genius-friend hadn't said that. I turn and see the bad news.

Oh shit...

A walking shadow, thick with desperation, and devoid of hope. A hollow man. An empty man. A hungry man. And dressed to change that. A black sweatshirt over denim jeans and leather work boots. A black hood over a black ski mask. And a black gun that gets shoved at the red waitress's face.

Their conversation is standard and clear. He wants silence and money. Now. He waves his gun at us, because he doesn't want any funny business. Funny. Criminals really say that?

He keeps the gun pointed at us until I dutifully push my head down, facing away. Damn it though, I put my cheek right on my stupid cheeseburger. Going to be sticky later. Nothing I hate more than being sticky. I chanced a peek at the old man, who'd slumped over, but missed hitting his soup. Snoring. Then at Barry. He's sweating too much. Cheeks flush against the table, hands over his head, eyes wide, dilated, and darting. Oh, no. Come on, bro, keep it together! Please don't start thinking that...

"We have to do something!"

"What? No! No, no, you stupid bastard!" I hissed. "Keep your head down. Don't look. Don't make a fucking sound."

"Tim, are you serious? He has a gun, we have to help her!"

"Right, he has a gun! He'll clean out the register and leave. No one will play hero. No one will get hurt." If any night revels in bad luck, it's this one. You don't fight an armed thug on the night your girlfriend—or sister—died. So I tuck my chin to my chest, watching it all on the window like a TV show. Can't help taking one more peek. The waitress empties the register, hands trembling, eyes watering. But respectable composure, all the same. She jerks back against the wall as he rips the cash from her hands. Did she expect him to patiently... Oh, damn. He's pointing at her pockets now. The bastard wants her tips, too?

"Tim! We have to stop him."

"Barry, please. Shut. The fuck. Up."

He's still clutching my forearm, temporarily unaware of a concept called circulation. But it leaves an opening to slowly crush his fingers. Nice and tight, ready to snap the bones if he tries to get up and get killed. He bites his lip, almost snarling. Blasted fool's got his head down, but he's still staring right at the robber. I mean, I get it. A young redhead facing death. Tonight of all nights. Can't blame him, but can't let him die, either. Thank god the thief's got his back to us. Finally Barry turns to the window. Good boy. Doesn't he get it? This world has no more heroes.

The old man slept right through it, even as the diner door slammed beside him. The shadow thief's footsteps echoed away. We look up to survey the pleasant lack of carnage. Just a shaken young waitress, an empty register. Bad, but about as good as these things get.

Slowly, some shuffling sounds creep out from the kitchen. Just one set of footsteps, but heavy, fat enough for two. It's a cook like me, just three times bigger, punching pots and pans. Most likely that he's sharing Barry's impotent fury. Then I hear all the heavy breathing. From everyone. Everyone but me.

Barry tore away from my grip. "When did you become such a coward?"

"When did you get so dumb? You think someone like that wouldn't shoot you right in the fucking face? Grow up! It's like this all the time, now. And Thornwood is no different. Sometimes it's an off-duty cop under those hoods, sometimes a desperate father or a junkie. And none of them give a shit about us! They want fast, easy money. Everyone just wants—"

"Shit. Shit, shit, shit!" The waitress quit yelling at the tiled floor and turned to us. "You fucking pussy ass cowards!" Red eyes swollen with raging fear, and tears, her bone-white hands clutching a pot of stale coffee. "You two! Why didn't you do anything! *Why didn't you help me?*"

The cook bellows, "Carolyn?"

"It's safe, Frank! Motherfucker's gone. No thanks to these two fucking losers that just SAT HERE AND WATCHED THE WHOLE DAMN THING!"

"Exactly," I said, keeping my tone the same as when ordering the ice-water I never got. "You're right. We didn't do anything. And thus, no one got hurt. Including you, honey."

Her glare hurt. Shame... yuck. I tried giving her that creepy, alpha-male, mirror-tested glare. I can sense that Barry's about to say that I stopped him from saving her. I know it. Just as his mouth opens I kick him under the table. Hard.

"Ow! What's your problem?"

The waitress spun on him.

"My problem? What's MY problem? YOU'RE MY—" the waitress screams, face burning like her hair. If she's going to explode, I'd like to get some of that coffee first.

"Oh, you would, huh? Are you fucking serious?" she screamed at me.

How did she...? I didn't say anything, again, what the...? No matter, this situation is spinning rapidly out of hand for no rational reason. "Listen, we were all hostages, okay? No one saw his face, no one gave him shit. He saw an empty old diner in the middle of a slummy street and took his share. Big deal. At least we're all—"

"I'm sorry," Barry said. "I'm so sorry. Look, my friend here is trying to say it was safer to let the guy take the money and go. He hangs out with people who know about these things, so…"

Ah, hush you fool! I kicked him again. His only counter was a daggered stare. I softened my tone, looking up at 'Carolyn the waitress' with practiced puppy eyes. "We'd have only made it worse. People get killed for no reason over shit like this. We didn't want that! Look, you're fine, right?"

She chewed her lips so hard I expected blood. Her nostrils flaring as she clutched the coffee pot. She pops in a fresh piece of gum.

"Go on. It's okay. Admit it," I said. "I'm right. And you're alright. We're all just fine."

SNAP!

"Fine? Fine! No, I'm not fucking fine! I just had a-a-a a gun in my face! And he took my shitty goddamned tips! The only real money I get for serving jerk-offs like you all night! And, and, and…"

All I see is Tracy not sitting with us, and gods fuck me, I open my stupid mouth and hear myself saying:

"Oh, so what? It's not *our* fault this place is empty. Maybe the food sucks. Look, it was *your boss* who left you and the cook alone for a graveyard shift. He lost a few bucks and you lost some tips? Big deal. You could have a *goddamned hole in your face right now*, and you don't! So you're welcome! Okay? You're alive. You get to go home and yell at… whoever. Just try and calm down."

"Tim!" Barry's looking at me as if I'm his embarrassing child.

What's wrong with all these people? Must be relief and the adrenaline dump mixing them up, slipping into rage, replacing relief with fear-fuelled anger. Don't they see how lucky we are? And what of the old man? Is the guy still sleeping, or is he dead? He didn't do anything either, or else he was smart like me. I'll try again… "Look, I'm sorry. Barry can cover your losses, so let's all chill out, have a cup of coffee and just—"

"Here's your coffee, dickhead!"

She misses my cup, but hits my head dead-on. The coffee's heavy, thick as sludge, like fiery mud water. It shoots through my shaggy hair, into my scalp, down my face, over my eyelids, the back of my neck and right into my Hawaiian shirt.

"Help! Witch! I'm burning!"

Blinded, frantic, I'm groping for something, anything, to salvage my face. Ah, there! Something soft, like cotton. I pull, but it pulls away. A living napkin! The madness! My mind is melting away! Must save what's left! I yank on it again, finally tearing it close enough to vigorously bury my face in, full force.

"Tim, holy shit! Chill out, you're not burning!" Barry shouts as he slaps me.

He's right.

It was all reflex. The coffee was cold, thank the gods. Survival mode convinced me it was scalding. It's almost funny, this diner's shitty service literally saving my skin. Still sticky, though. Now that I'm safe, I open my eyes to see what this sentient cloth really is. And realize that I'm clutching the bottom of the waitress's shirt.

Her bare navel is visible. I can see part of a rose tattoo creeping up from her waistline. Feel like gluing my eyes to the floor, but I manage to look up at her, trying 'the puppy eyes' again. Her pockets are as empty as the pot, her shirt is now stained with my face, and she's not buying the eye trick. She rips her shirt away, tucks it back in, all while raising the glass pot. Must dodge! Got lucky with the coffee, but glass is still glass. I dash backwards, bashing into the window.

"Fraaaaank!"

That's when we heard the bull thudding out from the kitchen.

"What's going on out here? Carolyn, are you okay?"

Hello, Frank… Frank is likely descended from mammoths and rabid elephants. Three hundred pounds of kitchen grease, hair, and Italian salami. A stubbly face, box nose, and pinched brow. Big ham fists. "The police are on the way! Who are these jerkoffs? They hurt you, Carolyn?"

"I've been better," she answers.

Still bitter. Not so scared anymore, are you, Carolyn? Seems like I washed away all that mugging fear. You're welcome. Again.

"What'd you just say, smartass?" Frank spat at me, face twitching.

What *did* I just say? I look to Barry, who's shaking his head.

"What happened to your shirt? Did the thief do this?"

"No, this skinny *fuckwad* did!"

God, I hate this city. I began an honest attempt to explain. Started at the beginning, and how we averted—

"Shut your damn mouth!" Frank commanded. "You just sit here and do nothing for Carolyn, then you have the nerve to insult her too? You call yourselves men?"

I scramble back into the booth, standing up on the seat. "Well, what the hell did you do? Cowering back there behind your stove! You could

44

have swallowed that punk whole!"

Barry's still seated, apparently quite fine.

He takes a bite from my cheeseburger before speaking. "Um, actually, sir... I *did* want to help, but my friend here insists it was safer to just let it be. I'm sorry, sir. We didn't mean to make things any worse for... Carolyn, is it? Here, allow me to—"

Carolyn gave him the stink eye, but then spit on me. Frank stomped forward. We should have heard sirens on their way, but the cops were far off, if even coming at all. The only thing for certain was that Frank was getting closer and closer, fists clenching into wrecking balls. Within the danger zone, time for fight or flight.

"Barry, let's go!" I shout, ready to dive right through the window.

Barry stands, calm, damned slow, fumbling through his pockets for cash. Coins fall beside my shoes while I seethe with rage, fear, and disbelief. He drops a wad of bills onto the table. Then calmly crisps them out for his new pals. "I'm sorry about all this, I really am. My brother here's terribly awkward, but he's got a good heart. He meant well. Didn't you?"

"Piss off, you bastard! Prepare for combat!" I raised my hands, trying to channel the swift power of the sea. Frank was more of a mountain with boulders for fists.

"Wow, look who's got some balls *now*." Carolyn spit at me again.

Taking a diaphragm-deep breath, I assumed a karate stance. Haven't done any since middle school, but muscle reflexes are like a great eagle swooping up from the volcano's blast. Honed into my very being. Thus I throw a right hook, preparing to deliver a front kick into Frank's chest and—

The cook smashes me right in my ear. I tumble over the booth. Now on my back, crunched up like a pill bug, I try bicycle-kicking to keep Frank at bay. Oh, Frank, you're so lucky! If I had my sword, I'd split you from nose to navel.

Barry grabs our two glasses of tap water but then sprays them on me. And he's laughing! Seems I've awakened his inner elf, and gods bless him, he knows how I loathe sticky skin. Frank's still trying to get past my furious kicking, and Carolyn continues to shriek and swing the coffee pot. I finally worm my way back to my feet. Frank snaps his jowls to Barry, teeth grinding, and fires another shot. Barry ducks, slips under Frank's greasy arm, and makes it to my side.

"Sorry again, he's drunk and can't take another hit in the head!" Barry laughs at them.

We explode out the door.

My eye catches the old man, still sleeping through the whole scene. We're turning the corner when I realize maybe he was never asleep at all. I'm still dizzy and shaking with pain as we stumble down the street, Barry giggling and pulling me along by my black Hawaiian shirt. We get around the corner to my car, and Frank is out of sight, hopefully collapsing from heart failure.

"Come back here, you shitheads!"

Nope.

Keep running.

Strange figures watch us run in the half-light. Pushers, peddlers, muggers. Enemy scum. We need to escape back to our island. To home-turf where the threats that are old and calculable.

We seem to open my car doors in half-time, falling into the seats, myself fumbling for the key, skinny fingers now as dexterous as sausage-links. Barry's looking behind, nervously slapping his hands against the headrest.

"Here he comes, Tim! Oh boy, he's pissed! Come on, man, gun it!"

At least he's having fun. Strange night for strange feelings.

My body follows Barry's command, but something else has arrested my attention...

Something alien and dead, something long past its time, revisiting our world. I barely believe what's in the alley. A phantom, the watcher always in the corner of your eye. The spirits you forget the moment you turn away. But not this time. I blink. Still there. I stare it down. So small, such delicate, amber fur. The white jaw and breast, black paws, black ears, and yellow, unblinking eyes. Blazing beside a green dumpster. This little red fox, staring right back at me. Vulpes vulpes, the perfect synthesis of feline and canine. Male and female. The meta-being. Contradiction given form. Unreal...

"No dude, this is very, very real! Stop mumbling and start the car already! You really are cursed, aren't you? Chaos follows you everywhere!" Barry is slapping my arm but I'm locked away. "Hey! Tim! For god's sake, drive!" He stops bouncing in the seat. Gets quiet when he sees the weird look in my eyes. "Hey? What is it? What's gotten into you?"

"Barry. Look. A fox."

"A fox?" Barry laughs. "Dude, are you serious? A real live fox, right here, right now? In Brooklyn? You must've taken a bad hit back there. Listen, Frank is real and he'll be on us with a cleaver soon!"

A bottle shatters across the rear windshield. Reflex tears my eyes away from the fox to my rear window. Frank is a persistent predator, I'll give him that. My trance flows away, down the slimy glass. No crack. Lucky. I turn the key, then immediately look back to the mythic alley.

Of course, it's gone.

"Dude, you're really losing it. I hope you're just drunk and crazy. It was probably a cat. You do remember that foxes are extinct?"

They are. Like so many great animals who tried to live beside our wicked race. The list grows longer each year. But thankfully the cats have not abandoned us. I know cats. That was no cat.

I spin the tires and peel away, leaving Frank and Carolyn's lives forever. The rhythmic pulse of dirty light bathes us as I follow signs toward the highway. We weave through the dreamless streets toward our highway escape.

The closer we got to the onramp, the safer I should have felt, but the concrete maze felt more and more like an ocean, frozen in time and turned to stone. Now cracking to life, threatening to spill through the condemned buildings and sweep us out into a dark, empty sea. My heartbeat drowns out my struggling engine.

Already the night feels invasive, like the purple, star-swollen sky, threatening to drip down and absorb us. Hapless morons coated in the ethereal slime, pulled screaming into the cosmos to be rent and torn amongst hungry, alien anti-gods.

No, no, not again. Not tonight. I can't swim tonight.

"Seriously, how hard did you get hit? Swim?" He was staring at my bone-white fingers locked around the steering wheel.

"What? I didn't say anything."

"Uh… yeah. You did." He was looking at me, a little afraid. "Maybe you should slow down a little?"

"No. We need to get home. Fast."

"Okay…" he said, tugging on his seatbelt. "Just, uh… drive safe, okay?"

It's the Curse.

It's closing in.

I fly up onto the highway, barely hearing the blaring horns protesting our arrival. Damn them, I won't slow now for man nor beast. We leap through lanes, slowing and speeding as needed to get into the fastest lane, racing toward that next SNAP when everything changes, defining all that came before...

Every moment preceding a cataclysm is significant. Time's smallest teardrops are equally precious and dangerous. Looking back, it seems so clear. You defrag, trying to tabulate every instance, every action, every breath taken. Because when things go terribly wrong, one can't help but wonder what factors you could've changed.

A few hours after the diner, I could only dissect how each piece fits our story. The waitress. The bloodlust chef. The quiet thief. The fox ghost. What could I have done differently? Had I not fallen under the phantom fox's sway, would things have turned out better? What if I'd stayed and fought? Spent just a few more precious moments bobbing, weaving, and being battered? Would that small fragment of time have aligned the wheels of fate in our favor, instead? And what of Barry? Did he act perfectly, or was there some glitch in the system that allowed him to fall onto the path he did?

Whatever the variables, they are terrible and many, and it's impossible to ignore the fact that taken as a whole, every sentence uttered, every action taken, every thought indulged, had one undeniable sum.

Was it was my Curse, or simply the random, grotesque math of existence? How ironic, that of all nights. Regardless of actions taken or not, I'll never know if our immediate future could've turned out better, or... even worse. But then of course, there's a third possibility.

The worst of all.

The one crashing down like a tsunami teeming with vengeful injustice. That maybe... tearing down the highway last week, on a noble quest to reunite mother and son on the anniversary of loss... I was once again an unwilling agent of fate. Walking poison. Cruelly chosen by their mother to race blindly into exactly what I deserve. And that's the only reason why Barry Cameron, guilty of nothing but association, was chosen to suffer.

Just to punish me.

Barry's Buddhist Bullets

We'd just passed Babylon when the coffee tore up my guts. Ice in the stomach, and a wave of nervous anger. Frank left my face feeling like raw beef, but that was the least of my troubles. This is a night without pornography, or toasted blankets. A night of flies. Still, I soldiered on, pushing my old car up to seventy-five. I think we've escaped the Curse. Although we're technically surrounded by water, north, south, and east, as we sped toward Thornwood, those crushing waves seemed to recede. The further from the fox, the more illusory barren sea became. Did I actually beat it this time? Left the Curse's ambush behind in Brooklyn? Maybe it was just a panic attack. Maybe everything will be okay. And, Barry was blissfully silent for twenty full minutes!

"You didn't leave a tip," Barry said, no longer full of bubbly glee.

"Shut up." I danced from lane to lane around the slow, wasted, and cowardly. More than three quarters of them would pull off of the S.I. Expressway before we reached our exit. The final exit, by no coincidence, I'm sure.

"Don't get so defensive," Barry continued the lecture. "I don't care about you throwing in, but the least you could have done was left her with a tip. And before you ask, no, saying 'Don't get shot during a robbery' doesn't count."

"Shut up, you cretin. I'm driving. It's an art." With a dash of luck...

"But you were right. Nobody was shot. And we didn't get beaten into burgers for Frank's next shift. I have to hand it to you, Tim. Sometimes your weird, nasty, logic, makes sense. Nobody got hurt in the end... Well, you did! Guess that's karma for starting a fight after a traumatic experience."

Caught him grinning at me via peripheral vision.

"First of all, I'm fine. Second, I don't start fights. I finish them. We'll have to leave this as a draw. One punch doesn't count."

"One hell of a punch, to nothing... I'd say he won. Wow," Barry ran his hands through his hair, "What a night! My car takes a shit, then Mom convinces you to save me, then armed robbery, *then* assault. And even after all that, you're seeing ghosts! An animal, not even a hu…"

His deflated voice left a heavy silence. He got excited and forgot. That's good, though. Right?

"What's good?" he asked.

"Um… that we…" I'm at a total loss. Has he become psychic? Distract him. "We still got a long way to go, so do me a favor and shut up. I have an epic enough headache as it is."

"I would too, if I got hit that hard."

"Crow-lords save me… shut up!"

The trip from tip to tip of Sponge Island always takes at least three hours at top speed. From the slums of Brooklyn, now out to the sandy fake shores of Thornwood. It's all local roads from there to the final stop, Tomahok. I prefer to drive at night, and I'm not really drunk, just like keeping Barry on edge. And we are still blessed with a few more hours of darkness.

Strange… Three foes in the diner. Three years since Tracy died… and about three hours until I deliver Barry to their insipid mother. Three hours and then I can return to my rum, to sit, sip, and cry alone on my porch, counting pebbles and stars. Ignoring Bernard's gibberish inside.

Humans can find patterns anywhere, I suppose. Speaking of, he'll be piping up again right about—

"Boy, I'm lucky this thing still runs, huh? Looks like you haven't cleaned out the back seat… uh, ever?" Barry was leaning into the back, scanning the interior of my loyal 1983 Voltaire. "It's like a three-dimensional yearbook."

I could see it through his eyes. Faded blue interior bathed in orange throbbing lights, a twilight land of woe for the many spiders living in the seats. The same used car Dad bought for me, a gift for not failing out of school. A gift we used and abused and keeps on kicking. A stick of incense burns in the broken air conditioning vent. Empty soda bottles, crushed coffee cups, and mud caked magazines carpet the floor. Barry's legs curl over a mountain of parking tickets and half a skateboard. There's a wetsuit with a huge tear down the spine draped across the back seat, just a dead shadow. The stench of stale coffee crept out of the Styrofoam catacombs below us. They conjure an altar to our guiding deity. So let us pause and worship our fuel at this dreadful hour.

All hail our weary lord, The Great and Terrible Caffeind, whose power makes the great magnet's oppressive pull far more tolerable! All hail our vein dwelling goddess! Her caffeine high that makes us run on broken legs! All hail—

"Jesus Christ!" Barry said. "Tim, did you even see that car?" His salami red face was twisted with concern. Red hair flared in the pulse of passing highway lights. "That car almost hit us! Damn, did you even see it?"

I didn't.

"Of course I saw it! How could I miss the bastard? Barry, you need to learn how to stay calm, or your reflexes just turn to shit. What good am I to us if I act like you, and get the fear? We'd swerve right into the divider. Trust me. Just stay calm. It worked during the robbery. Right?"

He laughed, chin tucked down into his crossed arms. "Calm, right. You know that you fight like a centipede on speed?" He rolled his head on the headrest. "I hope you never get in an actual life-or-death fight. And please, just be careful. Even for a highway, it seems dark as hell at night."

"Yes, I know, Barry. Most nights are."

"I hate this one." He sank into his seat. "The sooner we're at my house, the better. I need my bed, some good wine, and a good book."

Barry speaks truths. The night is ominous. All roads are wicked after dark, much less this artery for the suburban stench pit of Sponge Island. And that *was* a close call, although there's no sense in admitting to it now. It can only add to his impending freak-out. It will conjure vicious memories of the carcass-strewn roads of our youth, when the deer froze, before charging right into us.

"Most of the deer are gone now," I said. "The ones left just stand roadside, watching us pass. It's kind of creepy. Maybe they learned. The dumb ones are dying off like the pandas and penguins."

"That's evolution. The others are extinction. But remember the time that poor faun froze on the side of the road, and as we slowly crept by it suddenly ran head-first into Julio's Jeep? It looked so... it limped away with its neck flopping around. I felt sick for a week."

"It asked for it. Either way, there's so many less now. All those houses they built, it just destroyed what little scraps of woodland they had left."

"And the foxes. Nature will never forgive us for that," Barry says, finally making sense. Then he turns up the volume on my CD player. Didn't even know it was on. A heavy beat... definitely not my CD. When did the sneaky bastard slip that in? The rap lyrics are inescapable, can't plug my ears and drive... but for once this song isn't about the size of the rapper's Glock or his cock. This one is eerie, the beat is slow and sad. Like sun-up jazz, and his voice is fast but parched, aggressive yet still distant and tired.

"Who is this?"

"You don't recognize him? Listen!"

I snap the music off.

"Hey! I was listening to that."

"Driver's rules. I can't stand that shit." Still, who *was* that? The voice... it hit too close to the vest. Creepy despite the failed attempt at pretentious lyrics.

"Tim, you know that's Cook-Dough-Fresh, right?"

"That worthless Despot rip off?" Dear Julio had introduced me to some 'under-ground-hip-hop' years ago, and I must admit it was stunning in complexity and theme. Despot, Cannibal Ox, Breezly Brewin. Not this...

"Tim, he was our dorm-buddy! And he's not a Despot rip-off. Is he?"

"No, no, Cookie-puss is quite... something," I said.

"Well, even if you forgot him, I stayed in touch." Barry looked out the window. "The point is, he finally finished the album from college. It doesn't matter if you like it. Just thought you'd be happy to see someone else... He never gave up, you know? It's never too late. You could still go back. You never know, maybe you'll find some new direction, some new anything. It could only help."

"Help what?" I snapped. Seethe save me, if Barry only knew what I need help with. Starting to twitch, I want to feel happy for him, to hide my shame and let him live in blissful ignorance, but my gut is getting ready to tell him once more. "Is he going to help bring my family back? Will more college debt land me some stupid job that fixes... Just leave me the hell alone, man. Please."

"Whoa, sorry! God forbid you'd be happy for your friends. Wrong timing? I hope."

"What does that mean? Quit the subtext. If you have something to say, just say it."

"I just thought you'd like it! You're right, it sounds like Despot. That's why I thought of you. The songs are more like eulogies than party beats. And even those ones are bleak. Right up your dark, new alley."

"Well that's nice, but my *new alley* still hates vacuous rap."

"Julio loves rap."

"Your point?"

"You worship Julio."

"I worship cats, you moron," I said. Yes, like Lady Bast. Queen of the Feline. Surely, she's the one deity who could never lay a curse upon me. Do cats eat rays? Note to self: new experiment to conduct.

What would Julio do? He'd tell Barry. He'd man up and take the consequences. He would have done it years ago, the first night. He wouldn't have gotten into this quicksand-cesspool-guilt-trap.

"What was that?"

Nothing. It was nothing. What did he hear? Nothing.

"Tim. You're being a jerk. Which is almost normal. But I know you're not drunk. You're too... I know you're still hurt, but something about you is starting to creep me out. What's going on? Let me help."

"Help? Do you think *another* peer success story helps? I can't even flip burgers, and all I've heard tonight is 'this person is great, and so am I, and why aren't you?'. OH, and let's not forget 'Claude blew his brains out because he was just as sad as you are'."

"I never said that."

"And then an album from some twit from college! Real subtle sell on my 'failure'. Thanks Barry, I love having this rubbed in my face. You're not enough as it is. I'm sorry if I'm not holly-jolly, yippee-yay, woo-hoo enough for you! I'm not exactly happy tonight, remember?"

"Okay, I get it! Sorry that I care. Stupid me." He stared at his fist again, clenching and unclenching it. Unnaturally aggressive moves for him. "Not everything is about you."

I try to pass some stupid, big S.U.V. blocking the lane. Its horn blares behind us for three seconds too long. Not helping the mood. Seven hells, Barry's right. He's being a dick, but he's right. Just like his sister. Must be a family trait. He's patient, too. Despite my epic bitching about... everything... most of it is my fault. One way or the other. Cursed, yes, but he's just trying to do something. A true friend. After all, I'm the one who... *Wait a minute!*

Does he already know?

Is that what all this preening is about? He's always had an oblivious lack of humbleness, and for good reason. BUT... he's smart. Calculating.

And more dangerous than I give him credit for. We're friends for good reasons… so is he fattening me up with all these little ego jabs, before calling me out as the traitorous sister-fucker I am? Face feels hot now; in the mirror it's as red as a sunburn.

I look back at the road just in time to see a bumper coming in too fast. Manage to check the mirror and glide around as if I had it all planned. Slow down. What's wrong with you, man? Get a grip!

"Excuse me?" Barry actually sounded pissed. "You're the one who needs to get a grip. Hell, let me drive. You've almost killed us enough times already!"

This is going way downhill. Not playful downhill. Can't let him leave the car angry at me. But it's just too many memories, too many phantoms, too much for tonight. If only I could summon one of the old ones. Perhaps the Illithyd Mind-flayers, to offer up my meager brain in penance. Let it gorge those tentacle-lined jaws on my skull, shaving the last few minutes from my brain. Although I suspect they get a bit greedy once they start feeding. "Hey, what do you think brains taste like?"

He neither smiles nor responds.

The silence lasted while two more exits drifted by.

Considered turning the music back on, just to kill this poisoned mood. If I get the balls to tell him about Tracy and me, this is not the ambiance for it. But his voice comes out of nowhere, nearly making me swerve. Just a bit.

"It's okay, Tim. This is a tough night for you, too. Sometimes I forget how close you were to her. I'm sorry, buddy. Seriously, I know I said it already, but… thank you."

"Please stop thanking me."

This favor isn't entirely for him, best friend or not. It's for Tracy. And I've been wondering about that since I told his mother I'd drop everything and go pick him up in Brooklyn. Maybe it's a sign that… maybe tonight, I'll finally tell him? He practically left an opening for me just there. I stopped believing in coincidence long ago, so this must be it.

My throat tightens.

Risk owning up to the past. Tell him about us. There's no use denying that it's eating me alive, and I'm not getting any better with time. Not like him. But if Barry turns against me… Fuck it, I can take it. Yeah. Tonight. I can do it!

But are you really that selfish? Maybe a confession would make this all about me, just like he said. And that burned too raw for me to deny the truth in those words. So maybe the timing *isn't* right.

I can wait a little longer. Confess our affair to him... tomorrow? When we're not officially mourning her death? Oh, but Tim, that never ends. Are you still such a coward? Timid Tim, as Boil and the rest of those high school parking lot renegades called you. So afraid that Barry's friendship will die with your admission of guilt?

"You're talking to yourself again."

My whole body froze. Managed to steer smooth enough. I think. Bit down hard. Darted a quick look, but he didn't seem to notice, let alone look angry. He continued:

"It's getting creepy, man. Half-sentences and jumbled words. Random, like you have brain damage. Sounds like... I mean, what the hell are boiling renegade parking lots?"

"Huh? Boiling lots?" Hell, I have no idea. But can't lose control, I'm at the helm. Lie, until you've found the truth. You have plenty of practice by now. "I was just thinking about stuff. Spit-balling ideas, lost in thought, you know? Like you do with your stories."

"Yeah?" Barry sounds a tinge too suspicious. Must derail him and comport myself halfway sane. Get him talking about... Ah, that's it!

"Time, you know? Passing, things changing. Thinking pretty soon this whole freaking island is going to be one giant parking lot and... you've changed, too. You're getting published again, huh? Bet you couldn't imagine your dreams would really come true? It's all you ever talked about, even in middle school."

"It is awesome. Isn't it?" Barry smiled. "It's taken such a long time, but I still can't believe it. Like, I'm finally getting paid, almost enough for my rent! And even getting fans!" He was sitting upright now, letting the realization flood in. "It's really happening, Tim. Everything I've worked for. And check this out. I actually got laid once—"

"Congratulations!"

"I was going to say, by a girl in the audience. After a reading at the Korova! Never thought a writer could get action for... anything. Ha!"

Good, it worked. He's on a roll and I can just stare straight ahead.

"This new magazine editor said he has connections. Maybe this could finally lead to my collection if they're all this good. Then an agent, then a contract with a big publishing house. Then the best-seller list... It could happen, right?"

"Easy there, ace. One step at a time. I wonder what you'll do with all those… thousands of dollars. And groupies. So which gem of yours is this again?"

"The Buddhist Bullet, remember?" he answered. He mumbled to himself for a moment, counting. "That one got rejected about four hundred and eight times."

I nod, tune out of that and into the rhythmic pulse of rotten yellow lights above. If they'd all spontaneously shatter, my royal blue Voltaire would melt into the night. Sure, evil things thrive in the darkness, but you can use it to hide from the evil things hiding in the light.

Barry's still humbly self-congratulating himself.

Exit 43 slides by. We're halfway home now, leaving the promise of the city behind in a trail of screaming streets and haunted suburbs. On our left, the bloated snake of traffic struggles along. The coffee finally settled in my stomach and I felt my skin prickle. Ah! Truly, there can be no finer pleasure than flying straight ahead, while everyone else rots in frustration as they head west toward their cities. Many thanks to Velocitor, Lord of Speed, first cousin of the Caffeind, for these blessed high-speed hours, vacant and free!

Despite some slight rattling, my car is holding up. It's older than me, too. Sure, there's a bit of shaking at this speed, but we all shake here and there. Can't push too hard though. Gods be good, my sanity won't survive breaking down mid-island. This is the transition between city and country, a real mutant of a landscape. The creepy mystique of Brooklyn spasms and gnaws itself on the west end, and its psychotic inbred brother, Tomahok, rots to the east. This asphalt infection spreading between them accounts for roughly seventy-five percent of Sponge Island, itself stretching nearly a hundred-and-thirty miles. If you traveled across the whole nation toward either end, you'll either end up in Hawaii or Tomahok, with a machete slipped between your ribs either way.

The whole of this island is nothing more than a strip mall, surrounded by suburban homes growing over native bones. The general population is a doomed lot of lower middle class laborers, sentenced to eternal gridlock. This breed has a strange arrogance that comes from living on an island. The only claim to fame this shit-strip can boast is a handful of perfect beaches clustered at the end. Aside from that, which only one percent of the wealthiest enjoy, it's no different from any other blindly defeated piece of Americana.

In fact, we could do the whole world a favor, if the next time the Seven Great Waves long to taste human flesh, they devour Sponge Island first, thus losing their appetite for the whole wicked race. Then they can disperse, back into the abysmal depths forever more. Fuck it. I hope I'm on vacation when it happens. I never fully bought into that whole "joint stock company" idea anyway. I owe these swine nothing.

"...so in the end, I really owe these guys," Barry was saying. "I mean, I always knew it was a good story. But the rejections *were* starting to make me doubt. My lesser works seem to get bought with no trouble at all. But someone over at 'Paradox Layers' *finally* saw its potential, and that magazine is a bigger, better home for it. Actually, he said it was great! Agents check that magazine for newcomers. It's all fast, it's a lot to take in."

"I'm sure it is," I said. "Paradox Layers must have, what, three hundred readers? Barry, we'll be thirty in a couple of years. You can dream bigger. Hypocrite."

"Yeah, sure it's that, or it's the second largest international sci-fi journal." Barry laughed and crossed his arms behind his head. Unshakable. Admirable.

Unless I get the guts to tell him the truth. Can't decide, and we're running out of road. Yet he pushes on, unknowingly provoking me.

"So what *are* your dreams then, you cynical bastard?" he asked. "You'd better hurry up, you know. Despot says thirty is the new twenty, and dead's the new thirty."

"His name isn't... whatever. You sound like some dumb fan-boy. Do you have a pen name now, too? How do I earn an alter-ego?"

There's many awful ones I could claim, but I truly didn't hear his answer. I was stuck on the hip-hop wonder's wisdom. It was a joke, sure, but like all the best ones, truth hides in the laughs. I *am* running out of time, in a sense. What *do* I dream of? The past. Nothing more. I have no dreams left for the future. Just memories of a life when I had parents, a home, a girl I loved and who loved me the same, and every day was the only day that mattered.

When did the dreams of my future lose hope, decaying into blind fear instead? When I cast my mother's ashes from the Tomahok cliffs? When I cursed the ocean for keeping my father's corpse? When I hid while my girlfriend's corpse was laid into the cold earth? Too many choices abound. No more dreams, Barry, my friend. My future bears no ripe fruit, just ashes in my mouth.

"At least you two are doing well," I said. Glad Barry is still watching the trees pass; he can't see the falseness all over me. "I'd wager Julio is happy enough, and Burn, in his own way. That's a good majority of my friends. Anyone else actually pulling off... I mean, I'm happy you followed your dreams. Everything is working out in the end, after all. Ha!"

I could see the pain of his sister's death retreat behind his eyes, with that the promise of recognition looming. A vicious taste of shame tore through me. He took her death better than I ever could. I just can't let him know that. Because... because Barry deserves a break.

We've been best friends since five, lived like brothers, even if our parents never mingled. And thus I don't mind giving him a ride to his mother's house at this god-forsaken hour. I don't mind. No, really. I don't.

He hadn't gotten more than ten miles from his apartment before his own car kicked the can. No surprise, it being nothing but flash. All smooth angles, sharp reflections, and confident colors. A used 1981 Phoenix Firestorm G6. But the engine was loud and fragile, not built to last through true grit.

Wasn't lying before when I told him I was drunk-ish. I'd been nursing a glass of straight rum, alone, when his mother, that majestic bitch Helena Cameron, came rapping at my door. Being crafty and experienced, Barry called her up. She then had to drop the pills and booze, get a cab, and down to my place to bash the door, rousing me to action. My roommate, Bernard Saiyers, was absent, no note. As usual. It's up to me to, again.

"How come Burn didn't ride out with you?" Barry asked.

"He's M.I.A." I said. "I've gotten used to it. Not sure I'd even want to tag along for wherever it is he's going nowadays."

"Where? Doing what?"

"Couldn't even guess. I think he's been buddy-buddy with some lawyer or something lately, but I never met the guy. Most likely doing a lot of gambling out in Tomahok. Lord knows where he finds the money to do it."

Money. Helena Cameron could actually afford to send a cab to get Barry and bring him back. The family's money was disintegrating, but it was there. Yet she came to me. No gas money offered. No matter. There are few things more tedious than driving across Sponge Island in the dead of night, on a night for dead girls, knowing as soon as I get to the end, I'm headed right back. Helena was too numb on stiff drink and painkillers to care. So much so, that she nearly begged me to go fetch her son. Right now. But this was a mission that called beyond my own suffering. If it were any other night I'd have told her to buzz off. My debt to Barry hasn't been paid in full. Not yet. Maybe I could tell… Maybe this is the proper night, after all? It's going better now. He is a true friend, after all. A brother in soul, if not blood. Which… does not apply to Tracy.

Regardless, although it was Tracy who convinced me to finally get loans and scholarships for college, I let Barry believe his constant badgering was the key. A lifetime ago, when the escape from our hometown coffin nearly overwhelmed me. Even if it was the nearby community college. That new world that Barry dragged me kicking and screaming into the glow of college enlightenment. He was only doing what he thought best. He knew exactly where we'd come from, believed a break from Thornwood would change something in me. He didn't know why I lingered… But he did see me changing rapidly in the face of girls who weren't… her. Weird drugs, and fast friends. He saw me banging my head on our wall at midnight while he was studying, he saw me devour pack after pack of cigarettes and smile and cheer in front of strangers, and then sit silently on the couch for hours. He saw me stop reading books and start staring at lizards in the grass, letting ash fall from my lips. Not what he'd hoped for. But Barry never knew that I wasn't fully depressed. I was just counting the hours until I could return to Tracy. Until I dropped out, having no one to return to.

"Tim? We were talking about happy, fancy things. Dreams?"

You want to know my dream, Barry? I dream of being okay with not dreaming about her. All day and every night. I've been too close to Heaven to ever be whole again. That's my dream. So I tell him:

"My dream is to see your great success before it's my turn to cash in," I answered. I have to admit, Barry is a good writer and it's great that he's getting published. He has a call, a passion, something to drive towards, rather than escape… But tonight Barry needs to be with his mom. That's all the family the Camerons have left. I can do that for them. Would be nice if they invited me over, but I know Helena will shoo me down the driveway as soon as Barry opens the door. He'll come over tomorrow. I need to be alone. And he needs a better friend than me.

"So what's the issue?" I asked. Points for trying!

"The August one," Barry said.

"That's this month."

"Yeah. I get a few contributor copies. Do you want one? You want one, right?"

"I'll check it out," I said, reflexively reaching for a cigarette. A full second of confusion washed over me while my brain caught up. That was weird. I quit smoking in college. But I started again. But... no... then I quit, because Tracy asked me to—

"STOP!"

The brake lights swooped in like vicious little bats, coming right for our windshield. My forearms burned, the wheel turned, the road slid beneath us, and we glided across the shoulder, around the other car, into freedom.

"Jesus Christ, dude!" Barry said. His skin was bleached as he clutched the seat.

"I told you to relax," I said. Sweat rolled down the left side of my face, out of view. Don't betray yourself. I cleared my throat. "So remind me, what's the next story going to be about?"

Regret hit instantly. I sought to calm him, but opened the door to Barry's imaginary kingdom once again. I'll never shut him up now. It's okay, Tim. Reach for the radio casually, flip it on. Keep it low at first. Turn the rap back on if you must, just nod your head and listen. You'll drown him out soon enough.

"I just told you, The Buddhist Bullet! But I've got notes for... well, for a fantasy epic," Barry said. "I've never done the whole hero's journey thing."

"That makes two of us."

"It'll be set in the ancient past, a fantasy world with knights and monsters. But it's ruled by this horrid demon warlock. So you'd think that many heroes would step up to take him down, but there's this huge problem. You see, the demon lord has this cursed blade. If you're cut down by it, you vanish from existence. Completely. Everyone who ever knew you, ever loved you, instantly forgets you ever existed! Physical relics of your life vanish. No songs to sing of your heroism, no statue to commemorate your valiant effort. You're simply forgotten for all time."

A cursed sword. Damn. This is not what I need to talk to him about. I need to tell him about Tracy. My Curse. Whose baby she might have... Why her death might, just maybe, be my... God damn it, WHY CAN'T I JUST FUCKING DO IT?

Barry was staring at me as if I'd actually screamed. Did I actually scream?

"You look like you've seen a ghost," he said.

"I did. That fox. But it was real. It... I can't... I don't know, man," I was drowning. Found my lifeline and made a desperate grasp. "The sword idea, your curse? That's hard to connect with. How does that address the human condition?"

"You're kidding, right? You, of all people, aren't interested in demons and curses?"

"No, it's just that being forgotten is... man, I don't know. I like that story about the lovers foolishly merging their brains, better. You should finish that one. I'm sure it will be another hit."

Truth is, that idea he just pitched scared the shit out of me. Being erased forever? What a terrible idea he so casually batted around. Worldwide amnesia as a weapon? Jesus H. Christ. Barry was silent. He stared out the window. I watched his eyes track a dead deer, bloated, burst across the shoulder.

"Have you figured out which god cursed you yet?"

"Don't toy with me. And no. But I did do even more research. I'll narrow it down and then..." Then what? What are you going to do, Tim? Plead for mercy? Summon and bind it? Idiot.

"What'd you find?"

"Well, there's some kind of Taino religion. They have Coatrischie. If I offended her, the Goddess of torrential downpours and the storm servant to Guabancex, and also sidekick to the Thunder God Guatava... well, then I'm screwed thrice over. But from what I've read, she loves her work too much, a bit overzealous, so maybe I'm just one sad glitch in the system. The Job in her Bible. But I still don't see how *not* killing innocent sea life is worth being cursed."

"Sometimes intentions speak louder than words," he said.

What exactly does that mean? He must be humoring me. Yet he continued.

"Maybe their gods saved the fish, but that doesn't change the fact that you wanted to kill it."

"I did not! And it wasn't a fish. It was a stingray or something. And I was scared. And five!" I spit. Right onto my own steering wheel.

"Whether it's a grain of sand or a rock, in water they sink alike."

I stare at him in awe. This is the Barry I need. Don't deserve, but need. "Well, that... Damn, that actually makes sense. So you agree then. The Curse is real?"

He shrugged.

"It gets worse," I said, but actually felt something like relief. It felt like finding out this was all a bad dream. Or one of his bad stories. "As far as I can tell, those religions overlap, so there's the whole Baron Samedi and Papa Gheude sect I have to worry about, too. Get this. They're the lords of sex, death, and fertility! A neighbor religion, but who's to say that gods can't team up to screw around with—"

"Tim, stop. Are you okay?"

I glared at him.

"More than usual?" he clarified. He waited. And waited. Then got awkward again. "Ha, I mean, if all that's true, then you really are screwed."

"I'm fine. It's the world that's fucked. Claude apparently knew that. So he checked out? Must've been some king-hell type of secret that he couldn't shoulder."

"That's not cool, man. We have no idea why he..." A certain a flash of red hair and a young girl's face hit us. "...why he killed himself."

"Well, look at the evidence," I said. "No, no, I mean, let's not *list* the evidence, we don't have to waste our brains on that. You escaped home, right? Well, I stayed. There's nothing left. Our families are pretty much erased, most of our friends are gone, and the economy is so bad we have to eat each other alive just to get a catering job in some CEO's dungeon. No matter what we do, we're fucking doomed."

"Right. Cursed, as you put it. That's just your perspective."

"My perspective?" I nearly snarled. "Es la verdad, your brainless hick!"

"I'm just saying, you could try *doing* something besides sulk and research and drown yourself in paranoia. Change what you can, even if it's only yourself," Barry said. Still, calm, and smooth. "Accept a little responsibility, you know? Nobody's forcing you to stay there."

"Are you trying to imply that my negative world view stems from *my* internal state? That external circumstances don't apply?"

"Well, it's a combination," he said. He sighed. "Look, we both know reality is subjective to your perception. But you're locked in a loop, bro. A recursive loop of negativity that just exacerbates the external conflicts."

"Save the fancy words for your books. I get it." Now *this* feels like old times. Annoying, but challenging. Comfortable. This is why...

"Fine, then!" he shouted. "If we're all doomed from the start, then why don't you just kill yourself?"

Nearly swerved off the highway. Brake lights streamed by on all sides, anger my autopilot. Nearly snapped my wrists from gripping the wheel so hard.

"You know what, Barry? You're a fucking dick! How am I supposed to feel, living alone in a fucking garage with Bernard? My youth slipping away, my only prospects being the fry bitch at Burger Don and maybe, just maybe, by the grace of your god, making a manager position for fifteen bucks an hour? Which I *won't*, by the way, since apparently not smiling enough can get you fired."

"You hated it anyway."

"Well maybe I'd feel a little more fucking positive and smiley in my nice little wage-slave hell if I'd had some success, too."

Some silence passed. Some. Not enough.

"Just don't give up. That's what I meant, Tim. Please..."

"Give up? I'm fucking here, aren't I? I haven't given up." Would have done that a long time ago, at her side. But I hate this world too much to let it off the hook. Must leave some spiteful mark before I go.

More exits passed, faster, my foot growing heavier the longer we did not speak. Can't keep up this manic cycle, it's like one night with him and... I don't know. Getting too tired to drive, wasting my energy on this roller coaster.

"Hey, let's lighten the mood a little," Barry said. "I have an excerpt from the story with me.

"Oh yeah? Fantastic."

"Yes, The Buddhist Bullet itself!"

"Are you kidding me?" See, roller coaster. Up and down.

Heard paper rustling, like beetle skeletons wrestling in the autumn leaves. Barry smoothed out the crumpled pages. "You actually carry it around with you?"

"Yeah, I'm still tweaking it here and there, even though it's already being... do you want to hear some of it? The heart of it?" Barry asked.

"The heart," I chuckled.

"Oh, wait, I guess you've already read it, right?"

"Um," I stammered. I loosened my grip on the wheel. "Of course, several times. It's about the uh... sentient bullet that reaches enlightenment. But it's no use, since it can't protest being jammed into a rifle clip and fired into someone's guts?"

"Yeah. Pretty much, yeah." He leaned down and hugged his knees, then sat up quickly. "Tim, I need to tell you something else that's been on my mind and I don't wanna tell anyone because I'm afraid they'll think I'm crazy."

Wow. You and me both, buddy.

"Okay, but stop freaking me out, man. My heart can't take this manic bullshit. The whole car stinks of our weird-ass feelings. I swear I won't judge you, but calm down first, because I have a tranq-gun in the trunk."

He laughed. Good.

"Besides, at this point it's going to take a lot to make me think you're crazy," I said to my oldest friend.

"Okay, well, I think... I think I've been channeling Byron Brick's soul."

The words were hushed, timid, almost sacrosanct. I'm here dwelling on revealing the truth behind one of the most traumatic moments in both our lives and he's talking about channeling his favorite author's soul?

"It's like, I've read everything he ever wrote. And he died right around the time I was born. And lately, I've been having these really intense dreams, lucid as hell, and we're talking to each other. He tells me these ideas for stories he never got to write, like the Buddhist Bullet. And the other stories I said before. And then I wake up and the whole thing is already written in my head. It's like his spirit reached out and found a kindred spirit to cling to."

"So you're now telling me that your hot new story is merely supernatural plagiarism?"

"It's not plagiarism," he countered. "He never actually wrote any of it. It's more like... like his essence diffused into the natural world. Or spiritual world. Whatever. And he's been recycled, and we're just compatible. My love and respect of his work made me into a magnet for his spiritual residue."

"Gross," I said. "You ever wake up covered in his residue?"

"Don't joke, Tim. I'm being serious. It's not just Brick I feel like this about. Just, death in general. I feel like death. I feel like death is—"

I missed the semi-truck by a worm-burner. Nearly clipped the passenger side's mirror off.

"Fuck, Tim! Are you sure you're really sober? Slow down, please! There's no rush!"

I made my hands stop shaking, refused to return his glare, and swallowed. Pulled into the right lane and slowed down to seventy. Barry finally resumed breathing and arched his back in the cramped seat.

"There's something else," he said.

"What?"

"My car didn't really break down."

And we almost crashed. Lucky for us, my reflexes are better than I boast, and my mind was flipping between fearing a siren behind us and wanting to smack him in the face. "What the fuck! Why did you drag me out here?"

"I just... I didn't want to be alone. I thought you wouldn't... I'm not okay. Something's wrong and I don't know what it is. But I'm not okay."

A monstrous beast of a truck blew past, shaking the car.

"Damn! People are crazy out here," he mumbled.

There are no coincidences... I know what's wrong, of course.

It's me.

Okay, do it, Tim. Tell him about the affair.

"Barry, I'm not drunk. At all. Honestly," I slowed down to sixty, feeling sick. "There's something that's been on my mind. A long time. Something I need to tell you, too. Okay?"

When he looked at me, the skin beneath his eyes sank. "What?"

Seven hells, I'm sweating now, throat is tight. Do I just leap off the cliff, or... I can ease into it. Let the realization grow in his own mind before the bomb drops.

"It's uh, it's about the night we got rid of your dad."

He looked out his window and folded his arms. "So? What about it?"

"We never, you know, addressed it. Fully."

"This is a little out of character for you," Barry said. "Our friend kills himself and you don't give a shit, you lose your job to 'starve to death on a beach' on principle, but all of a sudden you want to psychoanalyze the worst night of my life?"

"The worst?"

He punched the dashboard. "Second worst."

"Can I just..." He'd almost dented the dashboard. His knuckles were raw. "Can I just explain it from my end?"

"I'm not stopping you."

"So here I am, you know, my parents are alive, and still in my old house, and I get this phone call from you at 3 A.M. and you sound like tear-stained glass."

"Again, very poetic."

"So of course I'm freaked out, and we both know what it is. Your father. And there's nothing I can do. My karate... Well, you remember how big your dad was."

"Yes, yes, I know all of this," Barry said, watching the trees pass and never returning my gaze. I see only the slope of his jaw line, the arterial vein stretch from neck to head.

"So I'm thinking holy shit, what am I going to do to a beast like that? Julio. Of course, Julio! He nearly beat his own father to death, so why not yours too?"

I laughed. He didn't. Returned my eyes to the road ahead. The red and yellow lights bobbing and weaving through the darkness, none ever overtaking the other. Blurring together.

"So Julio and I burst through your door like heroes and we see your dad holding you against the wall by your neck, your nose is busted, and his fucking cheek... his cheek is almost gone. All the blood... and that torn skin flapping as he screamed... Julio's pumped, but I'm frozen, I could almost see his teeth through it, and blood all over the floor, and we don't know if it's his or yours, and your mom just bashing him over the head, over and over with whatever she can grab. Lamps. Books. Doesn't make him flinch. And still, you dug your finger in his eye."

"Tim. Believe me, I remember."

"Barry, trust me, I have a point."

"Of course."

"So Julio, always the pragmatist, goes right for your dad's balls. He collapses, and you all descended on him like starving tigers, right? Even Bernard's there, a little late as usual... but still there, kicking him in the ribs. You guys are ripping him to shreds, tearing his hair, pulling at his eyelids. I'm saying it like this because… because I just watched. And I saw the staircase, and the only light on in the house is at your sister's door. So instead of helping, I leapt past all of you, and ran upstairs to her. And I just held Tracy, sitting there like a little… like a little girl, and a bit of her dad's cheek is still in her teeth. I pulled it out. I stopped her shaking. I kept her warm. I think… to your mom, maybe all of you, it seemed like I didn't help at all. Left you all to fight, just ran as usual. But the four of you beat him so bad. You didn't need me. Not really. And then the lawyers did the final kick in the balls, he's never… you didn't need me, but she did. You know? I didn't abandon you."

"You were upstairs with Tracy?" He turned toward me slowly.

"Yeah, uh… Timid Tim ain't much in a fight, right? To me it wasn't just about punishing your father. It was about protecting her."

"Right." He turns back to the black trees, thicker now than the suburbs, passing like a heart beat as another truck rocks us.

"So that's the truth. I was with her the whole time."

Come on Barry, connect the dots. Call me out. Don't make me say it.

"And… I left the window open so you'd think—"

"Ha. Brilliant idea, man," he finally said. True smile, wet eyes. "Very convincing. We actually thought you *did* run away. But I always thought it was you who got the police."

Something began its ascent, a great leathery flap of wings off the back of my neck, yet one claw remained hooked in my trachea. We're almost there. But it's not right to make Barry call it out. I have to admit it myself. Tracy and I were lovers and her death could be my fault. My love for her, my Curse, poisoned your sister. Come on, Barry! Figure it out, you smart little fucker! I can't… I just can't say it. Weaving through traffic, every stupid car looking like a hearse, waiting for him to respond. He sighed and leaned back in the chair, hands folded behind his head.

"Tim," he said. He laughed again. A relief laugh, without the tears. "I already knew all that. She told me how you held her all night, after Julio bolted from the cops, how you slept under her bed when the ambulance came. You always were like a big brother to her. I'd expect no less. And yeah, we've seen how good you are in a fight. You're a healer. Not a killer."

A healer? I'm the poison, can't you see it? It's all true, how many loved ones do we have to survive until everyone else catches on that I'm not crazy? Wait, he just said...

"She told you?" I don't know what this feeling is. Somewhere between hope and dread. His next words are vital. Seconds slow, holding my breath until he speaks. Can't wait anymore. "Did she tell you—?"

The front of my car explodes.

A gang of devils erupt in an orgy under the hood, shaking the very frame with their combustible abandon. Smoke jets across the windshield. I barely retain control, thudding across the shoulder, praying there's nothing hidden behind the smoke. Teeth rattling, metal screeching, pumping the brake so we don't spin out in the grass and eat a tree.

The engine coughs as we idle there, and I slowly pull back onto the shoulder, shaking.

"Fuck," I dropped my head against the wheel. "So close."

"Shit. Wow. Shit! What's wrong?" Barry asked.

"Age, maybe? Or fate," I answered. "One of those vile things. They come around to get us one way or the other."

"Both our cars breaking down tonight? Even more poetic. Maybe you're right about curses."

"You lied," I rolled down my window, spit into the grass, and then began gagging. "Or was that the real lie?"

"Tim you don't look so good. Hey, are you all right?" He grabbed my shoulder.

It just came up, coffee and rum and bad burgers, streaming down the side of my car door. No sleeves on my sacred Hawaiian shirt, so I wiped my mouth on my forearm.

"Nice," Barry said.

"Well, there's no point in dicking around." I coughed. "Let's get under the hood and tackle this bitch."

The night remains still, purple, thin and cool, sliced apart by streaks of metal cruising down the highway. A chorus of insects serenaded our arrival. I stood there for a moment in the summer air, utterly clueless. I popped the hood open, jerking back as steam shot out. I wrapped my t-shirt around my hand and started poking at things, leaning back as far as I could, my black and white Hawaiian shirt blowing like a cape as cars blurred by.

"Barry! Get your lazy ass out here and lend me a hand! Maybe you can channel a dead mechanic to inspire us."

He came over. We stood there, dumbfounded, trying to comprehend the strange inner workings of a burst combustible engine. This guy can spin worlds in his head, I can pursue mystical horror gods across space, yet neither of us know jack shit about a car engine. No matter. I can sit here all night if we just pick up the conversation again. We were so close. So close.

"So you know I didn't run away? She told you I was with her the whole time? She never told me. It doesn't... bother you?"

He didn't answer again, just stared at the steaming engine. Both our arms crossed over our bony chests. Dancing on landmines. Fine. Maybe I can lighten the mood before we dive to the bottom. I turned and poked him in the chest.

"Oh! I know why it doesn't bother you! Barry, I meant to confess earlier. I know your *true* secret, buddy, and don't worry. It's totally cool!"

"What the hell are you talking about? How are we going to get home?"

"You don't have to live in the closet, bro," I said.

"Tim, what the fuck are you talking about? You blew the engine. Maybe it overheated."

He's still trying to wave through the steam, not paying any head at my pathetic joke.

"Barry, bro, don't fret. It's cool if you're a gay. I always suspected you have a crush on me, and hey, who could blame you? I'm flattered, really."

"For Christ's Sake, Tim! I'm not gay!" Barry said. "Only in your wildest dreams. And if I was, I doubt a skinny, mentally ill loser in dire need of a haircut and a new shirt would be my type." He ducked under the hood.

I laughed, staring into the pipes and burning guts. "Oh, you're not that shallow. You said it yourself before, who but your mother could resist my charm?"

"Yes, yes, of course."

The steam had dissipated. I ducked under the hood with him.

"These damn things just break on you out of nowhere," I said. "So you were saying, about that night..."

"Do you have Triple A or something?" He stared at me, inches from my face. I didn't blink. "Um, you said you were upstairs taking care of Tracy while we did the dirty work. And you slept under her bed so she'd feel safe."

"Um... yes."

He ducked out from under the hood. Stood straight. I forget how tall he is when he stops slouching. He put his hand on my shoulder and smiled.

"You're a good friend, Tim."

"Th-thank you." Clenched teeth. Ah, shit. There's no right way to say these things. I have to just go for it.

"That'd be the best way," he leaned under the hood again. "Please don't kiss me. You just puked."

Shit! I said that all out loud? Again? No, not possible. Still... I'm stalling. Alright Tim, he might punch you. Kick you in the balls. Just take it.

"Barry, remember my mom's funeral?"

"Of course I do. Bro, what's going on? Your car just died. Don't you care? What are we going to do?"

"That's why I ran away from Tracy's. I couldn't stand to see her like that. My mom. Like a painted, dried, doll. Every single time I remember Mom, I see flashes of her in that casket. No matter what. Every single time. Every memory is wrapped in it."

"Tim..."

"And... also... I'm not convinced Tracy overdosed. Even the doctors couldn't tell us anything for sure. Even if she'd... I think she actually *was* pregnant. And I think I know whose—"

Bam.

Everything goes underwater.

It comes pouring through the pines, around the cars, hits full force. Gushing through trees and over silent cars. An ocean's ghost of waves crested in white froth. The grotesque math of existence... I'd let my guard down. It was just waiting since the city. Like always, waiting for the most vulnerable moment.

Sounds are distant. Sights are blurs. I suppose I heard the crunch of the other two cars, the skid of tires as they hurtled toward us, the smell of rubber grasping desperately to pavement. The angles are strange. Two cars sliding sideways off the road. I dove. One car clipped my Voltaire, spinning it into Barry, flicking him away like a bug. He hit a tree. I sat up, a three-car bonfire blinding me, a man hanging out of a windshield, starting to burn. Everything not bathed in fire looking like it was smashed with garbage bags full of tomatoes. Could hear the man saying someone's name. As I crawled closer, the screams behind me faded with my vision, trying to latch on to the words Barry was gasping.

But now I sit here in this hospital, waiting for Barry's mother, surely wrecked and pissed about taking a hundred-and-forty-dollar cab all the way to Thornwood's nearest, and only, hospital. Of course it's my fault, and she demands every detail. All I really remember is that Barry was standing beside me one moment, then boom, I'm lying alone and Barry is coated in red. I crawled a damned marathon to reach him. He lay crumpled against the tree. His body was limp, an abandoned puppet. But his eyes were wide open, darting back and forth. Those green gems burning into mine. Tracy, he wheezed. Hey, hey Barry! It's me. It's Tim! Come on, hold on! Stay with me! He kept whispering for Tracy.

I held him.

Even when the ambulance came and the cops gently pulled me aside, I never once glanced at the offending vehicles. The drivers could have been choking to death on their own blood, screaming for their children, for all I cared. All my attention was on my twisted friend.

They examined me up and down. They scanned me and spun machines and gave injections and filled me with numbing pills while he was far away in blinding rooms I couldn't enter.

Of course I was fine. Aside from some cuts and bruises.

My name is Timothy Dune. And I am perfectly. Fucking. Fine.

Barry can't die. Even if Tracy herself is pulling on him. I need him. He needs to see his dreams, he's so close. Just give him that one kindness. Then he can croak and leave me to a strangely hollow life that will forever be defined by his absence. That's how it goes in my world.

But somehow, nothing got that crazy.

Crazy is dinosaurs. Crazy is fireworks. Crazy is a dependable car that kicks the bucket for no good reason, leaving two best friends lined up for a perfect ricochet shot of fate. Crazy is Barry's mother losing her son on the anniversary of losing her daughter.

Everything between the accident and the ambulance is now gone.

Details.

Transitions.

I'm hunched over in an un-needed wheelchair in a plastic hallway, listening to the doctors. They've assured us that Barry is not going to die.

They swear to their god. They will protect him. I've heard that before. He looked bad, but hell, they promised he'd probably be walking again within a couple months.

The hospital hall is full of living bodies, and others beneath coarse blue sheets. Death was in the air from the very start, and the drivers of the two other vehicles are dead. One on impact, and the other down the hall just a few minutes ago. I shudder to think that he's now a spirit standing over my shoulder, trying to steal a witness's memory of his own death. Goddamn selfish ghost bastard. Get away.

But I'm already cataloguing the night's events, trying to look at the world through Barry's eyes instead of mine because I just can't fucking take this anymore. Trying to spin sentences to describe the true carnage of reality, finding metaphors to express the strangeness of it all. And I'm identifying the structure of the night, noticing that it all flows in a nice arc, and I'm thinking about Tracy, and her leather jacket and her one pierced eyebrow, and I'm watching Barry's mother marching down the hall toward me, and I'm smelling coffee on my breath and rust in my mouth and a smoke in my hair, thinking about Barry's fractured skeleton and his shallow breathing. Another miracle is that I even got a chance to see him, eyes still open, glazed. One goodbye before they stuck him into the machine for the night. He doesn't remember much after the diner. Yet.

I can't help it. The terrible nature of it all makes just enough sense. This is how it always happens. Right when something good is happening, someone close to me suffers or dies. So god help Barry. He needs to see his stupid story in print, and his collection finally come true. And god help me, because he was right. I've got nothing left, I'm going home to nowhere. I'm poison, growing more potent than ever. I'm angry that I got so close to coming clean. Angry that it's all about me again, and I can see it, yet I still can't help it. Angry that even after all this, I'm somehow still stealing his pain.

Hell Pump Lizard Teeth

"So is Barry gonna die or not?" Bernard asks through the sea-warped door.

I pinch my nose. "Damn it, Burn, did you eat road kill? Can I at least get a courtesy flush?"

Bernard is shitting out a two-dollar burrito while he digests the facts and I lay on the stolen mattress that we constantly fight over. I've got my left ankle up on my knee and already my foot's gone numb. My makeshift tattoo kit sits on an old table, old enough to have a glass surface, cracked and green, covering a pristine scrimshaw landscape. My supplies are laid out neatly, a safety pin, our last bit of hydrogen peroxide, a lighter, and a cap full of black India ink that Bernard pilfered from god knows where.

"Yo? Tim? What's up with Barry?"

"I told you. He's banged up. Bad. But he's stable. That's the problem. He's awake and bored, so I have to go do *another* favor for him now. Like I'm that family's damn guardian-angel-slash-butler."

"Aw, always another problem for you, poor..." he trails off. Probably wiping his ass. I try to wipe the image from my mind. "You sure as hell ain't no guardian angel. I name thee Devil!"

"Burn, I really did try to confess," I tell the door. "We got hit right before I could ease into it. BAM! Just as I was about to admit to... to..." He knows but I still can't say it without feeling some ghost's grip on my throat.

"Oh, well excuse me! So you finally, almost, *didn't* tell him about you and Tracy?" Bernard's sarcasm echoes through the thin door, along with his noxious stink. I hate talking during bowel movements, but he never, ever, has.

"Yes. We were just a few teary-eyed words away." I resume pushing the pin through my skin. Prick, pop, bleed, then the ink sinks in. Prick, pop, bleed...

"Hey, it's only been six years! What's another few days gonna hurt? Guess you've had enough time to prep?"

"She only died three years ago." Prick.

"But you were banging her before that."

I stab myself too hard.

One dot in this tattoo will be more imperfect than the others. I wait for Bernard to finish, as I finish the tattoo. Prick, prick, prick. The faintest line is made of hundreds of tiny punctures. Then an old but clean shirt, to wipe away the blood. It will join the laundry piles in our corner, waiting in vain to be washed, cash-free, in the sea. I smile as the image starts to take shape. Each time I smear the blood away, I can see the form emerging from the pain and random lines. Now that Bernard's silently crapping away, there's a peace about the shack. Our home is small and square, with bits of wood paneling on the inside and nothing but cold concrete outside.

Waves crash against the shore out back. They're audible through the rickety windows that must be stuffed with sweatpants and boarded up in November. Taking a break from the tattoo, my eyes scan graveyards of junk. Garbage bags. Old blankets that needed to be washed, if not burned. Chipped and battered surfboards still caked in wax, now turning green. My sword. Our skateboards. Boxes of tapes, records, CDs, and a T.V. that doesn't work. Micro-fridge humming in the corner, bean burrito spattered microwave balancing on top, both plugged into a tangled mess of cords, snaking up like sinewy muscle to a strip cord, hanging by another extension cord from the ceiling. Three beams run beneath the pointed ceiling, giving us enough height to pretend our "home" is larger than it is. I stare up at one of the few things in here that's not battered, burnt, stolen, or rotten. My father's suit, carefully hung above. Only wear it for funerals. It's always above us, the safest spot. Bernard thinks it's creepy, as if someone hanged themself but the body slipped out of the clothes. He's right, after a fashion. We hung our wetsuits on the other beams, but it didn't help. Looks like gallows. Everything in here is stretched too far. There's even a pile of melons by the deck-door. We only ate two. And a reclining chair rescued from the dump. Crusty microwave. Metal sink. Two recycling bins filled with trash. The whole thing smells like an abandoned museum, a gym sock tomb. Mold, memories, musk.

The toilet flushes.

Bernard comes out of the bathroom, a closet that can barely hold our tower of smut, let alone his lanky frame. No shirt or shoes, just torn jean-shorts and sandals. His curly black hair crowns his long, thin face. Stubble on his chin and nowhere else. Small beads of sweat run down his skin, tanned and cured by sea salt, high winds, and a diminutive diet. He's squinting, something menacing and profound swimming inside his dark irises.

"Hey!" and suddenly Burn is a kid again. He bends over, then springs up with throwing darts pinched between his fingers. "Rock and roll house darts! Let's play a round, bro!"

"Hell no!" Can't he see I'm busy? But I confess, the offer is tempting.

The rules are simple. The game runs twenty-four hours a day, seven days a week. You must scream "rock and roll" and then a nearby object. It's up to the other players to get the hell out of the way. But in this jumbled mess of adolescent wonder, this is a most dangerous battleground.

"Rock and roll... Rat-man Poster!"

I hunch into a ball, nearly knocking over my delicate D.I.Y. tattoo center. The dart speeds past me, putting another puncture in the 8th grade art above the mattress.

"For Christ's sake, Burn, cut it out! You'll ruin my damned tattoo! And there are more pressing matters at hand. I need your help."

"Sorry." He turns away, dejected, and limply tosses another dart. "Rock and roll Brontobud Skateboard..."

THUNK.

"Damn it, you man-child! Will you help me out, or do I have to sic another eldritch god on you?"

He spun around, tossing all of the remaining darts over his shoulder. Don't hear any hit... so they've joined this nostalgia-swamp that we call a floor. We'll never find those darts. He won't even bother. Great, yet another reason to wear shoes in here.

"Okay, Tim. Fine. I've decided."

I throw my arms up, bloody safety pin still in hand. "Hallelujah! The porcelain god has blessed you with insight! Please, oh wise and powerful Bernard Saiyers! Render thy judgment upon me!"

He kept his back to me, a life-long sign of his sincerity.

"It's simple. Be a man of your word. Just this once," Bernard said, slipping his thumbs into his pockets. "You said you'd bring Barry home. You didn't. And I know right now you can't, but you can still help him out. You know that you gotta go see him! Tonight. Just like you promised. Shit, you owe him, dude. Big time."

"What exactly do I owe him?"

"Well, let's just start with the best friends since forever angle," Bernard said. He rolled his eyes to the ceiling. He paced our cluttered cube shaped home, hands clasped behind his back and eyes on the ceiling, where the cement walls meet wood. "If it was me, you know that—"

"Then you should be coming with me."

"Hey, man! This isn't about me," Burn said. He scratched his lower back, buying time. "Plus, it actually is your fault that he's in the hospital. You're lucky, got to wheel yourself out the next day, but he's trapped there. All alone. You abandoned him in that... faux-god temple."

"Abandoned him? That's nonsense," I said. "I asked you for advice, not condemnation. And since when do you call hospitals faux-god temples?"

"Been hanging around you too long. But hey, man, whatever. He was in *your* car. *Your* car broke down. *You* pulled over. *You* asked him to get out."

"I needed help!"

"You needed help," Bernard repeated. He walked over to our small, brown fridge and yanked it open. "Do we have an eggplant left?"

"No."

"Orange juice?"

"Just fucking look," I said. I limped over to the glass door, leading to the back porch. The gray sea crashed against the shore. "His mom asked me for the ride, you know. I went out of my way to bring them together. Because of Tracy."

"Ah, and that brings us to the next point!" Bernard said. He spun around with his finger dancing in circles, all lit up again. "You owe them, and you know it! Jesus, you knocked up his little sister..."

If not for the fresh tattoo I would have leapt over the mattress and split his lovely, shaggy skull.

"We don't know that for sure! You rotten... scum sucking... parakeet!"

"What? Look, either way, you do owe Barry this stupid little favor. Go see him. Be a bro, bro. Bring him his whatever-it-is. Poor guy's been waiting alone for days." He stared me down. "Plus, we know what you really want."

"Yeah, Burn? What's that?"

"You still want to confess."

I resumed the tattoo. Prick, prick. Prick. Lots of careful detail, but just the face. Very difficult to do with millimeter stabs.

"What is that supposed to be? Don't get any blood on our mattress."

"A fox."

"Why?"

"I don't know." I put the finishing touches on. Wiped the blood. Poured the hydrogen peroxide on. Perfect. A slightly cartoonish, simple, yet elegant fox face. Staring with solid black eyes, just above my left ankle. "Grab me some Band-Aids."

"Uh... not sure we have any left."

"Just grab me anything that I can wrap this with. Anything clean. I don't want to die from blood poisoning."

He pushed around in the closet-sized bathroom and came out with two tiny Band-Aids and a box of gauze pads, probably unopened since our shin-splitting, skateboarding youth. He tossed them over. I used the Band-Aids to adhere the gauze and then carefully pulled my clean sock up over the whole thing. Felt like a hundred ants gnawing in my leg, but I also felt a release, like lying in the sand after a marathon, simply breathing. As I finished up, Burn found some weathered sandals to slip on.

"Dude I forgot. What does Barry want, again?"

"He wants books. Of all the *fucking* things to drag me back out there for."

"The dude's a writer."

"So? Barry wants me to get all the way up to that hospital again, just to bring him his favorite book collection," I said, flopping back. "He doesn't want to see me. He wants to escape."

"So what? Just bring him the damn books. He's probably super bored. All laid up. All alone. Trusting you like a brother. Slooooooowly healing, nobody to talk to. Probably high as fuck on painkillers, though."

Not sure if I'm ready to see him like that, tubes and wires and bags and blood.

"Okay, fine. But come with me. It's an extremely long walk with no car." More than an hour *with* a car. And no one's brave enough to pick up a hitchhiker these days. "He'll be thrilled to see you."

"Um, yeah, about that…" Burn squirmed. "Oh, so you guys saw an armed robbery?"

"Yeah. No big deal. Nothing different than shit we hear about every day."

"And you did nothing?"

"Yup."

"Smart move," Burn said, popping a handful of mysterious pills from nowhere. "So he's stressed, depressed, and stuck in the hospital. Thanks to you. Nice work, Tim."

"They have cable, magazines, and morphine. Besides, why can't his mother do it this time? She *has a car*. And the books. Maybe she can avoid getting shit-faced for a few hours. When did I become the de-facto father for the Camerons?"

"That's a very creepy concept," Burn said, eyebrows raised. He chewed and swallowed the pills dry. "You know his mother isn't good for anything. She's been a pill popping alcoholic for decades. I'm surprised she actually showed up at the hospital at all. I'm just saying… She's broken, man. Sad as it is, you're all the family he's got."

"But I don't have a car now! Remember? God knows when I'll get it back from the shop. And I don't have a dime to pay for it anyway. He can't be alone, can he? Didn't he make friends in Brooklyn?"

"That's far away. A different world and different friends. He *asked you*. What are you scared of?"

"But… I already played hero and failed. Lost my car, nearly killed Barry. What's going to happen this time? I show up, and the hospital bursts into flames, and locusts come pouring out of the morgue? How many times does this crap have to happen until—?"

"Stop being such a dick."

"A dick? Are you fucking serious?"

"Yeah, Tim. You're kind of a dick," Bernard said before gulping something down. I lifted myself up, just in time to see him chugging the last of our orange juice.

"You kill it, you fill it," I said. "And it's your turn to buy toilet paper."

"Don't worry, dude. I'll swipe some at Texan Bro later," he said. "Hey, can I borrow one of your shirts tonight?"

"Their toilet paper is too rough for me," I said. "It's like sandpaper."

"Just imagine if it actually was."

"Hold on, you sneak creep!" He tricked me again. "Where the hell do you get off calling me a dick?"

"You fucked his dead sister."

"She wasn't dead back then, *dick*. And please, don't... I didn't reveal that to you, just so you could torture me with it. Something called confiding? Friendship? Trust?"

"Right. Trust," he said, flittering his fingers under his chin. "Look, I'm as stoked as anyone that you got your shot at love. What happened sucked. Bad. But now you get to be like the rest of us and deal with the fallout."

"You'd hold your tongue if you ever lost true love."

He stared at me, so still, a cartoon caught in freeze frame. Didn't even blink. I forgot... he must know I didn't mean it that way. We're both orphans now. But Bernard didn't say a word, just marched across the room and hunched over my box of clothes. He rummaged through it violently, with the orange juice carton still in hand. When he didn't find anything satisfactory, he looked up, not noticing that he spilled drops onto my stuff.

"Hey, that black and white one you're wearing is nice," he said. "Can I borrow that?"

I snarled, "You're lucky we've been friends for so long, or I'd cut your throat where you stand."

"Yikes! Don't bust out your famous karate."

"I'm getting good with that sword. I could cut you in two and bury you in the dunes before dawn."

"Bury me under that new golf course. Then I'll rise from the grave and avenge us all," Bernard said. He turned around with a blue and orange Hawaiian shirt. "How about this one?"

"Fine, fine," I said. "Look man, I don't have a problem with bringing him the stupid books, but the fact remains, I don't have a car anymore. Or a job! So I don't have the money to take a cab over to his mom's place, get the books, then back to the train station, hope there's one even running at all, and then get all the way back west to that god-forsaken hospital, and then another cab... You see my point?"

He walked over. Loomed over me. Lit a secret cigarette, then squatted down to put his hand on my shoulder. "Look, I know how hard it is. But you're missing the point." He waved the cigarette in circles at me until I coughed. "Don't you see it, buddy? It's kinda funny. The circle? Now you need a friend with a ride. That's all."

"That's all? Where's your car?"

"My car? I don't... I've always caught a ride with you."

"Exactly. Did I tell you that his didn't even break down? It's sitting somewhere in Brooklyn right now, perfectly fine."

"Probably towed. It's been a couple days. Hey, I'm not your logistics-team. You asked for my help, I helped. You just needed to be told what you already know. That's all I know. Right?"

Sadly, the bastard's right.

But that doesn't help. We're stuck out here. Being a former resort town even before the last Big Crash, Thornwood's isolated. Barry and I were lucky, happened to get hit by the nearest hospital to Thornwood. The infamously irresponsible Hawkhouse. But that's still two towns away with only one pathetic excuse for a train station between them (it runs once at 6 A.M. and again at 11 P.M., if ever—the rich don't take trains anymore), and nothing else but highway. 'Just bringing him the books' was a bit more of an odyssey than Bernard realized. But he's right, I'm playing Barry now. I need more help than this, though. Who, who?

"Well, there's got to be somebody else," he said. He returned from our mountain of junk with the last of my dark rum. How'd he find it? He popped the top and guzzled the rest down.

"That wasn't easy to steal, buddy!"

"All for one and none for all, eh? You could get his mom to drive you, or loan you the cash. I could use some too, if she's—"

"His MOM? The bitch who wouldn't even go pick up her own son? Who hates my guts and blames all *of us* for her abusive husband's absence? Who's never even thanked us for *rescuing her family* from him? His mom...? Fat fucking chance."

"And then you banged her little girl, behind her back, while babysitting."

Not sure what happened next. Just felt the white flame's flare.

The bottle of rum was shattered across the room before my hand even felt the sting. "Don't even start on that shit! That was an ugly joke. Best friend or not, I swear to god I'll cram that cigarette down your throat."

Bernard stayed perfectly still, bug eyed. "You can be pretty fast. Ha, ha?"

I tried melting him with my eyes.

His eyes were glued to the floor. Face flushed. "I'm, uh, I'm sorry. Tim."

He was. He's a jerk, but he's one of the good ones. I'll let it pass this time. Get back on track. "His mom. Wow, are you just trying to get rid of me, or are you actually brain dead? You know Helena won't help me."

"It's 'cause you can't come clean!'"

"Burn, seriously, I will! I swear. But I have to actually get there to do it!"

"No. You won't. I'm not trying to be mean, but if you haven't done it by now, then you won't do it when you get there, either. We both know you'll take your secret to your sad, lonely grave."

"Gracias, amigo." I flipped him off, then crammed my bloody shirt, ink bottle, and needle into the corner. "You're so sympathetic. Such sage wisdom."

He sat down on the mattress and put his arm around my shoulders. "Listen, bud. You knew what I'd say. Hell, what good am I to you, if I don't tell it like it is? You'd just go twice as mad. So shut up and take it."

A rare moment passed, one where Bernard Saiyers would see me cry. Instead I said, "Burn, I got so close. Just help me get there. Better yet, come with me!" I sat up and stared out our sliding glass door to the ocean. "Shit. You're a pain in the ass and an awful roommate. But you're right. It's not the books. It's not the trip. Of course I need to come clean with him." I looked back at my friend. "I'm still afraid."

Afraid he'll hate me and I'll lose him too. I knelt before the glass door. The longer I wait, the worse it will get. Waves break and sand shifts outside. The ocean has no answer.

"I don't know if he'll be angry. And of course you're afraid. Hell, I'd be, too. Man up and handle it yourself. It's not like I'm gonna stand there next to both of you when it happens. Or if."

If. When. If not now, when? How did he even hear that? Am I still... Ah, shit.

"Are you still what?"

I got up from on my knees, wincing when my ankle tat burned. "Burn, you're right about... everything. But I can't do this alone. It's too hard."

"Kind of the point, huh? Shit, Jay already knows, I know, what makes you—"

A horn honked outside. Who could it possibly...? No matter. It's a car! Yes, some weird luck for a change!

Out on the abandoned street, an engine roared, rattling our grimy front window and shaking both doors. The wooden one, and the ancient garage door, forever sealed with rust and lots of crazy-glue. We were desperate for ideas... but it still seems to attract cars! It was a bright red convertible. A cherry painted rifle, idling on the long, vacant strip of road.

There could be no mistake, it was waiting for us. There was nowhere else to wait. My parents' long-abandoned gas station lay in a coma across the street, hearing that engine and wishing to rise and serve once more. A summer breeze whistled through the line of evergreens and pines that stood stoically beyond the yellow field, blocking our 'house' from the maze of tiny roads that led north, towards Thornwood proper. Just the station, our place, the beach behind us... and the barren desert of chemically killed grass from the neighboring golf course. Not another house in sight. Just my parents' old gas station across the street, and now this beautiful red behemoth idling before our home.

Another honk. Yes! A gift from the gods! Fate in vehicular glory!

"Whoops, I gotta go!" Bernard said as he pulled my borrowed shirt on.

"Wait, where are you going?" I limped after him.

"Tomahok!" he shouted without looking back. "I'm going to a party with Sergio. He's a cool dude. You should come chill with us sometime."

"Chill? Burn! You junkyard dog! What about Barry?"

Bernard hopped down the steps. The driver was an older man, with a younger, luscious Brazilian runway model beside him. She smoked a long, thin cigarette. Her copper skin, long black hair, and arrogant indifference suggested Brazilian. I think. Based on the last one that slapped me, at least. A living cover model, flapping her black mane beside the mystery driver.

He leaned across the smoking female, riding shotgun. He had a large bald spot and a flowing, platinum blond ponytail. He grinned behind purple aviator glasses that matched his purple silk shirt, unbuttoned at the top with a few carefully selected rogue hairs peeping out.

His radio was blaring some kind of whistling symphony. Sweet, sweet flutist passion danced around the convertible's curves. An air of magic wafted about. This magic was not for me. The normally dead beachside road suddenly felt as alien as the seventh grade cafeteria.

"Yo, Sergio!" Bernard said as he leapt into the back seat. "What's the plan, my man?"

"Bernard!" I yelled. I shouldn't be surprised, but that doesn't change anything. "You rotten son of a bitch! Don't you dare abandon me now! Traitorous free-loading swine!"

"Burny Burn!" Sergio waved. He squinted at me. "Hey, hey, easy on the harshness, my boy." He took a long, overly sucking drag from his cigar. His head was hanging back, his right arm draped around the woman's shoulders. He was grinning. Each of his strangely aligned and immaculately white teeth were begging for a swift karate kick.

Try diplomacy instead, maybe make a bargain.

"Listen, sir. I'm sorry you had plans with my friend." I hobbled down the sandy path, crushing beer cans. "Something's come up and I need his help more than you need his company. He should have told you. And clearly you've got... her."

"Tttchh," the model said, looking straight ahead.

"Bernard, who is this guy?" Sergio asked.

"Antonio Sergio, allow me to introduce my best bro, Timothy Dune. He's cool. He's just stressed. Doesn't know how to properly chill, know what I mean?"

"Properly chill?" I sputtered. "Our friend's in the hospital, and—"

"So sorry to hear that, but what exactly is this situation?" Sergio asked. He had that skillfully neutral way of being a dickhead.

"The situation is Bernard helping me get to the hospital tonight!"

"Hawkhouse?" Sergio waved for me to come beside his door. He took his shades down, chin tilted to the wheel, looking up just like I do when trying my 'creepy look'. "Tell me, kid. Are you just you, or are you Burn? Or perhaps my lovely friend here? Are you me, are we you?"

"What the hell are you talking about?"

He peeled his aviators off. His eyes shone gray. "You're on a Devil's Run, aren't you, my boy? I can see it in your eyes. Just keep this in mind. In your darkest hours, we are all facets of the same glittering jewel. You are your friend and he is you. So don't worry. Burn is coming with us, but you understand now, yes? We can never truly be alone."

I couldn't move. This felt... wrong. And familiar. He's certainly not a local, but his face is triggering some hazy, old alarm bells. Where have I seen this creep before?

"So I'm a creep, huh?" He didn't raise his voice. "Fair enough. And you must know me because, well... perhaps a few reasons. And if not, remember, I *am* you and vice versa, capisce?"

"Bernard, what the hell is this shit?" I asked him, nearly blinded by the sun and how quickly he'd sprawled happily across the back seat. "Look, whatever you're doing, please, I need a ride."

"Take a bus," the model said. She never turned her head, only used the mirrors. "We are late. Vamanos, Sergio. El chico es un cabron."

The engine roared. I shouted at her.

"Hey! I can speak Spanish, you punta de... de... mierda!"

Yes, I can speak Spanish. Kind of.

"Such language." Sergio shook his head. "Lo siento, amigo. But we're headed east, not west, and no time to lose! Keep that chin up!"

"Yo, I'll catch up with you later, bro!" Bernard shouted. "And tell Barry I said what's up! Thanks, Tim!"

Sergio flipped the back of his hand while gunning the engine.

They sped off, crushing a blue, plastic bag.

It was the newspaper. Who keeps sending these? I never pay, never get a bill, never see who drops them off. It must have sat out here for days. I pulled it out of the bag and looked at the tidings, still shaking off the shock of whatever just happened.

Ah, here we go! War! Three of them. Excellent. That means there must be at least five going on. If history is written by the victors, then you go to the losers for the truth. I hope I'm the one lying when all is said and done. So to hell with visiting Barry, there are terrorists to fight and jobs to create and morals to defend! The cosmic-will demands I put aside my life and fight for the common good. That great overmind, the devils running, or whatever Sergio was yammering about, it's calling me and my fellow citizens to outraged action! Surely Barry would understand.

When I looked up, the lawyer's car was long gone. Bernard's really gone.

Only the yellowed grass and sparse trees, peeking through the dirt-sand, remained. Alone in the light, facing the gas station rotting on the corner, once partnered with our makeshift garage-now-home, sitting perpendicular across the street. I looked north, to the line of trees separating Thornwood from this back-lot desert. The sound of gulls circling above. Open ocean to the south.

CRASH!

A bottle broke across the street. No one in sight... must be in the gas station. My parents'... Damn it. Nothing's sacred. No doubt it's hiding some pack of rootless teens. That place used to be ours. Back when companies like Texan Bro hadn't muscled into town. My parents' station was the only one on this stretch, the last chance for fuel before Tomahok. Last chance before the Sponge Island's end. Our garage, now home, once sported not only the finest beachfront view, but fair prices and competent service... so long as Bernard's father ran it. A good partnership between good families. We even had a nice little house down the street, with a swing-set up on the dunes. Burn and his dad lived further down the street, where no homes now stand.

The garage closed first and turned into a high-school hangout long before it became home. But the gas station plugged along longer than we expected. My dad managed the business, Bernard's pop ran the stations, my Mom paid the bills, and I got through high school.

By the time I had my degree, the bank took the station, Mom and Dad died, Bernard's dad split town, and Barry buried Tracy. Barry was almost done with college, and I was a little late to that party. Once I knew Tracy wasn't joining me, I just... left. Meanwhile, Bernard pursued his own local interests. Meeting all sorts of people. Like that... Sergio.

It all fell apart so fast. Their bodies weren't even cold before the suits foreclosed on my *real* house. The town of Thornwood bought it from the bank. Then the town tore it down, marked it as a nature preserve, sold it, and thus, some bastard threw up that fucking golf course next door. Today, only our shitty old garage remains under my domain. My inheritance, my legacy, is rent-free shelter in a cold shrine to warmer days. Not so bad, really. My parents couldn't leave me what they'd worked to death for, but they still left me enough to build a home.

Mom and Dad...

The dementia came on so quick. Dad forgot the little things first. His schedule, inventory, putting socks on, doctor's appointments, brushing his teeth, surf trips. Little things. And then one day he paddled out on his board and never came back. I still throw up whenever I see helicopters shining lights into the ocean. I imagined him out there alone, in the dark, cold seas, manta rays swarming him and ripping his surfboard apart. Sometimes I stare past the rolling waves to the serene glass and can't help imagining his corpse alone, rotting in some dark reef, tangled in seaweed and coral, nibbled by sharks and squid as whales and sailboats pass overhead.

Mom held on long enough, working at both the gas station and as a clerk for some soulless firm. But without the proper income to hire more mechanics, we couldn't hang on (I was too busy buried in magick books, ancient worlds, hiding with Tracy). We used to have neighbors before the houses were foreclosed and torn down to make way for condos that never came.

Mom made it all the way to my graduation before her heart gave in. Others died. We all lost... seems like everyone.

Cursed. Swimming the barren seas alone.

The weird garage/shack that Burn and I mutated into some kind of home, a semi-adult tree fort on the coast... that was all my parents could leave me. They didn't even own the gas station in the end, let alone our actual house. But it's something, something Bernard and I turned into a paradise. Purgatory. Something. We have no computer, but we steal electricity from the power grid and the golf course down the road (Bernard is good at surviving, resourceful to a fault, I'll give him that) and we have a big mattress and a working toilet. Thank god for the small things! Tracy said that if there is a god, he's one damned engine, spitting out sharks and doves with ease.

I saw it all, standing on the side of the road, waiting for Sergio's convertible to come back and save the day. Watching the past playing like movie reels overlapping like eels, fast forward in reverse. My chest felt tight. My lungs stuffed with stale cotton candy, my nose too small. Already, my fingertips grew numb. The edges of my eyes were sandy, sore.

CRASH!

Another bottle broke across the street. I struggled to catch a glimpse of some delinquent through the boarded windows. Those rotten little turds. Pissing, fucking and drinking on my memories. I should march over there and bash in their snotty little reptile teeth with a knotted stick.

CRASH!

Instead, I clutch the newspaper against my thigh and walk down to the beach. There's a cup of noon coffee Burn left sitting in the sand. I snatch it up and bring it down to the shore.

I consider covering my right eye and staring into the sun until the left one goes blind. Just a minute, that's all it takes. A sacrifice to Ra, Re, or Annu. Instead, I fall back on my ass and let the velvet touch of sand spill into my shoes.

At least the are no neighbors here. No parking lots for tourists. There are better beaches closer to snack shacks and condos and mansions. I can cry here all night and explain myself to no man or beast. This beach is forbidden, in its own way. This is where teens make babies and junkies sleep, but we all give each other space. Sometimes I find a needle in the dunes, or a used condom in the sand, smelling like lobsters and mushrooms. But I look over my shoulder at our porch, at the broken street lights and distant trees, and this beach is still mine.

Fluorescent umbrellas dot the horizon in either direction, but they are a very distant menace. Only the crack of irons striking golf balls, and a distant cry of "Fore!" can reach me here. Just barely see the greens down the way, now that there are only sticks and abandoned foundations where the houses were torn down and forgotten.

I reclined into a sand depression. I love the feeling of sand in my hair, my shoes, even my boxers. My foot pushed the newspaper into the sand, but a randy wind caught bits of it and pulled them free. The paper tumbled down the shoreline, taunting the ocean's lazy reach.

It's so easy to stare out over the sea and think of the horizon as the end of the world. The end of pleasure. The end of trouble. I used to lay very near here with her. Picking sand out of her red hair as she rested on my chest. A mile from our "houses", so we couldn't be found. Reading over her shoulder, both lost in comics or cosmos or theoretical this-and-thats. Sometimes the ancient mysteries, giggling at chaos magic. All thoughts of rays and curses banished.

Why was I given the one thing I wanted more than anything?

At this point my skin feels like a quilt of chiggers and worms, and it's abundantly clear that I need to lie down and meditate before something vital blows. I wiggle my ass into the sand and arch my spine back.

If I can't let go here, of all places, then there truly is no hope.

Now... just breathe. Let the immediate problems drift away. Think about something else. Decompress.

Don't think. Don't suffer. Namu amida butsu.

I let the fresh air fill my lungs, swirl around my bronchi. Solutions. Let them come.

Namu amida butsu. Om mani... um... padme hum? Fuck. Years

ago I could pretend to conjure some demon or ethereal spirits, to aid me tonight. I gave up, fell back, the sand spraying up over my head. Burn's counsel left me with nothing. Nothing.

There was nothing. It was good.

Then a spastic landmine burst behind my eyelids and Barry was running around my brain with a Kevlar vest and an AK-47, shouting to Bernard for cover fire while the President humped a dead wolf in the sand. Visions of Claude blowing his brains out in a Florida shower. Hair and brain splat on tile. Why do it in Florida, instead of here? Coward. Did he put the gun in his mouth? Did he even use a gun? I think so… Maybe he hung himself? I heard people shit down their legs after they hang. He always struck me as a wrist-slitting kind of guy. No, Barry said there was a gun. I should get a gun. Does everyone really fart when they die? Who said that?

I turn to the newspaper for distraction. My synapses scare me.

Snatched a few pages from under my foot. So it's war then, eh? What else? Did a paraplegic black woman in New Jersey win the lotto? Siamese twins earn doctorate at Yale? Maybe there will be a front-page story about a community banding together to push drug dealers and pimps out of town. Gay-marriage re-legalized yet? Neuroticism criminalized? Endangered species being cloned?

No.

Car bombings at hotels. Insurgent snipers aiming below GI helmets. The wrath of God spoken in tsunamis, earthquakes, and ritual genocide. Foxes extinct, cats expected to follow. Good God! Cats! Poverty isn't extinct. But apparently bats are. And… giraffes? There's a new sport now. Something in a cage with blood, but not *too* much blood. Flip the pages. Okay, orphans dying of thirst in sandstorms. Draught in the West, a season of blizzards expected in the East. Billions fleeing from one religion to another. Some country I can't pronounce was overthrown by the former dictator's regime. Buddha sighted on Mars. Unarmored Hummers burning like strips of empty insect husks. American bones for guts. Retaliation. Escalation. Thugs calling the shots on Capitol Hill, and thugs sticking sawed off shotguns under your chin in the subways. Wars and not-wars, vaccine-resistant polio spreading, financial flux flu, and pretty distraction machine version 5.0 releasing next week. Get in line yesterday.

Everywhere, worldwide, unfathomable potential and unmitigated cruelty, ignorance, and apathy. It should comfort us. Make us feel normal. Sure, our lives are shit, but whose isn't? Everything's okay so long as someone else is worse. And then the sun glints off a wave and I breathe in some slightly unpolluted breeze and I'm reminded of how utterly stupid I am.

Newspapers are awful.

If the news is always going to be this bad, it should have a little variety. Some better lies to spice up the rancid truth. Let the people separate fact from fiction, put a little fun in the crushing routine. The President has been breeding Siberian zombie dogs as Christmas gifts for Cabinet members. Not fake Christmas, the real one in November. And the endless war is really just an experimental reality TV program. All those poor dead soldiers, they're just pretending! Condoms spontaneously rip in unison across the nation! Local cops taser a skateboarding toddler to death because… well, just because!

I stood up and walked away from the beach.

I can feel it coming. The fear that fuels the white flame. The fear.

The melting ice working its way up from my feet, oncoming panic, and if it reaches my brain I'll lose it all. I'm dumb enough to fall into this mind maze, but still smart enough to recognize it. If this is going to strike, then things have to be in order. Just staring at the sea won't get my gears moving. Need to lube them with some passive violence.

I marched back up to the porch.

Through the sliding glass door, patched with duct tape, I saw it, leaning majestically against an unpacked box of Punk Hawk magazines. Grasping it in my hand, I strode back out to the deck, unsheathed it, and let the setting sun lash the sword with its solar rays. Beautiful, sharp, and folded over two hundred times. Or so Dad said. Before the disease, anything he said was law. The handle is ivory, lions and sharks and foxes and dragons carved into the spaces between the black crisscrossing X's that run down to the gold capped bottom.

A pile of crates sat by the door. I kicked the top off one, finding four lonely, nearly rotten melons staring up. My skills are not limited to basic melons, though I find them the easiest to steal. I am proficient in cutting many types of fruit, be it watermelons, cantaloupes, bushels of apples, pears, pineapples… and on one terrible night, an ill-tempered skunk.

I lifted each melon out, lovingly placing them on the banister. I balanced them to compensate for the deck's crooked nature. Then I stood in the corner, two melons in front, and two melons to the left on the perpendicular railing. A gray mountain began rolling in with the clouds. I pointed my sword to the horizon, letting the ritual movements free my mind. I am a veteran melon-cutting enthusiast, well on my way to being a professional. This act will clear my mind and lay the evening's twisted path before me, if only I can summon the calm dexterity to cut clean. Meifumado. Assume the forbidden karate stance. Prepare for violence. Barry needs his book. Barry needs support. We both need the truth. But I need my car. I need a friend. Jesus, I need so much back and there is nothing I can do. Nothing. Meifumado… Kuwabara, kuwabara. Praise the Lord (hey, you never know).

The blade shines. Swing, and a miss.

God damn it, what the hell happened?

Mom and Dad would not be proud.

It couldn't have always been this bad. I look around and see enough evidence that we've advanced pretty far from prehistory days, but I can't fathom how. Every day, the papers and pawns scream about our spiraling descent. If it's so obvious, why can't we stop it? I don't remember the world being this fucked when I was a kid. Sure, I was a kid, but I wasn't blind. I saw as much as could be expected of any child. It never seemed this bad, Cursed or not.

Diving eagle strike!

Miss the melon, but not the railing…

Pull the sword free and sigh. Why are we all fucking up? Animals are going extinct everywhere. We've lost the foxes. The whales are on their way out, komodo dragons, parliaments of insects, and a whole bunch of others I can't remember. Why couldn't we lose the stingrays and great whites instead of those wonderful, mischievous foxes? At least we still have the cats. For now. The loss of cats from this world would be a loss immeasurable. At that point, I'd join the dark sacrifices and welcome the coming of the King of All Tears. It would descend, wrenching me from this weird illusion. Foxes are… were… half cat, in my opinion. The strangely named author, Lovecraft, summed it up best:

For the cat is cryptic, and close to strange things which men cannot see. He is the soul of antique Aegyptus, and bearer of tales from forgotten cities in Meroe and Ophir. He is the kin of the jungle's lords, and heir to the secrets of hoary and sinister Africa. The Sphinx is his cousin, and he speaks her language; but he is more ancient than the Sphinx, and remembers that which she hath forgotten.

Damn straight. So is my slash, just catching the tip of my fruit-foe.

Just one wound, and then anything bleeds out. Like Thornwood. It's slow, the summer brings its cursed patrons, but overall the economy cannibalized itself. Our eastern resort is more of a rotted Wild West, minus any man-with-no-name. Not a moral one, at least. We have the heat. The world's heating up so fast that my shack will soon be in the ocean. Chaos dances in the wind, yet everywhere the sounds of slumber and electronic gods drown the outrage. If I had the income, my pocket would hold a computer with access to all the world's information, anyone I could possibly want to speak to, anywhere on Earth. Music I'd have to drive hours to find in obscure, dusty stores now downloaded for free right onto the phone, with games, and HD video. Hard to riot when you have that to play with.

Swing the sword down again. Too hard, goes right through a melon, spattering my legs with rancid juice. The blade is stuck deep into the porch. I push and pull, and fall on my ass as it comes free. I've kept it sharp. At least I've done that one thing right.

How did it all happen so quickly? I had parents and an education and dreams of fame, though I have no idea for what. It was all a dog and pony show. I already had my dream. Tracy. She made the pain tolerable. Love possible. Perhaps another could fill her place, but... I don't. Fucking. Want it.

Now I'm alone and wondering when exactly the President is going to nuke Manhattan. The fear of annihilation is very real for my generation. Silly, one of our many mainstream monikers actually is "The Doom Generation", and it has nothing to do with terrorism or super viruses. It's economics, politics, social stagnation. Little things adding up. Energy. Diet. Poverty. Not letting women run things again, even though it worked in the true past. And a plague of ignorant phobias. A great convergence of rotten ideals and promises raped, the blood smeared on the wall for all to see. Society set on self-destruct. Sergio's words echo now. All is one? A devil run? Everything reflecting on itself. Something like that. I can almost love it.

This time it's a wild slash.

Despite the many defenseless targets, I cut naught but air. But damn it felt good, the blood pulsing from chest through shoulder, down to arm to hand. The cutting edge an extension of my impotent rage. I'll swing and miss all day long as long as the ability to lash out still remains.

My parents talked of change, of power, of will. Where did they get it? Where was this well of optimism that so many drank freely from? Surely by now it's scrawled with graffiti and jizz. The monsters of today feast on the mutant children of tomorrow. A brutal revenge for our parents' free-form revolution. They opened the eyes of society and screamed their dissent... and then, hungry, tired, and shattered under the sheer weight of the establishment's resources, they got old. Their babies' food rained down in sneering trickles from the great Liberty Statue, while they lay prostrate in repentance before her. Their wide-eyed, enlightened openings were quickly filled with the steaming shit of the National God. They became festering sores. And now, just decades later, the pus is ripe and oozing around our sandaled feet.

But at least they tried.

Their groundwork was solid enough. It's my people who are lazy, *my* people who dropped the ball and let the wolverines catch up. No cause to maintain the effect. Time to go for broke, break out the technique I've never mastered. The Spiral Slash to Hell. This cut starts standing, then spins 360, lowering until I'm on one knee.

I blink, don't think, and... bits of melon plop to the ground. Sliding off slowly. Just like in the movies. A rather large wave crashes its approval. I smile into the sun, already red and weary.

Our sun is almost set. We won't rise, too tired from long nights of feeding our iFucks and stroking the Internet. Our connections are filtered through the blood-tipped black branches of an iron tree. We flail about impotently, looking to the light with all the passion of the crab's eye at the end of a stalk, waiting with open mouths and swollen tongues for the salt to become rain.

Jesus, how did our parents do it? I'm afraid to even have children. And not because of the world I'll leave for them. No, I'm afraid to have children because they'll get to be my age and see what a selfish loser I was. They'll see everything I didn't do.

That's the mean truth of it. It's guys like me that ruin it. A generation convinced we'd grow up to be rock stars and millionaires because goddamnit, we just plain deserve it. But no. No. I'm just another half-bright slug. Can't even deal with my own diseased mind. Can't keep myself from sucking the Cameron family dry while I wallow in the terrible screaming called silence.

Truly, I am a member of a lost and vapid generation. When the time comes for the next ones to throw dirt on our graves, no epitaph will suffice to fully capture the strange morality, skewed priorities, and overall spoiled complacency that defined us. We shall inherit an unholy debt that will enslave our grandchildren until oil pumps in their veins, and a large, voracious appetite that can only be sated by the misery of other men. We will never know peace again in our lifetime.

Well, so what?

When has the human race known peace? Fuck 'em.

I can still save Barry. Sort of. Right?

Even if it's just in this one, small way, I can be *some* kind of hero.

Strange obstacles lay before me, but someone once believed in me, no matter what. She said I can do anything, and I believed her. The path lays open, verdant and fertile. Sword in hand, I went back inside, slid a 2x4 in the glass door's groove, and checked the pot for stale coffee. None. Bernard finished it again. Then again, he mysteriously refills our stocks and hasn't brought police behind him, so it's okay. I'm almost there, almost okay.

Now go back outside. I stand high on our weak porch, watching the last bits of newspaper fly down the shore towards the golf course. So fake and green. I dwell here in the yellow and brown, but I can see blue, can jump in and wash and taste the salt and emerge anew each time.

This puts the Barry dilemma into perspective.

This is a *now* kind of problem. Nothing abstract about it. Many miles to cover in a short time, or a good friend will lay in bed, bored, broken, and alone. And it will certainly be my fault. But I can do this for him. I can do it for her.

So get to Barry's mom's house, get his precious collection of Byron J. Brick novels, get all the way back out to Hawkhouse... all with my car being held prisoner by psychotic Ukrainian mechanics in some underground garage up the island. They won't take any bullshit from me. But... forget that for now.

Almost no money, no transport, and no phone.

If only I dumped half my meager earnings into having another gimmicky gadget humming in my pocket. If only I could flip it open and find a ride from some piss-ant I haven't talked to since high school. But I'd hear a click. So who then? Tim, stay in focus, you damned fool! Pray to every dead god who will lend an ear. Barry is hooked up to disappearing machines and you're merely sick from feelings.

93

The sun is falling, the moon peeking above like a great gray skull. Nice of them to share the sky. I sheathe the sword, step back down to the beach. I fall to my knees, my bandaged ankle cooling in the sand. I press my forehead into it. What could possibly beat feeling fragments of ancient mountains massage your skin, as you watch seventy percent of the Earth ebb and crash at your feet?

Walk down to the water and lean flat, face forward, so the white wash just covers my head, leaving the rest of me dry. Renew. Water is the only thing that thrives at all temperatures, in all conditions, in three separate forms. We are composed of it. It can lift you. Sink you. Cushion you. Crush you. Cure your thirst or drown your lungs. In all aspects, in every way, I should be like water. Fluid, changing. Equally destructive and supportive. Bruce Lee said something like that. I should memorize it. Why can Barry channel Byron Brick's soul, but I can't get a word out of Bruce Lee? Bruce is long dead too, but maybe I can dig him up. He said a lot of great things that I never actually *do*. Fuck. This is going to be tough. Can I be crazy if I'm aware that I'm crazy? Does it matter?

Bernard's wrong. I can't be a total dick.

A cab would bleed me dry, especially in my newly minted welfare state (note to self: reapply for welfare). Need a trusted ally. With transport. And one in good spirits. The air is too cool and crisp this tropical eve to be sullied with a rotten disposition. That's my role. Yes, my weekend schedule is thrown out of whack. I must accept that it can't be salvaged. There will be no tee-shits this evening. Although me and Bernard's midnight trips to fill the golf course holes with steaming piles of contempt brings me great joy, it ain't happening tonight.

Back on the porch. Got the conviction but no solution. Still some melons left. I raise this sword, just an ornamental Christmas gift from Dad. Still, it's from Dad. The setting sun blesses it, yet the light reflecting back blinds me. No matter. We're going into battle. Spiritual. Mental. Pain lies ahead.

Another slash. The blade's path is precise, a faint hint of the Splitting Lotus technique. Four melons become slop, sliding into eight chunks. Now facing the glass door, squatting, breathing slowly.

The melons plop on the deck. The wind shifts, then settles.

Yes. It is clear.

Ha! How could I be so blind?

The red carnage makes me think of his glass eye. And though it increases the risks exponentially, there is only one terrible freak who might drop everything in his own weird life, just to drive me to victory. One friend who I helped rob a convenience store half a mile from our town with a BB gun, way back in 8th grade. One man who could be called upon in the dead of night to kick Barry's father in the balls and beat him half to death. Violence flows in his veins as freely as the secret honor I've seen in his heart. I can't phone him, but if Cthulhu's seed blesses me, I'll take the journey by foot and find out that he'll actually be home. Perhaps plotting some strange scheme or another... but he'll help me help Barry.

Mi hermano, Jay, a.k.a. Julio Sanchez Sin Corazon.

Oh Julio, you vicious cenobite. You wonderful, brutal, fire-cracking blood brother. I'm coming for you!

Run beside me!

Asphalt Nostalgia

The summer breeze ceased just as I stepped onto the street. My sword was sheathed in my hand. Stupid, maybe, but it felt like that kind of night. Cops have better things to do than hassle me at the height of party season. And that's *if* I even ran into any.

I turned back to my home and looked about the desolation surrounding it. Dried beach grass choked the roadside, like emaciated scarecrow fingers digging for sunlight. This is a good spot. Despite the threat of horny, shiftless teens prowling across the street, it is a quiet place. The tourists don't venture out here. Only nobodies. On a full moon, you can lie in the road for hours, sipping Atom Ale, watching the clouds as if you were an astronaut drifting over an alien tundra.

It was a night like that on this very spot, home from college for another weekend, when I told Julio Sanchez Sin Corazon that I'd finally lost my virginity. He was the first to know. At the time, the mixture of elation, relief, triumph, and fear made it likely that Jay might be the only one to ever know. Besides the obvious…

We were playing a late night game of 'Boom Boom Home Run Derby'. Julio used his cigarette to light a firecracker, stuff it into a wiffle ball, and send it hurtling at me. I swung, missed, ducked.

Pop!

He laughed. He was chain smoking, not coughing at all.

"Let's try two!" he shouted, stuffing more firecrackers into the next ball. We had plenty of both.

"Uh, how about on your turn?"

Too late. The sizzling wiffle bomb was coming. Swing. Crack. A double pop high over Julio's head.

"Not bad, homey!"

"Yeah, I'm feeling on point tonight," I said. Swung the plastic bat around like a pro.

"You're almost glowing!" he said. "Did you volunteer for some weird-ass experiment on Peach Pit Island?"

I was too busy staring up at my recent victory, tiny firefly bits of plastic falling alongside the browned ball, when the next one hit my chest. I dove onto the sidewalk just in time. Julio's laugh echoed with the small explosions.

"Fucking hell! You psycho!"

"Yo, you invited me to play. Aight, my turn."

We met halfway and traded the hollow bat for the firecrackers. A pile of browned wiffle balls lay in the grass at the corner, a little too close to my parents' gas station.

Time to let the news slip, casual, and slick.

"I got laid," I said, looking down at the ball. I lit, pitched, and crack, it came right back at me. Dodged left as it sailed past and popped. Sounds like a tongue clicking on teeth.

"No shit? About fucking time, son," he said, letting his cigarette bob between his teeth. "Fucking dude is in college and never had one girlfriend... It's like, you're not even ugly or nothing. Starting to think you were a queer. Which is fine, I'd just want first dibs on that ass."

"Thanks! And sorry, I'm not, but you'd be high on my list, too!" I said, taking the compliment, unsure if it was sarcastic, and too happy to care. I pitched another crackling ball of death. "It was inevitable."

He caught it in his hand. Laughed, then tossed it back at me. "My boy Timmy, finally popped his cherry. Took ya long enough. Hope it was better than your pitching."

"Like losing yours at fourteen is any better?"

"It is. So who was she?"

"Just someone."

I took a nice deep 'I'm not a virgin anymore' breath and walked over to my skateboard. I popped it up into my hand, did a few spinning tricks on the road. The full moon keeping us in bright, blue-white light.

"Just someone? What, like some skank at school?" Julio asked. He offered me a cigarette, which I waved away.

"I'm trying to cut down," I said. I skated in circles and tried a kick flip at the same exact time as I pitched. Too much skill, too soon. The ball smacked hard at his feet, rebounded up, and blew in front of Julio's face. He hardly leaned back. The brief fire pop framed his face, a devil with a heart. Yeah, I can tell him.

I pitched again, from on the board, but still and stable.

"Cut down? She couldn't be that bad. You've just started!"

Swing and a miss.

"Cut down smoking. Idiot."

"Duh," Julio said, lighting the stoge that I'd declined, while his still burned in the corner of his mouth. "Shit, I've been smoking these things since I was eleven, and look at me!"

"Yeah, look at you," I said. "And no, she's actually from around here. She's… actually not just someone."

"Well, shit, Tim, it took you long enough," Julio said, taking a deep drag.

"I'm a sophomore. That's normal."

"Yeah, a sophomore in college." He flicked his cigarette at my head. By the time I dodged it, he had another lit. "My turn."

"At least I go to college."

We switched spots again. My wheels made that lovely circular grinding sound. A wiffle ball bounced off the back of my head. Empty! Such a considerate bastard.

"Listen to Mister Middle-Class Educated-Elite brag, for once." Julio rolled his eyes.

"Hey, where'd you learn all those big words?" I said. "Lower middle class, now, by the way…"

"Momma taught me right after she showed us how to beat a piñata and roll burritos," Julio said. "Timmy, you and I both know there ain't nothing for me at college but some pussy and more debt."

"You'll see," I said. "After I get my degree, I'll sell this place and leave this shit-hole and all the rats like you behind. I'll bring her with me and we can escape…"

"Bring her?" he exhaled smoke. "Fuck are you even studying?"

I shrugged and felt small. "I can't live here forever, Jay. Beach or not, it's too… small. No privacy."

"Privacy? Whatever. I ain't planning on going anywhere," Julio said. He spit on the road. "I might move out to Tomahok, but that's about it."

"Tomahok? Seriously? With *you know who* still living out there?" I pointed at Julio's eye. The left one. The dead one. "You sure that's a smart move?"

"No, it's not smart, but he ain't gonna be living there forever. Some young gun always takes over the empire eventually." He thumped his chest. "Go big or go home. Right?"

"And that's going to be you? Sounds like suicide."

Jay stuffed four crackers into the wiffle ball. "Nah, what Jefe did to me… I'm over that shit. Like you said, sometimes you just gotta—"

"Woah, woah that could hurt!"

He paid no mind and threw it full force. "Move on."

That ball blew into pieces. I blinked. He laughed, that same contagious, slightly menacing laugh that freaks like Jay are blessed with.

"Someday I'm going to figure out how to see the world like you," I said.

"Like me? The fuck you talking about now?"

"With one eye. You say its flat, two-dimensional. Like on TV. That it's not black on one side, because black is a color."

"Aw, you *were* paying attention." Julio mocked me by hugging himself. Still smoking two cigarettes at the same time. Strange sight.

"It fascinates me. It's nearly impossible for me to see the world like you, and vice versa. But I'm gonna do it. Everything's going to change. Even with all that bad... the financial stuff... I'm going to make it. She... Look, I haven't told anyone yet, and this is uh, how do you say it? On the low down?"

"It's DL, idiot. So she's going to save your life, huh? This mysterious girl that pitied you enough to let you bang her out? Good luck with that. And hey, no doubt, I'm sure she's special," he held his palm out in defense. "But you're talking kind of... serious. Why tell me? Don't get me wrong, I'm honored and all."

"Are you joking? You're good with secrets. And you're my best friend."

"True that, but you have a quite a few best friends." He waved his hand toward the dark garage I newly called home. "Why not Bernard, or Barry? Isn't he like your butt-buddy or something?"

"I don't want to make Barry jealous," I said. "I told him I was saving myself for him until marriage. And Bernard isn't home. Just... trust me."

Jay walked over, the gravel crunching between the cracked road and his heavy boots.

"It's good that you don't pull no bullshit on me," he said, clapping my arm. "So how was it?"

"Magical," I said, clasping my hands. "We read poetry to each other and drank wine and talked until dawn. Did it at least... five times. Six times."

"Right, sure, bro," Julio said, pushing my shoulder. I almost fell off balance. He could probably throw me like one of the wiffle balls.

"Actually... we've been seeing each other for a while. We've been doing it a lot. A whole lot, ha. Even in my old house."

"Why not? Shit's empty, might as well use it for…" He looked up at me. His grin gone. "Sorry."

"It's okay, Jay. I can handle it."

That's when I noticed he'd dropped a handful of firecrackers on the ground behind me, all lit. I leapt away just in time.

"Good. Was she tight? The first time, whenever that was, Dr. Mysterio."

"Um… yes. Like Saran Wrap?"

"What the fuck is Saran Wrap?" Julio asked. He blew a plume of smoke out of his nostrils. His dual cigarettes flared beneath his chin.

"It's the stuff you wrap sandwiches in," I said. "You know, very tight."

He kept staring.

"She was a virgin too," I tried. "Um, like a glove? I don't know, I tend to view females as actual humans. Don't burn your brain out on the concept."

"Ha. And you still think you'll see like me?" Julio shook his head. "No girl out here is a fucking glove. Did she at least like your dick? You can tell if they don't, trust me."

"Uh… okay. Don't worry about my dick. And yes, we've been safe. Mostly."

"Did I ask? Speaking of, you want some of this?" He pulled a tied up condom out of his pocket. Pinched between his fingers, it sagged down with a pregnant bulge.

"Oh god," I said. "What the hell, you couldn't wait for it to get out of the mule's ass? Are you completely insane now?"

He tore it open with his teeth and poured the contents into his hand. With my eyes squinted, I made out a white pool cupped in his palm. My stomach curdled. I was relieved when he pressed his nose into it and took a deep snort. Of course it was blow, but with Julio… well, you just really never know what he'll do. And never why. If anyone could find a way to get twisted off semen, it'd be him. He held his palm toward me.

"I'm good," I said, turning away from his hand.

"So when was the last time you hit it?"

"I don't do coke anymore. Never really liked it, wears off so fast and makes me feel like shit. And talk as fast and annoying as Barry."

"Damn! No smokes, no snow, what's next, no booze or dope? Shit,

Tim, pussy is good, but not..." he trailed off. Staring at the sky. "So you get it all the time, huh? That's good. When was the last time? I can practically smell the sex on you. Stud."

"Last night, actually," I said. "On the beach."

"Sick. Did you get sand in your ass?"

"Yeah, a little bit."

"Nobody lays a towel... Wait, last night? That means you weren't even at school! You tryin' to pull one over on me, you shit? What about getting your degree and all that?"

"You caught me. Guilty as charged. I cut class. Should have known better. Whoops."

"Man, you don't even wanna hear about the last time I got laid," Julio said.

"Probably not, but go ahead."

He patted the sidewalk. I sat closer, the garage-house behind us, the newly closed gas station dark and dead before us. He leaned back on his palms, cigarette bit tight and smoke pouring between his teeth.

"Aight, so I'm just sitting in my living room, smoking a bowl. All of a sudden the back door whips open, and this big fucking *thing* comes right at me. BAM! Big ass wings flapping and shit."

"What was it? A bat?"

"No way, bro. It was a butterfly."

"A butterfly?"

"Son of a bitch had a three-foot wingspan." Julio spread his arms to ensure I understood just how massive this butterfly was. "Body was like... the girth of a forty. Just this... giant, mutant motherfucker." He sucked his nicotine down with relish, miming his words. "So here it comes, and I'm ready to throw down. Pow, pow! I punched its weird face. The wings felt like getting bitch-slapped, but crazy fast. We start wrestling, knocking over the lamp, spilling my bowl. You know, I'm basically just in shock. If I was anything more than stoned, I wouldn't have believed it. I mean, I'm punching this freaking butterfly, right? What the fuck? And it was *fierce*. Starts whipping me faster and faster. Loco. Then, I get the upper hand, beat it out the back door. Smack it with a lawn chair. It started getting slow and wobbly, and I knew I had it. So I plant that bitch down with my boot, and rip its god-damned wing off!"

"This is disgusting. Even for you," I said, hiding my face in my palms. "What does this have to do with sex?"

"So this mutant mother fucker, it's still alive, right? Flopping around and squirting this hot, green goo all over. Steaming. And I'm thinking, if this is how it's gonna be, giant bugs attacking my house, you know, I need to set a precedent. So I throw it down on that big fat stump by the ramp. And I'm just watching it squirm, and I start thinking... You know, my blood is pumping, I'm all worked up. This hot green goo is just oozing out of it, a big wound, pulsing and steaming, and…"

No. He's not that insane. Please, no. But with Julio, there's no good news or bad news. Just weird news or worse.

"Dude. Go. To. Hell."

"I banged that butterfly to death, bro. Right there in my own back yard!" Julio grinned. Legitimately proud. "Who else can say they did some shit like that, huh? Come on, who?"

"All right," I said. "Sounds like you've been reading too much of Barry's sci-fi. Your brain's twisted. I never want to have sex again."

"For real son, on my word, all true," he said, making the sign of a cross over his chest. "Damn thing probably escaped from Peach Pit Island. I should've used a rubber—I'm lucky my dick didn't melt off or grow a face, you know what I mean?"

I did. Peach Pit Island is a maximum-security level five biohazard research facility, nestled in a tiny cove fifteen miles off of Tomahok's coast. Many a local legend tell of errant fisherman—drunk, audacious, or both—venturing too close to the terrible Pit. Then they're either being sniped right in the throat, or blown up by the submerged mines dotting the small island's wicked shore. Tales of Ebola, the pox, airborne blood cancer, conspiratitis, goat-flu, foxfire, smilex, mustard-gas, and all manner of beastly plagues float from the secret cells of this government institution. Word has it that they also perform mind control experiments, broadcasting their evil rays across the eastern tip of Sponge Island. All of us, their guinea pigs. Dirty, dirty little zombie pigs. I heard of cows with human faces. Deer without skin. Maybe a giant, pissed off butterfly did escape… Jay's life was filled with odd things, losing an eye to a drug dealer, mixing up new drugs in his basement lab, working with cops right out of his kitchen.

"All right, so where's proof? Do you still have the corpse?"

"Nah. I grilled it. Too big for the fridge. Remember my last skate-jam? Dude, I served you all grilled butterfly burger. Shit was good, too."

Just then, a beam of light flickered behind Julio. Devil halo. But the rhythmic bob of it suggested a flashlight. Someone on foot. It glinted off the signs along the road, designated that nondescript strip as a "nature preserve" where my home, my real home, not the new garage-shack, once stood.

"Who's that?" Julio spun around, flicking his switchblade open. He pressed his fist to the street, leapt to his haunches like a jaguar, and waited.

"Dude, relax, it's probably Bernard."

I watched the back of his shaved head as he watched the shadow man approach.

"Burn walks in the dark. Screw the knife," Julio mumbled. He slipped it into his back pocket and pulled something from under his shirt. A knot grew in my throat.

"Where the fuck did you get a gun?" How did I not notice?

"Traded for it," he said as he bit his tongue and raised it.

"Jesus Christ, Julio!" I hissed. "If you're going to kill someone, don't do it in front of my house! What if that's a cop? Put that thing down, you shit-brained psycho!"

He looked back at me, then slowly laid the gun on the sidewalk, but kept his hand over it. I gripped my skateboard like a shield. The stranger was approaching slow and calm as he pleased.

"What'd you do if that's Savage Jefe?" Julio said, looking me dead in the eye.

"Jay, that is *not*... Why the hell would that scumbag be in Thornwood? You know he won't leave Tomahok anymore."

"He has. And does. Otherwise I wouldn't..." Jay tapped his eye, staring me down.

Is this some weird coked-up test? I bit my lip. Well, Savage Jefe is the top-dog drug smuggler, and violent as a rabid boar. I don't care if he dies. He's living on borrowed time, skulking about in his fortified bar-compound at the tip of Tomahok. I'd like to say he's an urban myth, as he does most of his work through kids. Kids like Julio. Sadly, Julio and his fake eye know, fact for fact, that Savage Jefe is very much real. "Okay, if it's Jefe, then go ahead and shoot him. But you bury him on your own. I don't want jack shit to do with that monster."

Jay smiled. "Claro que si, amigo."

The shadow man called out to us. "Tim?"

"Barry!" I shouted. "Good god, you weird bastard! What are you doing, creeping up on us? And why are you walking?"

"Tracy took the car again," he said. Now only ten feet away, we could see his sweaty, flushed features, glowing in the moonlight. "I really wish you'd get a phone. It'd be a lot easier than walking all the way here, hoping you're home."

"Yo, Barry! What up, son?" Julio said, slipping his gun back into his pants. He used his cigarette to light a firecracker, and tossed it at Barry. "Wanna play?"

"Hey, Julio," Barry said as he sidestepped the tiny bang. He sat down with us. "Not really in the mood. Where were you last night, Tim? I couldn't find you. Anywhere. Bernard couldn't either."

"I, uh… I got wasted and stumbled around Tomahok, ended up lost in the trails. Had a killer hangover all day," I said. "You're right. I guess I should get a phone, huh? Will you lend me the money?"

"Tomahok? You went out there alone?" Barry asked. He kept fidgeting with the ground, flicking rocks and not looking at me. "How'd you get—"

"Why, what's the big deal?" Can he see the sweat beading on me?

"Nothing, I was just wondering if you saw Tracy last night. She had the car then, too. Didn't ask me, just took it. Again. So I was stuck at home, doing nothing. We come back for the weekend, and she doesn't even say hi or ask about school or… It's my car! That girl drives twice as much as me, never fills the tank, never says when she's coming back, or where she's even going."

"She's fucking wild, bro. Here," Julio said. He lit a cigarette and passed it to Barry. Barry took it, sucked it down, then began coughing and spitting all over the street. "But she's smart. If the police aren't calling, then I wouldn't sweat it."

"When did you start smoking?" I asked Barry as I elbowed Julio, who finally got the hint and gave me a stoge, too.

"Who cares?" Barry said. He hunched into a tighter, knee hugging lump. "Tracy is… She barely talks to me now. I don't know… I'm just being paranoid, right? You're absolutely sure you didn't see her last night?"

"No," I said. "I mean, I'm sure she's fine. But no. No, I didn't see her."

Julio glanced at me, a quick, darting snake eye shot. Clever creep.

"None of her friends knew where she was, either," Barry said. "Mom got really freaked. She just vanished, and then poof! Back home like some kind of ghost. Passed out in her bed at five in the morning. I know I'm her big brother and probably just... I don't want to control her, you know? But lately it's hard to get her attention, let alone catch up, or bond, or... She's smart, brave, tough. But still, sometimes I worry about her."

"I don't blame you," Julio said. "What, with all those perverts running around? You're lucky she didn't get abducted, man. She could be a sex slave in Nicaragua by now."

"Fuck off," Barry mumbled.

"My bad, man. I'm kidding. Just trying to cheer you up," Julio said as he pushed himself off the sandy dirt. "She'd castrate anyone who even looked at her the wrong way. Probably has!"

"Barry, are sure you're okay?" I tossed my skateboard into the road.

"She's just freaking me out," Barry said. "She's always going out and showing up days later, looking all cracked out. Mom said she barely even goes to school anymore."

"Shit," I said. "What do you mean cracked out? You mean on drugs? She doesn't do drugs. Not like that. She's not cracked out. Is she?"

"How would you know? She doesn't even mention you, anymore. Maybe we embarrass her now? Or maybe... I think she's seeing someone. In secret. I don't know why. But I did see Lucas Boil in town. If anyone... You know how he is. He's a pusher," Barry said, still staring at the ground.

"Oh god," I said. "Where'd you see him?"

"At the pool hall," Barry said. "Funny thing though, Tim. He told me that he saw you and Tracy on the beach. He was smoking under the boardwalk."

Barry's eyes flicked up to mine.

"Really?" I cleared my throat. "When was this? Because I haven't seen that turd since—"

"Last night."

"Bullshit," Julio cut in. "That meat thief's brains are all fucked up, bro. He's a burnout, you just said so yourself. He wouldn't know his asshole from his mouth if it didn't stink so bad. I sold him a bag last week and for real, I think the Army's got his brain all scrambled. I wouldn't fuck with him, or tell him that, but you hear me?"

Barry took another drag from the cigarette. Mine was unlit, dancing between my fingers. Wanted Julio to keep talking, seemed to make my spine unclench.

"How did that jerk even get accepted with his record?" I asked, trying to deflect the conversation over to dreams of Boil's bullet-riddled corpse rotting in a sandstorm. Didn't work.

"So what *did* you do last night, Tim?" Barry asked, head down, but eyes directly on me.

Julio grabbed my hair and shook my head. "Getting shit faced, bro. He just told you. I got a little reckless last night, had my beer muscles on, ended up in Tomahok like a dumbass. Tim tried to get me out of there before I ran into you know who. Instead I made him take a shot, and another, and another. Ha! We got trashed, played blackjack with some losers, then smoked up in the graveyard. This douche bag lost damn near a hundred bucks. A hundred of *my* bucks. Wait, that was a graveyard, right?"

"On five dollar hands. You don't know when to quit. And yeah, it was." I glanced back at Julio. "You wouldn't want to pass out there, but we almost got back home."

Barry stared at both of us. Then down at Jay's hand.

"Is that a gun?"

"Hell yeah," Jay said.

"Huh. Cool. Is Burn home?" Barry asked.

"Nope," I said.

"Where is he?"

"God only knows," I answered. "He never leaves notes, either."

"Okay. You guys want to get some drinks later?" Barry asked. "I'm working on a new story and want to bounce some ideas off you."

"Absolutely," I answered too quickly.

"Nah, maybe. I don't know," Julio said, blowing smoke rings to the sky.

"It's getting cold. I'll wait inside," Barry said. He looked at the crisped wiffle balls and firecracker remains littering the street. "Finish up your games."

"You wanna play?" Jay asked.

"No," he said, still looking at me. Before I could speak, he turned his back to me and walked up the wooden planks to the front door. Wind blew over the sand covered driveway, sprinkling his legs.

"I'll be there in a minute," I called up to him.

Barry lifted his hand in recognition without looking back. As soon as the door shut, I turned to Julio.

"Dude…" I said. Let out a heavy breath and realized I'd crushed my unlit cigarette in my sweaty hand. "Thanks, Jay."

"It's cool, dog, whatever," Julio said with a prideful smile. He pulled another cigarette out and pointed it at me. I took it and lit it off his burning cherry. The brown crackling cloud flooded my lungs, piercing my will, letting guilty relaxation flow with the coughing.

"Thanks. I don't know what to do, I just—"

"Shut up. Look, Tim," Julio said, waving his finger at me. "It's like it's always been with us. You handle your business, I do mine, we hold it down if we need to, right? Otherwise, your shit is *your shit*. And I don't give a shit about your shit."

Well, he obviously knows now. "Thank you."

"What are friends for?" he said. He dropped his head back and smiled. "So it's Tracy? For real? Damn, bro, Barry's gonna fucking ice you!"

"You think?"

"I would."

"Yeah, but you're… you."

"A bastard." He smiled like a wolf, threw his arm around my shoulder and lightly slapped my face. "You treat her right."

It wasn't a question. And it didn't need an answer.

"You're something special, Julio. A gentleman and a scholar. And a murderous freak. Glad you're on my side."

"I'm on all your sides. But… I feel you. Tracy… Huh, that's funny. So how long you been hitting that? I mean, I know last night, but like, how long you been seeing her?"

"A pretty long time," I said. "And you're the only one who knows. Please, please, keep this between us. I'm thinking of telling Barry, but… I don't know. Could be real bad."

"Huh." He folded his arms, and accidently stuck a firecracker in his mouth. Raised his lighter. Thumb on the metal. Flick. Lit.

"Jay!"

He freaked just in time. Spit it out, just missing my face. The pop nearly blinded me. Heartbeat hurt. But then… Aha!

"I think I get it now."

"Get what?" He picked up the bat and started spinning it, his gun gone in one invisible move. A tiny sand-toad hopped out of the beach grass to replace him.

"Look." I stretched my arms as far as I could, until my fingertips vanished from my peripheral vision. "It looks like this, doesn't it?"

"One eye?"

"Yeah, you still see everything, and what you don't see just... isn't there, even though you know it is?" I wiggled my fingers, unable to see them.

"Yeah, I guess so. Maybe you're not as dumb as you look." He sat down next to me, nearly crushing the sand-toad. It vanished into the dunes.

"Neither are you," I said. We just sat there, the bat, the balls, the board lying before us. "Damn it, why does something wrong feel so damned good?"

"It always does," he said. He unclenched his fist and stared at the last of the cocaine. For such a big guy, he moves like a magician. "You love her?"

I stomped the stoge out on the road.

Looking over my shoulder, I saw Barry through the window. His back was to us. Alone, just sitting there, staring blankly at the wall.

CRASH!

The sound snapped me back to today.

I'm going to kill those kids...

Julio would actually do it. Then, and now.

It's been a few years since those awesome, devil-may-care nights. A long time since we played any Boom Boom Home Run Derby. I'd wager Julio's playing with dynamite by now. But we never completely lost touch. Just slowly stopped hanging, Tracy filling in more and more. So I seemed to vanish as much as her, I suppose. For Jay, Barry, Bernard, and some distant others, hanging every night became every weekend and so on. Our worlds always touch, no matter how different they get. A wicked Venn diagram that stretched with time, but never split apart. But only Barry chose to *really* leave.

Hell, I just saw Jay a week or two before the car crash. So he must be alive, that's a good enough start. Time to gear up and go get him. One step at a time, and by the end of the night, I'll end up at Barry's bedside. Somehow. Just got to have faith.

I scratched my ass, tore off a frayed shoe lace, and tied my sword to my belt, still black but peeling apart. It's lasted many years, but no need for a new one so long as it keeps buckled. The sword sheath smacked against my fraying shorts with every step. I pulled both socks high, to cover the tattoo and my shins. Old skating habit.

Okay. Here we go…

CRASH!

Damn those invisible thugs. Forget them, just get moving.

I began walking down the broken sidewalk toward Jay's home, shuffling my feet, the sun shooting red rays across my path. Hope he's there. Because he was right, about everything. Then and now. He's a nut, he's unpredictable, he's dangerous, a brawler, dealer, and yes, a criminal in the kindest ways. But he's my friend. And Julio's no fool. Mercurial, a gamble. But never a fool. Always a friend. Actually, he might be the smartest person I know.

Ruined

A path is clear, or at exists, at least, but I must still face facts. There *is* a chance that Julio's not home. It's Friday night. And if he's there, enticing him to drop everything for my sake might be a tough sell, regardless of past bonds. It could take more than nostalgia and a sense of obligation if he's in one of his more *eccentric* moods. Wish I had something to give in return. Regardless, my course is set.

Forget the variables, it's time to have faith in chance, luck, even fate. I can stay home and cannibalize the last of my mind with gluttonous guilt, or search out Julio and win his favor. For Barry, for Tracy, for myself, I must try.

For there can be no greater ally in the Hallway of Fire, no stranger bedfellow in the Coffin of Ice, than Julio Sanchez Sin Corazon. He's a weird force of nature, the kind of sparkling waterfall, polluted by fifty thousand barrels of toxic waste. Mutant toe-eyed fish leap through his hair, daring onlookers to question his savage grace. Perhaps a gift is in order? What odd offering is at hand to entice him? A leather bound Catholic schoolgirl, would suffice... but they're in high demand and short supply. I checked my pocket for pills, on the desperate hope Bernard had stolen my pants for a night and left something behind. Hmmm... One old Tylenol, a nickel, and some paper clips. Cash? My wallet snapped viciously at my fingers like a hungry wolf protecting its evening meal. I have taught it well. Just fifteen bucks, all in ones, with pentagrams and lewd comments scrawled across them.

It may as well be nothing. I'll just have to rely on my natural boyish charm. The gulls circled overhead, cackling. A clam shattered on the sidewalk. I shook my fist at the gulls. I was only a few feet away from home, when another bottle broke in the abandoned gas station.

CRASH! WHIP! SNAP! CRASH!

My *parents'* abandoned gas station. And what was that other sound?

CRASH! WHIP! CRACK!

That's it. Time to collect some fucking taxes.

Fists clenched, I storm back toward the ruins that once fed my home, hearing the high pitched cackles of juvenile destruction. Almost at the back door, boarded, but rotted and weak, ready to kick through. I steel myself for battle...

But then a fox darts out, a red-orange blur, streaking from behind the crackled brown walls, between the rusted pumps, leaping into the tall, dead grass. My inked ankle throbs.

Another fox? No, can't be. But... but I saw it! Just as clear as the one in Brooklyn. And no matter what you can say about my frame of mind, I am absolutely sober.

WHIP! CRACK! SLASH!

That sound... I turn from where fox vanished, drawn by the wet sounds of live meat being beaten. From within the lightless station. Strange and terrible things are happening in my parents' unofficial tomb.

This will not stand. What if their victim is a fox? Why not, given what I've seen? And if not, I can't imagine a substitution I could justify leaving to some punk's savage hands.

Marching around to the front, where the door-less entrance can provide some sunlight to see the enemies within, I grit my teeth and came to terms with the possibility of an adolescent ambush. Teenagers are dangerous, young, stupid, and strong. Even with something to lose, they'll react insane just to make the others blush. So barging in with a sword was probably a bad idea.

I laid my sword down in the tangled brush beside the pumps, then crept forward. The front door had long been torn off its hinges, so I angle my shadow to avoid entering before me. Breathe slow through the nose, it's quiet, but better than holding your breath. Don't hear anything now, to mask my approach. At the door now, but it's quiet. Someone must be inside—this is the only entrance or exit.

As I stepped inside, the lack of candy, soft drinks, engine oil, cold medicine, lottery tickets, light, or life reminds me why I haven't been back inside for years, despite seeing this place from my window every day. Smaller than our home, yet still so dark, grumpkins or clever kids could hide amongst the ruins. I'm making a point of not concentrating on the familiar gray walls, just the darkness, the floating specks of dirt, the dust and dancing ghosts of childhood where the register once sat. Fresh glass, dustless, sparkles on the floor. I creep around, focusing on the sound of shallow breathing. Could be two or more... There! In the back, behind the bare, dented aisles, stands my enemy!

A boy with spiky blond hair, and a red shirt with black stripes. He's staring at something on the floor. A thin silver cell phone peeks over the lip of his back pocket. So this boy is no bum, that's for sure. Daddy pay for that fancy phone? Couldn't be more than some-teen-years old... Cripes, he's half as old as me, at best. Makes him even more dangerous. The hormones are palpable.

Decided to avoid startling it, violence is not preferable here. I took a heavy step, cleared my throat, and waited for his attention. His shoulders heaved as smoke crept around the back of his blond head. Bits of shattered glass littered the floor around him. He held a cigarette in his left hand and a bike chain in his right. Unlike his cellphone, the chain bore no shine. Just dripped a musky red slime.

"You there," I said. "Hey! Look at me, kid."

He spun, the chain jangling at his side. His blue eyes burned with irrational rage. This was a stupid idea. Very nasty vibes. There's something wrong with his face. His eyes are too small, yet bulging. Possibly been hitting PCP Torpedoes? His mouth is a crescent moon, the edges pulled down to his chin. His nose is small, upturned, nostrils flaring. Something about his face is also a bit too familiar. Finally, he retorts.

"Fuck off, faggot!" Snot dripped down to his lip. He spit.

"Listen kid, this is my turf. You're trespassing. Forget the mess, I'll let it slide. Now bug off or I'll call the cops!"

"I said, *shut the fuck up*, old man. Now *you* get the fuck out of here."

"Really?" I put my hands on my hips, standing straight, chest forward, chin up, ensuring he realized I was over a foot taller. "Or what?"

"Or I kick your fucking teeth in."

He shifts his weight and I see something crumpled behind him. Something twitching. Something small, furry. Wet. Something struggling to make sounds that come out as bursting red bubbles, blocking air that exhales into death rattles.

"Is that a dog?"

"So?"

This punk is a pure monster. An uber-brat.

How long has he been beating animals in here whilst Bernard and I slept peacefully across the street? This will not stand! Not across the street from my home. Not where I played games and skated with my blood-brothers. Not where I walked with Tracy, hand in hand, to the home I once had. Not in the station that my parents bled themselves, keeping it alive for me.

Stay calm. Remember, at best, violence is just the nature of youth. Like Julio, a destructive instinct can mature, making room for new day of creation. I hope. Screw this. I've seen this sort of thing before. The first time, we were about nine years old. Tracy was only three or so, back then. Barry's dad took me, him, and Bernard out into the vast expanse of woods behind their big, white house. His dad had to put their neighbor's sheep down. Didn't answer why.

Used a shotgun. Point blank. The sheep's skull was so thick that its face blew off in strips, eyes, fur, and snout, hanging in clumps from a bloodied, jagged skull. Something to make Satan proud. The poor thing made a sound like a dying train, but still, it stood on buckling legs. So Barry's dad blasted it again. I peed. Just a little. Barry cried. An hour later, Burn threw up behind a tree. I still have no idea why he made us watch. Maybe to prove a point? He's the alpha. We ate lunch in silence while Helena, stoned as hell, watched TV with Tracy in their living room.

"Your move, bitch."

I hear him, but… as my eyes adjust to the dark, the picture's getting worse. That dog is still alive. It shouldn't be.

"What the hell is wrong with you?" I demanded. "You sick, twisted little vermin!"

"Why do you care? Who are you? Fucking creep, leave us alone or I'll break your bitch-ass face!"

There was a rustling in the corner. A girl came out of the shadows. Her face was round and pink. Her hair was bright blonde, almost white. She stood by the boy and didn't move, didn't speak. Not in shock, but nearly a blank slate.

"Look kids, just…" I couldn't take my eyes off the girl. What would Julio say in this situation? I know. He'd do what Barry's dad tried to. "Okay, enough. You wanna stay here? Then run your pockets, son! Empty them, now! Cigarettes, money, drugs. On the floor!"

He laughed. Julio would too, if he heard me trying to sound street tough. Note to self: practice different 'alpha male voice' to complement creepy eye stare.

"You can't have shit. It bit my sister!" he said, lashing his arm out and letting the chain snap into the dog's stomach. It didn't move. My lips tightened. There was no froth at its mouth, thankfully. The boy kept making demands. "I'll give *you* something if you kill it."

This really was a stupid idea. I could be halfway to Julio's by now.

So what if I went without gifts? Need to end this. I stepped forward. "Kill it? With the chain?"

"Kick it." His eyes narrowed.

"Fine." I stepped closer. My head was pointed down. He looked up to meet me. I used the stare. Where my eyes roll up and head tilts down, and all the pain and rage and anger can finally glint through. "No. Give me the chain."

He looked at his sister, who's never taken her eyes off me. He began to hand the chain toward me. I snatched it from him, feeling his young grip break under the pressure. I leapt back and swung the chain through the air.

"Ha! Dumbass!"

The boy stumbled back and tripped over the dog. He splashed in a thick sludge of blood. The dog wasn't moving at all. The girl broke her stare to look at her brother. I began swinging the chain wildly left to right, making circles and flicking it over my back like nunchaku. Something Bruce Lee would do. The chain bit into my lower back. I did my best not to wince. Show no fear!

"You rotten creep!" I shouted. "What did you do, huh? What made it bite her? Now give me everything you have! Out with it!"

Terror lit behind the little devil's eyes. He fumbled in his pants, pulled out a pack of Moose Lights, and tossed them at my feet.

"What else you got, boy?" I squatted down to snatch the pack, all the while arcing the chain before me. I glanced at the supposed sister. "Not you."

Something in his flickering eyes, a candle's flame blown erratically, said this wasn't the first time he laid helpless while an older man screamed demands at him. He pulled a prescription pill case out. Threw it to me.

Good.

"Now get the hell out of here and never come back," I said. I gathered the smokes and pills, then turned my back, proudly walking toward the door. Something Bruce Lee would not do.

He dropped me with a full-on kick into the small of my back. Caught myself on my hands, but lost the chain. I rolled over, right into a hellstorm of snarling and thrashing fingers. He tried to bite me, tried to claw my face, tried to kick my balls. It was a dance of parries from my back, and any slip would land a painful blow. But he slowed, so I planted my feet into his thighs and lifted. Threw him back like a doll. I rolled across the floor, over glass, grasping for the chain.

The sister had it. The boy leapt on me again, but with my considerably longer legs, I caught him midair, just below his sweaty armpits. I shifted our weight to the left and gave a mighty toss. He thudded into the old drink cases. Ha, countered twice in a row! But there's no telling what kind of endurance this kid has. So I made a mad dash for the door. Outside, I dove onto my chest and I snatched my sword from the ground, then spun and rose. But I lost my footing in the dirt. Slammed my back into a gas pump. I held the sheathed sword in front of me with both hands. I waved it menacingly at that black entrance. Waiting. Come on.

"Come on, you degenerate little dog! Come out here and fight," I growled.

The sound of wood snapping inside. Shuffling, hissed whispers, then silence. Nobody came out. I peeked in. The boarded window in the back was bashed through. They were gone, no doubt retreating into the maze of trails that run through the yellowing fields like a junkie's thinning veins.

Gone. I gazed at my shack, sitting proudly across the street on its little hill. There is great comfort in knowing the sea crashes just over the dunes that flank our home. But that comfort is corrupted by the disgusting reality that this man-child was hiding inside the remnants of *my* past, beating a poor old dog to death, while Bernard and I drank and played house darts and slept. Invisible in plain sight, just like how my kind slinks along the rim of Eastern Sponge Island, hidden from the celebrities, cops, and preachers. The germy underside of the toilet bowl. The crusty scum you know exists but won't confront. I thought my ilk of losers and users were the bottom, but it always goes lower, doesn't it?

The dog is dead. The kids are gone. The damage done.

I used my frayed shoelace to tie my sword back onto my belt. Then I stepped out of the two-pump station and into the past. Julio is east, but I can't help staring west, at the pristine green golf course, where a small ranch home once... where... after Mom died, my footsteps echoed across the floor. Empty. I'd sold the furniture. The pictures. Their bed. My bed. Tracy held my hand as we stood in the doorway.

Last day before the bank locked it up.

She was with me, both of us frozen in the front doorway.

"Is it lonely?" she asked.

"Not always."

She squeezed my fingers between hers. She kissed my cheek. "You can come live with us."

"No, I can't. The closer I am to you, the further we'll have to be apart."

"I know." She looked away. "What will you do?"

"That old garage-loft-thing down the road is grandfathered into their Will. Burn is gonna fix it up with me. I'll survive off the yard sale as long as I can. I have scholarships and student loans I can live off of for now."

"But you need them."

"I'm moving off campus. I'm coming home, so I can save more." I rubbed her back, staring at the dark beams. Our voices bouncing back at us. "I'll be here all the time now. Well, not *here*, but... No more waiting for the weekend."

She turned and hugged me. Her breasts pressed against my chest, her hair sank against my neck. She kissed my shoulder. I wrapped my arms around her, feeling the ridge in her back. Her piercings cold against my neck. I hung my head down, smelling her hair.

Now I smell that dog's blood on me. From the chain. On my forearm.

Wiped it on my shorts. Forced myself to move.

I was halfway down the road to Jay's house by the time the memory fully died. Staring at the pot-holed street ahead. A long, homeless stretch on the coastal edge. Lanky telephone poles watching me pass. The setting sun cast a purple hue over the orange streetlights that hum, buzz, and never turn off. Far to the north, over the thin fence of trees, loomed the swollen belly of the town proper. Traces of sunlight glinting off diamond encrusted mansions. Flamboyantly armored fortresses. Way too far to throw a rock, way too close to look away. The faint rim of the town peeking above the trees, winking like a broken whore with that new strand of HIV.

A quarter mile south, the beach was just out of sight around the bend, and the gray trees were hanging together in sparse clumps. Strange to see dying trees in this fertile season. It makes you hesitant to drink the water. But this view is spectacular. A stretch of paved desert, littered with ancient streetlights, the verdant green golf courses far behind me, a rim of forest to the left, and the magnificent ocean booming on the right.

Old rotted husks of homes, half-burnt in the name of insurance, faded 'For-Sale' signs standing in front of vacant lots. Only a handful of gray, warped, one-story hovels still dot the yellow land between my home and Julio's, and all are long since foreclosed. Truly a borderland, wrapped in the screeching hum of cicadas, hidden traffic and summer sport cars roaring, and the sweet smell of wet salt air.

The kids are all gone.

Once more I'm alone, sword in hand, and Julio ahead.

Everything else left behind.

Elvis Always Goes For the Throat

Almost there. Still alone. Only the insects' buzz and the smack of small waves to match each slapping step. Good. Is it wrong that I enjoy this privacy? This ghost street. Once a neighborhood. No police come here, now. Nobody comes here. Feel cool as a samurai, wandering with my sword. I love this thing. My comfort blanket is sharpened steel. Not so good to cuddle, but nothing is anymore.

Still, I'll admit that it's not exactly prudent to strut down the street holding a very large, very illegal weapon. Especially once you factor in the risk of some poor boy and his sister fleeing my gas-station, crying to the police about the crazy man who tried to kill them. But sealed in its ebony sheath, the sword could be tossed into the dunes at a moment's notice. Not that throwing it away was a true option. A samurai's sword is his soul. To throw it during battle was the ultimate dishonor. No way I could... Ha. Stupid Tim.

The sword is vital to enter Julio's home. Technically, he lives alone. But Jay keeps strange housemates, brutish members of the animal kingdom. The least dangerous of which is Jubedor Adobo, a Chilean iguana that's rumored to have once been slave to a woods-witch. Jubedor, with his rainbow scales and razor sharp tail, has full reign of the property. No leash, no cage, just like his master. Although Julio insists that his iguana is a vegetarian, I remain skeptical that any lizard can grow to over six feet long without a steady diet of rich meats. On more than one visit, Jubedor has been absent. Julio never knew where the beast was. I shudder to think the occasional missing persons alert is somehow connected. No doubt, Jubedor could swallow a toddler whole.

Alas, Jubedor Adobo is not the most dangerous of Jay's animal army. It's his vagrant gang of pugs that get me. When I visited three years ago to inform Julio of Tracy's death, dumb enough to waltz in, unannounced, I met the litter's new leader, Elvis Von Besos. Jay names all his beasts with full, formal titles. Sometimes I doubt he sees any difference between them and man. Elvis is squat and boxed, meaty lips, tar-yellow fangs, and just plain weird looking. There's about six or eight other pugs. Always hard to tell. They come and go with little explanation. But my suspicions always lie on Jubador or Elvis. Most people could punt the pug across the street. But in a group, cornered in a dark hallway with nothing between your crotch and their teeth… things are different.

So that night, witless in shock, I walked in and then… Julio heard me screaming over the snarling pack, rushed into the breezeway, grabbed Elvis by his hind legs, and delivered a vicious head butt, square into the pug's un-neutered balls. I have no doubt that Julio remains supreme master over his canine companions, but they will forever bow to no other man.

Sword or not, cutting down Elvis or Jubedor would certainly incur a savage beating from Julio. Even for me. But these are the sorts of things that must be taken into consideration when you dance with demons. I trust this man on any dangerous road, for he truly and deeply believes in an eye for an eye, and will stand by his friends through any hellfire. But I'll never presume to know what random company he keeps. Nor I will approach his castle without my own defenses.

And here we are!

There's the house, just a quarter of a mile from the corner of my road and his. Crooked, white paint chips peeling, something from the Midwest left behind on the corner of our lonely back roads, and only one vacant home left standing beside it, trying to slink away as it leans awkwardly in the soiled sand.

Many visitors have encountered disturbing wonders at Julio's childhood pad, then and now that his mother… Like I said, Bernard, Jay, and myself, all orphans in our way, now. But even back then, long as I can remember, his guests were as stupid, wild, or wondrous as his pets. Everything from alcoholic skaters to schizophrenic bums and limbless vets. Anyone who needs the occasional 'vacation' from reality. So… everyone. On more than one occasion, off duty cops were caught snorting coke in his kitchen, and gutted deer hung in the front yard. There are bats in his bedroom. Actually, Julio's two-story house is no different from anywhere else on Earth. Beautiful from certain angles, warm on certain nights, and certain to kill you when your guard is down.

I've been here so many times, even when his mom was alive, but right now an odd warning sign fills me with trepidation. See, there should be a rather large boulder across the street. It is—or rather was—grand and yellow, like a misshapen dinosaur egg. It served as the unofficial borderline between the residential area and the commercial. Julio's house was the first and last standing, in what was once a series of suburban homes. Devoid of trees, dotting the coastal road. This all lies north of the border-boulder... which, at the moment, is lying all about the street in large smoking chunks. Impressive chunks, but chunks nonetheless.

Now this is insane.

Nothing short of a burst of pure napalm-diaxitride could even crack this thing! Believe me, we tried many times. Especially in high school. Yet here it is, sprinkled along the street like smoldering confetti. Less than half of the border-boulder remains. A giant's skull split and fractured, odd ashy crystal shining from within. I'm so overwhelmed by the utter destruction of this monument, that I didn't notice all the goddamned noise.

Julio is quite the fan of violently aggressive music. Screeching from his windows, a torrent of death metal cut the air. But at the same time, he was blasting booming bass, pumping along with vulgar 'gangster rap'. Nothing like Barry's preferred hip-hop. Just in your face rage, any form, and he'll blast it, often at the same time, as if half his brain screamed as the other half digested light-speed, guttural screams.

But for the rest of us, this vile mixture of noise creates the atmosphere of an impending heart attack. This is why his animals are insane. This is what supposedly attracts giant, sexy, mutant butterflies.

There are a handful of foreclosed homes nearby, but only one was directly next door. A tree covered hill loomed up behind Julio's house at the corner. Once again, beyond that hill was the town proper, the thin pine forest shielding us from civilization. To the south, our Atlantic Ocean god keeps guard.

I tripped over a hot rock. No S.W.A.T. team destroyed this boulder. I look at the yellow chunks, faded crystals inside, edges burning like azure flames. His house was untouched. As always, his rusted, wheel-less town car sat on the piss-colored lawn, with a neon-pink penis scrawled on the car's hood.

There's another noise hidden in the music.

Barking. Hungry barking.

Elvis is already rallying his army behind the front door? Damn their special noses. I gripped my katana tightly. It suddenly occurred to me that I might be entering battle, yet again, without bestowing it with a proper name. It might be my sword's first encounter with a real enemy, and it was unfitting to proceed without title. Am I willing to kill one of Jay's dogs for this? I think of her face and her brother. Of things past and fading.

"From this day forth, you shall be Kitsune," I whispered to my sword. I unsheathed her. My tattoo flared up again, burning like a soccer kick in the shin. Thought of Barry's story, about a Cursed Sword that makes your existence nil. "Kitsune, serve me well, and you shall be remembered for ages! Celebrated in song and enshrined beside me."

The moment changed. It was as if the fake ceremony and weight of abandonment entranced me. Now I was slipping free, awakening to the dawn of reality. Like blacking out into light. Sounds fade. I float. For a split second I was not on the sidewalk, but up in the clouds, looking down on myself talking to a cheap sword. This was not the first time I found myself waking from a strange dream state frenzy. It is the Curse of those who try too hard.

As Barry Cameron once wrote in an acclaimed essay about artistic bullshit, "An automatic shutdown must occur, just to keep the engines cooled. You simply cannot help if you care too much at all times. But never mistake our standby mode for weakness. Trust that we are with you, that we feel the ground and smell the air as much as any of you, if not more. When we fall it hurts. When we breathe it stings. And when we are cut, we bleed a parade of clowns."

Ah, fuck you, Barry. You poor bastard! Bless you for seeing it all, as it truly is. Why do you write fantasy when you so clearly see what I can't? That all we live and breathe is truly fantastic?

A heavy rustling shatters my trance.

To the left.

A slinking rustle, low and dexterous. Heaven forbid, is Jubedor loose? I go into the Pecking Spider stance, a loose grip on Kitsune's hilt. This corner is now a battlefield seeking death and thus every detail is significant. The potholes that could trip me up. Chunks of boulder to stumble on. Even Kitsune's sheath could get caught during mid-slice, splitting me open instead. Or glints of sun flashing off her blade could blind me. Or...

Damn it, I hear the beast!

As if it knows, the tall grass stops moving. Where is it? If the monster moves, I might not hear it again, due to that horrible music mixing behind me and... now the lack of any sound... not even from Elvis and his pug thugs. No faint barking as they maul the door, trying to break free and nibble me to death.

Oh. Oh, no!

They're not *trying* to get out. They *are* out.

I'm being circled like a fat pig hunted by velociraptors. Right on cue, the snarls flare up all around me. Every direction at once. I spin wildly, trying to get a bead on my assailants. Twirling panic. These are no melons. They'll be coming for my ankles first, work their way up to the shins and then pull me down, piece by bloody piece. Gnawing through my forearms, dragging me down as Elvis goes for the throat!

"YO! Shithead! Fire in the hole!"

What?

"Tim, *back the fuck off!*" It's Julio, screaming from the front door. His fat gold chain shakes across his chest, the severed arm of an octopus giving a final death rattle. Big and burly, yet still smiling through his roars. He's waving a machete in the air.

"Jay?"

"DUDE! FIRE IN THE *FUCKING HOLE!*"

I leap into the grass.

There's no sound. The air sears. Metal slices past my skin. Something awful shakes my heart. The force shoots my feet up and over me like a scorpion's tale. I see Kitsune fly past me, while I fly over the street. Cracking into jagged stone. Everything upside down, metal in my mouth, and alarms ringing, as the sun... the sun is fading to black. Kitsune clangs beside me, but I can't reach, I'm still rolling, shaking apart, as fire eats all beside us.

Hellshock

I'm dead. Waking up in Hell. Brilliant.

It's not all that hot. But it's dark and smells like some hoofed creature's rubbed shit and ash around. A stench wells up behind my eyes, like piss on a fire, a bucket of rotten fish heads.

I am dirty and foolish. My soul is toilet paper for the gods' omnipotent asses. The air is still, but the noise is horrible. Screeching guitars, hammering drums, raspy screams, a deep, constant rumble, and rhythmic chanting. A mix of rage from two different, distant realms.

Head's still buzzing, skull feels like cracked eggs, brain boiled and blown. But some reptilian part of it activates, separates the sounds of earthrealm, the guttural growls and testicular braying. A savage voice screeches through a burnt and ravaged throat: *"A thorn from the holy cross enslaved but unchained, daemon pantheon sun eater reigns! My little nymph hacked to slivers lick her pain, her tears rain from a lacerated sky, she screams bloody murder as we embrace our sickness and submission, so this is how it feels to die! And it's okaaaaaaaaaaaaaay!"* At the exact same time, a deep voice rhymes over beastly bass, reminders of war and wicked streets above: *"I stack 'em high slinging dope as I fly by, get the fuck out way or you're staring at the sky, six shots live but got five extra, leave 'em so your niggas know who the fuck sent ya, down to the grave, my game ain't nothin' to mock, ya gave it a shot bitch now suck my cock!"*

Lovely. The swooning croons of Hell. And the horned lord's playlist is as grating and stupid as Julio's. He'll love it here. Well, I guess my last living thoughts were that soundtrack. Figures. Logic reigns, even here... Never believed in the afterlife, but I still assumed that even Hades would have the best death metal. Too bad. It fills the darkness, I can't move, see, speak, but I can smell.

The smell is right, fits the stereotypes, but it's too cold, no tormented screams of the damned. Hell is wrong. In this darkness, I don't burn. Skin is regaining sense. Is the ground...? I'm lying on something that should be soft, but as I wiggle, it's clearly cracking, crusted over with scum. Head is elevated. Uneven grooves. Feels almost like... a couch? But I still can't speak, and I swear my eyes are open but I cannot see.

Is this a coma?

Last thing I remember, I swear I'd stepped on a landmine, but I can still twitch my limbs. Like swollen little worms… Oh god. Here it comes. Bile creeping up, throat constricting.

The creeping fear.

The first hiccups of insanity, forced out after a violent assault on your senses. Judging by the memory of blinding fire, and the dull vibrations still echoing in my bones, it was most definitely an explosion.

Now comes loathing, the anger and the dread. Realizing that I am not alone. Something is breathing over me. Something large. Hot, smells like rotten cabbage. Starting to see a dim outline, like a shadow bathed in black. Its broad musculature is barely discernable in the darkness. It shifts its weight. Oh fuck the gods, please don't eat me, get away!

It stays just above my face. I wouldn't move if I could.

Oh, Tracy, I think it's finally happened. The stress has killed me. No way you are here, but I fear I'm in the lair of the Archfiend. Blown apart by something, my limbs likely sprayed across the street back on Earth. Will never be at your side. I'm indeed Cursed. Prey for surgeonfish. Future slave to The Nameless Nemesis, first-born of the Infernal Hag's Infertile Womb. Bastard born, eternal slave to epic evil's waiting to return. The Aborted Mother, her skeletal brood of Neverborn, and the Flagellator, Archon of Suicide, the Thousand Tooth Hunger! Dangling me over a pit of children's stomach acid. Immediate judgment from the Lords of Karma for beating that child, for being an unbeliever, for failing my parents, for abandoning Barry, for giving up too soon, for stupidly judging that innocent ray, for killing you, for loving you, for lying, for hiding, for failing—

"Damn, you *still* are a weird, whiny little bitch." The darkness laughs.

Flare, brief red bloom, flash. Smoke. Smoke blows into my face.

A cigarette has been lit?

For one horrible second I see my true enemy. Not the Archons of Woe. No! Worse. The cig's flare lights up a face I can't forget, if it's really him. Perhaps he died in the war? I'm dead, now bedfellows with my age-old nemesis. Childhood monster. Predator. Bully, beast…

Lucas Boil.

"Quit your rambling, bitch! We're alone boy, I'll slap the shit out of you," he growls.

"Boil?" I ask, voice sounding as weak as I feel. "You're in Hell? Ha. Jerk."

"Timid little Tim. You have *no idea* what Hell is. I'll show you, just give me the word." His voice still sounds like sandpaper that wishes it were gravel.

"No. You're enough, get off of me," I say. Or beg? If so, it was reflexive. I swear. Well… if we're stuck here together, I might as well be polite. Best I can do is say, "Long time no see."

I can see better now. Maybe it's just the voice, filling in the void. But I must trust my eyes, and they give a weak report. Boil's hunched on his haunches, balanced on the couch arm like a mountain lion. He takes a long, deliberate drag, letting the red smoke waft around his face. Suddenly leaps forward, slamming his fist into the couch beside my face. He's hovering over me. Smells like curdled cream. His cigarette crackles as he sucks it down, red-hot light killing the air between us. Oh Jesus, did he get used to man-flesh overseas? I cannot suffer that, not from him. My arm flops about, seeking Kitsune… finding nothing. I try sinking further into the couch, but it's like pushing yourself ass-first into a dumpster.

"Man meat and dumpsters? Did the blast scramble your fucking brains?" He slaps me. "Fuck's the matter with you? Shell shock?"

"What? I got… blast? Julio?"

He slaps me again. The cold tingling it ignites slips through the abyss and strangles my brain. Falling into blackout mode again. Fading. It's okay. I hear the slap, feel nothing. Hell is disappointingly lame. Dropping into myself, faster now, darkness is just echoes. It's okay, Tim. Just let go. Slide, fade away…

Swimming. Deep dark water. Lungs burning. Panic. Always panic, draining. Look for sun and struggle, follow bubbles, moving too slow, thrashing in water. Give up. You earned it. My mouth opens. Embrace drowning, waiting for chest to fill with salt and weight.

Yet I'm fine. I can breathe just fine. Awake? Feels more real than a dream, more real than the Hell hallucination, yet there is no sun. Just endless dark water, but I can move. Drifting. I look for anything, fish, seaweed, coral, an above, a below, even a shark, anything at all. Little white lights are approaching. I swim toward them.

They have limbs and faces. Frozen and paler than white, just drifting by. Three of them. An older man with my hair, my face but lined with hard work, clean shaven and in pain, and oh god, no, an exhausted woman, clasping his hand, floating behind… lovers, lost. I struggle to scream to my parents. They waver like thin, paper people. Their mouths move like fish, soundless. Their eyes blink, wide and scared, but black as the sea. Hollow. Holes in a sheet. They reach for me as they drift past, no matter how desperately I thrash they fade away.

Another one approaches. I try so hard not to look at her. Close my eyes, ball my fists over them, feel salt leaking out to join the sea. I have to see. I turn to face her. Preparing to open my eyes. Any minute now, heart hammering, cracking my ribs. Then something soft brushes my face, and I relax. I can look, I should, I prepare myself but…

Something huge rumbles in the void. Shaking the pitch black sea.

The water boils at it rises. Just as I have the guts to face Tracy, it whooshes into view, enormous, the face and chest so bright I can see its whole form, even if I close my eyes. How? Even if I turn my head, it's too big, and no matter what, it hovers between us, keeps us apart and I can't see her now. Can't reach, can't… A tsunami booms, blasting me back as its winged fins spread apart, and yet… I haven't moved any further from it at all. Blotting out all the darkness, the terrible horned outline glows as if it's hiding a distant sun. Somewhere there's a surface. It exists just to let me know. It doesn't even need to laugh. A long barbed tail gleams below the fangs lining its gaping, frozen maw. It wants to be a god. Water's getting darker again. But still, I can just barely make out the color of its underbelly, the milky chalk matching my parents' paper-thin skin.

I struggle to swim around it, but I can't see her. The god-ray flaps, pushing me back, and I can't see her, I can't reach her. Instinct makes me look back. Just in time to see my parents, tiny specks of white, floating away. A boom and my eardrums want to burst, I must look back to the ray. But something's wrong, more light, and I realize that maybe the evil fish-faced god is—

"A disgusting little prick!"

Boil is rearing back, desperate to escape the hot vomit that's dribbling down from my chin to my chest. Not much. Just a bit. Enough to push him away. I wipe it off with the back of my hand, flinging the hot glob onto the floor. I hear myself coughing up words, running on some kind of auto-pilot. Rub my neck and shirt on the couch arm. Clean enough. I'm alive, and know this isn't hell. Not this, not here, with him, not with anyone at all.

"Hope," I hear myself say.

"What? Get a hold of yourself. I'm sick of this. You're fine now. Get a grip, pussy."

Right. Need to get a grip on things. I could have sworn I was just standing on Julio's lawn, but Lucas Boil is supposed to be in the Army, and far, far away. How has it gotten so hot all over my skin? Why am I covered in sweat, nose clogged, bruised everywhere, and yet still floating in some clam sucked limbo with this vicious freak? The night's mission is already spiraling into chaos. Struggle, god damn it! Fight the shaking haze! You must get your bearings! Get a handle on this evil situation! Fight back!

"You? Fight?" He laughs.

Not sure what I'm saying or thinking... dangerous thing in the diner, more so here. Maybe. That's not the mission. I just wanted a ride from a friend for a friend. Now I'm burnt and broken, prostrated before our local devil. My sword... Kitsune is gone. Boil is going to pound me into meat and bone. Just like he always did, my whole fucking life. One big circle of failure and defeat.

Something growls in the darkness beside him. Something else slithers across the floor. Boil's lieutenants. On the left, Caninus, Lord of the Growl! A festering clump of mouths and noses, gnashing teeth and wailing beasts, torrents of saliva surging forth between glistening bicuspids. And in the center, the intelligent head, with coifed hair and furrowed brow. Pug Lord Elvis, and his Inbred Brood. To my right, the Serpent King, shark toothed, scales of silver and breath of fire, tongue of gold and eyes of ice. Generations tall, coiled about the mortal realm, staring hungrily at my crippled form. I came searching for Julio, but I am at the mercy of monsters, and I cannot scream.

"For what it's worth, we didn't see you." Boil sucked on his cigarette, and things don't feel any more normal. "I wasn't expecting a worthless little shit like you to get in the way." Boil spit into the dark and Elvis growled. "Didn't you hear us shout 'clear'? *Fire in the hole?* You fucking asshole, you could've got killed! Idiot... Even I don't want you dead. Too much paperwork."

"No. Thanks? I guess. Where is Julio? I thought... hell, I don't know. Boil, where are we? Why are you here? What *the hell* is going on?"

A faded light flashes at the far end of the room, as if a thousand fireflies are clinging to one another, coupling madly as they die, they condense in a cloud of sarin gas. Finally! This light harkens the coming of my fallen angel. The insane music fades away. Boots clomp on the floorboards. I close my eyes, swallow, and when they open, there's a blue plastic cup shoved into my face. I recognize the chewed fingernails around the cup.

"Julio?"

"Sup, Tim!"

Fire in my spine prevents me from sitting up. "Oh man, my back hurts."

"I bet, bro. That was fucking insane. Here, drink this," Julio said. His shoulder-length black hair, thick with grease and sweat, hangs around his face like ragged, limp bat wings. He pushes the cup to my lips. I trust him, but... When my mouth doesn't open, he pinches my nose, waits for my mouth to pop open, and then dumps the whole cup in. Before I can react, he forces a pill into my mouth, and I can't help but swallow since he strokes my throat like I'm his pet. "Be good! Easy, easy. Relax. There you go. It's all good now. You'll be fine in a few minutes."

"Thanks? What did you just give me?"

"Uh... water. And a painkiller?" Julio grabbed my knees and flung them to the side, forcing me to sit up. He flopped down on the couch between Boil and me. He's spreading his arms across the couch's back, forcing a cloud of dust mites and spider eggs to shoot out from under his weight. Between him and Boil, still sitting on the far arm, and both these brutes cut from stone, it's a wonder the couch doesn't tip onto its side and fling me off.

"Lucky he wasn't closer. Fucking moron could've lost a foot. What took you so long? I've seen men come out of shellshock quicker than this wimp," Boil said. He leaned across to snap his fingers in my face. "YOU WITH US YET? Wake up, asshole!"

"I AM. Clearly," I said into the dark. Can't face him yet.

Jay pushed Boil's hand away from my face. My brain still feels like a four-sided triangle, but the water starts bringing clarity. No surprise there, my worship of the element's divine powers is well documented. My senses start working in tandem again. The pit of hell was actually... well, not so far off. It was just Julio's living room.

My eyes adjusted to the extremely dim light. He always likes it dark inside. The true darkness I'd seen was fake, probably caused by my brain smacking the inside of my skull. The few lamps have no shades, bulbs seeming to float like ghosts. We're on his purple couch, marked with many holes, stabs, and cigarette burns dotting it like acne. The couch was in the center of the room, alone in a sea of discarded junk. A line of burst speakers crowded the walls. On the left, came the rap. On the right, the death metal. Both were turned down now, droning like a drunken army behind us.

Boxes of junk collected dust, some taped, some tipped over. Probably holding all manner of fascinations and hobbies collected through the years. Jay can't throw anything away. Faint traces of urine permeate, either coming from the floor or the peeling wallpaper, stolen from a party-store many years ago. This place has fallen apart, even for him. How long has it been?

Yet in many ways, the clutter and strange mutation of random objects was not too different from how Bernard and I lived. But we did have a small sense of order, and a bit more hygiene. Chalk it up to Julio spending most of the time in his basement lab, cooking up meth, napalm, raver glow-sticks, and gods know what else. Maybe fake sporting shoes. Huffers, rackets, blackjacks. Anything in demand.

And as my Mistress Iris, Goddess of Coherence, spreads her cool palms across my scalp, my demon captors are revealed in their true forms. Caninus was just Elvis and his hoard, mercifully at ease now that Julio was sitting by me. The Serpent King, clearly Jubedor, slinks around us in a circle. It quickly loses interest in us, lying patiently beside the couch. And thus, that must mean that Lucas Boil, the worst of them, was obviously just... Aw, shit!

It really is him!

The Nemesis of the Feline, archenemy to all who walk the Lunar path, returned from exile! Shaved head and a face only a mother could love. After she "accidentally" dropped it on the kitchen floor. Multiple times.

"Ya back with us, bitch?" Boil asked when he saw the recognition ignite in my eyes. Still has the same raspy, shit for nothing voice he's had since grade school. Still just as big, sweaty, beady eyes and wormy lips.

"So... you're back. Section Eight, I take it?"

"Not on your life," Boil said. "I'm just on leave. A little business trip. Brought some gifts back for my boy, here," he said, slapping Jay's shoulder. His boy? They're boys? Since when?

"How long?" I asked, hoping to hear he was on his way out.

"Oh, don't worry. I'm headed back to defend your freedom soon enough, dickhead."

I turned to Jay. His face showed no lies. The pieces forced together, and my gut felt full of shit. But the water helped, and the painkiller... don't like them ever since Tracy... but it's humming and buzzing. Still don't want to move, but I can speak, at least. "Jay, what is this? Business? Gifts? You mean he stole something?"

"Careful," Boil growled.

"Careful? How dare you... What the hell did you shoot at me? Don't tell me you didn't steal heavy ordinance or, or, something! Being a soldier doesn't make you a saint, tigers don't change their..." I was shouting, and actually feeling guilty as I heard it.

"And if he did?" Jay cocked his head.

Boil grinned. Crooked, yellowed, teeth.

"You seriously stole from the U.S. Military? I mean what, weapons, ammunition, explosives? And they're here, in this house? Right now?" I didn't care at this point. Wanted to run away, fast, no way the F.B.I. wasn't casing the joint right then and there.

Boil leaned over Julio, paused, and then smacked me in the head.

"Maybe. You'd be surprised."

"Yo, Tim, tranquilisate," Jay laughed. "You should see this shit, man! Real high class. You could blow a lot of fucking minds with these things. I'm talking scholars, lawyers, bank vaults, sewage lines. We got weeks worth of fun stashed out back. No more of that M-80, small time mailbox bullshit! Say goodbye to the Anarchist Cookbook, and hello to the next stage of my—"

"So you really blew up the boulder? I didn't imagine that, either?"

"C-4!" Boil thumped his chest.

"And the tree in the back, and Jubedor's old shed," Julio ticked off on his fingers. "And my old car. I was about to finish the rock, saw you at the last fucking second. Thank god. Shit's crazy strong, when you got enough. And we do! But you know that. Damn blast threw you across the road."

"Yeah. Cool. You know that big *rock* is probably a thousand years old? Maybe ten times as large underground. I think a glacier pushed it here. And you ruined it for... what? Fun?"

"Hell yeah," Julio said.

"And that means you also almost killed me."

"YOU almost killed you," Julio said as he started rolling a joint in his lap. "It's not like we laid a trap for you. You stumbled right on in, like a zombie, talking to yourself. Swear I thought you were bugging out on acid."

"No more," I said, thinking of her and the bad year after. "No more of any of that."

"He sounds like it. You should have heard the weird shit he was saying just now. Now don't freak, Tim. You're fine, but you got hit with concussive force, and thrown a few yards," Boil said. "Maybe some slight bumps and bruises, a concussion if I'm lucky, but I've seen far worse. So shut up, you'll be fine. I already checked your vitals. No breaks, probably not even a fracture. Guess you're tougher than you look. But you might have pissed yourself. Just a bit."

Did I just hear the words 'concussive force' and 'checked your vitals' out of that gorilla's mouth? I checked my crotch for dampness, but then a lump in my pocket called out. The gifts! I pulled them out and presented them to Julio. He took the pack of Moose Lights and the pills with a silent smile and a nod.

"Tim, my man! This is great. Is this Ventronal? Isn't that banned now for making dudes puke up their guts? Smokes too? Gracias, amigo," he said. "What is this, Christmas? For real, though, how'd you get Ventronal? You got a hook up? Yo, Luke, this is the stuff I need to finish my Devil Lotus Brew. Sick serum, you'll see. Now I don't have to knock over the pharmacy. Thanks, Tim!" He squeezed me like only a grizzly bear could.

"Indeed, thank god for the little things. I beat up a teenager for it."

"I call bullshit," Boil pointed at me. "Look at those girly arms."

"I think Tim could take a teenager," Jay said. He clapped Lucas on the shoulder, and then leaned back to me. "This will make the ride smoother. And who gives a fuck where it came from? I don't give a shit about your shirt. Your business is yours, mine is mine, right? Ya know, in the good way."

"In the good way," I said.

Our old code of honor of mutual trust and non-judgment.

Julio laughed. He reached under the couch cushion, fumbled for a second, and then pulled out a warm can of beer. He cracked it open and continued. "Tim here's good people, Luke. You'd do well to remember that."

"Oh, I'm very fond of Timmy," Lucas Boil sneered. "Though I

guess that means we can't finish blowing him up?"

"We gotta check with Elvis first." Julio laughed, ruffling his pug aggressively. It whimpered. The rest of the pack licked his hand.

I mustered a faint hearted laugh to match theirs. If you must dine with dragons, but can't breathe fire, or even shit knight skulls, then at *least* blow smoke. I might be doing a lot of blowing, if this bad feeling in my gut is right.

"What... what the fuck did you just say?" Boil looked truly shocked.

"Nothing," I answered. I hoped. Jay cut in, apparently oblivious or unfazed. Either's fine.

"I vote we flay him alive to teach him a lesson," he said. His head swiveled between Boil and I. His brow creased. "So wait... are you two friends?"

"Are *you two* friends?" I countered.

"That ain't your concern," Boil said. "Wait, Jay, you and Timid Tim are friends?"

"Okay guys, shut it, we're all friends in my domain," Jay said. He reached under the couch, found another beer, tossed it at Boil. "Aight, Luke, check this out. When I was eleven, I got arrested for the first time for stealing a stupid pack of cigarettes. The pigs wanted to make an example of me for all the other town rats. So get this, I'm sitting there in the back, not even cuffed, but mad as all hell, and then a friggin' rock smashes into the window! I didn't even have to think. I kicked that shit out right quick." He smiled and threw an arm around me. Stung a bit, on some unknown bruise. "When I scrambled out I saw this skinny little dork, already halfway down the street and turning the corner. All the other kids start freaking out and keeping the cops busy, and boom! I'm gone. A ghost!"

"And that little shit was you," Lucas said.

"In the flesh." I felt a swell of pride for the first time in a very, very long time.

Boil grinned. "I didn't know you had any balls."

"Have, Boil. Have. They still work," I said. I tried to grab my crotch defiantly, but it came off as more of a nervous fondling.

"Yeah, I bet." Boil snapped his fingers. Elvis leapt right into his lap! The pug curled up on Boil's thighs, growling low and steady as the brute stroked him, and never did either's beady little eyes leave mine.

"Yeah, so anyway I catch up to him. We make all nicey-nice, and I show him how to steal a six pack. An hour later, we're wandering around the trails, drunk as fuck. And the rest is history," Jay said. He drained the beer and threw it at Jubedor. The beast caught it with his fangs and chomped it in half. Julio patted his lap. Elvis leapt onto it. Julio gave me a fist bump. "Best buds ever since! Fuck man, if I'd killed—"

"And what inspired such bold action?" Boil asked. "I know little Timmy here in a very different light."

The different light was one that casts a pallid shadow over bullied victims around the world. Boil was a prototype toad-stomping, no-brained thug that terrorized the more intellectual of us back in the day. A real slope-browed brute. A grunt. Which is exactly what he ended up being in the Army.

Our mutual hatred began in middle school. I refused to aide him in tying two shaved cats to an oak tree by their tails, just so he could watch them claw each other to death. Truth be told, I ran away. I couldn't summon the courage to save those cats from Boil's twisted machinations. The guilt born of such cowardice is one that always remains, lodged inside like a bullet, aching on winter nights. Boil *always* wanted to do weird shit. Mess around with small animals, unspeakable things to a deer corpse, break into an old man's house for no reason at all, sniff glue. He never wanted to be alone, and I always saw him in that circulatory system of trails behind the Cameron estate. But I never agreed to his plans, and always got a shot in the gut or a black eye for it. I never condoned his actions. Yet I didn't have it in me to stop him, so I'd take the hit or get the wind knocked out of me for penance. But still, Boil was always alone. Unless he gathered Patterson Bathtub or Mikey Spitface to join his cruelty parade. But they never lasted long, he never formed a real gang. Didn't stop him, though.

"Yeah, they both moved on," Boil said. "Spitface went pro. Skates for Daydream Cleaver now."

Oh my. Stop thinking. You might be talking. No, stop stopping!

Anyway, further truth be told, I only rescued Julio to buy the compassion of someone bigger, meaner, and crazier than Boil. A diplomatic action for a wide-eyed wimp, and one that is still paying dividends to this day. Well... actually I was a town rat, too. We all were, and he was one of us. Seeing any of us in a police car for something like stealing smokes made me angry. I would've saved almost anyone. Sure there are the occasional situations when I am sucked alongside Julio that

I'd rather not speak of. But life is full of bumps and grime. I regret nothing. My selfish cowardice birthed a strange and unexpected friendship that's been as essential as any one I've ever had. And one day, I will see the world like him. The true way. It's not impossible. We're yin and yang.

Julio and Boil were staring at me. Jubedor, Elvis, and the pugs completed the semicircle, watching me. Waiting. Had they been talking, or was I? Cripes! Be clever. Be witty. Make it worth the wait.

"Yin and yang?" Boil asked.

"How long was I talking to myself?"

"Huh?" Julio looked up as he finished rolling the joint. "Wanna hit this brain dart?"

"Uh, I guess. Yo, Jay, I need a favor. Bad. Just a quick ride," I said. Crap, blew it, royally. I let the tension of my captors rush me into the objective. Abandon tact tactics, lose all leverage. Have to play it smart now. No karate stances can help. "Maybe not quick. But I need to get up island. Tonight."

"Yeah? How critical is this?"

"Alpha."

"Shit. Damn bro, I already have something… something that *has* to go down tonight. But if you can ride with us till it's done, I could probably swing that," Julio said. "We're about to go soon, anyway. Vision quest and all that shit."

"Vision quest? Are you looking for your spirit animal again?" Starting to feel like my normal self now. Took a hit off the joint. Sweet skunk.

Boil stood dramatically, propped one leg up on a sinus medication crate, and lifted a large, ebony, shining machete in one hand, a .45 in the other. He slapped the gun against his forearm.

"Vision quest, animals, whatever! We got serious business tonight. No pranks, no bullshit. No whoring around. Not that you'll have to worry about that," Boil said to me. "Lucky you. Tag along."

"Lucky me," I repeated.

Standing there, framed by the bulbs, I could see the word 'fukt' sloppily tattooed on his wrist. Boil had many hobbies in his budding delinquency, the most visible of which was his fondness of stick and poke jail tattoos. Just like the one I made an hour ago. No, not like me, mine mean… Anyway, there were many school day mornings where, if he even showed up at all, it was with a blotchy, runny scar on his body. When lunch time came, after he ran our pockets for tributes from me, Barry, and anyone else he could stomp, we were treated to faded black and blue renditions of his self-indulged 'body art'. To date, he has the following phrases tattooed, self-inflicted in sloppy black and blue:

Fukt, Fuck You, Fuck the World, Fuck Everyone, No Hope, Dead Last, Born Bad, I Eat Bitchez, Shitstorm, Born Ready, Rage Hard, Power Sex Money, Dickman (?), *Live Fast Die Slow, Stab Proof* (doubt it, but wouldn't mind finding out), *Anarchy, Renegade Machine, Mother, Luv 2 H8, Ice Scream, Thug Life,* and even more that have blurred into unintelligible blobs.

One legendary lunch-time, Bernard walked by and remarked that Boil's new "Power Sex Money" etched across his stomach was 'hilarious'. To our astonishment, Boil said nothing, and Bernard waltzed away. It's a wonder the Army didn't force laser removal on him upon enlistment.

"I got a new one," Boil said.

"A new what?"

"Tattoo, you dumbass. You were just telling the fucking dogs about them. Check this one out."

He pushed his right shoulder into view, although I could see clearly already, since he was wearing a stained wife-beater. It was actually really nice line work, contrasting colors, and elegant shading. Nothing like his style. Something pro. But the image…

"Our whole squad got it. Foxhound. Look, the Pitbull got a dead fox in its jaws. That's us, 'cause we were always rooting out little smart ass, IED planting motherfuckers, and blowin' away—"

"Okay. Enough. Jay, just drive me up island. Please. Please, you're my only hope and I must do this."

"What's the deal? I thought you had a car," Julio said.

"I did, up until a few nights ago. I also had a job, and a friend named Barry. Looks like all three are slowly going belly up."

"Say word? Barry's dying?" Julio dropped the joint.

"No, no. But he almost did the other night. It has to do with my car mysteriously crapping out, and then Barry being sideswiped by some witless fuckers without enough sense to keep their crash to themselves."

Julio stared at me. He turned to Boil, who just kept staring at me with his strange '*I'm gonna fuck you like a pig, boy*' eyes.

"What did you just say, you little punk?" Boil sneered. He pointed the .45 at me.

Panicked, shocked, utterly confused, I asked him the same question.

"That smart ass faggot shit you just said. About my eyes," Boil answered. His shaved head stretched forward as his whole face twisted sideways.

Holy shit, I've finally lost it. I really can't tell when I'm talking out loud or not. Christ, this house used to calm me, now it puts me on edge, and I'm in no mood to keep company like this. I wasn't prepared! Must pay attention to my lips, feel that they're shut, make sure no air touches my teeth while thinking. Julio is laughing. Boil is not. And suddenly I remember that I came here with a sword.

"Where's Kitsune?" I whispered to Julio.

"Huh? Kitsune? All you brought was that sick ass sword. It's in the kitchen," he said. He got up and elegantly lumbered away.

Boil was still staring me down, his ape arms tense, veins popping out like grave-worms. But his finger wasn't on the trigger. Just pressed along the barrel, aimed right at me.

"Sorry, Boil. I just meant you have very nice eyes." The only choice. Knock him off balance with the unexpected. He wants fear. He demands it. Give him homoerotic flattery. Prey on deep seated inhibitions and latent desires, just long enough for Julio to return with Kitsune. Then plunge her deep into his wicked heart.

"Man, I always knew you were a queer." Boil sat down on the steel crate. He laughed and whipped the gun over his shoulder, sliding it away. "But at least a queer with good taste. Thanks."

"What?"

"Thanks," Boil said. "My mom always said I had nice eyes. Emily has them, too."

Emily who? No matter. He looks lost, somewhere I don't know, and don't want to go. Current crisis averted, but confusion growing. No chance for relief.

He's still smiling. Even when he turns back to me. He's big. Please be thinking about that 'Emily', please. Just what exactly did the Army teach this Neanderthal? How did his primitive instincts cope with the lack of women and tidal wave of testosterone engulfing him? Am I really going to put myself in a car with this lunatic just to bring Barry his stupid books?

Damn my eyes… Yes, I must get the books and then turn around, go up the highway over an hour to the hospital. It's not impossible. Not yet. Despite back-alley whispers to the contrary, Julio does indeed have a human heart. But is he really going to do all this for me if he's already got something else planned? A vision quest? He only says that when he's going on some insane life-changing mission, like hunting down a shaman to steal his ayahuasca, or rob a mansion for sports memorabilia. I guess I can't hold it against him if he doesn't wait around to give me a ride home. As long as he can just get me to Hawkhouse. It's not his problem, after all.

"Yo, so Barry's okay then? I heard he's getting published in a book or something," Julio returned, handing Kitsune to me.

I rested my chin on my hands, and my hands on the hilt of my sheathed sword.

"Yes, and yes. Where'd you hear that?"

"Bernard. Barry's in, uh... what the fuck's it called? Chickenpox Slayer?" Jay asked.

"Paradox Layers."

"I like Chickenpox Slayer better," Boil said.

"It's the Bullet one, right, Tim? Man, that story kicked ass. Boil, when you learn how to read, you should check it out."

"Ha fucking ha," he said, walking away.

"When did *you* read that?"

"I don't know, like... a year ago, when he finished it," Jay said. He looked at the ceiling while pounding another beer. "He just handed me a copy when I saw him in town. Motherfucker was carrying them around in his backpack."

"Wait, you *actually read* 'The Buddhist Bullet'?"

"Yeah, I know how to read. Asshole."

"And you liked it."

"Yup. Didn't you? Is Barry going to be okay or not? Be straight with me."

"Yeah," I said. I rubbed my eyes again. "Yeah, but he's in bad shape. He won't be getting out for a while. It's a miracle he's alive, honestly. Lucky guy. He was actually conscious and coherent when I left him. Won't be getting out of bed for a while, but he'll walk again. Bruises and fractures and broken bones, but... it's a bloody miracle. Hey! You should come see him, too."

Boil's stared at us from whatever he was doing in the corner.

Something unspoken between him and Jay. Something serious.

"Aight, cool. But I'm not joking, we gotta do my deal first," Julio said, slapping his knees and leaning back. "You supposed to be there for sometime specific? That stupid hospital is at least an hour west, and I need to head out east. You don't have to get involved. I don't want you to, no offense. But we got a deadline."

"No, no, anything is fine, just as long as I get there. Oh, and… we need to stop at his mom's house to pick some stuff up."

"What stuff? I got stuff. I can bring him stuff."

"No, Jay, not 'stuff'. I'm sure they're pumping him with plenty of 'stuff'. It's books, or I may as well not even go. He wants some of his Byron J. Brick sci-fi novels. He's really bored, and alone. And he's probably going to be there for quite a while. I just don't feel like seeing his stupid mom."

Jay shrugged. "Aight, we can work with that. It's *you* she hates, not me."

"Seriously?"

"Don't sweat it, Tim, I got you."

Oh sweet honey heaven above us, thank god for Julio Sanchez Sin Corazon! I knew he hadn't changed! Can finally feel my back muscles easing up. Coiled strands of muscle unknotting like snakes falling asleep. "Fucking awesome, man! Thank you so much. It means a lot to me. More than a lot."

"Why?" Jay hit the joint and passed it to me.

"Jesus Christ," Boil grumbled. "Do you need us to change your diaper too?"

"Why, did you learn that in basic training?"

"Chill out, homes," Julio said. "What about visiting hours and shit? Isn't it gonna be, like, way too late to hang around a hospital? Even now?"

"I figured I'd just stay as long as I have to, or whenever they start again," I said. "It's not like I have anything else to do."

Elvis gnawed at Julio's leg. He kicked the pug away, looking to Boil, and at that moment, Elvis peeled his black lips back and flashed his rotted fangs at me. I saw Boil nod, and Jay returned it. Something inside me curled.

"Okay. Sure, whatever," Julio said. "Come on. Help load up my Jeep."

Blood Gun

Now that we're outside, the island air allows my head to clear (or clear up more, at least). On the off chance I actually have psychic powers, I concentrate on telling Barry, *"Sit still, you bird-brained worm. Things are moving!".*

The sun is nearly down. Darkness on its tiptoes, eager to invade. Ah, and there she is! The chariot on which all our hopes ride. The old roofless Jeep, built for days of wild teenage abandon and backwoods shenanigans.

Engine off, yet eager to go, it's as home here in Julio's backyard as it is on the open road, yellow, loud, and proud. Shadows stretch across my beloved freak's back yard as we work. Packing crate upon crate of mystery into Jay's Jeep, so I can help him and Boil, a brutal freak whom I hoped to never see again, complete a clandestine mission under the cover of night, therefore buying assistance for my mission, bringing books to our broken friend while he...

Okay, I'm trying, but I don't know what the hell we're really doing.

A drug run? Been to a million. Kidnapping? The metal crates at Boil's feet are too small for human cargo. Too large for adults, at least. No, Julio couldn't sink *that* low. But who knows, between these shiny metal crates and the explosions... Oh!

This must be a gun deal. Good god. This is big. But... I see her again and know she'd forgive me, yes, if it meant keeping my word to Barry by doing this, heck, I'd even become a total badass. Or an ass... Regardless, I'm willing to march into whatever this is to prove I still care that much for her brother. And I do. I really do. Gun running. For books. With Lucas Boil. Yes, I definitely care. Right?

Yes, everything is just swell.

The faded moon poked through thick clouds, shedding splinters of twilight on the fenced-in square of dead dirt, grass, and starving trees. Julio used to have neighbors. It's oddly quiet, not hearing them scream impotent threats, or shouting obscenities long into the night, while we grilled, skated, shot at bottles, and drank cold beers to toast ourselves. Joked about girls, and our imbecilic ideas of masculinity and our ignorant prowess. They hated us.

But like most of this 'neighborhood', they're all gone now. The house on the left burned down, and was never rebuilt. Suspected arson. But Julio merely shrugged when asked. Police found a hydroponic growing lab in the smoking remains of their attic. Competition? Julio kept on shrugging, tight smile and nary a word given. Then his neighbors on the right, they won some kind of scratch off ticket dream, moved to the better side of town, and never bothered to return to their original home, which one can only assume they kept for the pure luxury of it... before the banks took that too. Foreclosed and forever abandoned. A small scrap of forest still looms behind the back yard, a precious piece of nature, untapped real estate, no doubt devalued by this grimy thug who refuses to be evicted. Like my own, his mother managed to leave *something* to shelter her son.

"You gonna help or what?" Boil asked.

Didn't bother to answer, I was taken in by the surroundings, which those two hadn't yet blown to pieces. Julio's back yard is a mausoleum to all the great manic passions of young men. The mini-ramp, once a haven for all miscreants with seven-ply urethane dreams, was now half gone. The remaining half's graffiti was faded, plywood rotted by rain, echoing memories calling out from an old parking lot. Splinters of wood littered the ground. A pile of waterlogged skateboards and a rusty BMX leaned against its side. A crushed birdcage sat atop the rusted-over coping. Faded paintball guns and air rifles. And a tree stump with some kind of old, rotted green slime dried across—oh, no way! Paint. Yes, it must be paint.

Next to me, by the back door, is the musky, scum covered hot tub. Algae choked, plumes of neglect wafting over the moldy cover, lying by the busted air conditioner. His nicest bike, a Ninjabred 400, a true beauty of engineering, lay on its side, dead center of the yard. Vines snaked their way through the engine, frame, and wheels. It's a damn shame. When in top condition, you'd swear you could hit any jump, clear *any* gap, roaring through the sky like the fallen starlord S'igartha, on his winged Hellsteeds. On the Ninjabred 400, even I could kiss the sun. But no more. What horror to behold, in this fortress of passion! Each corner, each worn out toy, sat atop scores of fond memories, crawling around like shameful bugs. Bugs like the bacteria humans house until we die, and then eat their way out of us in the grave. So glad she was burned...

Does Jay even care? None of this had to happen. The Jeep itself stands in mute testimony to that fact. Idling to our right, where the driveway snakes around the house, the Jeep sits, maintained, rough, raw, but alive. The only passion to survive our past. Our peak. Hanging on with us.

The perfect vehicle for tonight. A sort of squat, yet elegant, bumble bee. Royal Yellow, a grand chariot for high school kings. A sturdy, steel beast, with an open top. Two doors, roll bars, room for four and a bit of trunk. Cigarette burns in the seats. Some forming a pentagram, a heart, a random starscape charred into the seats. Torn stickers for arcane bands like Artery Lotus and Angels' Filth haphazardly smacked all over the dashboard, faded slogans and tags, courtesy of paint-markers, snaking around the roll bars. Still smells of heady gas and old weed. Respectable engine, apparently unlike mine… but questionable seat belts. One must doubt the ability of duct tape to endure the rigors the road. Still, it's time tested. I've launched many eggs from the passenger window. BB guns aimed at mailboxes, and golf balls whipped at BMWs when they cut us off. Looking it over, I feel warmer days coat my heart. But I stop my biased inspection at the windshield. The past whisks away like smoke. There we were, the three of us reflected in the ugly present.

If there's one thing I hate more than math and bad magic, it's time.

"They're all kind of the same thing," Jay said.

Huh?

"Math plus magic equals time, yeah?"

Yeah. So there we are, reflected by the grace of our sun, and the fact that Julio actually still washed and polished this thing. Even wipes the pollen off. He could've kept my Voltaire as healthy as I believed it'd been. So there we stand, unfiltered by my eyes. Our visages reflected as the world truly sees us.

The driver, Julio Sanchez Sin Corazon: a brute, with delicately sculpted strips of beard and scruff framing his round face. One gray eye, and the other one cast in glass. The right drinks in life like a black-hole, but the left throws it back. Shoulder-length black hair now pinned back. A broad yellow smile and a fat gold chain ending in a pyramid medallion emblazoned with an inverted goat skull. Square shoulders, mule legs, and tufts of thick chest hair poking out of his old, once pink, tank top. Yes, pink. But faded, more the color of blood on snow. Fingerless leather gloves and faded black cargo pants. Smells like they may be the same ones he wore back when he was the fifth biggest kid in school. A cigarette behind the ear, god knows what else in those bulging cargo pockets. And strangest of all, his shit-kicker boots. Lovingly spray-painted to have a light blue and green camouflage pattern. And the final touch, his white silk overshirt, sleeves torn off past the shoulders, flapping in the wind like the cover supermarket romance novels. Spirit animal... most likely the nigh-immortal honey-badger. A vicious mammal that literally cannot feel fear.

Next, the client, Lucas Boil: half clad in standard issue military garb, half in the splendor of his white trash heritage. Standard white wife-beater tank top, too tight, with beer stain badges. Shaved head, square brow, little black triangle eyes and a boxcar champ nose. The aforementioned tattoos peeking out of every crack and crevice of his military physique, especially that stupid fucking *Foxhound* one. Smells of sweat soup and damp autumn leaves. Spirit animal most likely... bulldog. An abused bulldog. Unwisely un-neutered.

And myself, the hanger-on: Timothy Dune, a transmetropolitan scarecrow. Harmless freak with a taste for morbid, tropic flair. My ageless Hawaiian shirt, mainly black and white, with orange and silver palm trees sprinkled over it. Black torn shorts that were pants last fall, and standard black sneakers with toes fighting to peek out. Unkempt brown hair, alien to combs, daring to be tamed. Gold tinted ebony sword tied to my waist. Half a week unshaved. Brown hair, unkempt, hints of gray sneaking out strand by strand. Spirit animal... the humble stoat. Yes, I am tall, but it'd take three of me to match the weight of those other two. Soaking wet. Holding Jubedor. But I'm pretty sure I smell good. In contrast to them, at least.

"Tim! You smell fine! Now quit staring around and help." Julio pointed to the metal cases stacked by the grill.

Three steel military lockers. Time to find out.

"Jay, those are too big for... Please, don't tell me we're trafficking guns."

"Guns? Ha, guns! Aren't you supposed to be smart or something?" Boil shouted. He kicked one of the containers. A symphony of hissing and clawing echoed out. He flipped the steel latch back. The top popped open with such life that I swore it was Pandora's. I leaned as far as possible to peak past Boil.

It was filled to the brim with life. A slithering rainbow of guts. I blinked, hoping to clear my tainted eyes. But no, nothing changed. I saw a kaleidoscopic sea of limbs. Neon poison colors that could only belong to exotic, cat-sized, mutant insects. But no, it wasn't that bad. The colors adorned scales and angry, alien eyes. Wet fangs, flicking tongues, spikes, ridges, horns, and all manner of trembling limbs, and lashing tails. Smooth scaled beasts, crawling over each other in a desperate bid to escape, a rainbow's host of demons, some the size of Jay's fist, others crushed against the sides, some half as big as Jubedor, and all them as vicious as Elvis, himself. Boil stomped down on any that tried to escape. "No, not guns, you ass. Something far more rare."

"And far more valuable!" Julio said.

"To who? A zoo? One of those illegal restaurants?" I asked him. "Who would pay—"

"They're worth a fortune to our, uh... our customer." Julio spit into the crate. He pushed the lizards down with his boot, but gently. "Especially to someone so important."

Wow. I wanted to believe it. I did believe it. Boil stood guard as they hypnotized me. A hissing, churning soup, as if some monster melted every poison tree frog in existence to make a stew. Then used it as a dip for beasts born from an alien devil's designs. Too exotic to kill, too dangerous to run free. "Wow. Well, they are beautiful. But they're monsters! Jesus, look at the beasts! So strange and beautiful. Where did these things come from?"

"Timmy boy, you have the honor of seeing the Middle East's finest collection of endangered lizards," Boil said. As he smiled, his boot crushed the lid down. One had nearly climbed to freedom. The heavy lid snapped the poor thing's anklebone, an awful sound followed its retreat. Boil latched the case shut.

"Asshole! What good are they dead?" I almost shoved him.

"Better than free." He whipped his head side to side. His neck cracked, sounded like a tree splitting. "Scared?"

Of what? Nearly asked Jay if I could have one. He'd give me one, wouldn't he? But Bernard would let it escape within a fortnight. No, don't bother. But Boil nearly killed one already! I tapped the crate with my toe, immediately instigating a symphony of reptilian rage. "Are they poisonous? How secure are these cases? How did you even get them, let alone over here? Actually, forget it. I never even looked in those cases. I'm not even here right now. I have *no part* of this."

"Show him the really exotic ones." Julio laughed and popped open the Jeep's tiny trunk. It fit exactly one case. That meant two were getting crammed in the back. With me, no doubt.

"Well, I got another one of these babies at home," Boil said. He snapped open a different locker. "Presenting The Great Iraqi Horned Lizard!"

Lucas Boil was standing in front of me, stroking an enormous lizard, aiming it like a gun. This is too much. Gentlemen, I wash my hands of this madness! Good night and good luck.

"It's kinda like the Regal Horned Lizard, but rarer. And nastier," he said. The Great Lizard's face lacked elegance, completely covered in sharp, orange spikes. Asymmetrical, pale and gangly, not a lizard to cuddle. Its red eyes never rested, yet the beast hung limp under Boil's arm. "This baby can shoot a high pressure stream of blood, when threatened. From right here, see? That gland makes it look like the blood's shooting from its freaking eye! If *that's* not cool enough for you bitch-ass punks, think about *this*. The blood stream's got enough force to puncture human skin! Imagine getting hit in the face with that?" Boil aimed at me. The lizard lashed its tongue over its weird, derpy eyes. But then Boil spun around. "Or even dent sheet metal. Watch!"

Boil slapped the beast. It screeched, as a crimson jet shot from its eye like a champagne cork. It struck the side of the Jeep, like a paint-ball-sized comet. The dent and smear were small, but not insignificant. I gulped, taking a step back.

"Yo! Motherfucker, what's your problem?" Julio dropped his lizard case to vigorously wipe his Jeep. A brown smudge remained. The cases roared. Jay kicked it without a glance.

Boil was obsessively pleased with himself. He turned to me and raised his hand, ready to swat his living blood gun. I leapt behind the rusted grill, but no shot was fired.

A minute later, every lizard was safe, secured, and they were laughing. I crawled out from behind the grill, deconstructing the last few moments and taking stock. Who would buy all of these things, and how could they be worth more than Jay would get from even the basest and most boring of drug sales? Exactly how much money was at stake, and if by tagging along, was I entitled to a stake of that? Best not to ask, not now. Best to trust Julio, he's no fool. And hey, I love reptiles as much as the next guy. These things must be rare for a reason. Killed on sight over the years, no doubt. Somehow Boil defended democracy and still managed to steal an arcane reptile zoo. Beings so exotic and weird that I'd only read of their ilk in pulp stories, were here and now. Slashing, squirming, and gnashing before my eyes. Seeing as how I'd be along for the ride regardless of my desires, then for Barry's sake… it'd be best to become part of the team.

"Boil, I'm impressed," I said. The way he looked at me matched my reaction to his 'cargo'. "I've never seen anything like these. What are they?"

He ran through the list, and I won't lie. It was impressive. Worm-snakes, smooth-eared earth-chompers, granddaddy-wall-clingers, Fallujah-bed-hoppers, slender-glass-sand-creeps, ass crawlers, whiptail-milk-herders, broad-headed-skinks, *and* skanks, and even bronze mulletforgers that mimic glass toads, plus poisonous-golden-rods, and fat-head-belly-burpers. Each and every one of them looked like irradiated cosmic beasts. Such a broad array of fluorescent stripes and markings adorning their scaly, twisted bodies. I'm sure that on a healthy dose of acid, it'd be more beautiful. I'd roll around in the grass trying to cuddle them. Yes, I could imagine some Fortune 5000 back-breaker taking pleasure in such a collection. And yet something is still…

"I'm confused."

"No shit," Boil said, wiping his hands. "Don't worry, I know. You are a homo."

"Yes, of course, thank you for fixing my life, soldier," I said, turning my back to him and addressing my ally. "Look, Jay, don't get me wrong. As far as I'm concerned you're a swindling swine of the finest variety," I said, wiping the sweat from my brow. "Truly a gentleman and a scholar."

"Damn straight."

"But we both know that you're more likely to rob a pet shop than to do… whatever this is. Maybe paint some lizards and glue horns on them, not get this, this imbecilic cretin to steal an *actual endangered species*. What exactly are you doing? You're really selling them to one person? All of them? Tonight?"

"Tim, I told you, I got a friend of sorts. A customer out East. He's rich and unusually fond of lizards," Julio said. But as he spoke, he also turned his back to me. "We haven't talked in a long time. Lost touch. So Boil set everything up. What's so hard to understand? You want a ride, we want to get paid. Totally worth it. Right? Right."

A friend out East? Something is wrong. Deeply wrong. Only thing further East is Tomahok. A cold pit grew in my stomach. The ground shifted beneath my feet, crumbling like dry cake. My face melted and hung from my bony chin, dangling to and fro as my brain started drifting off with the sunlight.

And then it passed. Something inside shifted, some part of my mind clicked the wrong way. Subtle, but in something so fragile, even the slightest crack causes concern. But I'm okay. I can handle this. Time to get moving. Hit the streets.

What did we have to show for ourselves? A samurai sword, a zoo's worth of endangered, illegal freaks. Just another trio of broken boys in men's bodies. A hyena thug, a snake blooded ox, and a wily, paranoid, katana wielding cat. Oh, wait... No, those aren't right. Head is starting to throb. It's the pill, it must be. But I thought Jay just slipped me a painkiller. I feel less than pain... fuzzy, sort of... Ha, no, it's all okay. Right, right. They're staring at me, but who cares? We're too old to care.

"Look at us." I pointed at the Jeep's odd reflection. Speaking felt a bit sloppy, but not drunk -slurred. "We're too fucking old. Too old to be... to be us. To do whatever we're doing."

"What WE are doing?" Boil kept barking with his arms crossed.

"Bro, say it ain't so! You lost your edge, already?" Julio threw his arms to the sky. Then he laughed, but the smile died fast. "Whoa, whoa, whoa! Hold up homes, you can NOT bring that thing with us!"

He was pointing at Kitsune.

I raised my sword innocently. "But I need her. What if we run into trouble?"

"Her?" Boil mumbled.

"Nope, no way, dude. What are you, crazy? Driving around with that weapon? What if we get pulled over?"

They both waited.

The fuzzy okay feeling enveloped my chest, spreading, coiling around my gut. "Come on, Jay! Boil has a gun! I think!"

Julio grinned and lifted his shirt to show a revolver stuck into his pants. They laughed at me.

"There you go, shithead," Boil said, slapping my back hard enough to make my lungs bounce against my ribs. "Now get in, and quit holding us up. We actually have a schedule to maintain."

That we do.

Jay's climbing into his seat, Boil is pissing near the ramp. He can't see the dirty look Jay's shooting his way. We're all packed up, one crate in the trunk, and two in the back, with me wedged between. Other small bags and packets line the floor, random shapes and sizes, and surely nothing I want to know about. Julio fires up the Jeep. Her gentle rumble feels like a soft massage, long forgotten yet immediately soothing. The crates clang around. Barely enough room back here. Feel like a broken marionette between steel coffins. The lizards hiss their mutual displeasure. Boil hops into the passenger seat and punches the dashboard.

"Let's get this fucker moving, Sanchez!" Boil hollers. "Those guys got other meetings tonight. And I gave them MY WORD we'd be there with the goods. Hell, I served with Desmond's cousin, and *even then* I barely managed to put this meeting together! So screw the F.N.G. in the back! We got a job to do! Hoo-RAH!"

"Right, right, right. Vamanos. Amigo. Don't want to keep the boss waiting," Julio said. He wasn't whooping and hollering like Boil, but even still, his voice had a rare tone, recognized from only our worst high school days. The days that melted into dawns when no one spoke, wondering what went down the night before, and whose side we were really on.

What was that crap Sergio said about devils? That was barely two hours ago, at most, but already feels another world away. I tug on what passes for a seatbelt, hoping to click it in before Armageddon explodes out the gas tank. This strange delirious wave that's continuing to rise is starting to actually make sense. I'm Cursed, chained between a fallen angel and a rising devil. Shit. Doesn't matter that I'm doing Barry a solid, or that Jay's doing one for me.

No, because this weird, pleasing sense of nausea, gnawing into my sixth sense, is *trying* to tap a Morse code across my spine. Gibberish, but I get the message.

Their body language. Their exchange just now. The little details from the destruction of the border boulder, to Julio's devotion to *Boil's* schedule, for any reason at all, and especially over my humiliating, naked plea for his help…

It's not the raging reptiles. Not their queer mission. Not even Boil's mere existence that's wrong. As we begin to ride, I realize the hideous truth. In the end, although we're at Julio's personal palace, and Boil is shouting orders about *his* enormous contributions… Jay *always* calls the shots. Even in the smallest ways, clever or infantile, Jay never does a run that he doesn't run. Sure, he'll pretend or play along for fun. And this is Julio's Jeep, his deal, his risks, his profits to share, hell this is *his* turf, after all. And given the need for a ride, and a guide who's mastered not just Thornwood, but also Tomahawk's secrets—where to hide, who to bribe, where *not* to go and why, all the hidden roads and passwords in these infamously secluded towns—Julio's in control, he's Captain at the wheel. So it's okay. He's the one protecting me, and driving us all around...

But Lucas Boil is actually in charge.

Red Light Blues

"Tim, you're the tie-breaker! Do we kill the cop or run?" Boil is shouting at me over the wind. But I'm not paying attention. Just praying that I'm hallucinating, reliving some awful memory where I've already made the choice. That I'm suffering from some vividly lame PTSD by defragging a traumatic experience in vivid real-time. Maybe I've been drugged? It sure does feel too real. The Jeep's going too fast, the sounds around me too slow, my heart rate somehow deadly still, and yet pounding.

Okay, confession time:

Shocking as it may be, I'm not *always* as cool under fire as I may seem.

Like right now, with the police siren slicing through the glam and glitz of Thornwood, lizards shrieking behind us, Boil screaming, and I'm about to shut down, hoping to wake up in the aftermath and defrag my way through this horror.

Defragging is… Well, something computers do to maintain optimal functionality, but it's all the same to me. I defrag when a crisis strikes, like a true, snow-crash type, epic synaptic overload crisis. That's when my unique coping instincts take over. Some call it 'cowardice' or 'paralysis' or 'depression'. But I've always found it best to shut down, run on autopilot, and then wait for my mind to reboot in the aftermath. Try to make sense of it all via frazzled, half-dreamt memories. Usually, I end up discovering that yes, I *did* act. Once there's finally time to reflect, I may learn from the experience. But only after carefully defragmenting the recent past, transforming random, freshly coded synaptic recollections into coherent memories.

Which is to say, in Bernard's parlance, that I *'freak the fuck out'*, and then *'act super fucking lame'*.

But again, proper defragging takes time, a luxury I can't demand. For example, it's hard to do this refined process during a high-speed police chase, which is a big problem, since I'm actually defragging that right now, but that now which I speak of was really *then*, but back then, it *was* now, except… I think I'm running on auto-pilot now. Language muddles both time and death itself, which, although infuriating, is quite respectable. But still, it solves no problems.

We all have problems. Mine are legion, Boil's are too many to count, even counting those I know of, but Julio's biggest problem is now OUR problem. Amongst his many, many, subjectively eccentric issues, one is so severe that it's now a general characteristic. Usually it regards society, rules, regulations, limits, laws, and occasionally human rights. Right now, it's manifesting as a problem understanding traffic, safety, and red lights.

When Julio gets going, he *really* gets going, indoctrinating us with wild screams and infectious abandon. That's why I love him. Mostly. But when the Jeep became a disco ball of red and blue with that damned siren shrieking behind us, I was forced to reflect about certain recent decisions.

Back when we were sixteen, there was no fear of jail for our bullshit. Slaps on the wrist. Late twenties… cops aren't so lenient anymore. They *can* be, depending on who they are, who pays them, if they're legally honest, or morally honest, etc.

Now which kind of cop is this?

One Julio already paid off? One that he peddles drugs to? Or one of the best, most rare, cops in this dishonest corpse-called-resort? Yet even *those* are forced to meet their arbitrary monthly quotas. Seems like no matter what, I'm getting pulled over with these two freaks, and all the freaks in the crates, and I'm freaking out. There's nothing I can do. And that's the worst thing of all. Some days it feels like the only options when 'caught' aren't 'fight or flight', they're 'death or jail'. And while Julio could run a cellblock, let's not even entertain the idea of what would happen to me.

Right now, I already know the worst part. That innocent or guilty, I'm about to be caught with two known criminals with multiple kinds of illegal cargo. Jay can't help me. Kitsune can't help me. Nothing can. No choice, I'm going down with the ship. And so soon, having left less than an hour ago …

Immediately after leaving Julio's hidden oasis, we drove away from our low-income beach community, forced to venture deep into the prosperous scar of the town proper. The route that must be taken, but always makes sick with anger, envy, and lust. Driving into luxurious, majestic Thornwood, an ugly L-shaped Manhattan wannabe, with endless rows of—

"It it ain't that bad!" Jay said. "We kinda got it made out here, know what I'm sayin'? I hate this fucking shithole too, but where else could I get away with all this crap so easily? And it's still kinda pretty."

A little nervous about how often this is 'not speaking thing' is happening. Maybe I need to hold my jaw whilst thinking. In any event, Jay's right, I don't do my homeland justice. For better or worse, at the very least, we can function here. This weird ramshackle of architectural ages is kind of charming in a 'bad trip on weak acid' kind of way. It is vaguely amusing to see colonial shacks and misguided pueblos crunched between modern buildings. It can also be incredibly sad, if one is not well fed and rested. For better or worse, there is no place quite like Thornwood, and certainly no place quite like the heart of the town itself. It was these very lands that were first purchased from their native peoples for a handful of acorns and some pox-ridden blankets. We did them proud, keeping the names of their tribes for our towns' names... until our accents 'evolved' them a few decades later. With enough booze and a properly bad mood, you can still channel the furious spirits of a dejected, noble people, wandering the hilly streets and spitting on the living elite.

Here is where the view of the ocean gradually recedes behind a 1970s idea of avant-garde architecture, international banks, and elegant fashion storefronts. You can buy anything you don't need, and nothing that you do. We have no convenience stores, one small supermarket, and at least seven jewelers. And the 'town' is proud of it. The shame of what this place was, what it's degraded into, is celebrated for one increasingly long summer, each and every year.

My former employment at Burger Don was twenty minutes headed west up the highway, that just about paid for the gas to get to work, and that wasn't even halfway to the place holding Barry. Hawkhouse Hospital. Reprehensible, but the best hospital around, being the only one. Tainted with doctors of questionable education and malpractice suits. Still, Hawkhouse is—

"Hawkhouse is a cool name! At least they got that much right," Jay yelled back at me. "And I got a hot morphine hookup there in the winter." He saw the terror in my eyes. "Don't worry bro, I said I'll get you there."

"Just not as a patient, please."

My head still felt weird, like... purple? To take my mind off it, as we rode through twisted elegant streets, past wannabe villas and lonely estates, I marveled at the throng of invaders choking the sidewalks. These strange crowds migrate here annually in the summer. Smile, wave, make bigger demands and leave smaller tips. Then they leave us to destitution in the winter, but rest assured, soon as the ice cracks and the ocean welcomes us back in, they will return. The seasonal change on our tip of this floating assberg of an island is akin to a frozen, stroke-stricken brain, tricking your best hopes by suddenly becoming tumor-swelled, delirious, and over heated. Take your preferred pick.

"Whoo, eee! Look at that set of titties!" Boil whooped. "Thongs everywhere! Even at night! No fucking burkas! No turbans! No veils! Just good old solid American ass!"

"Jiggly jiggly goo!" Julio yelled. "Damn, hold up… are they middle schoolers? Gross. Man, I can't even tell anymore. You go to the friggin' beach and they're wearing thongs and two-pieces."

"Gotta make sure there's hair on the field," Boil said. "Who am I kidding, even that doesn't help. Sometimes. Ah, well. Fuck it! Life is—"

"Why check, then? Would that actually stop you?" I asked.

"Of course!" Julio whipped his attention at me, swatting at my head and nearly biting his cigarette in half. "What do you think I am, some kind of monster? You shit for brains worthless ungrateful cocksucker!"

"Look forward you freak!" I caught his hand and pushed it back toward the steering wheel. "I wasn't asking YOU! I'm asking your pet monster up there. For all I know, he's—"

"God, I missed this town," Boil said to himself, detached, at total ease. His voice stayed reflective. Interesting. He wasn't speaking to be heard. He just smiled to himself in a familiar, sad, way. "I miss America. I miss… I miss her."

"Yeah?" Jay's question sounded like an answer. "You gonna see her, Luke?"

"Gonna try," Boil said.

"Who?" I asked. He didn't look back at me. "Who are you talking about? Is it possible you're actually part human?"

It's like they didn't even hear me.

"Word," Julio said. "Shit, man, they're everywhere! Look at her! I guaran-damn-tee she's either a model or a porn star! And look at that walking sack of shit she's with, all bones and… Jesus, he has a CANE and can't even stand! I can't stand it!"

His mock yell of despair wasn't cheering me up. They kept their crowd commentary quite loud and conspicuous. But despite having only a roll bar for a roof and the enthusiastic jabbering madman at the helm, we drew little attention from the public. The early evening traffic was at a crawl, and it allowed me ample time to turn away from Julio and Boil and observe the people that I do such a good job of avoiding out by the coast. The coast that *they* don't like. Not yet. Someone will move next to me soon. Then another. And another. Like we did to the native inhabitants.

Individually, they aren't too amazing, or even all that bad. But packed together, refugees from a harsh world that doesn't understand their high-end needs, they do make for an interesting sport. If only I'd retained the cynical energy and witless testosterone of my youth. I would have been riding shotgun, instead of Boil, with a high-powered automatic paintball gun and a bag of golf balls, ready to take down any car too fancy or any upturned nose too snooty. But now the stakes are higher. There is no slap on the wrist for such hijinks. We're old enough to know better, old enough for a nightstick scolding to the base of the skull. Old enough to go to jail. Suppose that'd be justice, wouldn't it? We'd be the monsters, but… Damn… Nearly thirty, and we've all been too old for this kind of shit for a long time. Still, it feels almost…

"Here man, take one of these." Julio stretched his hand back. In his palm were two small capsules. Looked hand-assembled by a blind immigrant in a musty basement. Clearly his work. Certainly not over the counter factory-bred medications. Part time mad scientist. Something new from Jay's secret stash. Stuff is usually good… Once he gave me something that actually made me happy at work for three entire weeks. In the end I nearly got a twenty-four-cent raise. But other times, these gifts were pretty noxious experiments. Never saw a pattern to his actions, likely he was just as surprised when it went 'wrong' as I was.

"Thanks, but no thanks, Julio." Visions of a summer spent addicted to opium and stargazing returned. More of Jay's well meant Pandora gifts. "I'm going crazy enough on my own. Doing just fine without your help."

"Eh, whatever. Just remember who's calling the shots," he said.

"That's fucking-A right we're calling the shots!" Boil said. He rocked back and forth violently in his seat. His grin was large and smelled rotten. "Private, I order you to give me more pills!"

Julio flicked the capsules at Boil, who snatched them from the air and gulped them down in one ugly move.

"Well, then it's settled. I'll be the designated driver once they kick in," I said. "We should make it to Barry's mom's house before then. Right? And you two can just sit in the car like adults. Try to avoid causing a scene for five minutes."

"Yeah bro, wouldn't that be nice? If only things rolled so smooth," Julio said. He stared at more pills in his palm. "But good call on not dosing yourself again. No telling what kind of hell more of this shit will do to you. More could kill your metabolism, let alone your goddamned mind. Ha!"

"More? You—I thought that was a painkiller!"

He laughed.

Every tiny hair on my body pricked. There's that good old pit, cold ice in my stomach. A recent memory of Julio forcing a cup of water down my throat. And medicine to help. The bastard! The unrelenting evil fuck! Using me as a guinea pig for his amusement! Again! Stupid Tim, you should have been prepared for something like this! Don't even know what "this" is. I hugged Kitsune to my chest.

"You dating that thing?" Boil asked from the side mirror. "Very uh… phallus."

"It's phallic, you moron."

"Sure is."

Cursed as poison *and* poisoned. This is a problem not even Kitsune can weather. I'm dizzy and raw and full of bad juju already. The last thing I need is for Julio's mystery drug to push me over the edge. If there really is a Jesus, now would be a wonderful time to rack up a new convert. Oh Lord, expunge these rotten chemicals from my being! I swear I'll drink your blood, eat of your body, whatever weird things your cult does!

"He's losing it," Julio laughed. "Right in the middle of town too. Ha! Look!"

"Will you shut the hell up back there?" Boil said. He whipped around the side of the seat and glared at me with egg sized bug eyes. "You're going to spoil my trip with all that crazy nonsense! Even I need a break sometimes, okay dipshit?"

Fuck, I just did it again. It's either the stress or… No, it's the drug! *It* must be causing these weird brain-tongue hiccups. Yes, that's what's going on! Not my fault, no sir, not at all. Wronged again, innocent to the core.

"So what exactly did you poison me with?" I grabbed Jay's shoulder, tried to hurt him but it felt like a pinch.

"Haven't named it yet. Special homegrown recipe," Julio said. "Let me know if you have any ideas. I tried it out on Elvis once. He stumbled around and growled at a tree for a few hours, then pushed his nose into the sand, tried to jump over the fence, and fucked all the other pugs. Then he whimpered for a few hours. Then he shit constantly for a few more. Didn't kill him! So it's all good, yo! Of course, I gotta see how it hits a human, and you're always a good candidate. Strong constitution, survive curses and all that mystic shit, right? Take it as a compliment, and let me know if you need to bang something or take a dump. Or if you see bats. Tell me if you see bats!"

"Excellent." I slumped low in the seat, staring out at the boardwalk. "I'd feel a lot better if you at least rolled the roof up or something. We're so exposed like this. So exposed... everyone can see us. Like we're in a zoo..."

Of course. Here it comes. The fear.

When you know a panic attack is pending, it's damn hard to do anything other than scratch yourself into a fetal position. Curl up in a phantom womb. I tried to focus on the circus freaks crowding the sidewalk. The Jeep jerked from side to side, and if not for the lack of any thumps, I would have sworn Julio mowed down a pup without slowing.

They massed in Bermuda shorts, wearing sandals with too many straps and sparkles, carrying armfuls of equipment to make the beach as convenient as possible. Swinging designer bags beside meticulously sculpted hips. They crossed blindly through traffic, the drivers on phones, the walkers on phones, the phones showing books and videos and video games and playing songs, and no one paying attention to anyone. Their teeth too white, too straight. Living large on the backs of those finishing last. Everyone else was in *their* way, and now they were in ours. Thinking of earlier, that jerk with Bernard... Antonio Sergio? Yes, he'd disappear in this crowd. Hell, he probably already does. Bernard doesn't, which is exactly why he can sneak and slip like a snake through the cracks, smiling and keeping his wallet full and the drinks coming. Wonder what they're doing out in Tomahok right now? Jay pumps the breaks, almost rhythmically. We get green lights, but hordes of bipedal flesh pods race in front of us, perfectly trusting that Jay both notices and cares if he hits them. He honks the horn, curses, Boil does the same.

Still, the invaders ignore us. They think we like being here, and worse, think that we like *them* being here. They think this halcyon holiday of shrimp buffets never ends. Local business owners swear this influx of decadence is vital to our local economy, just before they jet set out west, leaving the fishers, farmers, hunters, builders, and gas-pumpers to try keeping their homes warm for one more winter.

"Sometimes you don't have to actually eat people to be a cannibal," I said.

"Sometimes you say weird shit that makes sense," Julio said.

Despite this list of woes, I lay in the Jeep, unable to shake the awful notion that everything might be okay. That maybe the sickness is in my head, this ugly paint-peeling world only in my eyes. All these shitheads might be a lot happier than me. No, they *are* a lot happier than me. Maybe this is as good as it gets.

Traffic forces us to actually stop at a red light.

The old make-out gazebo is on the left, center of the town park. And hell's bells, hanging over the railing is that blond-haired kid in his red and black shirt! His sister isn't with him. I leapt to my feet, gripping the roll bar and pointing.

"That kid! That's the one! I kicked his ass!"

Jay and Boil stared incredulously.

"Yeah? Looks like a worthy opponent for you." Boil said.

"Cool story, bro…" Jay agreed. Lit a cigarette, then flicked it at the convertible idling next to us. The driver's shout is cut short when he catches the glare Julio had ready for him.

But I watch the kid sucking down his own cloud of nicotine, the cigarette never leaving his lips. His eyes are glued to the grass. They scan up to a man in a nice orange jacket and a blue tie, holding a child's hand and guiding her through the park. The child is tugging on his arm, pointing at the jungle gym. The father is on his phone, looking at a thin tanned woman bent over her baby carriage. Tight ass. The blond boy watches. The family (?)… they never look back.

That damn kid. He doesn't seem so bad, not when he isn't standing over a dead dog. Where is his sister? The cloud of smoke washes over his face again. I look down from my perch to time the rhythm of Jay and Boil's puffs. Back to the boy. Oh boy, I used to, but quit, but she used to… I want to, even though the thought still makes me sick. What a powerful drug. What a passive aggressive path to suicide. A stinking cry for help, a manifestation of intent without will. That punk, he has no future. He's too young, too screwed. There's no good reason for it. Social conditions are cancer. Things, technology, us, forced to grow too fast, too wild. The kids. They can't be reigned in, they can't be tamed. And so they fester. What's his poison? Poverty? Dementia? Abuse? Boredom? Christ, now he looks so small. And I beat and robbed him. Barely. Still... dog killer. A new member for the Doom Generation. Technically he wasn't born within the right time, according to some charts and graphs, but details aside, he's more than welcome to drown with us.

He looks up and sees the traffic. Sees the Jeep. Sees me. His jaw drops. Then clenches. Then he gives me the finger while snatching up a large rock.

"Jay, how long is this damn light?" I'm getting antsy, hoping he'd blow threw it for once.

On cue, we crawl forward just as the boy throws. Hits the car behind us.

I flip him the finger. Watch the other driver swerve a bit, blare his horn, throw the car in park, and leap out. He's running after the kid, leaving his panicked wife behind. The old woman shrieks in the passenger seat, although the minor threat is over. Her flabby arm stomps the horn stupidly, causing domino hysteria behind her. I hear the brutes up front laugh. Feel like I'm floating, watching her waddle in frothing reactions.

Her flesh is fascinating. She's wearing a lavender one-piece, with a straw hat and dark glasses. Her skin is like burnt turkey, and her flesh like piles of pancakes buckling under the weight of melted butter. I swear I can see sweat oozing between her rolls like syrup. Bet she tastes like salty boiled ham. I lean out the back of the Jeep and point at her and scream, "Help her, you animals! She's having a stroke!" hoping to draw enough attention to let us escape this carnival of ridiculous honking.

We're snaking along now, but I can still see that kid running down the street, knocking shopping bags from bejeweled hands as his pursuer huffs along behind him.

This kid is not the worst by any means, yet he is still scum. An accident. A byproduct of the grand experiment. At best, the murderous punk will grow up to be like Boil, torturing animals and hopefully joining the military so he can do it legally and far, far away, instead of haunting

157

Thornwood. He'll have some other jerk-off like me, watching him, judging him, mining his despair so I can feel better about myself.

Julio spun around. "Yo dog, did you just say you're gonna jerk off that kid?"

"Told you he's a fag. Guess he's a kiddie fucker too."

"That's ugly, Boil. Real ugly," I said. "Even for you."

The Jeep lurches again, and my brain with it. The crates clattered beside me, and I pulled the duct-tape belt around me tighter, trying to sink. My arms felt like they were waving violently, despite my hands being tucked firmly into my armpits. An army of slugs began their orgy in my stomach. Whatever drug this is, it's been active for a while now… At least no bats yet. No yetis in the rearview mirror, nor heart thudding fast enough to make me mistakenly leap into the crowd, stumbling incoherently to a cop for help. No manta-rays or devil-rays or rays of any kind swooping out of the purple clouds. I hope this is the worst of it. Hope it's peaked and I'm about to come down, no matter how harsh that could be.

More sounds. A commotion. Louder. I can feel the direction. Ooh, no, I don't think I've peaked yet. Shit. I peek through my fingers. Somehow that rotten kid fought his way through the crowd and shot out into the street, right ahead of us. The old man is still after him, but his pace is pathetic. The kid's won. And then he looks back at the man and sees us. Now he's running toward the Jeep. Coming for me! He runs in front of us just as the car ahead pulls away. There's no room to go around. We're boxed in.

"Looks like he wants a rematch." Jay laughs and slaps my knee.

I bite my lip and then slam into the lizards' lockers as Julio guns the Jeep to the right, nearly running a sports car onto the sidewalk. The brat is leaping toward the Jeep, shouting something about me being a pervert. He's got another rock in his hand. No! No, kid don't do it!

Julio waves the kid over to us. The boy slows, then marches toward Jay, angry but curious.

THWACK!

The back of Jay's hand is red, as is the kid's face, and the blood dripping from his nose. The smack dropped his ass onto the yellow line. Now he's out of the way and we're on our way. Lucky a cop hasn't shown up yet, what with all this excitement dead center of town.

"What the hell was up with him?" Julio asked Boil. "Tim, did you really rob that kid?"

"He's a dog killer."

"Didn't think you had the grapes," Boil said. He lit a stoge. Turned to shoot smoke in my face. "You've grown a bit, eh? Little timid Timmy is the bully now! Any practice fighting girls yet?"

"Whatever, that little bitch is lucky," Jay cut in. "I just didn't want him tossing that rock at my ride. Not in the mood to beat his ass. Got work to do... Homeboy did look kinda familiar though."

"Julio, you're a fucking creep, a monster, and a goddamn menace to society! But thank you," I said. "Good call! Preemptive strike. If he got into the Jeep he may have let the lizards free." I shuddered, imagining their slick scales and claws sliding and tearing across my skin. "But Jay I love you, so you must understand! I'm calling the cops now, but for your own good! You'll understand one day."

"Sounds like that pill's kicking in," Julio told Boil. He laughed, turned around with tongue out and his middle finger up. "Go ahead, brooooo. Turn me in. You'll be dead by dawn. My heart aches at the mere thought, but, you know how it is, son. Eye for an eye."

"N-n-no! It's the pill," I said. "You've drugged me, traitor! Anything that happens falls on your head tonight, hombre!"

Boil cut us off. "Shut up. I got it. Wasn't that Claude Remington's little brother?"

"That brat?" Julio said. "Oh shit... It was, wasn't it?"

"Claude's dead."

"Say word," Julio said as he whipped the Jeep between the two lanes and under a yellow light.

"Word," I said, realizing Boil was right. "I just kind of forgot. Barry told me that Claude recently killed himself."

"Damn." Jay's head fell back on the headrest. He spit his cigarette out of the side of his mouth. "Claude offed himself? Bummer, man. Wonder why?"

"There's usually a good enough reason," Boil said. He's sounding dreamy, vacant, staring at the stars. Like before, when he missed things. "Maybe it just got to be too much, everything, the sounds, the smell of shit, the burning flesh..."

"Why didn't I hear about this?" Julio asked. "The fuck is going on in this world?"

"I only know because of Barry. He must've heard it through the grapevine. Hell, for all we know it ain't true. Plus he did it down in Florida for some reason. Actually... Boil, wasn't Claude's older brother in the service, too? Jack or something?"

We stare at Boil until his he blinks and looks back. "What, you think I know him just because he was in the army? You think we're all the same? The grunts, huh? Mindless drones to you, right Tim? You think they beat us all into one mind, one body? You think it always works, that I know every motherfucker in a uniform? Fuck off! People like you make me... If you weren't Jay's friend, I would—"

"But he is."

"Then you can both fuck off!" Boil's fist was too tight, and too high. I pushed my face as far back from it as possible.

"Okay, okay... We'll fuck off." Julio gunned the Jeep forward, flashing me a confused glance in the side mirror.

We drive on all of thirty seconds before another calamity strikes. Too many fast dopey mammals flittering about in a small space. A skeleton man didn't stop his wiry daughter from darting out in front of us. Julio slammed the brakes, my head smashed into the seat, and the father didn't even look up from his phone, or catch up to his daughter, now prancing through the other lanes.

Maybe she wasn't his daughter. Maybe she was his mistress. Maybe it was convenient for her to be smeared across the street. This place is a haven for people like that man. They come from all over America, thinking this place is special, that this place is different. It's not. It's just a pastel coat on the same old brick wall.

Need to escape. Feels like my flesh is scratching through my skin.

Whatever happens, we can't possibly escape to the highway now. We look insane, we act insane. Therefore, we must be insane. Furthermore, by all rights and laws of our world, we must die. For the greater good. The moon hung above the town, glowing in approval at our madness. Those who walk the lunar path thrive in these hours. Flips a switch, now I just might make it. But what of Julio? He's part cat, part moon... but maybe not enough? And Boil? Dirt, blood, spit, and snot. He can fend for himself.

The shining storefronts begin to thin out. We're almost out of here. Can see the purple haze above the ocean, the constant non-night that hangs over Sponge Island in August. Can see the ocean between the alleys and thinning traffic jam. The blessed curl of a wave could be seen between the real estate offices to the south. I watched the crest crash in on itself, then blast into a brilliant ivory chaos.

The ripple of the wave passed right from the shore and through the street, into the Jeep and up my spine. Julio and Boil are talking about something. Their voices became jittering bamboo poles with vacant, clattering skulls on top. Bone jangling, sounds like laughing. Don't they feel the water? We're going to drown, down in the depths of the barren sea. They don't see it at all!

Oh shit, here it comes. It was just warning shots before. Now we're getting down to business. When you're still sober enough to know how not sober you're becoming...

A red light bursts above, then disappears. Then another. And another. Now that he's got the space, Julio ain't gonna stop. Another bright red demand flies overhead. I clutch the roll bars and grit my teeth. Just one more traffic light on this road. Come on Jay, hold it together. Just one more. If I can do it, you can. Horns scream and drivers cry.

There it is. Green! Closer. Yellow... Closer...

Red.

A banshee born soul-searing shriek bursts behind us. I nearly break my neck, whipping around, catching a blast of red and blue. The banshee stole a cop car, and the bitch is gaining on us! Christ, she even figured out how to work the controls!

"PULL OVER!"

"There is no fucking way we're pulling over!" Boil said to Jay. Not a plea. It was an order.

"No shit," Julio said. "Chill. I got us covered."

The sudden acceleration sent me flying into a crate. Breaking my neck at a neck breaking pace. Kitsune flew up and I somehow caught her just in time. Although the sheath is strung to my belt, the sword itself could fly right out. I watched her float above it all, suspended, freed of the time illusion and ready to enter the sixth web covering our world, where time flows around corners man can't conceive. Where thoughts are shapes and feelings are colors. No, no, fight this weird drug, Tim. Stay here.

"Julio, I just... I just really need to get to Barry's house," I mumbled. Bile creeps up my throat. The terrible shiver of the banshee snuck across my back. "I have to get out of this car. I'm going to be sick. I'm going to throw this nasty drug up all over your bugs."

"Lizards!"

"Just shut the fuck up and let us concentrate, you whiny little shit!" Boil growled.

"Don't want jail… Want Hawkhouse… Want Barry…"

"Don't worry man, I'll get you there! You've got my word!" Julio shouted. He began laughing like a righteous cowboy lynching a horse thief. "Might not be so easy though, brother!"

By the grace of the Caffeind, Julio didn't kill any pedestrians as he weaved through the maze of SUVs, two-seat sports, long black cock-limos, and beaten pickup trucks with mammoth skull wheels. The tension in the air materialized as a swarm of static fueled insects, and they all wanted to burrow into my skin.

I think I'm screaming. The siren is screaming. The wind is screaming.

We're shooting forward, past the last restaurant in town, and out into the pine barren dunes. Then, BAM! We're skidding sideways as Julio whips the Jeep down an invisible dirt road. Careening through a dark patch of barren farm field, bordered by the back alleys of Thornwood, ocean crested hills and a dense woodland richly cut by vein-like trails. I watch the crisp flare of the main strip fade behind palm trees and wild beach grass. Ahead of us, before the Texan Bro gas station, a red rusted tetanus infested chain fence crumples over itself. It protects the neon gas station, the abominable Texan Bro. The first franchise allowed in Thornwood. For now. There will be more like Texan Bro, that mechanical vampire that bled my family's business dry. Fast food chains like Chicken Queen, to steal the meager business of our mom and pop diners. Texan Bro's electric white sign beams over this back-lot like a mechanical sun. A false god, signaling the divide between manicured mansion lawns, and the beginning of litter pocked, pesticide soaked dirt. Dirt which leads to the very end of Sponge Island, the Frankenstein province called Tomahok. Things are still crackling blue and red and red and blue and I think I'm going to puke. Jay and Boil are debating something.

"What?" I shouted at them.

"Tim, you're the tie-breaker! Do we kill the cop or run?"

"LAST WARNING! PULL! OVER!"

We bounce up and down, bones juggling joints, my teeth fuse, veins clench, eyes shake. This is dangerous ground for any confrontation.

Ravines, ditches, jagged dead trees. Crimson scrap. No place fit for police chases. A kid's place. A place to race quads after a good, muddy storm. But maybe, just maybe, the only place a nut like Jay could actually lose a rookie cop. Everything is flashing red and blue, even my skin, the sky, the very ground itself.

But we're gaining ground. We're gaining ground! And we grew up in these places as feral children, only to hustle old porn and cigarettes to fresh middle-school kids. We know these roads. With any luck, this banshee posessed cop is a transfer, out of his element, chasing three excitable dope fiends through no-man's land. We'll lose him, we'll lose him… we'll lose…

"Tim!"

What?

Julio screamed over the roar of the wind. "Jump out!"

"Jump?" My grip on Kitsune is so tight my knuckles nearly split open. The Jeep rocks up and down over the poor excuse for a road. The swirl of civilized lights bounced violently in the distance as the dust shields our Jeep and the leafy darkness seeps between the crimson-azure cracks.

"Bro, shut up and get ready! I'm going fly up behind the Texan Bro lot, and you bounce. I'll burn this fucker back out onto the strip to ditch this pig!" Julio shouted.

"But—but Barry, the books, the mission!"

"Barry's house is like… a half mile from there! Just hop out and run through the woods! Aight?" He punched the brakes. We skid to the side. The cop slides behind us, trying to stay on track. "Hey! You ready, aight?"

No. No, not all right at all.

The Texan Bro sign grows closer. Boil's throaty laughter echoes around me. This danger pit of sand is like home for this veteran thug. The kind of sunken meadow he'd smash dead deer in. He turns to glare at me. The sirens dance in his hollow eye sockets, over his nose, between his teeth. His calloused hands reach out.

"You heard Sanchez! Oscar Mike, boy! On the move! Go, go, go!" Boil roared. "JUMP!"

I try to fight his grip, but I am just a worm fighting an eagle. The belt buckle fails me. The side of the Jeep is cutting into my ribs, and my center of gravity is spilling over the side. And then the tornado of sounds and primary colors fall away. Julio spirals away from me.

No…

Sinking into myself. No time to think. Take a breath. Okay, just float like Kitsune. Enjoy the wind for one glorious moment. Gaia will snatch me back soon enough. Tuck and roll and keep the wrists and ankles bent inward, chin down to chest and—

TWHAM!

Ouch. God fucking damn it! Cracks and crunching and snaps. Pray it's twigs and trash, not me. The wind screams in my face and suddenly it's burning with dirt. The yellow Jeep goes into the dark, with a howling blue-red blur behind them.

My shoulders are killing me and Kitsune is skidding out of her sheath into the dirt. There are little rocks stuck in my skin. I lay in silence. Chaos passes Texan Bro's buzzing sign and it's dark enough to see the stars. I close my eyes, breathe, and see inside my eyelids. Exploding with fireworks, and lizards are laughing at me in the underbrush. The fresh tattoo throbs. The fox. I hope it didn't get scratched under my bandage.

The crickets mock me. Jump, jump, jump. I couldn't. I creak onto my knees and shout back at the ugly bugs.

"Silence, vermin! I'm not bred to leap, you freakish alien limbed freaks. You don't even have circulatory systems!" This drug is washing in to fill the gaps left by pain. I can only wonder what Elvis wanted to say when he went through this ordeal.

Okay. Stand. Kitsune in hand.

Cicadas and silence. Hum of the town far away.

Limbs light up like a pinball machine. Must move. I know where I am. A junkyard boundary between the clusterfuck of commerce and suburban homes. The divider between industrial coasts and shrinking forests. This is a bad place, built on an Indian burial ground.

Texan Bro's sign towers over the chain link fence that snakes through the underbrush. Stumble out of the weeds toward it. I'm dizzy and confused, but I used to drink Steel Stallion back here after class, so I expertly avoid the ditches and neck breaking falls. But still trip over the old lawn chairs. Brush past an ancient couch, covered in piss and lost virgin tears. Keep walking. Keep it together. Don't lean on that tree— that was the shitting tree…

Keep it together, Tim. Walk toward the light. Right behind the fence. Find it. Find the hole in the fence. Find the light. I get Kitsune sheathed and tied to my waist as I reach the fence. Cold and alone in the summer night.

There, the metal tear is still here. The old hole in the fence has never been patched, and before I know it, I'm standing on the worn pavement of an empty gas station. I'm tripping. I'm starving. My wallet is still in my pocket, and drug frenzy or not, I'm damn sure that station has coffee and candy. Sober up, Tim, because Texan Bro is the only store here for miles. Just the woods remain, and in them, Tracy's house. Barry's house. Doped up or not, just go on auto-pilot and trust your mind.

Okay. Go inside. Get food. Get to Barry's.

So simple, yes. But be cautious. Your body can fail. No warning. I've learned the hard way. Your heart ignores you. It never forgets. It will betray your mind. Despite that, my mind was the one thing I thought I could control... I think? Right now, Julio's chemical prank is playing games with my mind! I should have known. The fable about the fox and the scorpion, he and I. Playing with my mind! Crossing a line that... oh.

The sun's set. Now it's truly dark. Texan Bro beckons, the false light of man. Deep breath, Tim. Brush off and head toward that blinding false light. Doesn't matter if it's a trick, you're nearly there. You'll have the books soon, think about the rest after. Try to laugh. It's all just a joke, a trick, a harmless prank. Like the warm sun I once dreamt I could seize.

Forget it.

Move on.

The Dark Lobster's Neon Magic

Stumbling up past the pumps, I find there is no one here. Empty lot under thunderous corporate sign. Coffee and candy inside. Push into the humming incandescent convenience store. Just the cashier. It's only the two of us inside, but the attendant is making me nervous. This gas station was once a deli, here before our fathers' fathers. My first job, actually. Job… What was my job? I have a job. Drink books and find coffee.

The aisles pulse and shimmer. Jay's poison. The attendant wavers like a paper cut-out. He's staring at me. Speak. My tongue is being very disagreeable while trying to get directions to Barry's house. Had I not been poisoned, I would realize it's just a quarter mile down the road, waiting patiently at the end of a long dirt driveway, curved like the devil's backbone, nestled in the thorny forest of his brimstone chest. Okay. My lips cling to each other. I force a string of words out.

The attendant smiles through his scruff. The first thing he says to me is:

"Hi."

High? He's on to me? Already? This is too fast, he must have been waiting for some druggard like me. Another trap! He's a goddamned narc!

"No! Not high, low! Very low! Who smokes that stuff? We're good men here. You and I. Good, law abiding men. Both of us, yes. Only users lose drugs! Not me, just worshipping here. Legal men, friend. Thanks! Not sword. Just need coffee."

He points to the brown canisters behind me.

The tiles are dancing underneath my heels and it's hard to look this man in the eyes. Can't hear my own words over my heart. I think I'm saying something about cops. Need sugar. Spin around to peruse the small maze of aisles. Kitsune knocks something over. I stamp on anyway.

"Um, sir, can you pick that up?"

"Don't worry, the sword is fake."

Too many choices. They have all these coffees from Colombia and France and Hazelnut. Hmmm… Dark Magic. Extra strength. Extra dark. Must be the clerk at ease. Jokes. People like jokes.

"Dark magic," I point at the coffee container. "Man, I… I remember having to um… chant knee deep in ram's blood for a week… just to get a little of this. Ha? Not a fantasy fan?"

He hates me.

Good, must mean I'm sobering up. Got to go, though, since this kaleidoscopic chemical elixir is lighting up my chakra lines. Burning me brains. Sweating. Feel hollow. Okay. Walk past the coffee and grab a water. Five dollars. Back to the counter. All this light is making my head feel like a hive. Julio, you fudge fuck tart! You're next on my hit list.

"EXCUSE me? What was that?"

"What was what? No, nothing, talking to me about my friend! You're my friend, don't worry. I mean… not that friend. Other… I have friends."

He turns his attention to a porno mag. This was a bad idea. I creep to the back, near the sizzling nuked wieners. It's like a neon prison cell, with gas pumps standing at attention outside, waiting to shower me in foul dinosaur fuel if I escape.

I put the water on the counter. See a stand of sad, sad oranges. No good. Oranges are a volatile and untrustworthy fruit. Acidic. What the hell kind of color is orange? So sad, no rhymes, never in poems… No, I need different fuel. No more nightmare fuel, my tank is overflowing with it. Need something soft. Soft and passive. Something malleable that I can control.

Ah! The candy stand. Look at these colored wrappers! Astounding! Yet both alluring and confusing. What mad-man designed these? This should be my job! Or at least they could pay me to test the candy wrappers. Crimson reds and golden yellows. Deep moon blues and fat greens, all crinkly and shining. Bless Julio! He has finally freed me to celebrate these beautiful candy bars in all their glory! These creamy nougats and rich chocolates arouse strange instincts in me.

"Strange… instincts? Sir? Hey, are you okay?"

Oh crap, he's nervous again. He'll bring the police!

"Oh no, no, I'm never mind me. I'm good. Good. Passive. Nop a cop. Legally orange."

"You mean drunk?"

"Yes. Perfectly drunk. Am me." I smile and give him thumbs up.

He's so tense… maybe a new tactic is needed. Maybe I should grab the cashier by the back of his scruffy hotdog neck and plant a sloppy kiss on his purple lips. Be Elvis! Embrace the sickness, like a beast! After all, this man is only a pug. No, what am I saying? This is madness. I'm nothing more than another abandoned, failed experiment. Need a constant, something to latch on to and pull myself out of this flittering delirium. Munchomars! Chocolate and nougat. Yes. Wait, what the fuck is nougat?

"I don't know, sir. You didn't drive here, did you?"

Shit, doing it again. Find something, anything, to focus on. Reel it in, Tim, come on. His knobby brown hands. Fine. I stare at them, unblinking. Slap the Munchomars on the counter.

"No. Nougat yes, but no car."

Those damn hands. Those hands... I know this type of hand!

It all clicked into place. A setup. The clerk, he was a Vegas man, I was sure of that. My sword didn't faze him. He's stood his ground despite my unwanted mania. He's been around sketchy characters before. He's used to freaks. And besides, it's obvious by the way he handles the money. The slick confidence when handing back my change. It sang of younger days of stacking clay and peering through blinds. A casino veteran. Vegas man. Jesus, this could be dangerous. A Vegasian narc?

God knows what chased him from Vegas all the way out here. What predators could he have betrayed, back in the electric shark infested hollows of The Strip? Who's hunting this man for his debt? How much is the bounty? And what hideous retribution is waiting in the bushes outside? What deadly crossfire am I about to get entangled in? This man is nothing more than a target about to be descended upon by a vengeful pack of wild Vegas lobsters.

"For fuck's sake, man. We don't sell lobsters! You need help. Are you done? Is that all... sir?"

"Who are you? I've never seen you before," I said. "Coffee! Where are your credentials?"

"Do you need anything else?"

I gulped the water down.

"Beans," I growled. "Ground beans."

He's reaching under the counter. The panic button... or the panic shotgun?

Good god, I'm in too deep. I stumbled backwards into the candy.

"I think you should go. Now."

"Go to hell, you bet-welching creep! I'm not here for trouble!" Sweat pouring down my face. I took a horse stance and gripped the hilt of my katana. "For Christ's sake, man, just give me the FUCKING Munchomars!"

"Take them, you asshole! Just get out of here!" He threw them at me. The candy bounced of my chest.

Can't catch it, but at least I can feel my body now. Every thin strand of muscle, every twitching hair. But this man is alarmed. Like that fat cook, Frankenstein. He'll attack! What have I done to him? It's time to move, to act. Or play it cool and slow? Yeah. Back out slowly. He looks down at his tittie-rag while I back through the glass door. The bells jangle above.

"Just go and don't come back! Freak."

The door sweeps shut. Outside, still alone, buzzing from lights and cicada concertos. The station is still empty outside, but scores of teenage winos and celebrity celery creeps will arrive. This won't last for long. Too quiet, no… unless the mobsters already cleared it out. Shit, I forgot all about them. They've cleared out a killing box, setting up a trap for the cashier! Too late to warn him, but that's his problem. How many hidden guns are trained on me? Damn, if he comes outside I'll be perforated in the crossfire. Or be slammed onto my knees as a witness, guilty, with a 12-gauge between my teeth. Must escape, but what to do what to do? Boil would know what to do.

No, Tim. It's not that bad. You're just losing your mind.

Took a breath. Another.

Better.

Did Julio time this all? Bastard. Must get out of sight while I still can. I creep around to the back and use the tanks and crates to climb to the roof.

Good vantage up here. I scan the horizon for danger. The sky is stained by the distant streetlights. Like piss on a purple rug. But the trees ahead are rich and dark, the Jeep and the cops nowhere to be seen. There's no one to be seen. No headlights at all! Unless the drunks are speeding with their lights off, always a danger in this world.

This drug's eating my already sick mind. I can see it happening, can feel it, but do nothing! Feel slightly more lucid now, but how long? I can't remember what the cashier told me, or what info I'd given up. Memory is still spastic. No matter. Something glints at the edge of the station, by the air pump. Must be… yes, I think I see a sniper in the bushes. On a better night, in a different mind, I'd warn the poor clerk. Maybe. Instead, I dangle awkwardly from the gutter, collapse to the pavement in a heap, spring to my feet, and take off full sprint for the street.

I swear I can hear a muffled gunshot pop off behind me. The sharp crack of glass. I don't dare look back. That clerk wouldn't be the first soul put down out here. Just run, Tim run! Maybe I'm nuts, but Christ, what if, *just what if*, for once, I'm actually right? Keep running down the road. Use the dead, dark trees for cover. The forest across the street... that's the key. The hidden paths to the Cameron home. Tripping balls or not, it's finally time to dive.

Ah, I forgot coffee! Kitsune's hilt burns my palm. I relax, notice the crinkling wrapper in my left hand. Food. No matter now. In any event, the Munchomars are delicious, and safe. And for the moment, so am I. Things are finally coming together. What could possibly go wrong now?

The Wake of Sisyphus

Instincts do as they do, guiding my body toward Barry's home. I stumble down the dark road, away from Texan Bro, the woods forming high walls around. Even without streetlights I see the cracked tree, the mark of hidden passage, slashed by many teenage switchblades, hearts and arrows and machete hacks.

No time to hesitate, so I push past it into a trail I've not adventured into for three years. The instincts keep me moving through the branching trails, enveloped in a black sea of leaves, only the night above to give any light. Each step closer and closer toward their home, a house of memory and love and violence. Pure will yanks me like a doll, lurching through the wicked roots, bramble, litter, and squirrel blood. A trail of both dead and thriving trees. Blossoming tombs. My mind wanders, flits too long on the curve of a branch in my path, highlighted under the full-force moon. New obstacles have grown. Never used to be a thorn bush there. I get on hands and knees. Will have to push through, keep my eyes covered with one palm. It feels like an army of skeletal limbs caressing me. A thorn catches my arm as I crawl through to the end. Just another scratch, another red ditch in my flesh, threatening infection. And... bruises from falling out of the Jeep. Seem to feel it all at once. Even my ankle throbs, the tattoo burns. No matter. Must live through Jay's poison and get Barry's precious books.

Ah, or I could just end it all. Something truly memorable. Dive head-first into the thorn bushes that we've allowed to thrive, thousands of jagged little natural spikes ripping into me, an endless cascade of organic shivs that leave me stuck and bleeding out like a pig. My body left for the new children who haunt this forest labyrinth. A trippy thought... but not my style. Even intoxicated into manic waves of delusion and depression, my stubbornness recalls reading an argument against suicide called 'The Myth of Sisyphus'.

It had something to do with a cursed king pushing a boulder up a mountain, but no matter how hard he tried, it always rolled back down to crush him. A boulder covered in broken skull and blood, crystallized in veins. And he begins again. And fails just at the end. And begins again. A true curse. And at the end of this book by some smart, creepy author, there's a freakish anecdote about a mother cat eating her kittens. Should go back and tell the Texan Bro clerk about it... No, no. Gross, bad thoughts for this hour.

Well, too late to un-think that. Deprived of light, my eyes betray me, letting Julio's elixir of doom twist the canvas of blacks and shade that abound. Now shadows become severed catheads and small fish with hacksaw noses. They float out of the gloom, coaxing me along through the trees and new thorns, while the mighty rock of Sisyphus remains blown to chunks back on Julio's lawn. More cat's eyes, yellow slits peering through the brush. Branches become long witch fingers, tickling and scratching. More insects of indeterminable size hum, organic power-lines buzzing in the forest gloom. Owls hoot. Broken glass crunches below my shoes, bleached white cigarette butts litter the soil like gravestones for ants. I step on, push them deeper into the soil. Not cool, bro, bad for the environment. Too bad, move, before you puke and die out here. We poison as we move. Used to it by now.

There's no breeze back here. Cloud cover shifts, and my mind with it. How long has it been since Boil threw me away, at Jay's command? An hour? Five? All I know is that the Texan Bro's doomed attendant is far behind me in the murk of summer twilight. But as always, new troubles find me. For example: Did I lock the house before I left? That teenage dog-killer could get in, then jerk off in our bathroom and hide until I got home, just to cut my throat in my sleep. No, no, Julio dealt with him in the street, didn't he? Julio is the greatest dealer of deals and dealing with things that must be dealt with.

An animal shoots across the path.

I know what I saw, but it's not possible. They're all dead. Is it the same red phantom? Living in my mind? Or actually haunting this land? How lovely. Well, why not? This is the place of memory and ghosts. Or maybe it's really real, the last fox on Earth. Alone, unable to breed, waiting to be washed away like rain drops over the sea.

Seven hells, Tim, concentrate!

They're gone, they're not coming back! It's all just proof that this pill you swallowed merely... I sit down. Breathe slowly. Play with Kitsune, tracing patterns in the dirt. Stare up at the stars hiding between the leaves.

"Fox?" I call into the dark. It feels strange to yell, regardless of how sure I am that I'm alone. "Hello? Fox? Are you real? Am I nuts? Okay, bye!"

No answer. No sounds, no visions.

Good, I think I'm starting to *really* sober up. I can feel the ground now, and thoughts are becoming more coherent. But this electric energy in my stomach won't go. Standing again, my feet return to autopilot. Almost there. Must be. I bet Helena is guarding her last living child's books like Medusa, and ready to give me the same reception.

But getting there, even in this forking path of forks and forks and so on, means I eventually must set down one trail... Only one trail leads to the Camerons' vast, green, empty lawn. That means I have to return to... I'll have to cross through the fire pit. The love haven now turned into a shrine to pain, curses fulfilled, abandoned for good reason. I *could* try taking an alternate route, but that means hacking a new path through true, thick trees. Through a black forest of silken leaves and sharp trunks. Kitsune isn't up to that. I can't lie to myself enough to try.

But each step forward becomes slower. Colder. This is the sunken meadow. The twisted grove. The backwoods trails between the town proper and their homestead. The land of moss covered dead pets and shattered whiskey bottles. Native bones inches below the grass where memories of a different time, a different, better Tim, lie dead and restless with other spirits. In other words, the forbidden land of my youth, the danger zone, where the older kids sacrificed chickens and Boil tortured stray cats, unpunished. The place to smoke your cigarettes and pray the bus driver didn't find you. I'm too far off course! How? Subconscious betrayal? Am I about to fall prey to the descendants of savage, ass eating mutants? Will a fresh generation of Satan worshippers come tearing out of the shrubs brandishing Mommy's kitchen knives? Lucas Boil's spiritual successors... Vegas hit-men behind me, cannibal preteens lurking in the shrubs, and the vengeful dead below.

Hey, what happened to my Munchomars? Did I already eat them? Need that sucrose and creamy nougat dripping from my lips.

Sanity returns, just in time for me to fall again. I fold into a ball, a fetal loser lost in the past. Who was I kidding? I couldn't handle this sober, let alone in this crazed state. I'm going to fail. I'm going to let them all down again. Waves rumble in the distance, my lungs swell with imagined salt water. The Curse always churning behind me, that strange flooding roar you always hear underwater. A heartbeat in the dark. A black, barren sea for—

Huh?

I stare at it, eyes focusing on the shadow blocking my path. Bigger than a fox. I blink to wash it away. Just another drug-summoned phantom.

Just a hallucination. P.T.S.D. Blink and be gone.

Please.

Yet she remains. Moonlight, glinting off metal piercings. One from an eyebrow ring. The great fear is no longer creeping, it's leaping and bounding through me. No, no, no, no, this can't be happening. I'm nowhere near sober, I *can't be*. The only explanation is the right one. Julio's wonder drug slipped out of my brain and got into my heart. It's the location, a bad combo. My eyes are reporting things—strange, beautiful, dark. Things that are off limits to logic. I close my eyes so hard it hurts, get onto my hands and knees, and look again, ready to face the cold, empty night again.

But there she is, glowing between the black and blue trees.

She should be a skeleton.

Flesh hanging off in tattered clumps, and bugs nesting in her heart. Maggots dripping from her guts, flies in her mouth, chest rotted black. Stringy gray hair curling through empty eye sockets. Something more than awful.

She isn't.

She's beautiful.

Framed by black branches, arching over her like scythes. The moon showers her in twilight. I try to stand. Trip, fall to one knee. Look up to her. She shifts her weight, crosses her arms. Tapping her steel-toed boot on the ground impatiently. Like the last time I saw her, normal, without marble skin and those fluids spilled across her bed and ruined sheets and… Fuck no, no, NO. Forget then. Look at her *now*.

Somehow, I stand.

She's wearing that mesh top that you could just see her breasts through when she turned to the sun. No bra. Thick, black, bullet-lined belt. Chains dangling from pockets on her tight jeans, zippers, pins, fake spikes and black boots. Cold zippers running up the sides, nearly to her knees. The rings, skulls, and jewels. Short red hair, with that one long, purple strand, framing a gracefully strong chin. The piercings running up the crest of her right ear. The lips that never needed makeup. The eyes… Don't look at those eyes. Three colors saved for one soul. Thin blue rim, then thicker green, and a last ring of brown before the black center, always, always piercing me. They once hovered over mine, her breasts pressing against my chest, our breathing in rhythm. Those same eyes I see every single night I try to sleep.

Dry mouth hits first, then tingling below my navel, a weird sensitivity in the fingertips. Life down in my dead shorts. The strange call of the flesh. I try to shake it off. It's the damn chemicals. Julio's insipid wonder drug. Please gods, I'm already walking damage. Don't make me cursed *and* a necrophiliac. She'd laugh at that. I hear nothing. I'm standing but shaking and can't speak.

She steps forward. Reality buckles beneath her boots. The closer she comes, the more the world shimmers and shakes in protest. It's just shadows and dreams, *it must be*. She's just a shadow in the mist. This should be fantastic. So why do I feel sick?

Because somehow I know the truth. It's the drug. This is fake. It must be. Julio Sanchez Sin Corazon's funny little *fucking drug* is raping my mind. I'll never forgive this. You idiot! You knew you were sick! Why did you come here, of all places? I close my eyes before I can cry. Shake my head, trying to break free. Holding my breath. Won't look until this cruel joke is over.

"Hey there."

"Tracy?" I hear myself asking. You idiot. I finally look. She's smiling.

"In the flesh!" She's almost laughing, but the smile... it looks too sad.

"That's... that's funny. Am I...?"

"Damn it, babe," she says, then bites her lip. She sighs, looking down at the trail. "Why did you come here?"

What is she talking about? Why is it so cold now?

"Tim, you shouldn't be here. This place is for the dead. But you already knew that, didn't you, babe?"

I haven't been called 'babe' in over three years. I try that trick, staring up so I can't cry. It works. And she's right. This is a dead place. A tomb I've avoided. But now I'm here.

"But now you're here." Her head's down, hiding her face. "And I'm sorry. I'm so, so sorry."

"Wh-what? Why?"

"You've gone too far. Broke too many rules." Her eyes flicker up to mine. "You know what you've done. And what has to happen next."

Of course. I'm a bit shocked but... It'd be a relief. And a good death.

"You're going to kill me? Alright. Let's do this. Just don't be... scary. Don't turn into a monster or something, okay?"

I close my eyes, let go of my sword, and hold my breath, waiting for what comes next.

Nothing.

When I look again, she's leaning against a tree, failing to cover up a laugh.

"Ha, you dork! I'm not going to kill you! You brave, creepy dork." She's smiling. "Hey, relax, I'm just fucking with you!"

Don't feel relieved. Guess I really have lost my mind.

"Hey? Tim? Shit, I'm sorry."

"No, no it's okay. It's funny, ha. I would've done the same."

"No. It's not funny. I'm sorry." She holds out her hand. "Come here, babe. I love you."

And I cry.

"Oh, no... Tim, please! Don't worry, babe! You're okay, it's all okay!"

No, it's not. I want to tell her the truth.

This is hell.

Now I understand true hell.

The Sound of Her Wings

Her voice is so normal. It's terrifying.

She sounds so calm, and confident. And caring. No ghostly wail, no unearthly cry, no hollow echoes from beyond. Just a girl's voice. A dead girl. With a perfectly normal voice. I was so afraid I'd forget! Terrified that no matter how many conversations I remembered, word for word, that somehow, someday, I'd still forget the sound of her voice.

And I'm still crying.

"I'm sorry, I'm not scared," I say while pinching the tears away. "I'll stop, I just can't... If I'm not dead then I'm crazy. I'm fucking crazy, aren't I? Finally snapped after—"

"God, you're still so dramatic. And it's still cute." She's happy. As if she just forgot that she's dead. "Okay, I'll admit that maybe that wasn't the best joke to greet you with. But come on, Tim, it was a corny joke. I couldn't resist!"

I laugh away the last tear. Her hand is still waiting for me.

"It's okay, I'm... I'm not scared, I'm... Seriously? What the fuck! Tracy?"

"Yeah, dumbass. Hello! What, you forgot me already?"

"No! I'm sorry, no! No, no, never, I'd never—"

"Relax, silly. I'm just teasing you. Shit, where'd your freaky sense of humor go?"

"With you."

"Stop. No more jokes. Now take my hand! Please."

No more jokes, Tim. Go to her. Risk being a joke, you can take a little more psychic pain. I wipe my eyes, take a breath, and nearly fall over. When I look up she's hiding a smile with her other hand.

"It's okay." She put her hands on her thighs, arched against the tree, sneaky lips curled. "Get yourself together. You can handle this."

"Tracy, I—I'm trying. I'm trying to get to your house. I mean, I know where you live. I mean, where it *is* but... b-b-but I'm—"

"You're lost."

"Yeah." I fall to my knees. It feels good. And then I break. "I promised Barry I'd get his books for him because he's great and loves you and is happy but your mom asked me to help but I fucked up and freaked out but I had a plan and then Jay and Boil kidnapped me and I got dosed with some weird drug he made out of *something and I don't know what it is* or what it does but his pug shit a lot and gambling sharks beat me up I think maybe and some kid with a dog killed at my parents' place and the little sister cried but my sword couldn't help but still they blew it all up and hoped me too and the darkness I saw them and you but failed and I made a promise and Burn left me behind and Barry is not okay I lied and the police are after us but they threw me away when then cops, and, and, a car crashed, not my fault but—"

"Whoa, whoa! Shush, babe, I know. Take a breath. Calm down." Her voice is so god damned good that I *do* shut up.

Her hand's still waiting for me.

But she's not leaning on the tree, she's right in front of me. Her purple fingernails now inches from my face. "I know. This is pretty messed up. I won't lie to you. This might hurt. But you need it, and you can take it. I know you can."

"I can't, Trace. I can't take it. Not anymore."

Eyes shut, and then I feel her touch my cheek. It feels like daylight.

"That doesn't sound like the man I loved."

My whole body froze, then melted. I felt sleepy beneath her touch, as if she just pulled the toxins right out, sobering me up for the nuclear mind fuck about to come.

I raised my hand. She took it. Our fingers entwined.

I stand, and she turns her back, pulling me deeper into the darkness. She guides me down the trail, hand in hand as if we never missed a day. Her hand is soft cotton in mine, so fragile I hold my breath for fear of blowing it away.

In a night choked with madness, betrayal, and violence, this feels normal. This feels safe. We stop in the old clearing. The trees have crept across the trails, slowly reclaiming them. This really is a dead place, somehow unused by anyone else in all these years. In the center, that old fire pit slumbers beneath a blanket of ash. The moonlight centers on it, basking our private circle in a day-blue glow. Old beer bottles crunch beneath my feet. The two logs are still beside the fire pit. And it almost looks like an indigo flame still crackles there, an echo from another world. The breeze takes it, shimmering, but it holds. We just stand there, hand in hand, looking at this spot that holds far too much energy. A crack in time ready to burst. Let it.

She lets go.

We sit on the facing logs. My throat tightens. We both lean forward, faces just a breath away, eyes locked. But I don't hear her breath, don't smell it. Other than that, though… I remember sounds, the whip crack of fire and beetles popping. She looks so peaceful. She's not floating or glowing or translucent. Her eyes don't glow. They do reflect the full moon. No wings, no halo. But there are no sharp edges to her body, no definitive lines to separate her from the wind. Just soft blurs around young curves.

"Are you okay?"

"No. Yes. Can I be both?" I have to look down. Swirl patterns in the dirt with my feet.

"You usually are. In a vaguely healthy sense. You haven't run screaming into the night yet, so I'd say—"

"This is weird. Even for me, this is… this is too weird."

"Hell yeah it is. But you're doing good. Now."

I want to puke. Can't look at her when I speak. "I've wanted this more than anything since you… I've always wanted you back. Always dreamed I'd see you one more time. I'm so ready to believe this, and I *do*, but…"

"It's still a surprise when it actually happens."

"Exactly. If this even *is* real." Now I can look at her. "I mean, seriously, what the hell? Why, Tracy? Why now?"

She shushed me.

"Take it slow. You're still in too much pain."

It's true. She's dead-on accurate. Exactly how I remember. Always half smiling, far too at ease for a girl who either overdosed on pain-killers… or killed herself. Either or… just don't, Tim. Not now.

"So what's up with the sword?" She's pointing at Kitsune. "On your way to a duel?"

"Huh? Oh, ha. No." I swirled the sheath's tip in the dirt before unlacing it from my pants. I lay it against the log. "No. This… it's just a good luck charm."

"Hmm. Only a weird freak like you would use a sword for that."

"Funny. Actually, I finally named her! Every true sword needs a name, as you know." And now I smile. She doesn't. "It only took me a hundred years to get around to it."

"Her? Tim, please don't tell me you named it Tracy."

"Nah." I smiled. "No offense. Her name's Kitsune."

Her eyebrows arch, head tilts back. But she's starting to smile. Relieved?

"Kitsune? What kind of name is that?

"Just felt right. Since they're all dead now."

"What are you talking about?"

I shook my head. "Forget it."

"Okaaaaaay then," she said, slapping her knees. "So. Here we are."

"Here we are." I tap Kitsune in the grass. Now what? So many questions. "Um, so you're a... Shouldn't you have wings or something?"

"Wings? Come on, I'm not an angel," she said. "Wings. Ha! What about you? You look like the dead one, here. Have you been fighting gangs all night? Still rocking that old Hawaiian shirt, too. It's going to be rags soon."

"You don't like it?"

"Of course I do," she whips the strand of purple hair out of her face.

"No gang fights, but there's been, well, it's complicated, and my head isn't right. More so than usual. I think I'm drugged, infected, something. I tried to help Barry, but I'm poison and lizards and... Boil and bad kids... I got beaten and thrown away," I tried. Shutting down again. Battery fading fast. Darkness circling in. Got about six seconds before I faint. Tracy leans across the gap and flicks my forehead.

I'm fine.

I reach for her hand as she sits back. Our fingertips hook. Our arms make a bridge over the stone cold fire pit.

"You cool now?"

"Yes," I lie. "Why are you finally here? Why now?"

"Because I can't see you anymore. Not like this. You were my favorite light, Tim. But I've watched you slowly fading out."

She lets my fingers go. My arm hangs there, then falls back to my lap.

"Me? Fading? But I'm the one that's... th-th-that's still here." I lean back on my hands. Old grainy wood presses into skin. My palms must look like moon craters by now. "Fading, huh? Well, good. It's not like anything's getting better. It's worse than ever, Trace. All of it. Everything's awful."

"When wasn't it?"

"When you... when you were..." My jaw tensed. "Alive. That's okay to say, right?"

"Are you kidding?" She laughs, of course. "Babe, I know I'm dead. It's not the kind of thing you forget."

I know.

"If you're here, then that means there really *is* some sort of afterlife, right?"

"Maybe. If you even truly believe I'm here." She folded her arms, tilted her chin up.

I have to. "So how is heaven?"

"You'd assume that's where I went." She winks, does her cat hip shift.

"Very funny. There's no way you're in hell though, so… What the hell? Where are you?"

"Right here. Come on, is that what you really want to know?" She rests her foot on her knee, head on hand, waiting to pounce. Please pounce. I don't care how awkward it is, I've adapted this far already.

"Wow. You look so real. Sorry, not real, I mean, like, not fake? Sorry. Shit! I've never done this before."

"Yeah, it's a first for me too. Hey, we sound like two virgins again. Remember? Oh, I've never done this before! I'm nervous! Me too, this is weird! Blah, blah, blah. And a minute later it's no big deal."

"It was more than a minute!"

"Okay, two and a half minutes."

"And it was a very big deal."

She punches my arm. We laugh, the kind that barely grips onto sanity. The kind after realizing you're safe after escaping cops or sharks. My god Jay, what the fuck did you put in me? If I have a soul, every shred left prays for this is to be real. No hallucination has ever been like this. Please. Drugs, necro-magic, or if this is just true madness, then sign me up. She's completely solid now. No angle, no shift of moonlight, no blinking can distort her.

"Okay, I get it. I look real? So do you. What did you expect me to look like?"

"Expect? I begged, I didn't expect. I used to think about you all the time. I do think about you all the time. And now… here you are. But you can't be, because you're… You're sitting right there, except you can't be, because y-y-you're—"

"Say it."

Chewing my lip.

"Tim, just say it. Look me in the eye and say it."

"Dead." I blinked. "You're dead."

And nothing changes.

"Good boy! Now that we finally got *that* out of the way, you've got a lot of work to do. And we don't have a lot of time."

"We don't?"

"What do you think?"

"I think this is fake." I stare at my knees. Ice beads on my neck. "I'm afraid that I'm sitting alone having a drug induced anxiety attack. Talking to a phantom. You're just my own mind playing tricks on me. Again. Just making me see my idea of who you were. A lovely, deceitful hallucination. And… I'm not sure that I even…"

She sighed. "I'm a ghost, you asshole."

"Sorry."

"It's okay, you're allowed to. Don't sweat it, babe. And stop apologizing. You're not that kind of guy. I know you don't take shit at face value. Never was your style. Well, at least it wasn't your style," her voices has a hint of anxiety. "Listen, sulky, let's talk about something else for a second."

She's good. My breathing returns to a safely neurotic state. Okay. "Well, okay, but I need to ask or I'll just obsess. As you know. So what's it like? Being, you know, dead? Is it… fun?"

"I can't really talk about that stuff," she trails off, looking at the moon. "But all right, you little bugbear. I'll give you this one. Just *this one*, deal?"

"Okay." Yeah, right. Fat chance. There's so much more I must ask, and she knows it. I just hope, for both of us, that I don't have the balls to actually ask.

"Being dead, hmmm." She tapped her lips. "Well honestly, it's not worth thinking about. You kind of can't. Yeah, that's it! Your brain simply can't fathom it. I don't mean just you. No one can really conceive of it. I couldn't have, before I died. You're not hardwired for the concept."

"What? That's not an answer! That doesn't count!"

"Well then, try imagining a color that doesn't exist."

"I hate that metaphor."

"It's one of yours."

"Bleh. Fine. What about god? You got one up there with you?"

"Seriously? Like it'd change your mind. Always going on about your own occultish gods and half-assed spirituality."

"Please stop fucking with me."

"Listen, you got the wrong idea. You're like a fish trying to understand the ocean. Just forget about it for now and swim."

"See, now that sounds like something stupid I'd say." I curled up on my log. "The Curse. The barren sea. Makes me think this *is* me."

"Come on!" She stands up and twirls on one foot, my dead dancing goddess. "You've always been nuts. You believe in parallel worlds and alien churches trying to enslave us. And the never-be-named, and eldritch elders, anti-gods, hyper-gods, hologram worlds, mutant offshore labs, surgeonfish. Curses and ghosts."

I believe now more than ever. Hard not to, once you've seen the true face of horror. It's clever. It hides in the cracks between time. Once, it was when I made plans to bring the love of my life to a Brooklyn museum, but instead I'm brought to her bedroom, and she's spread face down on her red sheets like a swastika, covered in shit, piss, and puke. Cold and heavy. And I can't un-see that. Ever. That horror lives in me every time I think of her, like a flash cut in a projector. But not now. Divert, Tim, *do not tell her that.* "Yeah! You're right. I'm really starting to believe all this cosmic voodoo. Now that I'm sure the Curse... No, I don't give a shit about gods or devils right now."

Christ, I want a cigarette.

"I thought you quit." She spins into a bow, then slips back onto her seat.

"I did. Old habits. I guess I don't want one."

"So what do you really want?"

"I want to go dancing with you."

"You don't dance."

"I would."

She looked away. She stood up and paced around the fire pit, kicking ash and glass and bugs.

"You know I want you. And I'm not such a moron. I know I can't have you, but..." I coughed back bile. "Shit, I'm sorry, but, I think I really want..."

"Go on."

"Tracy, I'm so sorry, but some small part of me wishes..." Just admit it. "I wish I could stop wanting you."

"Good."

What? Good? I can hear her walking over but I'm watching the drops fall from my face. Her hand is on my shoulder. I look up at her, a totem with the moon standing in for a halo and the bruised branches make her wings. And just like that, it happens. All this armor falls off of me, plate by plate, phantom chainmail and helmets and gauntlets, all this invisible protection crashes into the dust.

"Babe, I want that for you, too. I'm not hurt. It's healthy. And I'm actually a bit surprised you even... I'm proud of you. Hell, it's hard to admit that to yourself, let alone to me. But that alone won't save you. I'm sorry, I can't keep watching you waste away. You're *so close* to gone. You have no idea. It hurts. And I can't save you."

"Save me?" I cough, feeling some rotted abortion in my gut trying to claw its way out. It hurts, and this pain is starting to get old. "Just tell me what I need to do. I'll do it."

"What do you need?"

"Answers. An end to this god damned Curse. Poisoning all I love, making them die because of me. I need to atone for all your deaths—"

"Damn it, Tim, that's just stupid! You don't actually kill people by simply loving them. Most people can't even admit they love anyone, let alone friends. No, you didn't kill any of us. You're not that powerful."

"Really? Because I'm pretty damned sure there's a body of evidence backing me up."

"That's not funny."

"No, it's not. So don't tell me it's not my fault." I shot up onto my feet, turning my back on her. Can't let her see my shame.

"You don't know if it was your fault," she said. "And I'm sorry, but you'll never know."

IT. She knows what I'm dancing around. I grab my stomach, swallow back the demon clawing up. "Why not? What if that's what's killing me, huh? Why can't I know the truth?"

"What truth?"

"You know exactly what I'm talking about."

"Tim... those aren't the answers you need. No answer will ever make you feel better."

"I appreciate your opinion," I say, a little too harsh. Pacing in circles, wanting to slash through all the trees. The monster clawing up. Ruining this. Anger? Now? But she must know. Know that I deserve to know. She...

"Babe, calm down. Look, there's no big secret! No answer that suddenly makes life okay and bad things stop. See, *this* is why you're stuck! This is why you're constantly in pain! And if you don't cut it out, you're going to die."

Marvelous.

"Tim, I don't just mean you'll 'never really live'. But that's also true. We'd be so pissed off if you wasted the rest of your life. We can't stand seeing you suffer every moment, feeling sorry for yourself and blaming a magic spell for everything. Yes, grieve. Mourn. Remember. But move on. It's... Fuck, it's getting pathetic."

"Pathetic?" I slam my first into a chunk of bark. I like the pain. Slam it again. Again. The monster is in my throat now, ready to break through my teeth.

"This is exactly what I mean! Look at yourself. My Tim never ran away, punching shit like a little kid!"

I can't face her. I punch the tree again. "You all get to leave me behind! Then you come back and tease me? It isn't so easy, you know. You don't just find a new mom and dad. You don't wake up one day and stumble into another true love. Sorry, *babe*, but no store has a fucking aisle for that."

"I know." A strong breeze could've covered her words.

"So what then? What do I need?"

"Not this. Not wallowing in self pity."

I slam my fist into my invincible enemy again. Twigs fall on me. I scratch them away. Bloody knuckles now. New white burns to match my tattoo.

"You're starting to remind me of someone," she says. I can hear her fire rising.

Don't say it. Don't you dare say your father. I stare at my knuckles, split up like the boulder, little shreds of red and brown, and the tree, old and wise and laughing at me. Barely catch myself against it, right as the monster escapes, sliding out in a brief burst of vomit. Wipe my mouth with a leaf, can't look at her.

"Is that what you want? You want to argue and hit things?"

I kick the tree to spin myself back around.

"How come you're so fucking concerned about what I want *now*?

YOU ALREADY KILLED YOURSELF!"

"STOP! You don't *know* that! Nobody knows what really happened! And you do NOT get to yell at me. Not you." She stops, lets the fires cool. Then seems to take a breath. "You're not going to survive if you keep obsessing. Look, it's not fair. Trust me, I know. But that's just how it is. Nothing will change the past. You need to accept that. It sucks. But you can't... You'll never know for sure."

"That's just how it is? Right. Well, I know one thing for sure. You. Left. Me."

"Tim, I... I don't know what to say. That's not why I'm here." She bites her lip and sits down. Is she going to cry? No, please. I can't do that to her. I bite my lip and wait. She picks a beetle up from the grass. "Hell, if there's one person I'd never leave, it's you. And *you* of all people should know that! Come on, look at this! You never yelled at me like this when I was here."

"Right. When you were here."

"For fuck's sake, what's wrong with you? I'm here for you right now!"

I'm at the edge of the pit, head mashed against a tree. How did I get here? This isn't a drug. This is worse. She's right. Good god, who am I? I wipe my knuckles on my shorts. I'm turning into a rainbow of black, white, and red.

"I'm sorry. Tracy? I can't make it stop. I've tried, but it hurts all the time. In the shadows, in the sun, in the ocean, on the sand. I know I'm going crazy. It's not like the movies. It's not fun."

"And it's not too late. You're running out of time, babe, but you still have a chance."

"Please, *please*, what are you talking about? No more talking around it. I can't take this."

"Yes you can. You just don't want to. The real you could handle anything." Her voice is soothing, patient, not combative. She puts her hand on my shoulder, her hair tickling my skin. "You're a weird, messed up, kinda creepy guy. The mysterious weirdo, who still has good people who love him. Friends like Barry, and Julio, and Bernard. You're... my boyfriend. So full of love that he even saw it in a screwed up little girl. Without you, the *real* you... She still would've died. But very slowly. And painfully. Like you—"

"You did die. I didn't save you. I am cursed. I should have just stayed away. I'm a fucking walking plague." I spit where I wanted a fire.

"Asshole, *you did* save me. You're cute dumb, but come on! Were you always this stupid, or do you just need to hear it? You protected me since I was born. You raised me, while my parents were off doing drugs and worse in my fucked up dad's fucked up fantasy world. While they ruined our lives, you and Barry stayed home, just two kids taking care of a baby girl. Barry loved me, but he had to. You didn't. So cut the shit. You act like you hate everything now. Life's unfair, and you're cursed, so you can't win. Fine. Then why do you keep trying?"

"Good question."

"You didn't follow me. Get it, yet? You're still alive. Even at your worst, getting drunk and letting people kick the shit out of you all up and down Tomahok... Even the drugs..."

"You were already gone, how do you—? Oh," I cut off. Must be spirit stuff. Can't believe I'm actually arguing with a ghost. I'm not. It's her. But she knows, somehow. "I got clean pretty fast. Kind of."

"I know. I was trying to compliment you, silly. My point is, you're living through the pain. That's not easy. Yes, you bitch and moan. A lot. But you're trying. I'm proud of you."

"I've thought about it," I said. Following her. Anywhere. Every day. "You said it before. That this was going to hurt. Well, here we are. I'm sad, I'm fading, and apparently I'm pathetic. I didn't die with you. I wish I did."

"Stop it."

I walk over slowly to take my seat across from her. The trail to her home is behind her, the trail to nothing behind me. Only two ways out. "Tracy, I'm sorry, but your Tim is gone."

"Not yet. Just broken. Really, really broken." She rubbed my shoulders. "But that's a rather bland statement for you. Where's that overly dramatic voice I fell in love with? Come on, babe. Give me a good hammy one. For old time's sake."

"Fine. But only because it's you," I smirked. Then I arched back and threw my arms to the sky. "I'm a shallow, festering husk, rotting in anguish and despair! Oh Lords of the Inverted World, strike me down with your archangel's sword! Princess of Hades, send your scorpion vanguard to rend my flesh! Chew my bones, drink my sorrow! Vomit me onto your Nightmare Children's maggot throne! Plant my soul in Ba'aal's field of teeth. Enslave me in the Invisible Kingdom! Make my grave yet one more stone on the Gloom Drake's terrible spine!"

She laughed. Ha, she laughed! That's cool. I like that. I returned to her. Step by step, looking down at her as she looked up, smiling.

"See? You're not totally gone," she said. "Yet. Shit. I miss that."

"Ha, anything for you. But seriously, I don't know what you're talking about, but I believe you. I do. There's this sense chasing me, like an oncoming storm, and I'm ready to just wash away. It's all gone wrong. I *did* curse all of you. Now I'm old and we're not married with kids. I'm not anything my parents thought I'd be. I'm not anything that you thought I'd be."

"And what's that? Content? Safe? Happy? Get a life."

"Oh, ha, ha. Nice one. No, it's more like… You said it. I'm stuck. Barry left to chase his dream. But he has one. Julio soldiers on, Bernard… does what he does. He's happy. But I still live in that half-house shack doing nothing. I had my dream, and it's over. Mom and Dad are dead, my house is a golf course. Everything used to seem so big. I could've handled all this, if you were still… with me. Like now."

"Well, Tim, I'm dead. Worm food. I'm probably just bones by now. I've shuffled off the mortal coil and it was one hell of a dance! Hell, you could say—"

"STOP IT."

She did.

"You're still a handful, Mr. Dune." She stares up at something I can't see. "You always said Barry and I were odd, but you're way weirder. Have you ever listened to yourself talk?"

"I'm afraid maybe I am right now."

"That hurts."

My head snapped.

"I'm sorry. I didn't mean… But you're different, now."

"So are you."

"I don't care. Whatever this is, right here, right now, I'll take the pain. I'll take the suffering. If it means we can stay here. Forever."

"Technically we do, but your consciousness won't know it."

"Oh. Cool? I guess?"

Okay, note to self, even precious lovers make strange ghosts.

"Yes, we do."

"Did you just like, spirit hear that? Or did I say it out loud? Because that's been happening to me a lot, lately."

She smirked.

"Seriously, it makes for terribly awkward situations."

"You certainly don't need any help with that."

I walked back to my sword. Spun Kitsune around. "So we agree, then. I've become a piece of shit and even you're sick of me."

"This is it, Tim." She stared at the stones and brittle black logs at the center. "That storm hits tonight."

Silence. She seems ashamed, hunched over beneath a secret burden. But she's a hellcat rebel. She breaks rules. Come on, Trace. Break them.

"If I break the rules then you'll never earn your future." She spoke, cold, deliberate, still as stone. "You've got to do this on your own."

"Do what? I am on my own. I've even poisoned Barry now! Hell, his life might be ruined, and it's my fault! Again. And I'll I can do is bring him some stupid books. Is that it? That's what I need to do, seriously?"

"No."

"Then just tell me. I won't stop asking."

"That's your problem."

"Go on…"

"Oh no, no. You won't trick me. I meant what I said."

"Well, all I can do is keep my word. That's what Jay would do. So I'm dropping everything to be Barry's delivery boy. Again."

"So bitter."

"Yes, because of my Curse. I'm sick of knowing this shit's my fault and you won't admit it! Your own brother is the victim now. Who's next?"

"So you admit it's your fault? Then go to him."

"To bring him some stupid books? That's going to make up for lying about us? Betraying his trust for years, lying to his face? For almost killing him too?"

"I think I need a cigarette now, too."

Fine. I'm done. I let Kitsune roll out of my hand. She clacks against the log, nearly slipping out of her sheath, then falls against the stone circle. Tracy watches this in horror, not even breathing.

"Ghosts don't breathe, dumbass." She winks at me, but still looks scared.

"Right. Tracy, let's cut the bullshit. We both know what I need."

"Okay. Tell me."

"Did I kill you?"

"I already told you. No answer will…" She's staring past me, at the sword.

"Then I'll always believe it was my fault." I walked to the other side of the pit, facing the path leading back to the streets. "And that's your fault."

The silence is too long. I start sweating. So I return, catching a bit of my shirt on a twig. Another slight rip to add to the other tears, and now a small branch hangs at my side like a thin, brown bone. I tap Kitsune with my foot, knocking her off the fire pit's stone and into the dirt. Tracy's smile is gone. Screw her rules, Tim, you've already risked a lot tonight. Just do it.

"What?" she asks, looking colder than ever.

"You were pregnant. Weren't you?"

"Babe…"

"That's why you killed yourself."

She picks Kitsune up off the ground and lays the sword across her lap.

"Tracy?" Were you? That's what they all told me after the… the uh…" I can't. Voice is already shaking. "They told me, after they did the autop… the…"

"Autopsy. They'll do one on you, too. I'm nothing special."

"Told all of us that you… you might've been pregnant. Then some bullshit about it was too early, they couldn't be sure. Same way they couldn't tell if you… you d-d-died. Accidentally. Or not."

She twists away, but I sit beside her, inching closer, feeling further apart than every. Gently place my hand behind her. Any answer is wrong? But the secret is too much for her to take alone, alive or… or otherwise. I can't carry half the weight.

"Was it my fault? I have to hear, to this day. All this bullshit from idiots still gossiping. Everyone betting over whose kid it was, like you were some kind of… a-a-a whore… but I know the truth. I know it. Another secret for you to bear. Alone."

She squints. Head tilts at an odd angle from another world.

I risk more and push again. "And when they found you, with all those pills and bottles dripping on the rug… Ah, shit. Okay. Trace. Please. Did you really overdose? Or did you kill yourself? I mean, you never did a lot drugs around me, but I know you liked to party, and if I got you pregnant and you freaked out, maybe tried to miscarry or—"

"Really? That's how it is? You think somebody knocked me up and I couldn't take it?"

"That's what they say." Never to our faces. Not to her mom or her brother. But all the local dipshits we grew up with still talk about it. For fun. FUN. It's always hiding in the town, the bars, the sun, the moon. Every wave, the gulls above and crabs below, every cancerous thought eating through my brain. I'd burn them all if I could. "Please, if you still love me, let me take some of the pain."

She fiddles with Kitsune. Legs crossed. Shades of purple wash over her. "How many times do I have to tell you? There's NO answer that will bring you peace."

"I'm not asking for peace. I'm asking because I love—"

She slams Kitsune to the ground. The fury on her face, the flames burning her armor away, the hurt fueled anger at my shred of doubt. But I smile. I look up to her with my rare martyr eyes, but it's no practiced act. She hands Kitsune back to me and brushes off the dirt. We're face to face again. But for one horrific moment, she flickers in the wind.

"It was yours."

I hold her hand. She squeezes. Never felt anything more real.

"So, Tim. Feel better?"

"No."

The Dead Can't Cry

Time with her is slow. Leaves take longer to fall. But I need to know more. So go slower. Please. She strokes my hair back, a sweaty mess, her hand pressing the chaos into order. Her fingers flow down my neck, to my spine, kneads into the muscle. The tension shoots out like trapped lightning. The same way she stripped my invisible armor away.

And she was wrong. No point in mentioning it. We both feel it. Our fire pit feels like it used to. Almost. So even though I'm definitely taking our secret to my grave, just finally knowing she was, and it was mine… is horrific. But it does make me feel better. Not good. It's awful. She was right about that. But better. That's something, at least.

She lays her head in my lap. "You're getting gray hair. A lot."

It's easy to forget she's not really here. She is but… not something I'm going to dwell on while this lasts. Could stand to lighten the mood a bit more. "Hey, since you seem to have been watching or omniscient or something, then you know there never was anyone after you. Only you. But don't worry, I'm not completely screwed up. I still jerk off. I do want sex. But I've never felt anything for anyone else. And I don't care."

"Such a dork. I don't want you to be alone. You might still have a chance, but you're running out of time. If you fail, you really will be alone. Forever. Not in the way you think of it, now. And before you know it, you really will care."

Sigh. "I don't believe you. Don't you get it? I don't want to feel good if it's only pretend. And I don't know how to save us."

"Save us? Are you still that thick?"

"No, I'm talking about the rest of us. Julio. Barry. Burn. Shit, that's about it, now, huh? We've been whittled down. Barry… it's like I'm *his* older brother now. Your mom can't do shit, no offense."

"None taken," she said. "Does that mean you're going to fall in love with him too?"

"Maybe." I looked down at her. She folded into my lap, my happy little fire cat.

"Well, I must admit, I've already had enough bad weirdness tonight to fill a year," I said. "And enough good to fill three. Christ almighty, the night's just getting started. What's next? Are you coming with me? Oh wow, that would be perfect! But I guess if they actually do pick me up, somehow, Julio will think I'm insane while we talk. Unless they can see you, too. Can they see you, too?"

"Tim, relax. For a guy who thinks he could be talking to himself, you sure got a lot to say."

I close my eyes. In the darkness I rub her back. She curls up tighter. "Trace, I'm scared."

She sat up. "What?"

"Why didn't I listen? To the counselor. The Curse. I did violate. I did poison. I think you're right. About everything. But... I've seen too much proof. I shouldn't get close to anyone. I can't bear causing more pain."

"Don't blame your fucking curse again. Please. Don't do that to me."

"I've already done that to you. I'm sorry, Tracy. It's my destiny. I've already caused drowning, heart attacks, cancer, car accidents, and... whatever I did to you."

She shoved me back. "You know what? You weren't this weak when your parents died. You dealt with it. With everything. The world spit in your face and you spit back. I can't believe I actually looked up to you. But now this 'curse' bullshit is your crutch. Do you even remember that you *did not* believe in it? It was just some weird story in your fun life. But it's making you angry and scared and pathetic. You're not the man I loved. He was awkward, nuts, but he wasn't such a coward."

She means it.

"I'm not weak! And I didn't believe it, and look what happened! I think that's why. What do you want me to do? Go back in time and stop that asshole from ruining my life? Tell myself not to touch a baby ray and *not* hurt it? How can you look me in the eye and say it's not real? Everyone started dying as soon as I let my guard down. Became happy and... and fell for you."

"I chose you."

"Well, I was ready and waiting. Then I violated you. Poisoned you. Just like the counselor said."

She shot to her feet and pushed me again. I nearly fell off the log.

"Enough! You seriously think any of this is your fault? That you have control over life and death? You don't sound afraid of god, you sound like you think you are one! Just because someone dies doesn't mean that your stupid fucking stingray bullshit did it! Do you really think your mere existence, your precious little curse, killed your parents? Your friends' parents? ME?"

"Yes."

She punched me in the face.

I rubbed my cheek, relishing the white-hot sting. Note to self, ghosts can—

"Ghosts can kick your fucking ass if you don't get your head out of it first! Have you ever stopped to think that the world doesn't revolve around you? That maybe, just maybe, *shit just happens?* Maybe babies starve and monsters thrive and it's got nothing at all to do with you at all?"

"Yes. Of course. I don't want to believe in it, but I've seen the proof. Time after time. And had to live with it. It becomes hard not to believe… it makes things make sense. Even if it's not right."

I thought she was going to hit me again, but she walked right through the phantom flames, to the tree I'd impotently attacked.

"You've seen shit… well, I'm glad you've found your crutch. Hey, dipshit, what if your parents just got old and died? Maybe Burn's dad did too? And Jay's mom? Maybe a car hit Barry because accidents just happen? Did you ever consider anything else? Like, *maybe* I got scared and ran away thinking, I was knocked up and maybe I got scared and just needed one night off from all the, the secrets and lies! The running around behind *everyone's* back. Do you even remember that it wasn't all fun all the time? That maybe I just took it too far and I fucked up? Maybe people try to wash the pain away but instead they just fucking die!"

Holy shit. She's crying. It's sick, but nothing could prevent my grin.

"What? Why the hell are you smiling?"

"Thank you."

She froze. Eyes twitching. Her tone dropped. "What?"

"You finally told me. It was an accident."

"I… You aren't supposed to…" She shook her head, short hair hanging, trying to hide her face. Only that long purple bit fell far enough. She chewed on it.

"So why couldn't I know?"

"Because it sucks. Because I've broken you. I can't stand hurting you any more."

"You didn't. Come here, fire girl. Please, come here."

She did. Then she sat closer. Then she buried into me. Her body trembled once. It's time to protect her again. Not from monsters downstairs, at the school, outside her bedroom. It's time to protect her— and Barry—from us. From me.

"Okay. Shhh. You were pregnant," I said. Thank god she's hiding in me, so I can speak without breaking down. "So your whole world got turned upside down. Again. You got scared. I can see how... how fear and panic might—"

"And exhaustion."

Oh.

"And exhaustion... I don't know why you didn't trust me. Because everyone would know what we did? But you couldn't predict how happy I'd have been. Yeah, I want it more than ever now. But back then, who knows?" My voice begins shaking. "It's so easy to forget that you were still a little girl. Twenties, yes, but... oh god I hope you know what I mean. I trust you do, Trace. I looked up to you. A strong, brilliant, mature... young woman. You survived so much. So much. A whole life of pain."

"I had you in the end." She digs her face into my lap.

I drape my hand over her hair. She shakes, sniffs. Tries to keep still. Note to self: even ghosts still cry.

"So," she wipes her eyes. "Do you feel better now?"

"No. You're right. As always. It's just as horrible as suicide," I cradled her. Actually, it's worse. She didn't want to die. My tears slid down to her. She started to wipe them away, but I had to push her back, twisting away to the darkness. "But at least I finally know. I can actually mourn... shit. I didn't even realize..."

Then I protected her from my vomit.

A geyser of bile, beer, and badness. Coughing, gasping for air between bouts of dry heaving. Throat is a furnace. Blood vessels popping across my skin. Tracy rubbed my shoulders. A cool, solid mist from my goddess of flame. I can keep the sickness inside. I wiped myself clean with my forearm, then wiped my forearm in the grass, then sat back on the log.

"Tim, what's happened to us?"

"We died."

"I died."

"That's what I mean. Without you, there's no 'we'." We laid down across the log. I pulled her against me. "Screw the rules. I'm sure 'whatever doesn't exist that I can't comprehend' will forgive you. If it doesn't I'll kill it."

She laughed.

"Why didn't you tell me?"

She chewed her hair, and it occurred to me that this feels so normal for me, then for her it must... but she answered, "It's hard to remember. I know that sounds weird, but it's true. Everyone would know about us. Because I was going to tell you, I really was, after... Everyone was stupid. They'd never understand. They'd all blame you instead of me. That scared me. I remember confusion and panic. Honestly I was so screwed up that I even doubted how you'd react. Keeping another secret day after day, after day. I just needed one night off. One to myself, one to run away and rest. To forget it all and be numb. It was so fucking stupid. Tim, I wasn't perfect."

Wasn't.

"Well, that makes two of us." I forced the laugh.

It worked. She bit my shoulder. We knocked our heads together, and I wondered if there were evening vagrants nearby, listening, peeping, or if we were in some weird necro-sphere, or... She bit my shoulder again. Just as I went to give a nip back, lightning strikes. Of course! I know what I need to do. "Barry can never know."

"Barry can never know what?" She's leaning up on her elbows, wiping her at her face.

"Not just us. Everything. The accident. The baby."

"Tim, look at me," she demanded. This time, she almost has a glow about her, an azure shimmer. "It's been minutes. Minutes! Did you already forget how much secrets hurt?"

"No."

She's keeps staring, I feel ashamed, but not sure why. Thought I got it right. "Trace, if Barry knows that you and I were together, perhaps he wouldn't kill me. Maybe even still be my friend. But if he knew I got you pregnant? That I pushed you into an overdose... What do you think he'd do?" She's still eye-stabbing through me. "Some things can be forgiven, but once they're done, they can't be undone. And no answer ever really helps. You said so yourself. Why cause more pain for him?"

"That's a totally different thing. Honor among friends? Blood brothers? Shit, call it bros before hoes if you have to."

"Would you tell him?"

She chews on nothing. "Tim, do us all a favor and think about it. Before the storm hits."

"No, Tracy. I've thought about it. So much, you wouldn't even— well you *would* believe. I can't lose him too. I'm honoring his wish with the stupid books. But I'll be by his side for everything else. Always. Recovery. Therapy. Everything. Except Barry can't know the truth. Not just for me. For you, and for him. Barry's been strong enough to struggle on. I can't pull him back into this. And how would I even... I need to protect all of us," I said. "And even your mom. Good god, girl! In some twisted way, I'm even shielding *her*. Imagine if she found out—I'd wake up with a gun in my mouth! No doubt she'd skin me alive, then roll me in salt."

She didn't laugh. So we do nothing. But there's no time to waste. Must reel us back in. This time is too good to waste.

"Hey, Trace. I have another question."

"Oh, Jesus Christ!" Her body language betrays her words. She IS having a good time. "Fine, go ahead."

"What do you mean when you say you're watching me? Do you sit on a cloud with a harp and spy on me? Are you watching me all the time?"

"You wish." She kicked at me. I slapped her boot away, remembering the song of leather and flesh. "I'm not a voyeur. You're the pervert here."

"Hey, I'm just saying, sounds like you have a lot of, uh, omniscience, concerning my affairs. It's kind of creepy. And yes, kind of kinky."

She kicked at me again. Trying not to grin. Good.

"It's not seeing with eyes. It's more like constantly smelling someone's dreams. It's not so glamorous or pleasant. And I don't have to if I don't want to. And that's only when I exist, which is... No, there aren't even words for that."

"Well, I appreciate you... smelling me."

"Well, your breath ain't smelling so hot right now. Do you have any gum?"

"Have I ever? Sorry, but you're one to talk. You're dead."

"I'm not a zombie. You're the one who needs a shower and a toothbrush, stinky."

True, she doesn't smell. Like anything. I wouldn't care if she did. And she's getting better. This 'event' feels like it's finally not all about me. We press foreheads together, and I could swear it was years ago. Can't we fall into the past, when none of our nightmare future was true? When we just made love all night, on the beach, in our beds, out here in the ash, and glass, and dead wood. But we're not that lucky. I don't deserve it.

"So you don't, um, smell me when I'm taking a dump? Or, uh, taking care of my personal? I'm too shy to believe that. I'd clog up and explode."

"No, just when you're wallowing in self hatred and being a whiny bitch. Which is more often than you take care of yourself."

"I'm usually thinking of you."

"Usually. Nice," she said. "No, Tim, there aren't ghosts watching you jerk off."

"I don't believe you. You said it before, you're not an angel." I pressed against her. "You think this date violates most major religious codes?"

She leaned back, swiping a finger across my cheek. "This is not a date. It's a karmic intervention,"

"It can't be both?"

"Nope."

The moon sweeps over us, bathing our brief relief, but it also a reminder that, slowed or not, time is still passing. Now our faces are necking forward, so close I can hear the absence of her breath. What would happen if I kissed her?

"Don't even think about it."

"What?"

"Kissing me! You creep. Gross." She slapped my shoulder.

"Goodness, my lady! Perish the thought, I wouldn't dare!"

"Sure you wouldn't," she says, all smiles now, her mouth, her eyes, that cheshire grin and her body pressing against mine. "Why, heaven forbid, good sir! Think of the consequences! Life and death locked in passion? Why, our very union could tear apart the thin veil of existence itself!"

"That's hot."

"Oh, you're *so brave*, Mr. Dune! But what if we violate the space-time continuum, or shatter the silver divide? We might flood the Earth with the desperate undead! Leave humanity prey to ancient, bound spirits. We could be the end of everything for just one kiss!"

"Would you believe me if I said it's worth it?" I put my knees up on the log, began leaning over her slowly, as she arched back below.

"For the record, Timothy, yes, I believe you'd doom everyone just to—"

I kissed her.

She tastes like a cloud, heavy with spring rain. We pull apart. Slow. Eyes locked. I kiss her again. Cup the back of her neck. But before I push further, I see her face. I'm a good kisser, but not that good. No, that shrinking flicker in her eyes... Oh crap. She's remembering life. The curse, violating all I love. Quick, asshole, save her! Make her laugh, somehow—

"Wow! I just kissed a ghost!"

"Wow. I am a ghost. But you taste like the dead one."

"Sorry. Been a weird night, to say the least. So, can I tell my friends?"

"You really want to risk that?" She laughed. Phew. Crisis averted. "They think you're crazy enough as it is."

"That's not a big concern right now. And Jay would probably get off on it."

"Yeah." She leans in again but stops.

"Well, Tracy Cameron, it seems we did not destroy the world. So if we can make out, then, we can probably, you know..."

"Seriously? I'm here to save your life and you want to fuck me? Tim... I really am a dead... I'm not... I'm gone."

"It's not like I dug you up."

She slapped me so lovingly. We're laughing through gloom yet again. Then a shadow slides over her. That moon. Time. Nothing ever ends. But nothing is forever, either. Feeling drained again. If you peeled back my skin you'd find wet, rotted wood. My eyes are hot and wet. Hers seem to shimmer, too.

Bit my lip. It bled. Just a dot.

"I feel so much better, except that I don't. But at least now I know. It's truly a relief, you have no idea. All these years, thinking you could possibly have wanted to die..."

"Sir, you have permission to feel better and shitty at the same time."

"Thank you, ma'am."

"You're not going to do something stupid now, are you? If that's the case, I'd rather you believe this is just a psychotic drug trip."

"What, like kill myself? No. And no offense, but I'm too angry to let the world get away without having to deal with me for as long as possible."

She rubbed her head across my chest. "You sound like my Tim. Go make me proud. Figure it out. Become the guy that I stole t-shirts from to stuff my pillows. Then... then move on."

Wait a minute... "Does that mean you can also?"

She shook her head.

It makes sense, though. Her choosing tonight. It's been strange enough already, explosions and mutant lizards, drugs, cops, and the living dead. But there's something more. What did that Sergio guy say about devils running and people being jewels? Such a strange beast of a night, and far from over...

"All that, plus the whole kissing me thing. You just made out with a dead girl, babe. Chew that one over."

"True. Now I'm a cursed-samurai-delivery-boy-necrophiliac."

"Seriously, if you actually pull your shit together, when you look back on all these years, they'll seem so short." She lifted my chin with her knuckles. "You are not poison. My one hope is that you'll do the right thing. And you'll stop being afraid to fall in love again. The best way to honor me, to honor us... is for you to just live. Earn the life you deserve. Please."

The moon's eerie shadows slide by.

"Why does this feel like an ending?" The tightrope snaps. I cry. Quietly.

"Babe?"

The stars are moving too. Streaking back into position like meteor tails. She's trying to push me forward, but the brutal truth of it all is too true and too brutal.

I look up to her. "It's going to be worse now, isn't it?"

"Probably. But... it was totally worth it. Right, babe?"

"Absolutely." I've never been more sure of anything in my life.

We sit together, staring at that one trail that leads to the open field before her house. I'll start with that. Just walking down that path and keeping my word.

"Don't just keep your word," she said. She sounds sleepy. "You always could handle anything, Tim. I wish that... I wish I'd remembered that when it counted most. Can you forgive me?"

"No. No, I can't forgive you."

200

"Why not?"

"Because there's nothing to forgive. I just I wish you'd remembered it too." I brush her hair back. I brush the piercings running up her ear. My hellfire cat. Is the world really shimmering, or is it just the tears?

She's smiling, of course, but something in her lips, her eyes, even her hair, is so distant. We both look up to that beautiful full moon, that glowing graveyard.

"You know, I almost told Barry about us? Right before the accident. Man, in some horrible way, I'm glad I couldn't. Would have made things even worse. I know what I have to do now."

She hangs her head, and I swear she whispers 'I tried', but it was only the wind.

"I hope you do. Fuck, I really hope you... Tim, you have to go."

"Why does this feel like an ending?"

She won't look at me.

"Hey? Hey," I shake her gently. "Are we... Are we breaking up?"

"We've been apart for years."

"Are you dumping me?"

Her laugh brings snot bubbles and quick eye wipes. She blinks too much before looking me in the eye. But she smiles, but not really.

"You're not coming back, are you?"

She shakes her head.

We sit side by side. Facing the trail that goes to that heart of darkness where the Camerons' home awaits. With the past dripping from the walls and screams of fear and joy creaking under every floorboard. Where her Medusa mother and her brilliant brother's treasures await me.

"Tracy?"

"Yeah?"

"Life sucks."

"Yes, babe. Life does suck."

Just savor this. Stare down that trail and don't think about the future. Just sit here with her and don't say something stupid. Just... lean on her, like you should. With my eyes still locked on the path ahead, I drop my head toward her shoulder.

I fall off the log. Face slams into ash.

Try scrambling to my feet, stumbling, slipping. Manage to stand. But I'm spinning, desperately searching for her. Shadows. Stomach acid. Heart beating like an icepick cracking my ribs. Like a puppet, some cosmic beast cuts my strings, and I collapse. Skull bounces off of the log. Sprawled out by the cold fire pit, in dirt and trash. Staring at broken glass just inches from my wrists. The summer night is freezing and all the insects are screaming.

Another sound pierces the darkness. An unearthly wail, something horrid and alien. The sound turns me to ice, shaking beyond fear. What is that awful, alien screech?

Then my throat seizes shut, and the sound is gone.

So cold. Wasn't there a fire? Shivering, but sweating.

I try rising, just onto my knees, only to fall again, nearly catching my eye on half a bottle. I'd managed to stop screaming, but the snot and tears are still dripping out. Try again. I can barely move, pushing my limbs as if I've been shot, pushing at ash, glass, cigarette butts, dirt, and bugs. A grasshopper leaps onto my head, then hops away. A beetle watches. Wait...

There's something else watching. Just beyond the trees. I flail onto my back, Kitsune now in hand. The bushes shuffle. There. I stare into its eyes. Where once the orange eyes held a black cat's pupil, there's only milky white. Vulpus vulpus. I know you. I reach out, fingers twitching like road-kill. The fox doesn't move at all. Just stares. The world says you're gone. But I can keep your secret, I swear.

Please help me.

It's gone before I blink.

The forest bursts back into life. The insects buzzing, frogs croaking, birds singing. The bugs, they're so loud. The leaves scratching in the wind, the creaks and moans and howls of the empty sky.

Using Kitsune as a cane, I slowly get to my hands and knees, still shaking. Blood sugar gone. Staring at the cold pit. The cold moon. The cold logs, cold gods. The smell of indifferent nature, pine and shit, dead flames and pollen.

Finally standing, resting both hands on Kitsune, bent over, coughing, losing fluid from every tiny wound. They add up, wasting me away bit by bit by bit. I make it to the trail, the edge of the fire pit, limping all the way. About to leave my sanctuary. Go. Don't look back.

Kitsune drags through the dirt as I lurch down the trail to their house, an inch at a time. Arms limp, branches pushed aside by my hollowed form. Scrapes, rips, sap, blood, and spit form new war paint on my face.

Almost there. Their house. The books. My word. More secrets to carry. Secrets hurt so much, she said. I can hurt for them, if I must. And so, like a zombie, I go. Shuffle. Trip. Shuffle. Trip. Leaking. Trying to rally, chanting whispers despite a sandpapered throat.

Alonse. Tulta munille. Namu amida butsu, and on, and on, and on, anon. Tonight would be a good death.

All that tough bullshit.

She scared the shit of me.

She still thinks I can handle anything. Her Tim did. I'm not him now. I felt like him, at the end. But the truth is that now I just look like him, weaker, bitter, the one who spit in the Curse's face. They cursed me for nothing. They took her away. Gave her *back* and then took her away again! She believes I still have a chance, but I've been too close to heaven to ever be me again.

Still running on nightmare-fuel, despite it's mostly fumes. Need... food. And water. Can't ignore the absence. How long—but there it is! The tip of the Cameron estate's ivory shingled roof, peeking over the tree-line!

It's clear now. I will survive Julio's mission and Boil's madness. I will get to Hawkhouse Hospital. But I will not tell Barry the truth. The truth only feeds our pain. If anything, I can protect Barry from further pain. That's what you wanted, Tracy? Right? I'm blasted by wind far too cold for August air. Only winter seas are this cold. It's not air, it's knives slashing by, cutting the intangible inside.

Tracy freed me from the invisible layer of armor holding me down. But it's coming back. Gauntlets, breastplate, greaves, helmet and all, pulled by the pain magnet. Invisible weight. Meant to protect, yet sealing in my toxic insides. Nervous system radiating neon green, rotten yellow bones, and old gray matter fusing together deep inside. There's only so much of this I can blame on Julio's drug. Even I know that.

I continue toward their home, acid churning inside, feeling a desperate need to evacuate from every end. Not looking forward to seeing Helena, especially in this state. Maybe I should risk breaking in?

Stupid. Just like the other night. The drive home... Good god, I nearly told Barry the truth! But the Curse struck first. Now the truth is worse than ever. I can't tell him. Imagine that conversation!

"Hey, Barry. Are you feeling better, bro? Good. Oh, guess what? I fucked your little sister for years. It turns out that she really was pregnant. Mine, of course. It

drove her to that overdose. Yup, she didn't kill herself after all. Great news, huh? Oh, here's your books. "

Her death was an accident, and I can't even give him that little peace, not without killing him with the rest. Just that piece, for that peace...

Just... What an ugly word. No. Barry must never know. More tears cascade down my face, tracing a path down my neck to my chest. Still? When does it end?

Tracy, I forgot to ask.

When do we run out of tears?

BOOK TWO:
The Devils Run

Helena Cameron:
The Sarcophagus Queen

Any further delay is likely to bring misfortune.

I'm standing outside the Camerons' tusk-white home, feet planted firm as a gunslinger in the shadows, unclear of how much time has passed. It seems the moon is in relatively the same position, but I'm just telling myself that. There's no proof, no reason to trust my mind. Not after what just happened back there... Or didn't happen. Can't trust anything. But I fall to one knee, bowing to this temple still standing in the heart of our woods like the scab of a comet's crater. To the garden snakes, it must seem I'm being knighted with my sword. I feel like one, after all that's happened these past few... hours?

I lay down, for just a moment. My eyes close on their own accord. Just resting, not hesitating. I swear. The grass is cool. As soothing as a lover's hand against a fever. Running on empty. Despite what she said, I can't handle this.

Barry's in the hospital. Bernard abandoned us to go gallivanting with some lawyer. Julio, the genius psychopath and my only hope, is setting up a shady deal with my nemesis, the predator Lucas Boil. This is a heavy dose for just one knight. And on top of all *that*, I've spent most of the night being poisoned, puking, crying, bleeding, knocked out, beaten, bashed, drugged, and generally just freaking the fuck out. I'm constantly slipping in and out of delirium, and I don't know how much of that I can blame on the drugs. And the kicker, seeing Tracy. Or thinking I did. Either way, it was so painful and so awesome. That alone made this night the best of the worst nights in my life. And there have been many worst nights.

Get up, Tim! This night is far from over.

Straight ahead, their dilapidated, once ivory, three-floor home beckons. Gleaming against the abyss of pitch black encircling it. Just like a skull in the shadows. A poorly drawn skull. Fitting, to come stumbling out of the trails, panicked and ashamed, and then find myself face to face with *that*. The bony fortress hiding a faux-Botox-Queen. The ageless vampire, Helena Cameron!

Helena's distain for me is well documented, regardless of her actually stating any *reasons* why. At least to my face. Don't care. Can't care. Need to get in there. Boy oh boy, will she be shocked to see me. But at least the thought of seeing Barry's insipid, arrogant mother dries my eyes.

This won't be a fun surprise. But things are different, now. If she tore into my chest, split apart my skin, straight down to the web of nerves, the veiny vines, rending and tearing a path to crack my sternum apart like a butterfly crab, she'd find no heart to mock inside. Just a rolling black cloud of silent thunder. But if she was feeling *really* mean and hugged me instead… I'd run like a gazelle, praying for rain to hide both my tracks and the tears.

Run and hide. The Dune way.

I'm still hiding in the shadows. Seconds away from the home, the books. Paralysis or shock, or cowardice, call it what you will. But there's so much light ahead. Light streaming from the windows, the front door, back door, the second floor. Spotlights, everywhere. The house is alone, neighbor-less. Vulnerable and shining, at the end of a long, criminal friendly driveway. Perfect setting for a murder. Not that I'm considering one, just finding a human emotion within Helena. Something to relate to. Fear. But it's still it's far too much light for that one lonely, wasted, bitter bitch. Hard to believe she fears anything at all by now. After all she's seen… after all she's done to barricade her heart until it's numb. She still despises me, and inspires no love on my part.

For a brief moment, the sky flickers, as if tuned to a dead channel. I feel the flicker, like one last shot of ecstasy before coming down. Always coming down, realizing what I just ran away from, and what I'm now running to. Need to believe it was real, need to believe I can handle what lies ahead.

Dead-locked between the ancient twin spirits, logic and belief.

Faith. So easily mocked from behind my cynical bars. Almost feel bad for making fun of religions, now. Well, in a carpet bombing way. I can see why some believe, why they *need to believe*. Because it's so terrifying to have nothing. Yet the extremes are… wasting time on this, delaying. Extremely paralyzed at the cusp of actually getting something done.

New tactic needed. Perhaps I'll find perspective by finding some miniscule, acceptable in-between. Use logic to believe. Yes, faith via science! The way of Barry Cameron. Sound of mind and body, but bat-shit crazy in his own manner. Swallowing my pride, I try chanting Barry's favorite mantra: *Reality is subjective perception.* Three times feels just right, more than enough… Barry says that shit every single chance he can possibly get. Especially when high. But I must admit, it does dissolve my apprehension to indulge in faith. Faith that it was all real. She was real. Yes, the cocky way of Barry Cameron is right. I need it to be right. Because I can't look back, can't go back down that trail. Just relish what was, rise above greed, fear, pride, and embrace the unknown sins to come.

I puke on their lawn.

Yup, Julio's drugs may still be circulating, treating my weakened form like some biological amusement park. I puke on my puke. But less, at least. Don't need to clean it, either. It's just grass. Verdant, dark grass, manicured by underpaid illegal immigrants. More victims of this place, a great white shark feeding on any unfortunate to simply be smaller. Helena won't know that I fouled her grounds until dawn, might even blame her underpaid army. But she needs no excuse to piss on my soul.

No, quit stalling, Tim! Put Barry first, you idiot. Do whatever must be done. If you can't go knock on the front door like a man, then climb up back, into Tracy's old room. Sneak in and out! Helena will be too drunk to notice. Yeah! Yeah, that's healthy…

Do it, face her, endure her slights and arrows. The scorpion king's stings don't matter, you're already poisoned. And alive. You bear the badges of battle, both body and soul. Flesh sings a symphony of rug burns and dead ash, humming cuts and scrapes. The true wounds burn inside. Hidden. So quit moaning, quit hiding.

Just hope I don't look the same as I feel, guts turned inside out and drying like acid. Spine needs an oil lube. Man, I could sleep on this lawn for a thousand years. Sleep now, for the waking world does not forgive, and you were never bred to survive. Awake, and Hail the Kingdom of Fear. When the sun rises and you'll forget just enough. But I'm a slave to the moon, and the longer we live beneath that cosmic pearl sphere of graves, the older and colder we become, we focus more on who is dead and gone, rather than still with us. And the sun rises and you get just a bit better. And it falls, and just when you're at your best, where Barry thinks he is now, the memories crush your heart. You realize that all those days you managed to live without her were just a beautiful, delicate illusion. Time to start over. Worse now. Swimming up from a deeper abyss. Feeling the cold in sunlight. The absence of life in wind. Hearing the whispers barely beyond the gray veil.

Okay, maybe I'm not fully sober. But there is a mission to finish. I stand. Rubbed my forehead, squished my eyes, making sure no dirt stuck to the lashes. Looked around. Lightning bugs mate with stars. Branches barely cover the night sky. End of the woods. So far from the fire pit. On the rolling lawn before the Cameron estate, waiting for me across the open, tree-free lawn. Barry's books inside. No cover from here to there.

My first objective. A possible win. Go seize it!

It's been three years since I've actually seen this house that I half grew up in. Strange how it just looks... the same. I crouched on the tree-lined boundary, scanning the pool, where Tracy once swam. Then she would lie on the grainy tiles, the sun smiling down, with the grass in the cracks tickling her wet skin, letting the natural world dry her back. Once in a while, Barry would catch me catching myself gazing despondently. So I would turn to him and say something poetic or stupid.

And there's the yellow, moldy fence. Many years before we came together, when she was still just my best friend's little sister, I ate some shrooms alone. A secret experiment, while following the gang around all night. When we crept up the driveway to Barry and Tracy's house, I hallucinated a man made of logs, sprinting beside that fence, vanishing through the sliding doors behind the pool. When my friends all turned and pointed to the doors, gasping with *"Oh shit!"* and *"Did you just see someone go in there?"* I had a panic attack, then passed out on this very lawn. They rushed inside and found no one.

The same porch light glows above their circular driveway. Running along the grass just behind the driveway was a low voltage electric fence, built to keep the neighbor's horses at bay. When we were eleven, Barry and I held Bernard's hand while he peed on the fence. We weren't sick, just testing a theory. We were scientists when young. While youth and ignorance still equaled bravery.

Haven't been brave in years. I checked the trail behind me, just one more time. Nothing. No ghosts. No animals stirring in the foliage. No insects chewing on leaves. A dull red thing scampers by, but it could have been brown. Regardless, the ankle tattoo burns anew. Shouldn't be wearing shorts, need to...

No, stop it, Tim. You're slipping back into that vile trip.

Even with the first objective so close, I don't think I ever fully believed I'd cross the glass chasm and make it here. Yet here I am. Still crippled by the strange jealous anger of Tracy dying without me being there. Hiding from her wake, absent from her funeral. Yet I take a filthy pride in knowing the truth. That I'm inextricable from it all.

Now, time to face Helena, get the books, and get the hell out. I bit my hand, hoping pain could summon more sobriety. Before I know it, I'm at the front door.

It was once pure white. The three-story rodeo-era house swayed back and forth as I fought the influence of Julio's devil drug. Forget about what you just saw. Forget about what's ahead. Just go in. Get those goddamn Byron J. Brick books and get the hell out.

I caught my reflection in the window. Such a mess. Dozens of tiny scrapes, rips in my clothing and skin, bits of scab and blood and bruised up shins. My stupid jail style tattoo probably getting infected under the bandage, while dragging around my stupid sword. Stupid, stupid, stupid.

I hid Kitsune in the porch pillar's shadows. Placing her gently, praying I wouldn't need her when facing Helena Cameron. Oh for fuck's sake, Tim, what kind of thought is that? Yeah, she may choke you to death just for showing up. But didn't she impose the same sudden intrusion on you not so long ago, when she was too blitzed on painkillers and wine to go to Brooklyn? To go pick up her own son? Hell, it's her fault I have no car now, her fault that he's... No. Fair is fair. Should it actually come to blows against my best friend's mother, I won't dare sink so low as to use the sword. But I'll bite.

"Namu amida butsu, Kitsune," I whispered. Yes, I kissed the sheath. Then I crossed myself just in case. Hey, you never know.

Knocked on the door softly. Waited. Nothing. Knocked a bit louder. Pressed my ear to the door. No footsteps, no sounds at all. Knocked again. Every light in the house is on. Is she playing games with me? Finally, I slammed my fist on it.

Starving incestuous gods were stacking the odds against this night from the start. They still are, cheating unknowable bastards! It's annoying, not knowing if the game is fixed. But it's infuriating to not even know the. Fate wants to play chess? Fine, I'll play checkers. No retreat!

I banged repeatedly.

A slow, steady, beat. *Bam*. I'm. *Bam*. Not. *Bam*. Leaving. *BAM*. Open. *Bam*! OPEN!

BAM BAM BAM!

Brave fist banging, I nearly bopped her nose when the door tore open. I took baby steps back. The plastic renegade wrinkles on her face twisted toward her nose.

"Oh! Sorry, um…Ha, hello, Helena."

"Timothy? Fantastic. You look like you were hit by a car. And dragged here."

"Funny, since I don't have one anymore. No thanks to you."

"Right. What do you want, Timothy?"

"It's my turn for a favor Hel—Ms. Cameron. I'm going to see Barry, and he asked me to bring some things with me."

"You should have called. Oh, that's right. You don't have a phone. Unlike the rest of the human race." She continued to stare, then finally turned her back and stepped inside. "Very well. Make it quick. I'm busy."

She was in a pastel blue nightgown that whipped like a vampire's cape as she turned away. Would the sight of my blood inspire some insatiable lust in this sad monster? Terrible. Yet somehow she and her infernal mate spawned my two favorite people. So I followed, painfully aware of how loud my steps echoed through the empty house, compared to the quick patter of her bare feet.

"Why, what's the hurry, Ms. Cameron? Do you have company?"

She vanished around a corner. "I do now, unfortunately."

I passed into the orange hallway and drank in the nostalgia. The old Pear 2GS Computer in the study, off to the right. Where we once waited fifty minutes for a grainy shot of boobs, back in the days before the Internet was just another utility, like water. Why hadn't she replaced this relic? As we aged and the Internet got faster, midnight rendezvous with the Pear also opened our eyes to bestiality, golden-showers, and all manners of sadism. As noted before, we once were as brave, naïve scientists, pumped with curiosity and feverish hormones.

More relics, unchanged since we ripped her vile husband out of this place. Forever. For which all but I was thanked. Well, *by her* at least. Jesus, this is morbid. Everything is the same. Barry lived here for quite a while after we lost Tracy. Refused to leave his mother alone. Good man. But nothing's changed. There are still scratched leather couches, same ones that sprawled across the living room, just visible around the bend. The liquor cabinet Julio would raid, just beneath the facing staircase. Directly below Tracy's room. Our skills in espionage blossomed under the mystic call of the whiskey shelf, watering it down when we realized we'd drank too much.

"You're a mess," Helena said. It was just a statement. No concern. She vanished back into the kitchen.

"I'm okay." I touched the bumps hidden in my hair. Barely bleeding.

I followed her in and stared out the sliding glass doors, finding the exact spot I had been lying in moments before. Had she seen me? Waiting as I wiggled about the lawn, wildly hallucinating? The lion queen debating the safety of her den, amused, watching me the whole time? Considering calling the police on the young man thrashing on her perfect grass? Curious? Fearful? Lustful? Woah now, what—no, no. Bad thoughts. It's the drug! Yes, the drug…

"Excuse me?" Her question held enough pause that I assumed whatever I'd said wasn't clear enough to damn me.

"You're excused. Ouch."

Her arched brows and needle-point eyes did not waver. "Are you sure you're—"

"No really, I'm fine. It's just a gash." Then I noticed some blood on my finger tips.

"Your standard of fine has always been lacking, Timothy."

She handed me a paper towel and let me dab my sweaty hair. While I looked her in the eye. Like stones. Slowly eroding stones. I dropped the paper towel on her counter. Just a bit of brown and red on it.

"Thanks."

"Mmm, yes. So, Timothy. Are you really going to see my son? I figured you'd have found some excuse to flake out by now."

"When I tell Barry I'll be there, I actually show up. Unlike you."

She spit in the sink. She plucked a cigarette from the table and lit it. She left it pinched between her lips, bobbing and flaring with her breath as she leaned cross-armed on the kitchen counter. Just like Julio.

I had to admire her for a moment. She had Barry while still so young, and Tracy just a scarce six or so years later. The small benefits of such a mistake were evident in the continued contour of her hips, the curve of her chest and the smoothness of her skin. Her red hair flowed effortlessly about her shoulders and around the nape of her neck. Good god, she must have been… Shit, she when she got knocked up, she must've been way younger than we are *now*. Despite our mutual dislike, must give credit where it's due. Helena is still a MILF.

"I'm a… a milk? What does that mean?"

Oh, fuck. Divert, ignore, you have no reputation to save. "Barry has some books somewhere. Brick novels? Want to fetch—um, find them for me?"

Her eyelid twitched.

For a moment I entertained asking her for a ride to Hawkhouse Hospital, then immediately thought better of it. No way I could take an hour and a half ride with her, sweating nervously in the passenger seat and pretending to be sympathetic. Or I'd probably have to drive, since she was likely already halfway through a bottle of white wine, oxyvicodins, and fifty-milligram para-percodans. Like every other night. Hence her not even picking up her own son on the anniversary that her daughter died. Hence her sitting here alone. Hence all the lights, filling an empty, hidden house. Hence…

For a moment I felt sorry for her. Okay, now this hellish drug's potency is confirmed. I'm hitting the second tidal wave. Hanging on like a hermit crab pinching your cuticle. One of the big ones. Size of a baseball. It happened to me once. Hurts real bad, I swear. It's like an aquatic vice. My stomach feels like an ant farm. Why can't I feel my tongue? No matter. Just. Try. To talk.

"Come on me. All I, need are… I just need b-b-b—" Boobs danced on my tongue. Damn it, don't say boobs! Oh, but she does have a rack. Ah, fuck you, Julio! He warned me about Elvis, the sex drive, and the bowel disruption. This isn't funny anymore. "I just need some b-b-booooooo-ks."

She arched her brow. Small wonder it's not frozen that way.

"Well, they're probably up in the attic with all his other junk," Helena said. Her weight shifted, her hips cocked out to the side. A living hourglass, determined to never crack.

"Great! I just need to boob your tits."

Mouth agape, she can't even speak. But her hand is inching toward the kitchen knives. OKAY, play it cool. You are really losing it, buddy. Only one recourse here. Make *her* the crazy one.

"What's your problem, Helena? Are you *deaf*? Why are they in the *attic*? You just couldn't bear to leave all his belongings in his room?"

"Because he moved out," she snapped. "Why do you still talk like that?"

"Talk like what?"

"Saying 'his belongings' instead of 'his stuff'," she said. "Or shit. Or things. Why don't you talk like a normal person? Half the time you speak gibberish. The rest is stuck up, pretentious bullshit."

I wanted to proudly declare that I was not a normal person. But... no. No, if I had any real spark at all, I'd just slap her. Then maybe indulge the subtext beneath her anger. Her obvious attraction to me. Yes, have my way with her on the kitchen floor, right then and there. Leave her panting and wrecked. That's what Julio would do. Of course he'd finish off her pills and booze too. But he'd bend her over that gleaming counter and plow right through her vampire cape.

"Excuse me?" Helena snarled, her eyes wide in disbelief. She leaned forward and dropped her arms. "I must be extremely drunk. What the *fuck* did you just say?"

"What?" I said, stammering, feeling like a rat died on the roof of my mouth. Can't convince her that she's crazy. Need to end this fast. "I didn't say anything. Yes, you are extremely drunk!"

"Don't act like you don't know. You said something under your breath!" Helena's fingers reached forward, accusing, sharp. "Something about having your way with Julio on my counter."

Um...

"Look, look, look. I'm sorry," I said, shaking my head and backing toward the main hallway. "Haven't slept in a couple of days. Disoriented. I've been real worried about Barry and all. Stressful times. Must be hallucinating from all this."

"I'm sure," Helena said. She paused, looked, away, and then attacked. "Are you turning my son into a faggot?"

"Turning him into..." My awkwardly respectful fear of her whipped into anger. "What the hell kind of question is that? You ungrateful, homophobic—"

"I know what you're about, Timothy Dune. You're a lonely, pathetic, little boy. A loser, feeding off your betters! Just another sad user."

Note to self: Anger burns this chemical weapon out. I can function through fear if I just embrace rage. Counter vile with venom! Be nasty! Be Elvis!

But before I could say another word, she advanced with savage confidence. Like a sexy, female Lucas Boil. I backed into the hallway toward the staircase, watching Helena's reflection in the sliding doors creep closer. She marched forward, shoulders high, fists clenched, cigarette nearly bit in half. I climb the stairs slowly, cautiously, as if caught in the gaze of a tigress raring for savage blood sport.

"I'll just be a finite," I mumbled. Didn't dare turn my back as I ascended. She watched me creep backwards like a crab, gripping the railing and slipping every other step.

"You're not even making any sense. Are you on drugs, Timothy? Are you tripping out? Or nervous because... Damn you! I know your games!" she shouted, each word growing pregnant with bottled rage. "You wretched little... goddamn... *queer!*"

It was a gamble to turn my back, but I hurried up the stairs and snatched the latch to the attic. The stairs slid down like a sleeping giant's tongue, with fetid air to match its breath.

"Loser! Homo!"

She really is like Boil. Why does everyone always think I'm gay? And what's wrong with that? Just proof she wouldn't love her son, that's all. Monster. How was her daughter the exact opposite of this witch? Goddamnit, I should tell her that Tracy knew I wasn't... No, no ugly thoughts. No time for that. Wrong rage. I'm not a monster. I'm not a monster? I'm... thinking too much.

I crept up into the family's archival grounds, tasting the musky still air, hoping maybe it would clear my head a bit. No such luck. So hot up here. Hot, stagnant air breeds disgusting head viruses. The sooner I'm out of this wretched place, the better. It's like an ancient cathedral overrun with tributes to neo-fascist gangs and punk rock ghosts.

I began sifting through the avalanche of cardboard boxes with Barry's name scrawled on them. There were a lot of old clothes, ill fitting at any point in his life, plaid and polo, and comic books and action figures, belongings—excuse me—"shit"—like that. I found the elaborately decorated "incense box" that was once under his bed. Yes, it held incense, but it really housed a kaleidoscope of uppers, downers, hash, and plain old weed. I found half a bottle of snorelazen, the little anxiety killing wonder drug Barry used to slip me. These innocuous looking bastards are a real pinch in the 9-to-5 gulag. When I worked at Burger Don, I'd have to mix up a rather noxious brew every morning to power through the day. It consisted of half a cup of extra strength coffee, a quarter cup of orange juice, a splash of Crimson Bull, and one finely ground up snorelazen. Sometimes two. Maybe this will purge me of this poison? I popped a few in my mouth and swallowed via saliva.

"What the hell is taking you so long? Are you done yet?" Helena called up through the hatch.

"Spitting! Just a minute!"

Blasted warehouse in here.

A couple boxes later, I hit the jackpot. Barry's extensive Byron J. Brick collection. A smattering of pulp philosophy glittered before me. So many. Two different editions of *Looking Through A Dark Glass*, a hardcover *Maze of Alien Intrigue*, *The Lunar Clan Revolt*, *Psyche of the Spider Mother*, *Illicit Androids and Unruly Sheep*, the ill-received *Scott Too*, *Veronica the Human Hourglass*, *Sleep Walking In the Deadlands*, and my least favorite: the rare, highly coveted, limited edition printing of *Thank You Death Robot*.

There really was no telling which books he wanted, so I just snatched up three without looking. Next to that box was a tattered briefcase. Only one clasp locked properly. A rocket ship was carved into the side. Barry's stylish answer to the common college backpack.

I popped it open. Dust and spider sacks. I shook them out, banged the briefcase against the floor a few times, and threw some books in. It would hold. Briefcase now in hand, I descended through the hatchway in triumph. My feet hit the hallway floor, bursting with satisfaction.

First objective complete!

Mission update: Escape! Rendezvous with the maniac mercenaries!

There should be some kind of triumphant music playing, like I just found the secret treasure in The Legend of Ouroboros Part Six, or whatever that game was. I just remember it played in an endless loop and you couldn't beat it, the freakish thing having no true ending. Great soundtrack though. Ah, shut up and go!

But striding toward the stairs, I'm struck by a soft pink light, cutting across the hallway.

Had my brain simply blocked it out before? How could I not notice this eerie slice of light before? It came from Tracy's former bedroom. Door slightly ajar. The light from her pink panda bear lamp creeps out, washes everything in innocence. I creep in. Helena makes dramatic noises downstairs. Strange that she'd leave the light on in here. Did Helena turn it on? No, that's... that'd be nice of her.

"What the fuck is taking you so long?"

"I'm a jar..."

"What?"

I'm losing my tongue. But no matter. Right now I'm a tomb raider. This was my escape, my cave in the blizzard. Now it's a mausoleum. A pristine time warp to her final night. Tread softly. Disturb nothing. The riding crop hanging above her bed, the magazine posters pasted to the walls, the collection of knives scattered across her desk, the books piled high, the boots and belts and ancient stuffed animals. The scuff marks on the windowsill, from when I used to leap out in the dead of night. Hit the grass and roll, look back up for one more smile, maybe a flash of tits, then dart across the lawn into the shadows. To the fire pit. Snaking my way home.

Her bed… The sheets are splayed out, dripping onto the floor. No doubt, these subtle creases were left as her body was lifted out. I leaned down, gently placing my palms so they wouldn't disturb the shrine. I smelled the sheets. Strawberry sweat. This is wrong. The sheets wouldn't be this clean. When people die, they… Juices come. People… You can live with dignity; you can't die with it. That's all. So they were cleaned, then placed back here? And these imprints are manufactured. She pressed Tracy's imprint… Oh god, Helena. Oh, this isn't right. This is sick. Right below me, it's wet. Fresh.

I wiped my eyes and backed away. Idiot.

The room feels diagonal, falling through space. Memory and memoriam made form. Like the top horns of the pentagram, symbolizing the triumph of matter and duality over unity and spirituality.

Three years. Jesus. Not a speck of dust anywhere. Her panty drawer still open just a bit, and her journal most likely hidden inside. Pictures of her youth pasted across the mirror, from four to fourteen, then some boys, crushes, and then nothing after fifteen. All those photos, those phantom memories are left in me now. Sure, Barry and Helena know some of them. I don't know all, but I know much of the rest. Fucked up fake dead sheets aside, you'd swear Tracy walked out ten minutes ago. Helena the curator, keeper of the eternal flame. Queen of the living tomb, the dried womb with no pharaoh to lie beside. What pain must fuel her. How much pain must burn in that hateful heart? Helena, I'm sorry. I'm so, so sorry.

I place Barry's briefcase on the dresser, between a coliseum of pictures celebrating friends, rock star crushes cut from magazines, and some local high-school predators. Everywhere are the stickers, band posters, carefully ripped clothes, childhood toys, and manic pastel scrawlings on the wall. The black light posters that stood watch while we slept in secret. These relics betray the strange synergy of a beautiful human girl, a tortured, pressured product. Fuck. I'm so sorry.

Turned back and saw something awful. What she must have been planning to wear the next day. It was Tracy's favorite pair of pants, tossed over the beanbag in the corner. She wore them often. And the sweatshirt I bought for her birthday. The one she cut the sleeves off of. But the pants... I lifted the white khakis with one hand, tasting their well-worn dependability through my fingertips. Maybe not khaki, I'm ignorant of fashion, but they were... they *are* nice pants, something *fancy*. They were about my size, as Tracy liked wearing larger men's pants. I looked at my own torn black shorts. Covered in the new filth, blood and nature, spirit tracks, tears and fear. Then back at the white pants. My size.

Well, the night is getting colder... the ocean breeze and all... Julio's roofless Jeep...

"Oh good God, Timothy! What the FUCK are you doing?"

Helena stood in the doorway. Her cigarette dropped.

Admission is suicide and I'm out of options. I stumble with the words, wishing her face were a blank page for me to ponder and pound out the correct phrase at a proper pace. Instead, I stare at her breasts, a strategy sure to help. Her tits remind me of Kitsune, and I reflexively reach to my hip.

Where the fuck is it? Ah... the porch, behind the enemy. My shorts are on the floor, and I'm caught halfway in her daughter's pants. And you know what, fuck it. They're a perfect fit. My wallet and keys have already joined my hairy legs in calling them home. Whether she likes it or not, these white trousers are walking out with me.

Also, don't forget the briefcase. Grab it first. Slowly, so as not to arouse excitement.

This will require careful timing.

"I really don't know what to say," Helena said. "You've outdone yourself. This... this is unbelievable. This is beyond idiotic. It's *sick*."

"These are mine," I said. "I swear, I lent them to her!"

"No. I bought those for her birthday. You really are some piece of work. Get the hell out of my house! Pervert!"

She really didn't, I really am, and I really should.

"Please, Ms. Cameron. Helena. Please, let me keep them. I know it doesn't make sense, but I'm cold, and... And. You know, I'm Barry's best friend. Whatever you think of me, he thinks very highly of me. We might as well be family."

"Get out," she hissed. "You used to be… You've turned out to be a terribly disturbed young man."

Fine, let's throw down. I rested my hands on the dresser, back to her, staring up at the ceiling so my eyes wouldn't water.

"Look, I can see what you did for her. I can see it." Pointed at the bed. "I just need something to hang on to, you know? She was… I mean, I—"

"Timothy, don't." There was no edge to her voice now. "Please. Don't."

"I loved her like a little sister." I looked over my shoulder, accepting to be struck hard.

But she nodded, eyes stuck to the floor.

"So I'm going to take these books. And tell Barry you said hi. And you love him. And you're going to leave everything to me now, just like always, and you know what? That's okay. I'm not even going to ask for thanks. And I'm not asking your permission for these." I tugged the white pants on, slipped my feet back into my shoes.

She was leaning against the door frame, face hidden behind her arm. I squeezed past. I was halfway down the steps when I looked over my shoulder and added, "And believe it or not, your daughter thought very highly of me."

"Oh for god's sake, you little worm. Just get out."

She's right, I need to go, but I need validation. Need to clear out this ugly anger before I start lashing out crazy bullshit again. Lucky I haven't been killed or arrested yet.

"I'm a part of this, whether you like it or not!" I said, feeling red rush across my face. I flew down the steps, knees jerking out to the sides as the briefcase bounced above me. Reached the floor, just a few feet from the front door. "Who did you turn to when you were too wasted to pick up your son? Who, Helena? Who watched your daughter while you went on benders and didn't call home for days? Who helped rid your home of that evil beast you married? Me! Me, the filthy little animal! Whether you like it or not, we're bound by threads of cosmic fate!"

"Get out. Get the *fuck* out of my house, NOW!"

She's given too many attacks in short, hurried breaths. She'll either begin tearing up or have an orgasm at this rate.

Now at the front door, finally trusting my own words once more, I spin around on my heels, tip a hat that isn't there, and smile. In a quiet, measured, tone, I say, "Well, I believe I have everything I came for, madam. Thank you once more for the hospitality. I'll be taking my leave now."

"Yes you *will*," she said. Lit another cigarette. "It's been a pleasure as always, Timothy."

I stare into her deadly emerald eyes, the eyes of the abused and survived. It's not her fault she hates me. I feel strange. Hot and quick, blood ready to squeeze through my pores. My bowels clench. My teeth grind.

Oh. Shit. I can't leave yet.

"Um, on second thought, can I use the phone before I go?"

By the time I seized the kitchen phone, she was screaming that if I wasn't out in two seconds, she'd have the cops string me up by my balls.

The line is dead. Dead. Dead. Dead.

My core folds in on itself again. How? Why?

No matter. I forgot. There is no one to call now. Since I don't have a cellphone, I don't know Jay's number. He was my last, best, and only hope. I have no way to get in touch with him. That car chase... Please don't be in jail. Please let him make good on his word. Somehow. Come save me.

And fuck you, Bernard! Where are you? Deliver me from this foaming bitch! Give her a hard kiss and a devil's goodbye, and let us be on our way to our beloved friend! Of all the nights to indulge in his erratic, fanciful whims...

"It's been dead all night. A branch fell on a power line. I've been waiting for hours for the fucking phone company to fix it," Helena said behind me. "As you can see, I have quite enough going on without you bothering me."

"What about your cell phone? Can I use that?"

"I don't get reception out here. No one does. Now go! Go, go, GO!" She had her wine bottle in hand like a bludgeon.

I stride back to the front door, full of righteous indignation. I turn to give her another verbal joust, but I am arrested by a hot, evil squirt. No... Julio's words echo as the trickle of muddy shit coats my boxers. *Elvis got real horny before he shit himself.* Fuck you, Julio. Fuck you!

"FUCK YOU TOO!" Helena screamed. She grabbed an empty

bottle of chardonnay and fired at my face. Not a warning. I barely ducked in time.

The next thought I have is far from the front door. Kitsune gripped in my sweaty palms, the briefcase tucked tightly in my armpit, tiny bits of glass in my hair and shit in my boxers. Helena is laughing in short, sharp rasps as I worm my way down the long gravel driveway. Leaving her alone. Can't hear what she's shouting at this point. Don't care. Gave her what she wanted, as always. She's alone. All alone.

Ice Cream Shores

Down the driveway, around the bend, the neighbors' horses watch through gaps in the trees. I hurry past, eager to escape the mute judgment in their eyes. The trees are closing in overhead, a natural lightless tunnel, hidden from the full moon. The leaves are varied and beautiful, but I'm highly reluctant to use any to clean myself. My senses are as poisoned as the family of oaks, sumacs, and ivies that infest these woods. The last thing I need on top of all this is to exchange swamp-ass for an ass-rash.

Fatigue is clouding the most basic tasks. Need coffee to keep going, but… none… No. No caffeine, no cheeseburgers, no fuel. Nothing but ghosts, books, mud, and vengeful matriarchs out here. Nothing to eat. About to collapse in this pebbled driveway. Shit in my pants, toxin in my veins, and sticky all over. It's only natural to run out of steam. Where are you going? Where is Julio? What makes you think you'd even find him? Why keep fighting?

Just sloam it, babe, that's what she'd say. That was her word. For when I got all freaked out and needed a break. Sloaming. I created a deity for it. Drew a picture in my notebook and everything. The Great Sloam, sister deity to the Caffeind, and fellow exile of the Jubilant Grove. A beautiful beast of elegant sloth. Tri-headed cigars pinched between bejeweled teeth, gravy veins, and chandelier tits. Climb up its silken snow capped belly and nestle in the neck that smells of bee hives, laundry detergent, and Sunday mornings. Jelly! Sweet, sweet gleaming jelly oozing from buttery eyelashes!

That snorelazen might be kicking in, because for the first time in forever, sloaming seems possible. My heart is beating cool. I kneel down beside the little white rocks that they call a driveway. Yes, the grass poking through is just as soft, moist, and cool. The little bugs part for me. I can rest for just a minute. Even with shit pants. Yes, babe. I will sloam it. Just a bit.

The sky is beautiful, free of spirits, night rays and phantom kings. No risk of being run down here, as the driveway is long and twisting. A horse farm lies through the shrubs on the left. There's a very small, very private graveyard on the right. That's where she… I see the carved stone, the grave beyond the fence. I see that the clearing around it, immaculate in a sea of leaves.

Yeah, these anxiety meds haven't gone stale. That, or the other drug is wearing off. No matter now. I lay my head against the white fence and can't help but sink into memories again. Staring across to the other side, the electric one meant to keep horses at bay and young boys perpetually retarded. No, think about… think about something good, Tim. Something to rally.

Like the first time my uncomfortable role as a surrogate older brother became corrupted. We were alone, lying on the beach. It was a little weird, not being with her, not laying side by side on the beach. But when she so casually laid her head on me. Figured it was just total trust, and tried to forget, as she confessed that she was a nerd. Like me. Liked puzzles and difficult reading. Not school crap. Banned books, weird, arcane books. Philosophy, horror, history. All the same in the end. She didn't have any friends that appreciated her interest. Not surprising. So I told her how I would read alone on the beach, with the skyline like fluorescent ice cream and the sound of surf pounding. It got colder. She got closer. The ice cream skies melted. We settled in a deep groove we'd molded into the sand.

She didn't want sand in her hair. That's all. Wordlessly, her upper body inched over, and she laid her head on my chest. There was a heartbeat, both mine in her ear, but another in my mind, where platonic shifted to romantic and suddenly life didn't feel like something to endure, but a privilege to enjoy. It was that quick. Didn't matter whether the feeling was gestating for years, growing slowly as we both grew older, or if it was triggered the moment her knee slid up over mine. I gave in forever. Her touch like an ancient incantation from long forgotten tribes, the atoms of her skin swirling into the base of my skull, ravaging my brainstem. Like a benzedrine bath cascading down your spine, leaving every part of your body numb, like blue styrofoam soaked in sweat. Sleepy. Enchanted. Perfect dumb.

My eyes slipped off the page to stare at the top of her head, the line where her hair parted. She kept on reading. Little angel fuck. What innocuous lines she'd crossed. And in that moment, feeling her damp hair on my naked chest, I felt bigger. Thicker. I felt like everyone else looked. In that instant she gave me all I never knew was missing. It was like a drowsy adrenaline, injected right into my neck. And then I remembered how I read to her, when I babysat her a decade ago as a child.

I felt wrong and sick and just horrible all around. But at the time I didn't know, let alone dare dream, about how right *she* was feeling about me.

Because of her, text became more than an escape. It was a fix. We would read together, sometimes huddled on the winter shore, sometimes in the ultimate sanctity of her very bedroom, while Barry wrote one room over. Trusting. A perfect excuse for fingers to brush by accident as a page turned.

I thought it was all in my head, it was too good to be true, and often I was sick with shame as her breasts grew and she got tall, got hips, grew an identity that she carefully crafted and chose. The small town boys swarmed her. Everyone my age ignored me, or I ignored them. Either way, she became proud to read side by side with the older boy who couldn't catch a football or pick up any girls. I would never make the move. That wasn't in question, and not even because if I was wrong, I was dead. So I buried the idea, but not the bond. But a couple years later, she picked me. Those days... I never suspected those days were coming. Or finite.

Time is a motherfucker.

A horse screams, snapping me back to the present.

It's got to be late. Jesus, I'm so alone out in this driveway. In this town. A shrunken head thrown into the Euphrates and rotting. Sleep comes less often these days, and I never wake up fully assured that my identity wasn't just imprinted on a blank slate the night before. Never convinced that I'm older than a few brief, horrible moments. Who are these actors keeping me company? Whose nervous mouth is this, yawning in my chest, clouding all judgment and direction?

Come on, Tim! Rally! Get up! Stop sloaming! Just get to the road. Tie Kitsune to your pants, grab the case, and get marching. Forget the beach. There's a long way to go, and the first step is getting that thumb outstretched. Fancy as the hope may be, Jay may never return. Not a problem. Yet I can still feel Tracy's head on my chest, like when you hold your dead cat, wrapped in a blanket, so soft yet so firm, and you ache to feel that cold bundle squirm. So impossible, you know, but your heart does not. Maybe just this once? And you hope and hope even as you shovel dirt.

But I didn't follow her. I have the books.

Fueled by the awkward pride in surviving that kind of loss, I move. Before I know it, I'm back on the road, at the end of the Camerons' driveway, a mile or so from the trail I'd first entered. Back in the twilight empty public sphere. Nothing here, no cars, no lights save for the distant glow of Texan Bro to the east.

Something flashes at me from the west. Something big barreling down the road. I'm frozen by horrid recognition. I can smell coconut suntan oil, salt, and musk. Dead minnows. The Bahamian devil gods. Standard bearers for the Curse.

It's been bleeding me dry for years, and now the Curse has finally come to finish me off. The flash comes from a pair of blinding eyes. The eyes of a devil, storming out of the negative space and into our world. I'm done for. The devil lord of the ocean has come to devour all vestiges of my pathetic past. For most he's a shark, but not me. No. Not me. Here he comes, oh god, I can see it, a great stingray, screeching down from the sky!

For fuck's sake, man, get a hold of yourself! This is wrong! Fish don't live in the sky! It holds no authority here! You're in control now. Ah, but what if the sky is just a hole in the sea? Then… then… it's just another wicked hallucination. Must be. Regardless, I drop the briefcase against my leg and unsheathe Kitsune.

Okay, there's no doubt about it. The trees are glowing bright, and the beast is careening toward me. Strange that this monster is yellow… I'm about to be swallowed whole by a lunatic stingray god, and it's not even the right color? I'll be impaled on its harpoon tail and be swept away to that bottomless barren sea. Or worse, it's flying past to get Barry at the hospital, to snuff out another precious life that got too close to me. Leaving me even more alone. Unfit to even be acknowledged, trembling in my dead girlfriend's pants.

Seconds away now. Blinding light glinting from Kitsune. Tighten my grip. Better to die in battle, I suppose. If a good ghost can visit me, then why not a demonic sea monster? After all, she said time was running out… Too dizzy, blinded by its fiery golden eyes, the roaring shakes my bones. But instead of running back down the driveway, or diving into the foliage, I toss the briefcase aside and step right into its path. Sword before me. Trying to sound defiant, screaming like a loon.

"'Come on, you filthy beast! I'll split you from bone to core! Let's end this once and for all!"

Make Us Stranger

I assume the Pecking Scorpion style. Arm stretched up high, arced over my head with a blade hungry. Ready to meet fate with a steel song. I will strike down this Demon Ray and feast on its entrails. It shrieks, and oddly enough it sounds exactly like the mournful wail of a car horn mixed with tires burning to a halt. Street pebbles spray like shrapnel. The ray rumbles. Stinks like rubber too. Shielding my eyes, but the light's burning through my fingers. Can't see a damn thing. I sidestep around it, trying to flank its side for a fast cut... and see the shadow of a man. Does the counselor ride this eldritch beast?

"Yo! What's good, sexy?"

Julio?

"Come on, samurai! Get in!" He shouts over the engine.

I grab the briefcase, sheathe Kitsune, and try not to shake, taking my time to look cool while walking over. There are red smears dripping down the sides of the yellow Jeep, streaking it in—oh god.

This thing is covered in blood.

What did these monsters do to that cop? No, no, it was that weird lizard Boil wielded like a weapon. Julio's lips are pulled back in a tight grin, but I see tension swimming in his iris. Like Elvis, he can smell my fear, and it naturally puts him in attack mode. Boil is a hungry shadow behind him, just a glint of teeth.

"Perfect timing, huh?" Jay squints at me. "Shit, man. What happened? You're a fucking mess!" Julio holds his hand out. Something steaming in his palm. "Here. Drink this and get in."

Coffee! Hail the Caffeind!

"Julio, you rotten son of a bitch." I snatch the styrofoam cup. "What happened to me? You threw me out of a moving vehicle! And what the *fuck* did you drug me with? It could have killed me! Do you have any idea what I've been through?! I've been tripping balls all night! I saw... I had to face Barry's mom, and... and... Fuck you, man! This will not stand!"

"Easy, homes. I already told you, I tested it on Elvis, and *his* dose was twice as strong. I knew you could handle it. Hell, I thought it would feel good! Dude, chill! You never used to get pissed like this. Sorry, aight? I'm sorry. Now shut up and get in."

The coffee's scent rises, coating my nostrils in sticky brown relief. The caffeine hooks its fingernails into my ribs as I gulp the whole thing down. Bam. In my aortic valve. The pump. The awkward fear and longing of the Cameron estate slips away. Things seem clearer and brighter as my inner strength comes crackling back.

And just like that, it's gone.

One drug overtakes another. The buzz travels down my throat and burns out in a hot flash. Soon the motivation will creep away and leave the coffee to tear a new merciless path through my intestines. No quarter asked and none given. Just brace my asshole for the shock and use the energy while it lasts. Coffee is just dirty water. And gummy candies are made from horse bones. So what? All I can say is—

"For fuck's sake!" Boil snapped. "Get in the goddamn Jeep already."

I climb into the back. The reptiles hiss and shake inside their metal crates. I don't care if these guys are psychic psychos, hearing my thoughts. I don't care if I'm speaking out loud. I got the books. I got her touch. And the truth. I'm doing good. Just have to ride out their little deal in Tomahok, and then he'll bring me to Barry. Everything will be all right.

"Of course it will," Julio said. "No doubt. It's *all* good when we team up. When have we ever failed, son?"

Him and me, or him and Boil?

"Sounds like your baby's jealous." Boil spit on the roadside.

Who wouldn't be?

"Yeah, who wouldn't be?" Julio asked as he reached around Boil's headrest to look past me. He floors the gas, lets the Jeep fishtail, then he guns us in reverse down the twisting dark driveway, pebbles spitting upward. The horses snort and stomp in the distance. The Jeep explodes down the road, sliding into a drift, right into the proper lane. We tear down the street. Flush with moonlight, hot breeze and silence. Julio then takes his eye completely off the road and starts twiddling and twisting the radio, which hisses violently in protest.

"Jay, I'm thrilled to see you. But I can't help but notice you're not in jail. What happened?"

"With the pig? Ah, he was a friend. Not even one of my customers, just a buddy from back in the day." Julio is now smacking the radio and still not looking at the damn road. "I wasn't sweating it, I got most of them in my pocket anyway. They profit when I profit, so they cut me just enough slack, and I cut 'em in. But you remember that dude Tim?"

"I am Tim."

"The other Tim, not you," Boil said. "The cool one, from school. The one that's not a fucking lame, bitch-ass loser."

I don't know who that is. And I'm not whatever he said. But it's a common enough name, and I'm too relieved in general to give a shit.

"Well, turns out the other Tim's been a cop for years," Julio said. "He finally cornered us when I tried to pull down Sugar Drive. When he saw it was me, we both freaked. Like, good freaked. We had some laughs and split a beer. Dude actually enjoyed the chase. Said he's been bored as hell on this shift. Fucker still stuck it to me, though. Like, when it came time to bribe the bastard. But whatever. Boil covered half of it. S'all good."

Hold up. Odd… A local cop that Julio doesn't know? Let alone a classmate? The tides are changing for sure. That's beyond odd, and less than good.

"It *is* all good, bro. What's got you so tight?"

"No, it's not all good! You almost blew me up, then fucking drugged me, then threw me out of your Jeep! You abandoned me for hours after promising—"

"Actually, I tossed you out," Boil said. "And you're crazy light. Hit the gym sometime, you bag of bones."

"Dude, it's only been like an hour," Julio said as he punched the static-spewing radio. "You got whatever you needed at Barry's, right? And I swung back around to get you, just like I said. You know better than anyone, my word is bond. And I even stopped for coffee, you fuzzy little freak. So shut up for a second, drink it, and relax, aight?"

He was right. "Amazing. You magnificent bastard."

"Now let's really get this night rolling, amigos," Julio said. He nodded his head at my briefcase. "What's that shit?"

"This?" I lay the briefcase on Tracy's—my—pants. "It's a bomb."

"Perfect," he said. "We're gonna need another."

"What's that smell?" Boil sniffed around the back seat.

"Shit," Julio said. "Something totally smells like shit."

"Something smells exactly like shit. I will never forget that smell as long as I live," Boil said. "Fucking Iraq, whole goddamn country smells like flaming shit, day in and day out. Had to burn it in the street. Every god damned day in old barrels. Never forget it. You can't escape it! Shit,

shit, shit, shit. Bodies, bullets, blood, and *shit*."

"I'm sure you fit right in," I mumbled. And then squeaked out another wet fart. My face reddened. Going to have to take care of this soon.

"How could we smell it with the wind—" Boil whipped around. "It's you, isn't it? You're the shit!" His eyebrows meet. Face twists. Something weird is going on inside his head. Like an actual thought being born. He's staring at my crotch. A horrible grin spreads across his face, like a pederast running into a fondly remembered youth. "Looky, here, Julio. Timmy Poon got a makeover! Where'd you get those nice new pants?"

"Alright, come on. Poon? I know you're grasping for puns, but that's weak. Stick to whatever it is you're good at. Being a dickhead," I said, caffeinated with confidence.

"It's kinda funny," Julio said. He was finally ignoring the broken radio and driving like a normal human being.

"Dune. Poon. Like, getting poontang. It means pussy. Something you wouldn't know about, Timmy Poon. Except for being one."

"Very poetic, Boil."

"Well, I'm in such inspiring company," he said, waving his hand about.

"Why don't you leave the metaphors to me? You can regale us with some boot camp brainwashing songs if you must. Assuming you can even remember any."

"Whoa-ho-ho. This pussy has some bite!"

"Yeah, sometimes my man does," Jay said. "Better watch your back. But yo, for real, Tim. You got dragged across razors or something? You look busted as *fuck*. You got changed at Barry's?"

"Um, yeah, I was cold."

"Wait a sec. Those pants look..." Boil started.

The radio suddenly hissed like a snake.

"God fucking damn it!" Julio pounded the dashboard. He hit it harder and harder, but the snake could only hiss louder.

Bernard once told me that while a passenger, one should pay attention to the driver's music. It tells you a lot about what they're leaving unsaid. I must say, he impressed me with that insight. I repeated it to Barry, taking the credit for myself. So the hissing, the white noise, crackling static—

"Is driving me insane!" Jay shouts. Then he slowly reaches under the seat, still steering with his right hand. And he pulls out—oh lord—he pulls out his mean motherfucker of a .44 Magnum. A big steel dick. There's no denying it. And capable of dropping even bigger game. Punch a hole in a bear's head. My stomach turns.

Then Jay presses the barrel against the radio. Pulls the trigger. The roar drowns out the wind. Bits of metal and plastic shower us. Time freezes, we don't die, shrapnel passes, and time resumes. Not much to defrag this time. The dashboard now bears an unsalvageable wound. A booming gunshot is our driver's sweet song.

The blood pounds in my ears as the normal sounds of life start trickling back in. I'm still marveling that the blast didn't tear into the engine block and ignite us. Start shaking the bits of radio out of my hair. Glass and dirt and blood and plastic bits. I'm a walking collage.

"Luke! Marching songs! Start singing, pendejo!" Jay demands. He howls at the moon. "Come on, we need some music. The radio's shot!"

He's still laughing as Boil swats at his head.

Jeeeeesus fucking Christ. Are they still on drugs, too?

"Jay, seriously, my heart can't take much more of this." I'm gripping his head rest with bone-white fingers, yelling in his ear. His long hair, no longer tied back for some reason, whips into my eyes. Stings, as I plead, "You have no idea what I've just been through. I was running through the woods and then I saw something out in the trees. Something… Forget it. Then Helena got all crazy with me. I swear I thought she was going to rape me, feast on my bones. And then I had a panic attack out in the dark, alone… and now here's you two."

"Shit, I'd let that bitch rape *me*," Boil said. "What a piece of ass! Just like her daughter, what's her name… you know, the one that bit it?"

My teeth nearly broke against each other. I'm definitely sober now. I want to grab the back of his shaved head and slam it into the dashboard. Take Julio's Magnum and jam at the base of his skull and make him say her name before begging for forgiveness. And then still cock the hammer back and let—

"Chill, son. Tracy. Her name was Tracy," Julio said. "The poor girl died, man. Show some fucking respect. You should know better, soldier. That shit's just embarrassing."

Boil crossed his arms and slid down into his seat. "Just remember the soldier part."

Julio, I love you.

"I love you too," he laughed, driving with the gun still in his hand, pressed against the wheel and angled up toward the gods.

I stared at the chicken-scratch prison tattoos wrapping around Boil's biceps like sad, inbred-styled Sak Yant. My gaze is broken by another light tearing the darkness. A sick artificial light. A city-type light that hides stars.

We're headed back toward Texan Bro?

"Where the hell are we going?" I shout over the wind.

As he turns his head to respond, his wrist slackens and the .44 nonchalantly tips in my direction. "Gotta fill up before we hit Tomahok! That place is a madhouse, and the bastards rape you at the only gas station. End of the island and all that. And they damn well know it. God damned shame, your family got ran out, and those thieves didn't."

Oh.

Shit.

Hazy memories from earlier. Before being with her, it's a blur, but I do remember being there recently… Something with mobsters and dark magic and… wait a second. "Do we really have to go to Tomahok?"

"Yeah! No comprende? I thought you were smart," Julio sounds annoyed. "It won't take long. Just gotta drop off this shipment. I swear on my life, you'll get to Barry, even if I have to give you the keys and stay behind! Okay? Don't sweat it."

Wow. If he says it, he means it. Can't imagine why that'd happen, but yes, he is a noble beast. And he even came back with coffee. All hail Julio, El Dio de Diablos!

"Damn straight!" he shouts. "Let's be quick, boys. We'll grab some road sodas. And look, I have no problem going to see Barry, but this night was planned long before you showed up. Which is fucking great, by the way. There's nothing I love more than nearly blowing my buddy to pieces before a night of hard work!"

"Oh, that's just… muchos gracias, hombre," I say, slumping down and resting my head against a cool metal case. They hiss inside, so I pound on it. I know, little lizard lords, I know. I too, have a reptilian brain. But at least you're safe.

"Don't worry, baby. I'll protect you." Jay reached back and shook my knee. That hyena grin again.

"I'm starting to think you're a fag, too," Boil said to him. "You two seriously got something going?"

"Whatever, jealous bitch," Jay responds, and although he's joking there's a slight growl to his voice. "Don't you army guys shower naked and jerk each other off?"

I imagine Boil as more of the 'rape the locals' type.

Boil spins so fast that I shudder. Oh no—

"TIM! I can't fucking take it anymore!" Boil screams. He slams his fists on the dashboard. Little strips of Magnum-stripped plastic fly up. "You stinky little shit! Did you actually crap in your pants?"

Thank god the rape comment was in my head. Best be grateful and take responsibility for the smaller offense. "Yes, Lucas. You're right. I shit my pants."

He stares at me, dumbfounded, then turns back forward.

Silence.

Okay. Strange. All of this. This night. I almost like it. But something strikes me as off... A drug deal—excuse me—a *lizard* deal, out in Tomahok, eh? Fine. Boil smuggled them back, Jay had a connect to sell... No. No, Boil said he had the connection, so why is Jay involved at all? Well, it could be worse. Better off staying out of it, just like they want. After all, whatever does not kill us makes us stronger.

"It makes us stranger!" Jay shouted with both arms pumping skyward, and the Jeep coasting into the other lane.

I've survived stranger. For example, last fall I awoke swearing that my stomach lining burst and my liver leaked onto the rug. My mouth was sandpaper, and my tongue a pregnant worm. Everything stunk of old clams. Bernard was curled up in the far corner on top of his surfboard. Gray light trickled through the ratty blinds and danced on the back of his curly black hair. My cries for help fell on deaf ears. There's no moving a sleeping surfer. That's a fact you must face, even in the worst of times. The old clam smell faded, so I could enjoy our crowded pad's normal stench of sand, sweat, and salt. Still couldn't move, I felt caught, waiting for the hammer of doom, like a doped up bum found taking a dump inside an ATM vestibule. Turns out our malaise was the result of a special powder that Julio brewed up and gave to Bernard. When he finally woke, Burn confessed to using it as a spice for our meal of discount ramen, hoping to induce some chemical euphoria for dessert. Why Bernard would mix anything from Julio's nightmare lab into our food is beyond me, but the road to hell might be paved with friends strong enough—or stupid enough—to stick together just a bit too long.

God, aren't people our age married with children by now? Tracy, I couldn't blame you for hating me if I quit now. I'm lame. Life's not... maybe not horrific. But it sucks. Oh man, does it suck. This needs to end.

"You want a pill?" Julio asked me.

"NO. No more pills."

"Come on! At least now we know it won't kill ya!" He smiles, until my laser like glare burns it away.

"If you ever dose me again," I begin, "I swear to the old gods and the new, I'll cut you open from balls to brain."

He smiles again. Feebly. He means well. He must.

Texan Bro's Babylon tower sign is burning hot now. So close. And Jay's right. His stupid pill didn't kill me. And what happened out at the pit was strange, to put it lightly. But I'll never be sure just how big a role the pill played.

Did it put me in the right frame of mind, and I wandered into just the right place, in just the right state? Maybe the fire pit is an ironic Gateway to the Deadzone? Just so happens to rest above one of Earth's mysterious, precious Leylines? So maybe, thanks to Julio's chemical magic, I was able to tap into the source?

Maybe all of those. Maybe some.

Or none.

Just drugs breaking a broken man, triggering psychedelic post-traumatic stress. Nothing more, nothing less. But it doesn't matter. Not after peeking back-stage to see her. To hear, to hold and kiss her one more time. If nothing else, it was a moment with her, and I was happy. Already becoming another memory to piss and moan and pine for.

But she knows I can be stronger. She knows I can figure out how to stop the coming storm. The only thing I know is that I'm alive, she's dead, and Jay is right. Yet again.

Petting the sword in my lap, I mumble what he'd said before. "Whatever doesn't kill us makes us stranger."

"That's the spirit!" Julio looks back at me, grinning with those large yellow teeth. Eye not on the road, he speeds up while spinning the .44 in his hand. Then aims it at me. "Click, click, BANG! If tonight goes right, we're all gonna wake up really fucking strange!"

I'm starting to hope he's wrong.

Radiation Turned Me Into A Beautiful Unicorn

Conspiracies.

You're only paranoid if you're wrong.

Something's off. Not news, I know, but the bad feeling in my gut is growing like a nuclear ulcer, despite being as close to the toughest, nastiest, most loyal friend I have. It's not even Boil. It's the little things. Adding up. String the tiniest details together, and you end up with something larger, something too big and dark to hide in the shadows. And it's easier to sniff out the details once you're already in the conspiracies' shadow. This plan of theirs, the lizards, the mystery buyer, even the insistence on helping me, is a bit odd. And Julio being a diehard diamond solid friend being an odd factor, is the strangest thing of all. Am I still drugged? And yet...

"Your timing was strangely impeccable. What would you have done if I wasn't at the house?" I asked Jay, once he and his gun turned back to face the road.

"Left your ass in the dust," Boil said.

"I would've gone inside and got cool with Ms. C," Jay said. "I'd wait as long as I could, and trust you to show. No biggie. You *had* to get there, so I knew you would."

"But what if I didn't?"

"You said you'd do it. And you did. What's the problem?"

"Nothing, man. Forget it," I said.

Well that's a vote of confidence in my favor, and right now I need as many as possible. This feeling is nasty. For *something* is waiting in Tomahok, slumming, teeth gleaming, snoring soot and ash on the horizon. A nearer future than Hawkhouse.

Now, as Julio gunned his Jeep toward Texan Bro, the single vestige of civilization on this stretch, I felt the wave come crashing down inside. Julio's strange drug, the actual chemical aspect, not the effect on my mind, is FINALLY flushing out. You just know it when you feel it. Out of my brain, down my spine, organic highways they've left slick with sickness. There is always shame when coming down. No matter how happy the high, your body always finds a way of saying, *"Hey asshole, you tainted us! So if you want to play, now it's time to pay!"* Much like being caught jerking off to porn in your father's study, but then he asks to stay and watch. Which I swear never happened. Barry's metaphor...

Getting a hold of myself, but the nervousness is still inching ahead. It's not even the drug deal. Something about these lizards, Boil and Julio's mania, really eccentric even by his standards, it makes me sick. Angry, confused sick. Like when you realize you can never really understand anything. Like these human rats are dragging me out to a bug party. That's where healthy men purposely have unprotected gay sex so that they can catch HIV from others. Diving into the worst abyss on purpose. Jay told me all about that concept, after making a huge delivery to one. Supposedly. His reaction was more of shrugging off interest than horror. What phases this beast? Certainly not the lizards.

Something worse is going on. He and Boil, they're on edge. Good at hiding it, sure. But I know. They drugged me on purpose, dragging me along on their twisted vision quest or whatever. But it's clear now. Very slick, boys. *Too* slick.

There is only one explanation. Violence. Jay is a hand grenade, someone else needs to pull the pin. But Lucas Boil is evil. He causes pain and fear for fun. Like a terrorist? Yes. It's time. Time to lay the cards on the table. Don't go out like a punk.

"Boil, I've got your number. You're nothing more than a goddamn terrorist!" I shouted.

The Jeep lurched as we spun 180 degrees, veering onto the shoulder. The brakes clenched hard, nearly dislodging one of the metal cases. We rested in darkness, just out of sight of the Texan Bro gas station. Why did—

Julio raised his Magnum into the air.

BLAM! BLAM! BLAM!

The gunfire echoed down the empty road.

"What the holy HELL?" I collapsed into a phantom womb. Can't fake warmth. He's a proven genius, but is he also just smart, or lucky?

"You goddamned shit brained dope addicts!" I shrieked.

"Hey!" Julio growled. He waved his finger in the air, staring through the mirror. "We're drug enthusiasts! And you need to watch it, man. Terrorist?"

"Damn straight," Boil said. "Show some respect. I've broken men's necks for less. Lucky you're not a man."

"Seriously, what the hell is wrong with you tonight? Are you really going to sell *lizards*? It doesn't add up. Who cares enough to pay you to smuggle them across the world?"

"What do you want to hear, Tim?" Julio was on the edge of angry. "You'd rather I got in on the sex-trade? Because there's a hell of a lot more money in that, and it all flows out here. Makes lizards and seem a little tame, huh? You gonna moralize me about selling H now, too?"

Point taken.

"It's exhaustion," I mumbled.

Julio threw the Jeep back into motion, spinning around to head back to Texan Bro again. My cheeks flushed. I felt like a total toddler. Ashamed.

"You're tagging along, getting your ride. Shut up and keep low. Dumbass." Boil pushed the Jeep's cigarette lighter in. The lighter popped into readiness. He pressed it into his cigarette, took a deep drag, and then tossed it out the window.

Julio did a double-take.

"Dude, what the fuck?" he shouted.

"What?"

"You just threw my fucking lighter out the window!"

"I did?"

"Yes, you did!"

"Ah, so what? You just put a fucking bullet in the radio a second ago," Boil said, kicking his feet up onto the dashboard. His seat arched back, crushing me further.

"It was *my* radio," Julio growled.

"Can you two focus? Come on, level with me. What's the real deal here? I'm here, so I'm in on it, whether I ever get out of the Jeep or not."

"No! And you're replacing my burner." Julio put his finger against Boil's head.

"Julio Sanchez Sin Corazon! I'm on this blasted road with you, now tell me the truth!"

He jerked the Jeep into the left lane and waved his Magnum at the sky. "No, no, I can't do it, Tim! For your own sake, stay ignorant! Stay ignorant! Stay innocent!" His face was so twisted with mock concern, his fingers curled and pleading, and he really should have been looking at the road instead of back at me. "Truth is, son, I'm sick."

Sick? Hospital sick? White sheets sterile sick?

"This guy, it ain't about money, he can provide something." Julio grit his teeth, burning his attention down the road. "Something *no one* else can ever give me. So he wants the stupid lizards. Whatever. I'm getting something far better."

"What is it? An organ? A cure?"

Jay laughed, deep and secretive, almost relieved. "Yeah man, a cure. For sure."

Boil let out a moan, tilted his head back, and fell dead silent. Then a pleased cry came roaring out as a high-pitched whine.

"Yeeeeeeeeeeeeeeeeeeeeeeeeeeeeessssssssssssssssssssssssssssssssss. I FEEL IT!"

Julio swatted at Boil like the man was a swarm of flies. "Cut that shit out, we're going into public! We barely made it last time!"

"Enough! You're both going to drive me crazy!"

"Crazier. Join us on the dark side. Everything is sideways, inside out and right side in," Jay mocked me with the deepest voice he had.

Boil kept hissing in joy until "Johnny Come Marching Home" blared from his lap. He dropped the act and flipped open a black cell phone. He gestured to slit our throats and pull over, which we did. We'll never get to that damn gas station like this.

"What's up?" He listened to for a moment, then cupped the phone, glared at Julio and put his finger to his lips. "It's them."

Julio nodded, looked me in the eye through the rear view mirror, also putting his finger to his lips. Yes, yes. I get it. Boil continued his clipped conversation.

"Yes. Of course, I got them. All of them. Yeah. What, do you need to speak to one? They're fucking animals, you twat! Seriously?" Boil looked at me, signaled that I had to put the cellphone near a metal crate. I did. Boil knocked on it. An aria of hisses, snaps, and shrieks arose. Boil took his cellphone back. "Happy now? No, it's fine. All good. Yeah, no doubt. We'll be there. We? Me and my... cousin. I already told you, it's not my fault you forgot. All right? Yes, my cousin. Right. We'll be there, no worries on that. Good. Peace." He flicked the phone shut. "Oscar Mike, Julio! Game on."

Oscar and Mike? I don't know everyone out here, by any means, especially when you add in the tourists, but—

"It's a fucking military term. Means the mission's a go."

Julio's barely constrained energy burst out. He spun us back onto the tree lined street. The Jeep lurched left and right as he shouted, "What do you mean it's on? Of course it's on! It's been on for the past month! You never said it could ever not be on!"

"Yeah, but now it's really, really on," Boil said.

I punched down on my seat.

"*What's* on?"

They stared at each other. Julio shrugged.

"Aight, fine. Here it is. Our contact is a mole for the FBI. They're working together to snuff me out," Julio said. He shot a glance over his shoulder.

"FBI?" I whimpered.

"They've been testing chemical weapons in the hills. Radiation waves shot out from Peach Pit Island. Mess with our heads. Control us. They know I know," Julio continued. "Some *rat* betrayed me. And the government is gonna snuff me. Or at least try. Heh. Figure once I'm out of the picture, they'll use Savage Jefe's connections as a front to spread their sick conspiracy. How's that sound, Tim? A proxy goon to rule our infected Sponge Island! Shit, man, it's America at its worst."

"It's America at its best!" Boil jumped in.

Are they serious? They sound serious… and it fits the serious creep-on that's been eating at me. This *is* a conspiracy, my god! Barry, what have you gotten me into?

Boil spun around, eyes bulging, bits of spit flying as he spoke. "You stumbled into deep shit, Timmy Poon! Once they gain control over a third of the island, they'll keep creeping up through the underground, dealer by dealer, until they hit New York. Didn't you notice the tap water, Poon? That nasty egg taste? They've been poisoning the wells. And testing their brain beams on us. We're really spreading the lizards out to some dedicated guerillas. They're poised, and trained. They're living beacons, gonna be injected to spread germ warfare. We're gonna take those cocksuckers down!"

"Yeah." Jay sparked a fat blunt and took one king hell of a hit. As he spoke his mouth was a volcano, billowing clouds into the wind. "Those fucking lizards man, the lizards absorb radiation, too. Genetically bred so we can regain our will, man! The will to fight! Revolucion!"

Good gods fuck me dead, it all makes sense now… but Jay wasn't done.

"We've been washed in that shit for months now. Hell, Tim, we're covered in it right now!" Julio whipped around and snarled. "That's why they're endangered. That's why Boil put his life on the line to get 'em. That's why we're gonna trick these NSA goons into thinking we're delivering the lizards *to them*. Good, obedient slaves, we are. But we'll hand them off to the guerillas first, then ice those government assholes. You ready for a throw down? Because you might wanna sit this one out, bro. I didn't want to get you involved, figured I'd give you the Jeep and just vanish, ya feel me?"

"That's, um, very interesting," I said, chewing on my empty coffee cup. "I feel you."

Julio went full on manic, rocking in his seat, the .44 flailing in every direction. "But we're still DOOMED! All their god-damned radiation is mutating us! Bastards are turning me into a beautiful unicorn!"

Enough. I snatched Julio's greasy hair.

"Julio. Stop fucking with me. You had me for a second. Now this sounds like one of Barry's stupid stories!"

"Dios mio, Tim! Help us! When did I sign up to be a unicorn?" Julio shrieked. Didn't even flinch as I tugged his hair down. "This is justice! *Justice!* Don't you love justice?"

"Shut up!" It was more of a plea than an order.

"Look at this," Julio said. He spun around, teeth grinding, and nearly tearing his hear out. I lost my grip. He thumped his forehead. "Look, right there! You see that nub?"

"There's no nub."

"It'll be a horn before dawn! Time is of the... the precious!"

"Essence? Soooo... You'll be a unicorn if we don't give these lizards to eco-terrorists by dawn?" I rolled my eyes. "Okay, you boys get an A for effort. You have somehow managed to drive me even *more* insane. You've scared the shit out of me too! Congratulations. There's nothing left to squeeze out. So. Get. Real."

"You wanna touch it? You wanna rub the nub?" Julio giggled and stared at me, his eyes so wide the lids nearly split.

"There's no nub! Watch the road!" I shouted. Bless the empty roads, we're still at the pre-party hour, before this stretch is overflowing with drunk drivers whipping back and forth from Thornwood parties to Tomahok ones and back again.

"God, Tim, it hurts! I already feel my bones stretching! I'll have hooves by dawn. You have to help me, hombre!"

"We just passed the gas station," I lied. We passed it quite a while ago. Nearly back in Thornwood proper. Hoped he might just get so into his game that we'd end up too close to Hawkhouse Hospital for him to turn back.

Alas, no. Jay snapped to and then whipped the Jeep around *again*. Had to hold the crates down with each arm, briefcase and sword between my knees. "I didn't sign up for this shit! You don't want to tell me the truth? Fine! Probably IS for the best. But get your act fucking together! You're the goddamn pilot, and I trusted you!"

"It's no act." Boil grabbed my knee. His fingers dug in like a steroid spider's legs. "But you're the key, Timmy. The first sacrifice! We'll make a drum out of your skin. Feed your corpse to the lizards so they get a taste for human blood."

"Nothing like a good bloodlust." Julio nodded.

"Get your hand off me. Now this is just annoying. I don't even give a shit what's going on, just stop." Felt my stomach drop around my ankles like an inner tube. "My heart, Jay! I'm weak enough. My heart can't take any more."

Boil was about to speak but Jay gently grabbed him. They were quiet.

"Don't worry, buddy. Nothing's gonna happen to you. Relax, I got your heart right here in my hand. See?"

Well, that's sort of true. Damned manic depressive, genius-rock star-drug slinging-gun shooting-bat out of a jail cell-neo-terrorist-prince. Couldn't help but respect him, crossing my arms and holding my laughter in.

"Gay." Boil crossed his arms, too.

Jay threw his arm behind Boil's headrest and looked back at me again, his glasses nearly falling off his head by this point. Too much earnestness in his eyes...

"Tim. You ready to die tonight?"

I actually considered it.

"Yeah, Jay. I think I am."

He turned back, then tucked his .44 under the seat. The rear view mirror betrayed him. He wasn't laughing. His skin suddenly looked like old curtains. Drooped. Unshaven. Tired. My eyes locked into his one. Eye contact, always, even when it sucks, maintain eye contact.

"You ain't gonna die. Heh. Not while I got your back. But first things first, right?"

"But not always in that order," I finished our old joke. I smiled.

"So let's get gas and booze and get this done." He smiled.

Boil sighed, arms folded.

"Tim, for real, though, you know any run I make is gonna be dangerous," Julio said. "See, I'm always ready to die. But no matter what goes down, I have a plan. I wasn't bullshitting you. You got my word. You'll get to Barry. Even if I die. Word is bond."

Word is bond. He threw me off the trail yet again, but I feel better. Somehow, still in the dark, I truly feel better. Because his word *is* his bond, and in this day and age, that's quite a fucking thing. Ha, word is bond! I wonder if anybody still says that.

Wonder if anyone else still *means* it.

Screw it. Jay does. That's good enough for me.

Impossible Is Acceptable

Thank you, Jay. Even if he dies, he'll make sure I get to Barry. That's nice... Wait, if he dies? He said that in his 'non-performance' voice. No, he'll be fine. My Curse has had countless times to catch him and still hasn't. Ironic. Boil is the safest from it, since there's no love there to poison or violate.

"Violate me?"

"Ah, uh, yes. Yes, that's what I want to do." Just roll with it, nothing to lose with this meat-head. "Boil, I want to poison and violate you."

"Wicked." Boil lit another cig and smoked it along with the blunt.

I slid deeper into the seat, letting the cold steel of the lizard cases soothe the nape of my neck. There was a slight comfort in the darkness ahead. No oncoming headlights. No witnesses. I can trust Jay. The years have proven that time and again. Five minutes ago negated any neurotic doubts. But Boil is still the wildcard.

"All right, Jay, you were trying to get a rise out of me. I admit, it's kind of easy and sometimes even fun. But you, Boil, I haven't seen you in years. You were a crazy nasty brute back then, and I seriously don't know if you're kidding around or not. You're the last person I'll risk getting killed for."

"Killed? What do you know about killing? You gotta kill those crazy motherfuckers before they kill you," Boil said.

"The only crazy motherfucker I see right now is you."

"No, I'm not crazy. I'm not. And the only mother I fucked was yours."

And that's when Julio smacked Boil across the back of his skull so hard that I almost felt it.

"Tim's mother passed away."

Boil stared into the woods. "Sorry."

It's fine.

"But don't forget I'm a goddamned patriot, got it?"

"Christ, Boil, just because you signed up to kill people doesn't mean you get a pat on the back from me. I won't condemn you, and yes you're brave and do great things, but spare me. My dad was a veteran. I know good soldiers, good men. Doesn't seem like you've changed. You're no hero."

He spun around. Veins popped up along his skin, winding across his tattoo roadmap. He nearly bit the cigarette in half as he spoke. "Shut your damn mouth right now. I don't remember seeing *you* there. I went to war, not you! You think it's about being a hero? You dickless little know-it-all. *I know* what the fuck is going on. This is a job for private contractors. Guts for grunts, guns for grudges."

Strange talk to hear from this guy. But at least it's halfway normal.

"Okay. Okay, maybe I run my mouth when I'm stressed. And I don't know as much as you, are you happy now?"

He was silent, but the aggression seemed gone. Julio seemed at ease, too.

"So... uh, so you saw some rough stuff over there, huh?" I asked.

"Yeah, I saw some *rough stuff,*" Boil said. His natural growl returned, signaling that perhaps their little show was finally over.

I actually anchored them in. Back to ugly old reality.

"War is hell, huh?" I pressed, trying to make up for whatever I did.

Boil sighed. I could almost hear him roll his eyes.

"War is true. After that, there's nothing. You think I haven't changed, huh? Trust me, boy, your approval is the last thing I need. But if you must know," he huffed, as if strained to explain. He wants to talk. But not to me. Boit lit another cancer stick. "You can't come back from war. You don't really come home. Ever."

"Oh. Are you going back?"

"Not soon enough." He spit smoke, then slapped the outside of the Jeep. Hard.

"Uh... well, if you don't mind me asking, how exactly did you smuggle dozens of lizards out? Seriously, I am impressed. Did you run around the desert and catch them yourself?"

"Hell no. I got kids to do it for me, or just traded for 'em. And anyway, no one gives a shit about what you bring back, as long as it's not guns or gold."

"But you have guns," I said.

"Bought all that crap stateside. Much easier to get guns stateside."

Good, good. It's working. This is almost a real conversation.

Suddenly the vehicle swings to the right, rearing up on two wheels. Boil lunges past me like a mad python, shoving his arms around the crates as they threaten to spill out the back. The lizards shriek. So do I, clutching the roll bar and bracing my knees.

The Jeep bumps over the curb and into Texan Bro's lot. FINALLY.

"Fuel!" Julio shouted as he slammed the brakes. The Jeep was perfectly lined up with a gas pump. He hopped over the door. Happy as all hell.

"This is no good man, no good." My heart-rate was strangely even.

"What's the big deal now, pussy?" Boil asked.

"We're going in circles. Backtracking. We need to keep forward momentum. And I can't be seen here again. I have an awkward history with the attendant. He already thinks I'm a burnout, and you two are tripping balls." This could get ugly, and I doubt the poor guy inside will hesitate to call the cops on someone like Julio.

"So stay here." Julio took two steps away from the car, then abruptly spun on his heel. He grabbed the side of the Jeep and thrust his face in, stopping inches from mine. "Pobrecito! You know we're just playing," Julio said. He ruffled my hair. "I won't screw your brains no more. You wanna hear something crazy? Me and Luke are totally sober."

That is actually far more upsetting.

Jay rested his arms on the Jeep. "Seriously, Tim, you okay? You seem a little crazed tonight. Like, more than usual. Thought you'd laugh, for real."

"You're saying I'm crazy? Ha! Took you all these years to figure that out?"

"Bro, you've been more than a little off tonight. Not just weird. Mad wound up. Know what I'm sayin'? You've been all fucked up for years, but now you're, I dunno... more sad than angry? I'm used to you being an asshole, that's fun. You're a selfish prick, but now you're totally set on this mission. Seeing Barry and bringing some fucking books? Specifically tonight. What the shit is going on, man? Is Barry really okay? Are you lying to me?"

"No, no he's fine, all things considered. He's a walking miracle. If there's one thing Barry is, it's lucky. Got hit by a fucking car and lived! Sure, the recovery will be long, but he'll be mostly normal again. Docs said maybe six months. But cut the crap. You dosed me, and almost blew me up! Not cool. You're wondering why I'm a bit off? Shit that was something you tested on your dog! You could have killed me! And you wonder why I'm acting strange? Bastard."

"Heh. Well, that's why I tested it on Elvis first. And now that you came down without dying, I know I can start selling it." He rested his chin on his arms. So casual. "You're still my favorite test piggie. And I'll throw you a cut for your trouble, aight? Maybe name it... T-Doom? Cool, huh?"

"What an honor."

"Always and forever, bro. But for real, I'll leave you alone. I just thought you needed a little fun."

"Jesus, are you two gonna start making out back there?" Boil asked.

"Don't be jealous." Julio kicked the Jeep.

"I'll be fine, Jay." I wasn't completely lying. "I've just seen things tonight... things you'd never believe. Learned bad shit, and—wait a second, you guys took the same pill I did. Before the cop in town! I saw you take it!"

"Us? No fucking way, hombre. I wouldn't touch that shit," Julio laughed, leaning back from the Jeep. "Shit, I had to be responsible, know what I mean? We just ate some painkillers."

He slapped the lizard crates, spun on his heel again, and marched inside. Boil grabbed the driver's side seat and pulled himself into the back. I recoiled in horror against the door. So close, no wind, I can smell the boiled swine sweat coating him.

"He's still lying for you. We've been doing lines all night." He winked.

"Of course." Jay on coke, booze, or pot isn't enough to destroy me.

"He's protecting you. But I don't care." Boil leaned in closer. His jagged teeth glinted under the fluorescent lights, his tattoos seemed to glow as he whispered, "So you *really* want the truth? We're going to kill Savage Jefe."

"Suuuuuure you are. Even if he wanted to, Jay would've tried that years ago. I'm above your level, so quit trying. Please, go back up front. Go!"

"You know I could snap your neck and make it look like an accident? I've done it before. It's real easy. You just grab the base of the skull here..."

I put my foot against his chest and leaned over the edge of the Jeep, hanging out backwards. He sat back and actually caught my foot, pulling me safely back in.

"I'm sure you're proud of it too," I said as I slightly unsheathed Kitsune. "But I'll split your veins and piss in them before you can bleed out."

"Wow! That's the spirit, Timmy! Good for you. I mean, fat chance in hell, I'd tear apart like a little girl, but good for you."

"You mean you'd tear me apart like a little girl would? If you want to make fun of me, you need to… Your grammar is, ah, forget it."

He leapt out of the Jeep, leaving me with my briefcase, my sword, and the crates. I leaned back against the seat. Sigh. Even with my eyelids closed, white light filtered through my eyelids. I opened them and saw the Texan Bro sign leering down at me, a twisted neon circus clown. Mocking me. It spit on my family legacy. Capital vampire.

CLUNK.

Boil slams the nozzle into the gas tank like a Neanderthal trying to mount a tiger while ripped on a neo-level PCP. Every action so aggressive and lacking any grace.

"A PCP tiger? You really are one odd son of a bitch." Boil sniffed the air. "Ah, the best part about pumping gas is the fumes, ain't it? Never get sick of that smell."

I don't either, actually.

Aw, crap. My stomach rumbled again, recalling the muddy mess in my boxers. Shit, I hope it was just a squirt. I crept out of the Jeep, praying the clerk didn't see me. Slunk around to the back of the station to clean my ass in the single-person bathroom. It stank of piss. The toilet was clogged. Graffiti covered everything. Paper towels lay soaked and crumpled on the floor. I managed to completely clean my ass, but I had to ditch the boxers. There was no saving them. Your sacrifice shall be remembered. I tried wetting some toilet paper in the sink and using that, but it just left sopping wet balls of mush in my ass hairs. It was like smearing toothpaste with a sponge. Ultimate cleanliness is impossible, so it must be acceptable. The mirror, cracked and stained, reflected my face. Sallow, dark rims under my eyes, sweaty hair shooting in all directions, scratches on my cheek, dried blood near my ear. The water was cold, but it felt clean and cooled me down, inside and out. I washed my arms as best I could, getting the grime and blood, the vomity residue and sweaty night soil off of my skin. Worked well enough. Felt recharged, ready for more abject insanity.

Back outside, happy, free-balling in Tracy's pants, which are still pristine thanks to my boxers' noble sacrifice. True, boxers don't really offer any protection, but I like the idea that my nuts are behind a cotton curtain. Now I feel the cold zipper, the lining of the pants. Deal with it. Testicles are kind of stupid. Hanging out, vulnerable, silly looking. I know why they do, but evolution wise, they should be tucked in. Like ovaries. But I treasure and protect mine, nonetheless.

I stared around the gas station. Little, but part of a vast chain encompassing the whole country. A suture meant to let green blood seep out into the right hands. Seep out from small business owners. Seep out of my parents. Screw this place. Stupid oil conglomerate gas station whores. It's not a brilliant epiphany, but the rage is tangible. I kicked the bathroom open, took my shitty boxers from the trash. Using them as a paintbrush, I smeared a pentagram and "YOUR CHILDREN WILL PAY" on the tiled wall. Washed my hands, proud, until I realized that no CEO would ever see that. Ever. Some poor dude, maybe even the clerk inside, will have to clean it up. Well… too late now. I'd wager Jay and Boil are waiting for me.

I exited the bathroom cautiously. Back out front, and one blink later, we're not alone! Where did they all come from? A bunch of SUVs and sports cars, station wagons, and pickup trucks, taking in every pump. Blonde broads hanging onto twisted men with thinning hair, nighttime shades, ugly shorts, and silver watches. Young fools with plastic hair and lame jokes, braying for their vapid dates. All of them, any age, prancing as if the world owed them luxury. Yet it's a blessing, having no one paying attention to us. I got back in the Jeep just as Julio did. Refreshed. Lighter. She's right. She was always right. I can handle this. Nothing easy is truly noble.

Julio dropped a huge case of Uber Ale Dark next to me. He tore off the top of the case. His hand became a snake, darting in and recoiling with two beers pinched between his fingers.

"Want one?"

I hesitated.

"Dude, just take it."

I did, and tried to twist the cap off. He laughed and stuck the bottle tops between his teeth. He looked like a stubble covered walrus. Then he snapped both bottles down violently, and a carbonated hiss shot out mixed with his vile breath. He handed the beer to me as he proceeded to drain half of his in one shot. I sipped mine, eyes darting around at the other people. No one gives a crap about what we do. May as well be invisible.

Boil finished filling up and jumped in. We pulled out of Texan Bro without incident, and my Uber Ale tasted kind of good. Nutty and bitter, with a hint of cocoa. Sweet seaweed. Nothing like a swig of the hops to put things into perspective.

We drove on, finally heading back east. Toward the edge of our world. Past the heavily wooded strip that hid the Camerons' house, up some hills, faster and faster. Strange, the farther I go from Barry, the closer I come to reaching him.

Zipping along, the space between the houses grew. The trees thinned. Streetlights gradually appeared again, but sparse. Dim beacons. Grass gave way to an amalgamation of dirt and sand. The vast starscape spread above. The ocean took the night off, lazily gyrating against the shore to our right, just behind a strip of motels that border Thornwood from outer Tomahok.

"Seriously, we just drop these off at some nut's house, get the money, and head up island, right?" I asked, draping my arms over the steel crates, briefcase between my knees, Kitsune tugged snugged beneath my seatbelt.

"Uh… yeah," Julio said. "You seem better."

"Ha, you know, a minute ago, Boil was trying to convince me you two were going to snuff Savage Jefe."

"Really?" Jay glanced at Boil, then back at me. "Ha, fuck that noise. I'm not that crazy."

"The buyer might want to talk for a bit," Boil said. He chucked his beer bottle into the darkness and opened another. No respect for nature, our only asset left out here. "We served together."

"Really?" I said.

"Really. He moved out here after our first tour. He's throwing his own PMC together. If that fails, join Blackwater or something. But he's done with the national military, and somehow slipped out through the cracks."

"Wait, you're serious?" I sat up sharp, spilling beer on my shirt.

"Yeah, you twit," Boil said. "Always serious."

"That's kind of cool." I leaned back again.

"Yeah, he's a brave man," Boil said. "Now shut it. Be grateful. You're aiding the war on terror just by sitting there, doing nothing but whine."

"That's all the honor I could ask for."

"Why'd you think Luke was a terrorist?" Julio asked as he let out a terrible burp before tossing his bottle into the night. He's a litterer now, too?

"I was trying to play along?" I said. "I almost wish you were selling weight. I'm used to that. But all jokes aside, lizards?"

"We told you, they're for my friend," Boil said. "He's really into the things, and uh… he was stationed way out in the middle of nowhere. It's like a gift, ya know, reminder of the old times. Except we gotta charge him for our trouble. And he'll pay, he's stacked."

"No. Jay, I've slept on your couch while you moved blow to pirates. I slung weed with you in school, rocked bottles of liquor on Main Street and broke into mansions. What's with all the jokes and secrets? And this asshole is obviously your new partner in crime. What are you afraid of, Park Rangers? ASPCA? This doesn't add up."

"When has anything?" Julio shrugged. "I just do things. A lot of that stuff was fun, man, but you stopped when, um… you had better things to do, know what I mean? When you had something to lose. I didn't ditch you. You saying you're down to ride again?"

What kind of question is that? I have less to lose now more than ever. The ocean has no answers. The faster we go, the slower it waves, purple and spacey blue, just within sight and out of touch.

Boil shifted around again. "Where *did* you get those pants? Swear they look familiar."

A chill wind seized my spine.

"I told you, I got cold and changed at Barry's. They're his."

"You got cold in the summer? Well, you still look like gay as hell," Boil said, turning back to the windshield.

"Glad you noticed."

"Yeah, because you're a fag."

"That, that was such a lame—will you cut it out with the homophobic bullshit? You sound like you're twelve. Statistically, your homophobia makes you the most likely to be gay."

"Yeah, Boil. It's not cool, and that crap hasn't been funny since we was little stupid kids. Gay people are just people," Julio said. But Julio seemed to be in another car, perhaps a child with a father who forgot him long ago. Tiger on top of the mountain mist, tired, probably pissed. He has that weird body silence, the kind that turns into a vicious sucker punch at bars.

"Stop changing the subject. Lizards!" I pounded my fist on the lizard locker. Mistake. That sound, ah, nails on a chalkboard, motorboat on a manatee's back. Christ!

"Whatever, Poon, you're still a whiny bitch-ass pussy who shouldn't even be here. If you want me to quite calling you a fag, do something about it." Boil laughed, so pleased with himself.

"You know my dad was queer?" Jay asked him, staring straight ahead.

"See, Boil? Julio evolved with the rest of us. You can be tough without being afraid that some man is going to treat you the way you treat women."

"You better watch it, Tim," Boil said, arms folded, so tense I could feel the heat coming off him. "Keep talking shit. Go ahead, see what happens. You think I give a fuck if Julio's your butt buddy? Keep pushing me and I'll break your fucking skull."

"Jay, are you really going to let him keep—"

"Yo! Both of you shut up!" Jay spit on the dashboard. "Luke, I ain't playin'. My dad was gay. That's why he left, you shit-brick. Take the fucking hint, aight? And you, too Tim. Don't be such a baby."

Damn, he's a knife. I take for granted that I always get the blunt end. Julio turned to Boil now. His mercurial mood flipped from somber annoyance to festive again. "Speaking of babies, Luke, what's good with Selena?"

Boil didn't answer. Guess he didn't hear. No problem, I need that sweet sound of silence. It's not always a scream. The night is so clear and clean as we coast along, tossing trash in our wake, but where is this storm? Vague clouds in the distance, but no static in the air, no purple sky and rolling waves. No tornados, no crackling air heralding thunder and lightning. Either this oncoming storm is late, or it's...

"Shit. Who the fuck cares about that cunt?" Boil's chin dipped down to his chest. He lit yet another stoge, staring into his private nothing. His cigarette rocketed out of his mouth, around the back of his head, nearly blinding me. I watched the meteor fade to an ember behind us. "Selena's a whore."

Think I shall sit this one out.

"Yo that's cold, even for a guy like you." Julio put his lit cigarette in Boil's mouth. He accepted it. "Calling your baby's momma a cunt? C'mon, show some class, you ass. What about the kid?"

Tim, go blank. Don't even think a word. Just in case.

"She sent me one letter while I was deployed," Boil said, looking down the sloping hill on his side. "One letter. Saying I could still see Emily when I got back, but... you know, she doesn't want to see me anymore. She said... Selena said... fuck it. Fuck her. She can't keep Emily from me. Whatever."

Sweet Lady Bastet! Lucas Boil is a *father*? Perhaps he is the one foretold to bear the Nightmare Child?

"Yeah, you're right. It is a nightmare," Boil said. "Sometimes."

Oops!

He continued, mechanical, like the drone he asked to be. "It's stupid. I hate the bitch. But I miss her. Selena, duh. But... both of them. Selena said she 'needed more security'. Her and Emily." He sank for a moment, then exploded like a mortar. He punched the dashboard so hard I felt the frame shake. "Security! *What the fuck is that shit*? Does she have any idea why I joined the stupid army? Stability! Security for our fam—Stupid cock sucking, lying, cheating *whore*!"

Emily. No, Boil, please stay perfectly evil for me.

Yet he's got a child. A little girl named Emily. I always thought if me and Tracy had a daughter, I'd suggest naming her Eowyn. From an ancient European language, basically an elegantly feminine way of saying "horse master". Powerful, and the nickname is Wyn, still feminine, obvious phonetic connotations. Tracy liked Aria as well, both for the song and for a female assassin she'd read about. But neither name flowed with Dune. But that discussion, it was all just fantasy. Long before the Curse took her. It was just... fun. All couples joke about it, right? *"Oh, so it's your kid, huh?"* she had mocked me. She laughed as she fell on top of me, on top of the empty king size bed that had been my parents', the room blue and cold and the talk of phantom children warming us. *"And what if this hypothetical child was a boy?"* That was tough. Need hard consonants. Chase? No. Jase? Her suggestion, short for Jason. His initials would be J.D. she said, while tracing my neck. I smiled and got us some drinks. And in the end... I have a feeling it was... it could have been a girl. The Lord of Death really scored on that accursed night. Took two beautiful souls for the price of one.

And now I find out this butcher has spawned.

Emily Boil. Huh. Papa Boil. Papa... Lucas.

"So, um, Luke? How old is she?" I asked. Boil didn't speak, didn't move. Wasn't even sure he was breathing. That'd actually be kind of okay with me. Boil always struck me as the 'hit it and quit it' type. Maybe that's how this started. Ah, I really hope I didn't say that out loud. "Emily is a nice name."

"Thanks. It's my mom's," Boil said. "She's three now. And, uh, sorry about your mom. I didn't really mean that before. Sorry she died."

"You didn't know," I said. "It was a long time ago."

Silence.

"It's never long enough," Jay said. He cracked a beer while sparking another blunt. Apparently he'd been rolling it in his lap, one hand on the wheel, one hand cracking the leaf, emptying the tobacco on the floor with his .44, sprinkling the bud and rolling it tight with one hand. Damn. If we get pulled over... No, don't even give it a thought. He passed it to Boil. He hit it. He passed it to me, blindly. I hit it. Then again. And again. Back to Jay. The cycle continues. The tree line gave way to more rolling slopes of sand. I turned right, facing the dunes with Boil.

"When's the last time you saw her?" I heard myself asking my foe.

"I saw Emily yesterday. At my mom's place. Selena dropped her off. But she was long gone before I got there. I ain't seen Selena since... shit, since right before I went on tour."

"Rough," Jay said. "Shit's fucked up, man. What happened, yo? Why's she playing you like that?"

Boil spit, threw his cigarette into the wind. The wind threw it back at me. Could just barely feel the heat as it passed over my hair. "Can you *please* flick those at the road? You almost blinded me. Twice."

Boil didn't react and Julio shot me a stink eye in the mirror.

"So how many times have you been to Iraq?" I asked, trying to stay nicey-nice. Not so hard now. Somehow.

"Enough times." Boil said. He seemed lost between thoughts. Dead radio, and more dead silence. "But enough is never enough. I'm going back. Haven't thought further than that. No point in planning. Never works out anyway."

True.

Another stretch of silence, wind and breathing and beer caps popping and cigarettes burning, lizards clawing and scratching, metal screeching. Julio mashed the pedal. Good lord, this rancid highway never ends. Not sure you can even consider a two-lane road a highway, but it's east or west at high speed, with nothing but dead-end turn-offs, so we do. This highway, stretching between Thornwood and Tomahok, is a thirty-minute drive at a human speed, about ten the way Julio's driving. Like I said, only two choices, forward or back. It never feels forward. All the side roads are short dead ends. We continue, quietly, passing one car, rushing to Tomahok like minnows into the gaping maw of the reviled angler fish. Ugly beasts.

Yet the stretch is somehow beautiful, the ocean rolling on south, to our right. The Atlantic Ocean is our border, hiding monster gods like Ceto and her Seven Serpent Bastards of the Sea. And to the north, our other border, a sandy desert named the Creeping Dunes. Once we leapt from them as kids, doing flips off fifty-foot-high mountainous dunes. They continue to creep annually, shifting about three feet per year with the aide of coastal winds. As we age, they crawl on. Rising, devouring, leaving vast sandy craters in their wake. In fact, just one hundred years ago they were on the south side of the highway. Well, there was no highway, but you understand.

Beneath the Creeping Dunes is the Phantom Forest, an eerie cemetery for trees that were suffocated by the encroaching sands. You can still see the tips of the tallest trees, as tall as they are stubborn, craning their necks above of the sand. Some thrive, some are naught but leafless branches, skeletal claws grasping at el Sol. Tracy and I would take long, off-season hikes there. Camping over the edge, in the really remote edge of our deserted dead forest. To hide, to make love, to just plain get away from everything.

In all ways, and especially tonight, there's no going back. No traffic lights, no tourist traps. Just motels and bars crammed against one another by the water. The main problem is that, out here, we have no definitive setting. It's a landscape of transition. And without a setting, you can't have any proper footing. Without footing, you have no stance. And without a stance, you just can't make any goddamn moves.

So it's all waiting. Waiting for weird watcher-gods to blink. Waiting for the warden to throw the switch. The stretch is Thornwood's mucous membrane, ready to burst out from a brain, flailing out around a bullet like a torn parachute. Bone fragments. Sand. Seaside hovels. And one building that houses a seasonally changing club, terminally destined for failure, and new restaurant ventures. And thus, the true prize. Tax evasion.

Few cars pass us, and none shine ahead or behind. At this point, you've decided where you fit, in the decadent low-brow madness of Tomahok, or the decadent high-brow madness of Thornwood. We're in that awkward hour, when clubs are just opening and the more refined patrons chow on entrees that Burn and I could survive on for a week.

But in just a few hours, the stretch will be a parade of drunk drivers. Not to mention the ones four-wheeling down the beach, lights out, running over teenage couples screwing under towels, hiding from parents and police, lust blanketed in the dark. Crushed. Bodies burst into each other, ribs melded, blood pooling into the sand, compacted by the heavy tires. Most go unfound. Terrible. Terrible. Everything here is a tower of maggots, dead pets and shit, swaying under its own weight, a giant mutant worm.

"That's freakin' disgusting, man."

We pass the speed limit sign, the one that marks where Julio threw a narc out the back of this very Jeep when he was seventeen. Means we're almost there.

Now the road forks, but it's a cruel trick.

Both roads lead to Tomahok. You're not choosing a destination, just your path. In fact, they converge perfectly like a wishbone at the town limits. But the left one arcs up, toward the sky, deceptively inviting. Taking the left fork, the "New Highway", is the sign of a yuppie, looking to escape the menagerie of poor housing and opulent semi-mansions vying for space on the water's edge. And that edge is the lower fork, the "Old Highway". Very creative names, I know. But still, they're not true highways. Just normal, potholed, two-lane roads.

The New guarantees plenty of wooden signs declaring that you're near a state park, although you can only see the tips of evergreens sloping down the southern shoulder, ending at brown water and red sands. But the Old is no bullshit. A twisting roller coaster of potholes and blind curves, steep climbs and sharp drops, mere inches from poor excuses for sidewalks. It rips through rolling hills, lined with both very poor and mysteriously rich real estate. Students call it the Coaster. Skaters call it the Devil's Backbone. By any name, it's definitely more fun, and more deadly. Famous on a stretch already famous for DWIs and premature deaths. Makeshift crosses dot every turn. Suffice to say, it's the riskiest choice. Julio makes his choice. Jams straight down the Old Highway.

My usual unease swells. There's no use in denying that Tomahok *is* fun. It's the farthest tip of this long island. The eastern-most tip of the

American Empire. The last giddy dingle-berry dangling off its ass. And that's how we must play. Nothing is taboo. Anything less than excess is a bore.

If Thornwood is a cracked diamond covered in dirt, then Tomahok is a ramshack carnival. A curious tourist trap that devolves in the desolate winter months, before the annual metamorphosis into a summer husk of intrigue and decadence. But when the sun is farthest from the Earth, the axis tilts, and winter's long night blankets the land... then our true beasts emerge. The bitter frost season of pure Tomahok locals. Prisoners of all kinds, creeping back into daylight. Blinking in the wake of summer madness.

But tonight, at the height of August lust, it's full of the new breed, the old guard, and their tepid fluids clogging the gutters as they dance above. It's populated by people, plain old humans of all kinds. Even mine. Tomahok does not discriminate, mixing up a turgid froth of alcoholic fishermen, winos, coke addled yuppies, weird hybrid crawfish, post- and pre-op transhumanoids, deposed broken backed natives, sniveling hormone drenched teenagers, smoke brained scummy haired burnout surfers, craggy old living corpses, illegal immigrants, legal immigrants, ex-patriots, vagabonds, misogynistic tribes of cis-men, friendly homosexuals, poly, bi, and meh lovers, even asexuals, agnostics, religious fanatics, hipsters, hetero-fascists, pimps, pushers, peddlers of painted crab shells, preteen Colombian boys, hackers, exiled Third World dictators, malfeasants of all shapes and sizes, cenobites, librarians, babies, fried chicken, Hollywood royalty, renegade paramilitary commandos, journalists, counter intelligence mercenaries, skaters, riot aficionados, smokers, dopers, eaters, beaters, hair-trigger pacifists, outlaw Buddhists, pederasts, serial spouse abusers, professional chefs, vacationing politicians, nu-wave pirates, and the largest family of Great White sharks on the Eastern Seaboard.

Given this volatile mix, in the winter, Friday nights are divine, Saturdays are fatal, and the rest of the week is spent trudging through a stupor of failure, despair, and minimum-wage hellscapes.

In the summer it's a carnival, a filthy spring break where booze replaces water, meth replaces coke, coke replaces weed, and weed replaces... well, nothing. And if you're dumb enough, or desperate enough, the high grade dope trade always flows, the steady red blood cell beat of the end land's economy. And all of it, every vice for sale, first runs through Savage Jefe. He is the heart of sin, pumping the junk, keeping us jumping and humping and forgetting that every sunlit soaring rise ends in a deep, sunless dive.

Okay, yes, there was a time when I thought Tomahok was a blast.

But those days are long past. I'm not yet thirty, but I'm already too old for the tourists and too young for the locals. If you don't already live in Tomahok, there's no point in going. Unless you're good at fucking or fighting. At the moment, I'm not in the mood for either.

But if a storm *is* brewing, this must be where it'll hit. I'll just have to deal with it. Stand by Julio's word and my sword, clinging to the bony brimstone underbelly of this demonic Jeep, flapping its wings over a sea of lava and anywhere else it may please. Perhaps I'll cross paths with Bernard. And wring his neck. After hugging him.

Regardless, I stretched out across the back seat. Tough to manage, but I make do. Pop open another Uber Ale. Drink, breathe, try to remember that I'm just along for the ride. I'm not in control. For now. And apparently, someone still believes I can handle anything.

That was quickly proven false a moment later, when violence exploded around us. Just around the bend. A bonus brutality, right as I relaxed, accepting the coming storm.

Once again, I'd let my guard down. Dared to smile.

And the Curse struck.

BONUS CHAPTER!
The Secret Death of Julio's Left Eye

I'll let you in on a secret.

As stated, we drove head-on into a brutal scene, and it was partly because Julio is half-blind. But I'm one of the few who knows the truth. Despite years of rumors and misinformation built on heavy threats, I know how Jay *really* lost his left eye. Whispered legends say it was a skateboarding accident, or a gang fight in the city, or my favorite, that he popped it out himself on a dare.

But once again, I'm saddled with the truth.

Julio sold weed, cocaine, and ecstasy in high school. He was supplied by a then-thirty-year-old baron named Henry Jefe, whom he met during a bar brawl down at the Tomahok docks. Jefe was impressed that Julio not only got into the bar at age fourteen, but then proceeded to decisively win a fight against three full-grown, ex-con, nasty men. A thus, a business was born.

Jay's motives are legion. Fame, respect, cash for peanut butter and jelly sandwiches, clothes, the mortgage on his mother's house, the absence of his father. Julio got it all and more in tiny little Thornwood. And Jefe got an amiable young puppet to access the schools, parking lots, homes, that Jefe could not. Anywhere a profit waited, Jay was Jefe's respected mule.

It seemed so ideal. Julio pushed one portion of Jefe's poison while the lazy bastard slowly built his drug empire, man by man, school by school, kid by kid, cop by cop. Corpse by corpse. It only took a couple years before Henry Jefe could officially set up shop out on those docks. Safe upon his seasick throne at the end of the end, the desolate Tomahok Tiburon Dockyards. The ones that had no tourist mobs, no visitors save the men who toiled day and night on their ships, and the hand-picked noble scum that served Jefe.

Sadly, Jay actually is a genius, and morals aside, it's easy to believe he saw his future not as a tool for the CEO of crime, but as the king himself. Before long he skimmed product on the side, started turning over scratch and not tipping it into Henry's hat. And Henry found out.

Jay told me the truth. That Henry Jefe confronted him during a cash drop-off/product pick-up out at Tiburon. Between Jay's temper and Jefe's ineloquent inquiry, let's just say… shit went down. I suppose Jefe was right to assume he could beat some punk kid back into obedience. But no one ever pulled that off on young Julio. And so… well, they both learned something that day.

When Julio got the upper hand, Jefe, unable to suffer not only defeat, but the added threat of being exposed, needed to castrate young Julio's confidence. Plant a seed of fear, insurance to eat away plans for future escalation. For both titans knew this was a true clash of unstoppable forces.

So, faking that he'd lost, Henry lay bloodied and limp. And Julio took the bait. As he leaned down to spit on in his former boss's face, Henry seized Julio's hair, yanked him down into a head-butt that split his nose.

And then bit into his eye.

Jefe hung on, biting deeper, clawing at Jay's hair to prevent escape, even as Jay struck him in the neck, the balls, and blindly attacked Jefe's own eyes. In the end, a grown man stood over a kid's bleeding, unconscious body. And so, witnessed by Henry's elite and loyal servants, that bastard was re-forged into their vicious, undisputed, and eternal baron. The Savage Jefe.

As Julio lay in Hawkhouse's ER, as doctors salvaged the boy's mangled face, cheers and blood-oaths sounded across the Tiburon Docks. Julio's steel-willed pride caused his fall from grace, and also crowned his new nemesis, the legendary Savage Jefe.

But how did Jay escape alive? Why did Savage Jefe let that happen, instead of tossing the young upstart into the sea to drown? Julio laid it out straight for me, spilling it all while I stood vigil by his bedside. The strangest thing is that he laughed. Perhaps it was the morphine, but as Jay recounted it, too calm for comfort, I could see the roiling blood-thunder behind his remaining eye.

"You can get away with a lot on this wicked island, but murdering a kid is a tough sell, anytime, anywhere," he said, wrapped like a mummy in the hospital. "Tim, don't sweat it. Don't get involved. Don't open your mouth, and just trust me, hombre."

"Yes, of course," I nodded, still in shock.

He grabbed my arm, hard, pulling me down closer. "But no one can ever know. Not you, not the doctors, not the fucking pigs, and especially not my mother! NOBODY. You hear me, Tim? *No one can ever know.*"

You'd never know the eye is glass. Attached to the muscle, it moves in conjunction with the right one, even reflects light properly. The funny part is, Jefe paid for both the surgery and the amazing prosthetic. Certainly a cold, calculated gesture. I suspect it's part of a multi-pronged attack to subconsciously undermine Julio's thirst for vengeance. But it worked. And by the gods, Julio actually let it go. By the time he returned to school, Jay's rep was solid, his reputation feared, the truth buried. But he didn't give up! He secured his own sources and continued to sell. A smaller but consistent, lucrative business.

Jay adapted fast. It's what he does. Some people don't even realize that he's missing an eye at all. Whether it's skateboarding, bare-knuckle brawling, driving, throwing darts, still his skill surpasses the norm. So everyone knows he lost an eye, but the how and why is left to conjecture to all but his most trusted friends.

Bernard claims that one time he saw Julio unscrew the front of the eye and pull out a tab of acid. It's about as likely as Julio's story about banging a giant mutant moth. Still, the idea of hiding contraband in his eye is plausible enough for me. I've seen crazier. Even more amazing, but completely verifiable, is that both of these dealers have kept out of each other's way. For over a decade. Julio and Jefe both have plenty of customers, though Savage Jefe clearly owns the bigger market share, sitting atop the island's drug funnel. Ships come in, pay their dues, the goods sweep out to the mid-level guys, and somewhere down that line, Julio buys his stock. No bad blood, but no contact. Never again will the two meet, an unspoken acknowledgment of mutual self-destruction.

Easy enough, as there's never a dearth of customers. Bored teens or hopeless, broken people. Those seeing no hope beyond the highway. Or having no one waiting at home. Or someone to avoid going home to. Or just jackasses like myself, who just wanted to feel good, even if it's only pretend. We're all sick out here. They're not doctors, but damned good anesthesiologists.

Despite Jay's assurances, and the utter lack of *any* retribution from either side over nearly fifteen years… I worry. Jay's too stupid to slip, but if Savage Jefe decided to throw logic to the wind and… No, no it would have already happened by now. But I still get the fear when Jay's eyes snipe at a shadow, when he slips out his knife, when a car follows us for too long, or I see an awfully rare, nervous sweat upon his brow.

I never told a soul, not even Tracy. But I still worry. Big surprise, huh? But as we get older, the protection offered by being young and legally tough to kill erodes like mountains beaten into sand. Unspoken, chipping away. I still fear being caught in their crossfire, eating a bullet while crossing the street, getting the Glasgow smile while grabbing a drink. I fear being hung on a hook, flayed alive, simply because I happened to be with Jay when he gets taken out. A funny inverse of my own Curse.

So within a year, Julio Sanchez Sin Corazon got a new career and a glass eye, and Henry Jefe got a fearsome rep to build his empire upon. The scoreboard is even enough. There's no benefit to either in escalating the conflict. Perhaps Savage Jefe did break Jay in the end, like an abusive father that you can finally beat to death, if only those crippling memories of childhood trauma would cease. And perhaps Jefe sees no point in poking Julio's hornet-nest patience. So few know the truth about his eye, the financial backing for the operations, and most miraculous of all, that Julio not only lost a fight... but actually *let it go*. Now she's dead too, leaving me as the sole keeper of his secret. I think. Regardless, 'tis yet another secret I must bear for my friends and family. And an honor.

But make no mistake! This terrible wound will never define him. When it comes right down to it, this force of nature truly has a human heart. Because when everything falls apart, when things get real, and real changes life forever, you want Julio to get your back. Or seize the wheel. Now, we know I'm no good at math, but I can tell one thing about Julio Corazon: when you're at the edge, when it's do or die, the amount of fucks he gives is far less than zero. But not for his friends.

Congratulations on finding this secret, you lucky, inquisitive creature!

And now, back to our blind rush into chaos...

Blind Rage

Julio flew down the Old Highway, then took a hairpin turn left, just a *little* too fast, just a *bit* over the line. Everything exploded with such ferocity that the shock stopped my brain. The only shot at sanity was to once again defrag the memories. Restart like any other computer, praying the motherboard hasn't crashed. Reorganize the files, prioritize everything before it overheats. Awash in the adrenaline, feeling it fade into that horrid dump, I keep calm by looking back. Breaking the sequence of events down, piece by piece. Separate them from gunfire, crashing metal, and screaming, into something resembling order.

It always happens so fast.

Looking back, slow. I'm processing the last few minutes with Barry's briefcase pinched between my knees. Kitsune clutched against my chest. Near deafened by squealing tires, the savage metallic orgy, screams of terror and rage, roaring Magnum rounds. But some inane clattering pierces all. It's my teeth.

Okay. Breathe. Go back, defrag.

It started when Jay turned to look at me, navigating the crests and turns like an old pro. There was a conversation... before the turn. Come on, Tim, piece it together!

"Hey. You want to hear a secret?" Jay asked.

"Sure."

"Promise you won't flip your shit."

"Impossible. But I'll do my best," I promised.

Boil laughed, like he already knew.

Julio tossed an empty bottle right past Boil's head. "I never drugged you."

My stomach drops. We dive down a hill. Skid around a corner.

"Bullshit!" It's not possible. Just another awful joke. It must be.

"What, like I ain't ever pulled a prank on you before?" Jay laughed.

"I felt you stuff the pill in my mouth! You forced me to swallow!"

Boil laughed. Our tires bumped up onto the mercifully empty sidewalk.

"Did you actually see the pill?"

"Do you see the fucking road?" I shot my finger at his face, forcing him to turn forward.

"Did you?" he repeated.

No, I didn't.

"You gave me... I lost my mind! I hallucinated, I got horny, I shit myself, all the things you said would happen! I had an awful panic attack and, and, and then..."

"Exactly, bro. Everything that I told you would happen."

I could see them both smiling in the rearview mirror. Jay, playful. Boil, cruel.

"Okay, Jay. Let me get this straight," I spoke each word carefully, trying not to scream with rage. "So you're telling me that I'm delusional? That all the insane crap I endured was psychosomatic? That you could be such a piece of... Really? You expect me to believe that?"

"You believe a lot of weird shit! And I never called you a psycho." We took another sharp turn, all banging against the Jeep. "And what exactly did you endure, huh?"

"No, psychosomatic means... Never mind." I dropped my head into my hands. "This is the worst prank. Ever. Stop lying, man. Stop. I can't take it. I can't possibly think my mind could do all of that. That it can make her—"

"That your mind controls your body. I'm no moron." Julio rolled his eyes. I kept watching his face in the mirror, testing it for the telltale twitching of a liar. He laughed. "Tim, it was just some painkillers, dude. Just like I said. The first time, heh."

I swatted at the back of his head. The Jeep lurched side to side as he ducked, looking back and laughing. "Bullshit, I know that fuzzy cloud high! This was NOTHING like that! I don't believe you! And slow down, you blasted fool! We're on the Devil's Backbone!"

Except, maybe, with all the... heaviness, the grief, the anger... I saw a ghost. Or an imitation of a person I knew too well... NO. It was real. Whether I was drugged or not. That still leaves me mad.

"Yeah, you should be mad," Boil said. "We totally punked your ass! Hoo, boy, that's fucked up! Now you gotta believe your *best friend* would slip you hashed up drugs, just so you can believe you're not insane! Man, that's whack. Ha!"

Mad, mad. I am going to lose it. No, I have to do this, I have to get to Barry. I don't really get why. But if I don't, I'm going to die. I don't know how, I don't know when or why, but I'm going to... The truth is, after she died, I cared even more about her than I ever did about him. And I swear I do love Barry like a brother. But things need to change. I can handle this. This is just another joke, another test, another lie.

"You've drugged me before, you imbecile! Why not this time? And even if you didn't, that just means my mind is so strong that I can actually drive myself crazy. So... so that makes me totally badass! I'm walking death metal."

"Sure, sure," Julio laughed. "Whatever makes you feel better." He reached down between Boil's legs, then tossed the beer over his shoulder at me. Trusted me to catch it. I did.

"You're lying. You definitely dosed me. The evidence is insurmountable."

So many lies. Lies upon lies, unknown danger ahead and freak lizards beside me. The New Highway towered above us on the left, creating a jagged, forested mountain. Low-income housing was crammed along the coast below us, a thin guardrail keeping us from spilling down onto their roofs. All it takes is one wrong turn...

Right then Julio took that blind, hairpin turn. To the left. Now, it's entirely possible that Julio simply couldn't see the car in the other lane for two reasons. One is the aforementioned glass eye. And the other is because those *rotten shits* in the other car didn't have their lights on. Regardless, yet another perfect storm of exotic angles, bad timing, and cruel random math brought us crashing together. Flashes of Barry hit. Then I'm clinging to the roll bar as my bones quake.

The front driver's side of our Jeep shredded against the same part of their red sedan. For a second, the roar of metal meeting metal shrieked across the hills. Sparks rained. Our bumpers crunched. The cars began to spin around one another. We flew away from the other car while in reverse, skidding along the guardrail. The other car slammed into the hill below the New Highway. For one blissful moment, there was naught but smoke and silence.

"YOU CRAZY SPIC!" The driver was leaning out the window, shaking his fist. He had a thick blond beard and hip, neon blue sunglasses.

What is it with these people wearing their soul shades after dark? So many souls to hide, eh? His passenger was a scruffy man with no chin and even less hair. He was leaning across the driver, giving us all the finger.

Julio stood up on his seat. He had one hand up, trying to calm them.

"Aight guys, just chill out for one sec. No one's hurt. Yet. So calm down."

"Did you even see us? What are you, fucking blind?" the driver shouted.

Racial slurs. Blind. Not taking his first, reasonable, calm, reaction. Oh boy…

"YOU didn't have your lights on," Jay spoke, like a serpent to a child's tantrum. "Just calm down, fork over some cash, and we can—"

"Suck my cock, you fucking cunt!" the passenger chimed in.

"Gentlemen. Please, if your headlights…" Julio tried. Despite his genius vocabulary, Julio never says 'gentlemen' during a confrontation. This is bad.

"Oh fuck," I whispered to Boil. "Have you ever seen Jay calm before a fight?"

"Nah, I've never seen him fight. Why?"

"Just… just get ready. He never loses. He never, ever loses."

"Get a fucking license, you illegal trash!" the driver screamed.

Please stop screaming.

"So?" Boil shrugged. He was leaning back against the door just watching. "That's a good thing. You want him to lose?"

"You dare ask for cash, you fucking wetback? You got insurance, huh? Who's gonna pay for MY car? YOU?" the driver screamed. "You job stealing Mexican piece of shit!"

"Is he Mexican?" Boil asked me.

"No, he's American, you—look, we don't want him to fight these guys. Julio's fights are either one punch, or five of us pulling him off a bag of meat that used to look like a man."

"Sweet." Boil rested his head back on his folded hands, one leg up over the other. He waved. "On with the show!"

Jay's hands were no longer relaxed, palms forward.

The driver hopped out of his car, pinching his cigarette between his fingers. He snarled and flicked it right at Julio's face. It must have been the Curse. Had to have been. Too many tiny little terribles coming together. Because the goddamn thing hit Julio dead on in his right eye. And he screamed. Not a pained scream. A primal one. For such a big guy, he's damned fast. Looked like his Magnum teleported into hand.

Boil keeps casually talking to me, like we're just watching a movie.

"Man, those guys have some really original racism, huh? Shit, I could out shit-talk both those dipshits. Tim, you know what kinda gun that is?"

"The kind that puts us in jail! Who cares? Boil, he's about to—"

"It's a Colt Anaconda. Real nice. Probably blow right through that guy's head and straight through the car."

Jay had one boot on the door and the other on the seat. Boil sat up and raised his arms to catch Julio in case the kickback killed his balance. Jay bit his tongue and aimed.

Nooooooo......

BANG.

BANG.

Their windshield shatters. Their rear tire explodes.

I thank the gladiators' gods, and anything else that's watching from beyond the veil. Makoto, Jamiri of the Windless, Asura, Scion of the Outer Church. Any of them. Even The Golden Triangle. Please, please, let us all leave here alive! And soon.

The driver is falling back on his heels, his face twisted in fear. Julio leaps onto the road, grabs him by the collar, and with one arm, lifts the foe back to onto his feet.

"I was *trying* to be *reasonable*, you motherfucking pendejo," Julio said, one hand eating up the driver's shirt and the other pressing the .44 against his cheek. "And for the record, *amigo*, pendejo means you're a dickhead. But I think you're more of a fucking piece of inbred white-trash. Is that what you are?"

The guy spit in Jay's face.

Aaaaaaaand... Jay pistol-whips him, right in the mouth. In public. Middle of the road, between two crashed vehicles. The driver goes limp in Jay's grip, as if his off switch got hit. The guy spits out a tooth as blood dribbles down his chin.

"You're right, Timmy!" Boil slapped my shoulder in pure delight. "One-hit wonder!"

Except now the driver's lanky buddy is out of the car... and he's got a sawed-off shotgun in his hand.

"I... did not see that coming," Boil says, yet still relaxed, hardly moved at all, elbow rested on the door. Just another show. Now I finally realize just how much Boil's life is entrenched in violence.

I'm trying to keep my legs from shaking. Trying not to piss myself.

"Get on your knees!" the passenger shouts.

Julio, still holding the limp driver by his collar, pushes the gun against his throat. The driver's stupid sunglasses are on the ground. Julio crushes them without taking his eyes off the passenger.

"Fuck off," Julio growled. "Or I'll paint the road with his fucking brains. And then I'll stick that shotgun up your ass, you walking abortion."

The passenger pauses, starts to tremble, then lowers the shotgun. Julio spits and pushes the driver away. The guy stumbles back, slams into his car's door, clutching his bleeding mouth.

"Get out of here." Julio's voice is calm again.

They climb in and gun the engine. It coughs, sputters, but does its job. The wheel's rim shrieks against the pavement as the car struggles, fishtailing around the corner. It slides off the road, then slams into the trees.

Julio flicks the Magnum open, empties the shell casings onto the road, pulls fresh bullets from his pocket, and reloads.

He sauntered back to the Jeep, paused, then sat.

Boil grabbed Julio's arm and pulled him down.

"Very fucking badass, Julio. But don't forget we got a schedule to maintain. Remember our mission? Don't waste anymore time on these jerkoffs."

"Whatever. Fuck them. I'll eat their hearts."

"You don't gotta, you already—"

KABOOM!

Julio dropped into Boil's lap just in time.

"Those dirty *shits*!" Boil said. "Fuck it, Julio, ICE THEM!"

"Oh, I'm going to," Julio snarled, kicked his door open and rolled out onto the street.

Smoke rose from the missed shot, just a few feet from the Jeep. Julio duck-walked over it, weapon ready. Boil flexed, cracked his neck, but didn't join in.

"For Christ's sake! You're not really going to kill them? Are you?" I shouted. He didn't look back. "Jay?"

The two men scramble back out. The chinless passenger reloads. Clumsy. Shotgun or no, they are nothing more than man-shaped gelatin, quivering before the indignant rage of Julio Sin Corazon.

Lights flicker on in the shacks down the hill. Dogs bark. A baby cries. Boil laughs. Julio gives chase, squeezing off shots that echo across the coast. His prey scramble uphill toward the New Highway, trying to disappear into the foliage. Julio walks after them, slow and cold, like a Terminator. Firing methodically. Just like that, Jay's gone. And here I am, briefcase between my shaking knees, sword clutched impotently against my bony chest.

"Boil, go help him!"

"He doesn't need it. Julio can handle himself. You said so."

"But you're a soldier! Go! That's... um, that's an order!"

"You're out of your mind if you think I'm leaving this shit alone," Boil said, waving at the steel creates. "Julio can handle himself. Now sit down, and calm down. He'll be back any minute. And don't you ever even pretend to give ME a fucking order."

"Yeah? What about your stupid mission, Boil? Huh? What exactly is your grand plan? Just sit here until the cops arrive?" My voice trembles. Then it fills in, becomes flush with fierce exhaustion. "Screw it. I'm done. That's it. I'm done. I *am not* cool with this. Sit here and wait if you want, coward!"

I grab Kitsune and try climbing over the side of the Jeep. But his gnarled hand seizes my arm. His fingertips dig into my bicep, as if his fingers were tiger teeth.

"You're right," Boil growled. "We're going to sit here and wait. Your boyfriend will be back soon."

"And what if he isn't?" I demanded. "I'm not going to just let him go off and get killed or... or kill someone else!"

He squeezed harder. Damn, can feel his fingers biting into bone.

"You think that stupid sword is going to do anything against a shotgun? Take your own advice. Have a little faith."

"Okay, tough guy," I said. "Maybe you don't care, or maybe you're the real pussy. Let go and give me your gun."

He lets go to light a cigarette.

But I'm frozen exactly where he stopped me. Then I stumble out of the Jeep. Slumped against it, letting my knuckles crack against the road. The sword clatters beside me. Head hanging. The ocean roars miles below. Any second now a cop could round the bend. Or an innocent bystander. Screw that, I'm the innocent bystander. Jesus, has Julio finally lost it? I look up at Boil, still totally unfazed. Combat experience calm. I bite my knuckles.

"I can't believe this. I can't fucking believe this."

"Believe it," Boil said, gazing over the guardrail.

"Why? Why are these stupid lizards so goddamn important! Go help him! Please!"

"I am. Julio paid me good money for this cargo," Boil said. "He'd be disappointed if I just left it here. Mission priority, boy. And for some reason he seems happier and more relaxed now that you're here. The second I turn my back, you'll take off like the little bitch coward you are. So stay THERE."

BANG.

The gunshot echoes unseen.

"Jeez... Here! Go save him."

I look up from the road. Boil looms over me, extending his handgun down. The grip faces me. He's chewing his cigarette, staring me down. If I just slipped, hit the trigger, the bullet would shoot right through his jaw. An accident...

BANG.

"That's the Anaconda, Timmy. I haven't heard a shotgun yet. Have you?"

"No, but..." I have nothing to say, suddenly shriveled outside the Jeep, wrapped around my sword. Boil dangles his handgun in front of me.

"They're not shooting back. But go ahead. Come on, cowboy!"

I stare at his gun. I've never held a gun. I don't know how to shoot a gun. But I reach for it. Then lights wash over us. Fantastic timing! Here it comes, it's just light, just a millisecond, but I know what's coming. The flash of red and blue will follow with that awful siren. My skin tries to tear itself free and flee.

We're caught. Doomed. Death, dishonor, or jail?

I could dive under the guardrail. I'd tumble into the unknown. I could break my neck on the way down. Or I might land in barbed wire, at the foot of a hungry Rottweiler. Or an understandably freaked homeowner might end me with a rifle. Or shovel. No option brings comfort.

Or I stand and fight? Prison is not an option. No prolonged half-life of suffering and rape for me. We'll have an Alamo instead. Something to make them all proud. But not with Boil's gun. I'm not a thug. I'm a samurai. I'll use the sword if it comes down to it. If I'm to be a monster, then I choose a cop killing samurai. Only in self defense, of course.

Just pretend my foes are the fruit that I'm so good at destroying.

Yes, I can see it. Kitsune glinting in the flash of gunfire as I'm torn apart. My bullet-ridden corpse tumbles down the hill toward the hungry crabs below. Swallowed up by that barren sea, just as it should be. Fulfilling the prophecy.

Or I could use Boil as a human shield.

It's funny how many thoughts flash by in that kill switch of a second.

But I rise. Each limb trembling like a leaf, I rise. Placing the briefcase on the road, I grip Kitsune. Slide her out. She'd look more beautiful in the rain. The lights abound to round the bend, the engine is roaring. Boil is shouting something, Jay is gone but I hear gunshots in the dark. It's all about to hit. For a moment, I'm night-blind and deafened by all the confusion.

Sorry, Barry. Guess this is what happens when you run behind devils. Ha, well, at least I tried. Failed, but tried. Please consider my blood debt paid. Hope fate spares the others. Even Boil, if need be.

Just let this Curse die with me.

Kuwabara, kuwabara! Heaven forbid the lightning strikes us.

I take a deep breath, certain it's the last. Waiting for the impact, or the sirens and barked orders to drop our weapons. Yet the light is just strolling over, taking its sweet time. Is it just the adrenaline? Come on already, turn the corner before I lose my nerve! Finally, Kitsune shines, my legs slip into a horse stance as the doom arrives.

But there's no siren. It *had* to be cops. Had to be! Gunshots echoing all over the road? A car crash? Someone must have called the police! Yet for once, the Fortune Egg cracked, and out spilled a golden baby chick, instead of a slimy still-birthed eel. Instead of a black and white cop car, we were confronted with a red convertible. Sunshine and flowers and pink butterflies flood my cells, washing away all the pain and fear.

But Boil was not so pleased.

He was standing on the passenger seat, one leg propped up on the mangled dashboard. His trapezius muscles were flexed in full force, like a cobra's hood. Veins popped beneath his skin, a fleshy roadmap to Armageddon. His head was hunched forward, neck tense, legs rippling with potential energy.

The convertible's high beams click off.

My suspicions are confirmed.

The driver is a balding man in aviator shades and a purple silk shirt.

His ponytail hangs from his balding scalp like a horsetail from its ass. He's not phased by the scene before him. The sedan smashed against a tree, the Jeep with one headlight plowed into the guardrail, the shaking freak with a sword in the road, or the ogre standing with his hand hovering over the gun tucked in his waistband.

As I lower my sword, Boil whips out his gun and takes aim.

"Boil, NO! They're friendlies!"

Too late.

Bang.

The Stand

The shot went high and wide.

Even I was surprised, truth be told. But I did it! I'd saved their lives by swinging Barry's briefcase into Boil's calves. He buckled, did not fall, but still missed. I didn't even realize what I did until it was done. Expected cheers, applause, but the following silence was just awkward.

Boil broke it. "Easy, boy! It was just a *warning shot*. You almost got somebody killed!" He snarled down at me, speaking nice and loud for his former targets. He laughed, as he lowered his gun. "Sorry about that, folks! This guy is an idiot. I'm U.S. Army, and we have a little situation. I thought you were their backup." He nodded at the empty sedan. "No need to panic, I'm securing the perimeter."

What an ass. I wanted to kill him, but just let the lie slide. Because it's a double dose of relief now, oh boy! Sweet hallelujah! Of all the random cars...

"You know them?" Boil's head snapped back to me. His facial muscles lost some tension, downgrading from a murderous snarl to his standard grimace.

"Obviously!" I tried to sound tough, but could hear the squeak in my voice. Waiting to see how they'll react.

Sergio's staring at us, contemplative, but very much at ease. Looks as if he's used to these 'mishaps'. Deliberating on whether he's intrigued or just annoyed. An auburn cigar cracks between his teeth, his left arm is draped over the door, dangling limp above the road. His wrist is cupping the wheel. The purple silk shirt cascades across his chest, little gray hairs peeking up from the collar like albino spider legs. Finally, he smiles.

That smoking hot Brazilian model is still riding shotgun like a bored heiress, a scornful look of disdain creasing her perfect olive skin. Stretched across the cramped back seat is that lanky bastard I can't help but love. He reclines proudly in my blue and orange Hawaiian shirt. Quick as a snake, he leaps out of the convertible and strides toward our Jeep.

"Bernard!" I slide Kitsune away. "Holy shit on a dog's tits, am I glad to see you!" I flung open my arms to hug him.

"Bernard?" Boil asked.

"Everything's okay, Boil! It's Burn!"

"Whoa, dude. That was bonkers. Tim! What's up, man?" Burn said, ignoring my open arms. Then he saw *who* tried to shoot them. "Holy shit! Is that Lucas Boil? And isn't this Julio's Jeep? Where's he at? Man, you look terrible. What the hell are you doing here?"

"I have no idea," I said, shaking my head. "One minute we're fine, the next, Julio's beating a guy to death and we're getting shot at, and now he's running around in the woods after them!"

"He's just taking care of some business," Boil said. "Tim's overreacting."

"Overreacting?"

Sergio got out, leaving his convertible running. He strolled over to the other mangled car, hands in the pockets of his leather pants, whistling while surveying the damage. A near visible cloud of synaptic lust formed over his head, most likely calculating liabilities and payouts. This slick fuck is the one who kidnapped Bernard in my moment of need. And like his date, he's not even fazed. His transition into pleasantries springs out as fast as Boil's gun had.

"Hello, hello! Oh, this is just precious," Sergio said. He turned to us, extending one hand toward the empty vehicle. His cigar bobbed above his cleft chin. "This is truly amazing. Fate, it is! I know this car!"

"They're your friends?" Boil asked, hiding his weapon.

Uh-oh. This might actually be quite awful.

"Far from it! Good work, lads."

"Thanks?" we said in unison.

"Clearly, these men are to blame. Their engine's on, but the lights aren't. They've fled the scene of an accident. So are there any witnesses that weren't involved? Are you looking to press charges? How soon do you want to sue?"

His hand darted into his shirt, and then reemerged, business card at the ready. He handed it to Boil, who accepted it without looking. Sergio truly perplexed him.

"Hey, Sergio," I said. "I'm Tim. Remember? Bernard's roommate."

"Hmm? Do I know you?" Sergio said, peeling his sunglasses down. He extended his hand, another card between his fingers. I didn't even see him reach for it. "Antonio Sergio, attorney at law. Pleasure to meet you, Tom. Tell me, what do you remember regarding the mitigating circumstances of this little incident?"

"*Tim*. We met a few hours ago."

"Oh yes, Tim. Right. Of course! Don't forget what I said about the jewel."

"What?" I vaguely recall some inane nonsense he spewed before stealing Burn away. I brushed my hair aside and tuned him out. He just as easily returned to inspecting the battered Jeep.

"Is he for real?" I asked Burn.

"Nice shirt," Boil said.

"Thanks." Bernard pinched the shirt from his chest with satisfaction. "Dude, Sergio's a lawyer. He's used to this kind of shit. So what are you doing here?"

"It's a long story. Sparked by your lack of assistance. Wait, are you guys headed back west now?"

"Nope. Actually, we were having a great time out at the Sugar Shack, drinking, gambling, and then Sergio spots these two hillbilly losers and decides he wants to tail them. He was dead set on it, almost pissed! I've never seen Sergio angry."

"Oh what, in the two weeks you've known him?"

"It's been a month, I think?"

"I'm quite sure now. I know who they are," Sergio said. He thumbed over his shoulder. "The lowlifes driving that car. Yes, yes I've met the scum before. We weren't far behind. Looks like you good boys got to them first."

"My friend is dealing with them now," Boil said. "You might have a murder case on your hands soon."

"He means *my* friend, Julio."

"Excuse me, did you say Julio? Julio Corazon?" Sergio strode past me and over to Boil. "Ah yes! That Jeep! It is him after all!"

"Yeah. So what's it to you?" Boil grilled Sergio, but the lawyer didn't notice.

"Julio's an old friend. All the facets of the same jewel. Right, Tom? And your enemies here are low-level associates of one of my... former clients. One who's acted quite unprofessionally, I'll have you know. One who I'd like to catch up with. Just to settle things, in a manner of speaking. It seems my boy Julio is on something of the same trip. Are you boys all on this devil's run together?"

"Settle things?" Boil eyed suave Antonio Sergio. He looked at the card again. "Lawyer, huh? You got some sway with cops?"

"Certainly."

"Hey, guys? Where's Jay?" I scanned about the smoke, trees, the distant shore. All silent. When I glanced at the model, she sighed and turned away.

"So who do these punks work for?" Boil asked.

"Henry Poole," Sergio's tone was both cold and optimistic, like a scorned human and a polite robot speaking in one voice. "I hoped to catch up with them. Nothing illegal, I assure you. Just to pass along a message to Henry about unpaid debts. Curious. I don't know why, but as soon as I saw them, this uncontrollable urge to find good old Henry arose. Indomitable. There certainly is something strange in the air tonight."

"Hell yeah, there is." Boil cocked his head to the side. "Let's talk."

They strode around to the back of the convertible. The taillights cast them in red while the model pinched her necklace open and stuck it under her nose. Snort and a sigh of relief.

"Burn," I turned to him. "What the devil is happening?"

"Maybe Boil needs legal counsel. I don't know. Isn't he supposed to be in Iraq or something?"

"He's on leave. Plus he's got some kind of bizarre business with Jay. Tonight. In Tomahok."

Sergio and Boil shook hands. They returned. Sergio clapped Boil on the back. Boil's fists clenched reflexively. Sergio didn't notice.

"Truly divine intervention, my boys!" Sergio said. "These circumstances lend themselves to a most propitious collective future." He looked directly at me. "A shared future, an aspect of the collective over-mind, yes, Tom?"

What is with this guy? Why is his date just sitting in the car, unfazed? She took another snort. Ah, of course.

"Cool, cool. But what the hell's up in here?" Burn asked. "C'mon Tim, fill us in."

"I did…" I began, but the moment the word 'us' hit my ears, I faded away.

The internal world sways on its axis, twisting about my core while the outside world remained solid. My stomach boils. It's been a long time since I've eaten. Need something powerful and exotic. Corn. Bacon scallops. Snow crab legs. My skin is tracing paper. I'm hollow, a man shaped half-mast boner, ready to flop under the slightest pressure. My mindset is one of pre-dawn hours, when every blade of grass is wet and sharp. I'm leaning against the Jeep, with the guardrail behind me and a sharp drop to the shacks, pueblos, and beach below. I hate Boil. I love Burn. Sergio just creeps me out. The woman is an alien. And we're all waiting on the one friend I really need. Right now.

They keep talking, maybe even to me, but I just stagger away, limp sword, sounds fading. Adrenaline dump. Feel so heavy. Fall to my knees. They'll be broken before the night's through. Then a strange smell wafts down from the upper hill. Something like a stoner's corpse, ripe and spilling out. A musky green odor, faint yet impossible to ignore.

"Tim? Hello?"

Snap snap!

"You in there, buddy?" Burn asked. He kept snapping his fingers in front of my face. "Dude, what's up? You're pretty pale."

I smacked his hand away. "No, Burn, I'm not okay. I'm really, really not okay."

"Because?"

"Because? Cripes man, look at this scene! We just got in a car crash, and now Jay's acting like he's in some spaghetti western! We're all just standing around at the scene of a very heavy crime! You don't even want to know what else I've been through tonight."

"Well, *they* hit *us*," Boil said.

"Serves you right, Tim" Bernard said. He leaned against the dented Jeep. "I mean, what the hell are you doing heading out to Tomahok? Aren't you supposed to be visiting Barry? That's selfish, man. I thought better of you."

"You thought better of—he's your goddamn friend too! At least I'm trying! What the hell have you done?"

"Not put him in the hospital."

"Look, I'm trying to get there. Very, very hard. That's exactly why I'm in all this god-damned chaos. No thanks to *you*, you rotten creep." I held the briefcase up, letting it dangle in the air. "See? I got the books. And at great personal risk, I might add. Julio was going to drive me out there after he got rid of…" The crates rattled and hissed. "Those."

"Cool," Bernard's eyes lit up. "What's in there? They sound angry."

Sergio didn't react, and the model kept snorting at her necklace.

"Yeah. Cool. Boil smuggled some weird lizards out of Iraq. One of them shoots blood from its eye like a cannon. They're selling them to a friend in Tomahok, and then Julio promised to drive me out to Hawkhouse after, but seriously, Burn, I'm not even sure that—"

"Julio, my dear boy!" Sergio shouted.

We all turned to see Jay bounding down the hill, letting his heels dig into the dirt, sliding between the trees, Magnum hanging lazily at his side. He stepped out onto the road. That dead pot odor trailed him. His right leg was slick and brown. Blood. More fucking blood. Oh Christ, no…

"Well?" Boil asked.

"Ah, you know how it is," Julio said. "I chased them. I shot. They got away. I wasn't really trying to hit them, just scare them off. Buy some time for us to bail this scene before they report it, know what I'm sayin'? No big deal."

"Then what the hell is that?" I pointed at his pants.

"That? Ah, I saw a skunk on the way back, and the bastard was ready to spray me. So I capped it." He looked up from the stain and did a double take. "Yo, what the fuck! Sergio? What's up, old man? What's good?"

"Fate! Pure fate, indeed. Most fortuitous, golden, lovely, fate!" Sergio answered. He reached out so that he and Julio could clasp each other's forearms.

"Is this guy for real?" I asked Bernard.

He shrugged. Boil crossed his arms and straightened his back.

"My, how you've grown into a fine young man," Sergio said.

"What's it been, something like ten years?" Jay tossed his gun into the Jeep as casually as dirty laundry.

"I believe it has. Well, it's good to see you're not in jail! Looks like you've finally learned how to handle your legal issues on your own," Sergio said. "I sincerely apologize about… for my absence. I had to concentrate on my practice back home in the city, you understand? No hard feelings?"

"No, I guess not. Mom always thought you were cool, so…" Julio said. "Well, it's good to see you, Serge." Jay looked around the scene now, as if taking it all in for the first time. "Uh, what's going down now?"

"We've been making the rounds," Bernard piped up.

"That's what you call partying?" I asked.

"Oh, what up, Burn," Julio nodded at him, then acknowledged me. "Bro, you never told me Burn and Sergio hang!"

"As if I ever know what the hell is going on." I turned away from them again, staring out at the silent sea.

Sergio waved Boil over. "Your friend Lucas and I just negotiated a mutually beneficial deal."

"Oh really?" Julio arched his eyebrow. He thumbed over his shoulder to the vacant car. "You know you're my man, but I don't think these bone smuggling meat-thieves are gonna press charges. Ain't like anybody's innocent here."

"No, no. Nothing concerning those dregs," Sergio said. "But we do have a common goal. And tonight of all nights! Come, let's talk."

Sergio wrapped his hairy arms around both Julio and Boil's shoulders, leading them off for another private chat. They spoke in shadows. My irritation grew.

"Will you all just shut up?" I shouted. "We're standing around making chit chat after a gunfight! Did you forget that police exist? Let's get out of here!"

"I guess he has a point," Burn said.

"Boys, boys, relax. Let me handle the police," Sergio said to the group, before confiding with Jay and Boil again. "So it's agreed then. I'll follow you back to Tomahok."

"Bernard," I said. "If you have any info, now's the time to spill it."

"I dunno. About what?" He shrugged. He really doesn't care.

Jay jumped back into the driver's seat. Boil clambered into shotgun. I stared at the convertible as Sergio got behind the wheel and Bernard slipped into the back seat. The woman took another snort of coke from her necklace. Two cars full of mutants. Don't know which option is worse.

"Tim! Vamanos!" Julio shouted.

I hunched back into my seat, briefcase, sword, and beers pressed between me and the steel crates. Julio whipped a U-turn, just brushing the guardrail. Our vehicles were now lined up facing opposite ways. Just as Sergio was about to get behind us, the fun started up again. The model leapt to her feet, teetering on the car seat. Animated like a harpy filled with lightning, she shouted at our Jeep. Boom, she finally decides to speak!

"Estos gringos, puedes cree esta mierda? Jamas volvere a esta ciudad condenada, y menos con estos hijos de putas! Antontio, porque te asocias con estos ninos?"

278

Now it was Julio's turn, bolting up with one foot on his crumpling dashboard. I watched his Magnum teeter on the small of his back, tucked into his pants with the handle hanging out. When did he do that? Speaking faster than I could hyperventilate, they volleyed back and forth.

"Oye puta, sientate y quedate callada. Nadie te pregunto tu opinion," Julio snarled.

"Callate! O te arranco la verga!"

"Y se la meto en la garganta de tu madre!"

"La tuya deberia haberse matado antes de que tu nacieras!"

It was fiery and fluent. But like any explosion, it was over just as quick. And with that, Julio whipped the Magnum out and raised it into the air.

Everyone immediately reacted. A grotesque dance of waving arms and alarm, Sergio pulling at the model to sit down, her still yelling and pointing at Julio, Boil grabbing Jay's elbow, trying to pull him back, Bernard squirming like a squid, and me melting between the lizards' crates. My Spanish isn't that good, but I think we all got the general idea.

Sergio whispered sternly into her ear, Julio's chest heaved up and down, and Boil finally convinced him that we shouldn't be wasting any more time. Jay sat down. He gripped the wheel so hard the veins in his forearms nearly burst. Then he rolled his head back. He pulled a vial out of his cargo pant pocket and spilled some coke in a fat line across the dashboard. He blew it, howled, and gunned the engine.

"Don't be stingy," Boil said.

Julio tossed the vial. Boil caught it, screwed the cap off, jammed the whole thing into his nose. I heard Bernard giggling from the other car. Barry, I know you're hurt, but I bet right now you've got a steady chemical drip keeping you sedate and placid, while I slip further and further into the mouth of Yamaraja, with Belial driving, and Sheol riding shotgun.

Reached for the seatbelt, but by then the engine roars and we're speeding down the Devil's Backbone once again. With one headlight. I pulled my knees up to my chest and kept Kitsune pressed between my legs, sticking straight up as an unintentional show of phallic power. I slid down into the seat, trying to get my knees to press into the space between Julio and Boil. Whenever possible, one's knees should be presented confidently. Due to my fresh pants, I couldn't show my gnarled knees, but their presence was felt nonetheless. The knees are a symbol of vitality, grace, and balance. Wearing shorts that cut off just above the knee is ideal. Don't shy away from craggy, scarred ones. They show wisdom, much like the tree's rings or the scars on a wolverine's back. An animal that actually doesn't feel fear and can eat a poison snake without dying, and take a machete blow to a head with ease.

"What?" Boil turned to me, sneering.

"Homeboy here is right. Knees are crazy sexy," Jay said.

How long, oh lord? How long? I cracked another Uber Ale and finished it before I could savor the taste.

"You know how they do runs like this upstate?" Boil asked, so excited, getting a chance to drop knowledge instead of bombs for once. "Check this. The dealers fully tint all the windows on a black car. Then they wait till a moonless night, strap on a pair of night vision goggles, and just fucking burn rubber. Always way over a hundred miles an hour, and not on the highway, either! On the damned shoulder!"

"No shit, genius," Julio said, seeming to concentrate on the drive for once.

"If a cop even notices them at all, it's just a blur zipping by in the darkness," Boil said… to me. He's having a conversation with me. Huh. "Not a chance of catching them. What you think about that, Tim? You rather be with us or in one of those whips?"

How about being the cop, sitting in my patrol car, bloated stomach glazed in sugar and coffee? And then suddenly some horrid, invisible beast streaks past. Me just sitting there in shock, knowing if anyone was going to do anything, it'd fall on me. What would I do? "Why don't they just lay those tire shredders across the shoulders?"

"That's a god-damn dumb idea," Boil answered.

"Yeah man, liability and shit," Julio said. "Pigs cause an accident for some innocent hick and they're toast. Their asses are always shackled by lawsuits and caution."

Right. Of course. Lawsuits and caution.

"I gotta get my hands on more night vision goggles," Boil said.

I buried my face against the briefcase. I kept it there, listening to the occasional car pass, listening to Boil's phlegm coated breathing, and Julio whistling. Shortly, these sounds are drowned out by a distant bass, thumping like a war drum. It's a sinister sound that excites the basest of my kind, an undeniable sign that we have arrived. We round another sharp bend and see the faint orange glow. I steal one last glance down at the purple surf pounding on the shore.

The town's glow grows as we descend faster into the heart of Tomahok. The war drums are joined by a thin, whining sound. Insects mating in pebbles. And just like that, we fly up and over one last hill. We're here. Lord almighty. I've never been so happy to be in this wretched place. It means this is all almost over. Pretty soon it'll all be just another bad memory.

Tomahok's main street splits like a trident. The top fork leads out to the desolate lighthouse. The middle prong begins with Main Street, forming the heart of the small yet densely populated town. Squeeze through that, and you end up at the farthest point, the affluent docks, the home of yachts, seabreeze cruisers, day ships, whale watching, and the like. It's the diamond in the rough, flanked by the ancient lighthouse to the north, and the seedier dockyards to the south. The lowest fork, the path of the shifty and shiftless, curves down and around the town proper, out to the scummiest dockside, the Tiburon Pier, with only one infamous bar beside a vast parking lot graveyard.

Of course, we pound right through the middle prong, straight into the crowd. The war drums come from Main Street, where the Old and New Highways reconverge. Julio slows down as we press into a crowd of young men and women spilling across the street. Wandering from bar to bar, grinding against each other, spilling drinks, lighting joints, and shouting whoops, hollers, and wild yips. We crawl along, just another float in the parade, with Sergio's car close behind.

A bullhorn blares in the distance. A cop car rolls through the street slowly, grinding bottles and beer cans under its wheels. The officer is desperately commanding the crowd to disperse. In the winter, the handful of cops employed are more than enough. So bored they make sport of running down and executing deer, or ticketing the hardcore winter surfers. Beating librarians and such. But the summer is a whole other mess entirely. Yet the town is too poor and too cheap to up the man-force, even just for one season a year. We're all quite okay with that for various reasons.

The street is thick with lust, abandon, desperation, bestiality, and lobster shells. Still, I follow the ways of the noble ostrich. Lay low. This is no longer my place, these are not my people. Those days died long ago. It sounds like the humping throng is in the car with us. Something pops up ahead. A gunshot? Or fireworks? Impossible to tell in this manic sea.

"Damn, yo. I think someone's heated up there," Julio said. I looked up just in time to see the cop car's siren snap on, trying in vain to turn around in the crowd. Blowing its bullhorn at the stumbling young drunks (at best, if not more eccentrically inebriated).

"Nope," Boil said, sipping his beer and then slipping it back out of view.

"Just fireworks," Julio said. "Bummer. Tim, remember that game we used to play?"

"I hate this place." I slowly wrapped my fingers around Kitsune's hilt, letting the miscreants around us know I was armed as the Jeep crawled through the street. Any of these freaks could reach in, and they need to know I mean to lop off any errant limbs. A most authentic zombie horde experience.

I look over my shoulder to Sergio's red beast. Bernard's head is just barely visible between Sergio and the Brazilian. I wave. He returns a dopey grin and a thumbs up. Blessed space cadet. Like he's got nothing to lose. I want to be Burn someday. When I've got nothing to lose but bitter patterns, darkness and shadows. Get out of this world. Ironic, I once loved this town for the same reasons I now hate it.

"Man, I'll *always* love this town," Julio said. He draped his arm across the back of the seat and hung his head upside down, a diseased twinkle in his eye. His dry lips peeled back, about to split. His right shoulder was shifting, and despite the roar of blissful chaos around us, I heard a soft clicking in the front seat. Playing with the Anaconda in his lap. I mean... did they hear that? He's spinning the .44's empty chamber in his lap. It's okay if they hear that...

I felt trapped on a sinking ship of sin, somehow still aflame as it slips into an endless whirlpool, the bottom being the gaping maw of the Drowned God, one of the old ones, with black teeth and seaweed draped across its barnacled skull. My enemy by my side and my brother at the wheel. This whole scene is bad weirdness squared. Too much to be a coincidence. Bernard befriends a powerful lawyer from Julio's past? And then tails the same goons that we slam into, and we're all just one big happy family now?

No. I know what this is. It's the Curse, setting me up for a big one. This must be the storm. I can picture it now, the great sneering ray, moving pawns across the cosmic chessboard. What moves can I make?

Are things what they really seem? Did I stumble into their secret game, or did they all stumble into mine? How many more must I drag down with me? Please, take Boil as a sacrifice! No, I guess that would be the antithesis… but an offering nonetheless.

No matter. Now that Burn is with me, I can't help but give in to that second creepy feeling. The one that swarms about this Jeep like a school of spirit piranhas. All this horror and violence, chaos and secrets, and yet… it's kind of exciting.

Perhaps I've just awoken, but the game is nearing a checkmate. And no matter whose game we end up playing, one thing is increasingly clear. You can accuse me of being many things. Cursed, weak, pathetic, cynical, selfish. But I'm not stupid. I need to step up my game, before another piece gets knocked off the board. But it's all too clear now. Regardless of how well I play, someone will die tonight.

Sin Corazon

Our one-eyed monster-helmed Jeep rumbles forward slowly. A caravan of bent bankers, twisted runway superstars, and high school football heroes stagger behind. Like cows circling around to the slaughterhouse. Blinded, blissful, butchered.

"Jay, I have a problem."

"No shit," Boil said.

"I'm serious. I'm sick. Might be losing my mind."

"Nah, you've always been like this," Julio said. "You're just stressed. Have another beer."

"No, hear me out. I keep thinking that I'm just thinking things. But then it turns out I'm actually saying them out loud. It's been happening all night."

"Word, you've been mumbling some strange shit. Well, like, stranger than usual." Julio shrugged. "Fuck it. Things happen. One time I swore I could read Jubador's mind for a week. Boy, that's one perverted lizard."

This from the butterfly fucker.

"Whatever," Boil said. "That's your problem? You're lucky, man. If you ever saw the shit I saw, the real problems people deal with… Dudes killing people for fun. Kids running around with one arm and gushing blood at your feet. Constant rape. Your friend's limbs rocketing into the sky. Babies that end at the neck. Food covered in flies, everywhere, and people too hungry to give a shit. Waking up covered in your best friends' guts. Can't even hear their last words over the explosions."

"I'm very sorry that going to war sucked, but your suffering doesn't invalidate mine," I said. "Granted, maybe yours is worse, but it doesn't make mine go away."

"MAYBE?"

"Yo, chill, chill, chill. Check *her* out." Julio pointed to a tanned girl marching her neon green thong through the crowd.

Boil whistled. His blood was still pumping, but at least now it wasn't from anger. She was well tanned. Nice ass. Swaying hips and a shallow curve up her bare back. Can almost… almost… Her skin looks so smooth and oiled… No, catch yourself, deflect.

"Hey, want to know something funny about tans?" I jumped

forward to push myself up front. This was information I shared with Tracy years ago as we tanned naked, hidden in the Walking Dunes. "In ye olden days, a tan was looked upon with disdain. It meant you were lower class, since you spent your days doing manual labor outside. Pale skin was in vogue with the elite. So was incest-bred hemophilia, but anyway, now it's all reversed. People who work for a living tend to do it inside, poisoned by chemicals and cancer rays, while the elite spend all day soaking up their cancer on the beach. Pretty neat, huh?"

"What? The fuck are you going on about now?" Boil asked, still staring at the parade of tits and ass.

"Yeah, Tim, no offense, but I don't give a shit. They can tan all they want," Julio said monotone, his head scanning all the nubile flesh that prevented our progress.

A midnight parade of party-goers so thick we may as well be at a rock concert. Wish I could surrender to it. I've tried. Lord, I've tried. Since she died everything is just... muted. No desire. Everything feels like ash and concrete.

"Ash and...? God, will you shut up for five minutes?" Boil snapped.

"See! That's *exactly* what I'm talking about! I truly did not realize I was talking just now!"

"Relax," Jay said. He tossed a lit joint over his shoulder. "Hit this."

It fell by my waist. "I don't think that's helping." I found it before a whole new hole got burned into the seat.

"Or go ride with that lawyer. Julio, you didn't pay me enough to ride with this jackass. You're lucky I don't jack up the price."

"There's no room with them," I grunted. "What's the deal with Sergio anyway?"

"Mutual friends," Julio said. "We go way back."

"Then why don't I know him?"

"You seriously don't recognize him, do you? Eh, I guess you wouldn't have seen him much. Most of the sleepovers were at your place."

"You two had sleepovers?" Boil laughed. "That's just so precious."

"Bitch, shut up. You're just mad jealous."

He did shut up. Because Julio was right. I can see baby Boil, alone in middle school, wondering why nobody invited him to sleepovers. Growing colder and meaner every day. Would he be different today if we'd just included him in our reindeer games? Why was he excluded to the point of becoming a jerk just to—

"Damn, I want to bang the shit out of these hoes," he said. "Just tear that pussy apart. Am I right, or am I right?"

Right. That's why.

"So Sergio knows this mystery friend of yours, too? The lizard guy?"

"Uh, yeah, I guess so," Jay said, staring straight ahead.

"Curiouser and curiouser," I said, rapping on one crate. "Weird and rich. So he's both your friend and Sergio's, and also Boil's ex-military buddy who just moved out here?"

"He is weird, and he is rich," Julio said, voice flat.

"He sounds crazier than either of you. Dagon protect us, I don't want to meet this guy," I said. There it is again, that itch. The mystery is like a rash, flaring deeper and hotter, aching to burst like an ingrown hair. I cleared my throat. "So uh, I don't want to scare you, but I've been getting this feeling. Like we're in danger."

"No shit, ace," Boil said. "We just had a shootout twenty minutes ago."

"Well, that's my point," I turned to Jay. I hate talking to the back of people's heads. "You're being pretty liberal with the violence tonight. It's just... If we keep running around like this, someone might get hurt."

They're silent.

"Or worse than hurt..."

Still no response, like I just flicked their off switches by accident. Praise Nyarlathotep, if that's even possible.

Boil's cell phone rings. Johnny Come Marching Home again. Sigh. He flicked it open.

"What's good?" Boil listened. Nodded. Dropped his head back in annoyance. "Right. Yeah, no problem. Look, I said we'll be there. Yeah, just me and one other guy. Huh? I told you, my cousin! Don't you ever fucking pay attention? You think it's easy to catch these things? Plus I gotta keep them alive? Feed them? No, *no you* listen. You got a problem with that, we can cancel the deal right now. Yeah, I'll wait."

Julio shot Boil a furiously concerned glare. Boil put his finger to his lips. Julio ground his teeth. Boil kept talking while leaning out to smack a passing ass. The girl actually laughed. The guys with her yelled something as we rolled away.

"Listen, your boss ain't the only guy with a taste for these beasts. People got fetishes for exotic reptiles all over, so I'll unload them one way or another. Remember, I'm doing you the favor," Boil continued. "Okay, fine. All right, I said okay! I got it. No, it's cool. Don't worry. That's fine. Aight, see you then. Peace."

Boil snaps the phone shut.

"What's the deal?" Jay demanded. "Did you just screw us up?"

"Bitch, please. It's just a slight delay. They aren't ready for us to come by yet, so we gotta kill some time. Just an hour or two. They got some other deal they're still finishing up."

"Great, let's go smoke a bone!"

"Smoking a bone doesn't mean giving a blow job," Boil politely informed me.

You've got to be kidding me. I'm about to tell him off... but get caught. Deal? Boss? Something feels shady over friendly. Something here's not right. More not right than I already knew. The doubt gremlin is clawing at my back.

Julio waves his hand at Sergio, then makes a sudden right turn, bumping over the curb. People dive out of the way, shouting insults. Luckily Julio doesn't care this time, and we're suddenly off the main strip, into open air and with twenty-foot high dunes ahead, the carnival spiraling behind. Sergio and crew are right behind us, cruising around the beach-bordered back roads.

This road leads to the southern fork. The strip runs for half of Tomahok's meager eight-mile length. There is a small branch of hotels, restaurants, and bars huddled along the shore. Their strung-up lights and neon signs bathe the coastal road in pink, green, and purple. Ridiculous, all of them right next to each other, some even sharing walls, and all expensive as hell. I know this first-hand. Tracy and I managed to sneak away and spend a whole weekend here, once. A hundred and fifty dollars a night minimum, but hell, that was worth every dime. I'd sell my organs on the black market to pay for that weekend again and again. And again. The motel that we stayed in, which I thought was the cheapest, was Shagalots. The stupid thing was built right on the beachfront but still had a heated swimming pool for those who just want to watch the ocean while they swim. It's not hard to imagine this place, a decade from now, when the Earth's fever burns us out. The hotels will merge into a seaside mega-dome, with a giant wave pool. Generating endless, static waves. Rows of yuppies, yammering and drooling on their vid-phones, all in perfect synchronization while pretending to surf. A row of hollow apostles, husks, Bitcoin drones seeking one more minute of pleasure to dull the pain, the pain they might not even feel, gumming up their souls and waiting for their savior, clad in full dry suits that will always tear.

"You stayed at Shagalots?" Boil asked.

"Yes? No?" Hearts thundering. How much did I say? Jay's fine, but Boil must not know my secrets.

"You just said you stayed at Shagalots and gummy people were surfing there," Jay said. "Forget it, Luke, it's just his usual weird bullshit."

"That's it? That's all I said?"

"Yeah bro, chill out." Jay swings another hard right, seemingly into a wall of thick beach grass, but we know better. It's like a spy movie. We plow right through the fake wall of monstrous sharp grass and into the dirt-soiled sand wastes.

This is a secret trail. Another secret area for locals who want to get drunk and screw just beyond the prying eyes of others. We park in a large clearing, the ocean night framing one side, and the glow and hustle of the party world on the other. Sergio's ride comes clambering in behind. Parked in the bottom of a deep bowl, dunes framing us with the ocean so close that we can hear its roar just out of view.

"What's this now?" Sergio shouts over the idle roar of his fantastic car.

"Smoke break," Julio shouted. He's hunched over, splitting a blunt in his lap.

He cracks it and dumps the guts onto the dirt-sand while Boil flicks the weed's stems and seeds into the brush. The Brazilian looks absolutely furious, arms crossed, head down, defiant eyes straining back toward Main Street. She obviously wants to be at the party, not in the shadow dunes with us chicos estupidos.

Bernard's head pops up. "Sweet!"

"You got any to throw in?" Jay asked him without looking up.

"Yeah, I got some good bud," he answered, flicking a plastic bag into the Jeep.

"What the hell, Bernard? You got money for gambling and drugs but not for groceries or toilet paper? You know, necessities?"

"Weed is a necessity," he said.

I trust he was genuinely confused by my annoyance. And then I flicked Boil on the shoulder without even realizing it. "How do you guys keep pulling weapons and drugs out of nowhere? You're like cartoons."

"Yup," Jay said as he licked the blunt, sealing it shut. "We're just full of surprises."

Boil laughed. Too deep. Too knowing.

So now we're sitting in a circle, except for the model, who hasn't even unfolded her arms, let alone left the car. Sergio is with us, but failed to convince her to join. Our rides frame us, their headlights casting an appalling glow in the absence of fire. Bernard is to my right, Kitsune sheathed across my lap across my crossed legs. Julio's stretching out on my left, Boil to his, and Sergio to his, completing the circle. Our shadows melt into each other, flickering limbs in what feels like a warm firelight. The merged shadows look like the All-Father's Lost Legion from the Dawn of Sorrow, a silhouette of twitching corpses fused around one pulsing core.

"Oh yeah, that thing ruled!" Burn piped up. "That was the last boss in uh... whatever game that was. Tough son of a bitch. Every time you hit it, one of the bodies falls off until it's just like... What was that thing inside? A brain with hands?"

Burn, Barry, and I beat that game a thousand times. But I can't remember the name either. The blunt makes its way around the circle. Lap after lap. Crispy and crackling, a smell of spit, old chocolate, and armpits. Something is in the air, but it's been there all night. We are totems. Demi-gods on shattered earth. Bone and dust, hair, meat, and piss. The old boys club.

"Yo! Tim," Julio says. He sits up, now cross legged like me, elbow propped up on knee, staring down at the blunt as he blows smoke out. Like he's speaking his transient escape instead of me. "Tim. Yo."

"Yes? Yo, what?"

"I gotta tell you something." He blows a thick, forceful cloud across the cherry. It flares through the poison air. He's a shaman. "Yeah, yeah, I gotta tell you somethin', dude."

"Right here? Right now? You sound... Do you want to go for a walk?"

"Nah, we're all friends here."

I eye Boil. His head is wafting about oddly, as if he's unsure of his surroundings. Surely this mere weed isn't rocking him so hard. His eyes are lost, searching for something among the dirt, the litter, the hard, dry beach grass. Deep in thought, if he's capable of such a thing. Regardless, this is a special moment. The Chief is singling me out in front the tribe.

Cool. It feels just as cool as ever, back when the other jerks gave me crap until Jay praised me. Gave me some small town respect.

"I'm skipping town."

What?

"What?"

"Tomorrow, I'm getting out of here," Julio said. He looked me in the eye, head down, blunt still burning in his hand. "This place is dead to me, man. It's time to move on."

No. No, come on, not another. Don't. Don't do this.

"Seriously? What the hell, Jay? Of all the people to leave! You're safe in Thornwood. Hell, you're a king! You've got clients, cops in your pocket, a home. Friends!"

"A home... Ha. Doesn't matter though. See, man... the thing is, tonight, how do I... Tonight I got to do something that—"

"HOLY SHIT!" Boil shouts. He's propped on all fours, pointing right at me. Eyes cracked and red. "I can't believe it. Now I know why I recognize those pants! Timmy Dune, you sneaky little player! You're wearing what's her name's pants! That hot little bitch! You were at her house before!"

I speak, all teeth, skin burning, heartbeat fast and violent.

"Tracy. Tracy Cameron."

"Yeah! Tracy. That's right, of course! Your friend's sister! They're not his pants, they're hers! I seen her in them at parties and shit. Whoa, you're messed up, Poon. Dude, *why the fuck are you wearing her pants?*"

"How do you know that they're hers?" I asked. Can't hear my own words, just have to trust myself. Speaking feels like gulping. Getting tunnel vision.

"I tore those lame-ass pants off her with my teeth! Right before I banged her out, right here in this *exact* fucking spot!" He whooped and clapped his hands. "Hoorah! What a sweet little lay she was! Damned shame she bit it. Bitch was in her prime! What a waste of good pussy. Man, now I remember! That girl could suck—"

Things are weird. Jay and Burn are completely silent, stoic, ready. My heart's beating so fast it hurts. Ribs fracturing under the weight of the pulsing. Strange chemicals and hormones racing through me, burning out the weed, burning out the beer and Julio's fake-phantom drug and anything else impure. I am completely here and now. I'm on autopilot. I'm who I used to be. My hand tightens around Kitsune.

290

"HOLD THE FUCK UP!" Jay jumps in, hoping to stop the oncoming storm. "Boil! Come on. Be cool."

"Would you..." My words are hushed. Swallow. Crack my neck. I force my hand to stop shaking before continuing. Afraid to raise my voice because I'll either cry or scream. "Could you... repeat that, Lucas? I'm afraid I misheard."

"I said I fucked that slut. Right here. Oh man, she was a freak! God damn, remember her, Julio? Shit, how could I forget? Damn. Ha, I miss her. Always wanted to put it in her—"

"Here, here, now kid! Be a gentleman," Sergio says. "There's a lady present. I think. Somewhere. Where is she?"

Sergio gets up and stumbles back toward the convertible. Bernard is struck stone.

"What is it, Timmy?" Boil asks. "You broke off a piece, too? Oh shit, hell no! Don't even tell me we stuck the same honey pot."

Julio cut in. "Hey, Luke, you're making a mistake. You're fucking high, trust me. You're mixing Tracy up with Tara. Or Jill, or maybe Brittany. Yeah, she had red hair -"

"Nah, shut the fuck up, I'm never wrong! Wow! Damn, Tim, I still can't believe it. So you nailed her, too?"

"Boil. I know... I know you're trying to provoke me. But there's no way in hell an angel like Tracy would ever even talk to disgusting piece of shit like you."

"Angel? Angel? Man, what planet are you living on? Yeah, you really are losing your mind, man. Shee-it."

I stand up. Legs are leaves in the wind. Stomach cold, far away. No matter.

"Boil. Shut. The fuck. Up."

"We were so wasted," he says. He's standing now too, back to me. He's walking in funny little circles. His body sends a warning his brain can't. Muscles flexing rapidly. "Shit, we were on vikes, percs, methadone, something. I couldn't get my dick up at first. But when she started—"

I'm already across the circle before they react. My fist hits his ear. He hops back, lands in a perfect fighting stance. Fuck, he's Army, and he makes me feel it. Left right combo, head explodes in light and pain. Falling backward, knee in the stomach. Headlock. Crushed between his ribs and armpit. Neck in a vice. Can't breathe. Walls of throbbing red closing in. Blacking out, vision just flashes yellow veins and blood spots.

Everyone shouts from underwater. This is happening to someone else.

That's it. This is my story. Another red fox prances across my heart. Stops. Bares its fangs.

I bite.

Tastes like a mouthful of salted steel, but my jaw locks down. Blood seeps around my teeth. Boil screams and lets go. He's red from head to toe. Just warming up. Cast in shadow by headlights. Ocean behind him. Realize Kitsune is still tied to my waste. The fire rises. I grip the hilt, inviting her first kill.

"TIM NO!"

Tackled from behind, face first, arms pinned as we hit the ground. Eat dirt. Sand in my eyelids. Recognize Julio by the smell of burnt crabmeat and mowed grass. Trapped, I look up at Boil. Like a fucking gorilla, ready to rape me. Spittle on his mouth. Bloodlust in the eyes. So tense. But I relax. Julio gets up, slowly. Eyes still locked on Boil as Jay gently pulls the sword from my hand.

Can't breathe. Suck it in, slow. Hands on knees. Straighten up.

"Aight, we cool?" Julio is whipping back and forth between us, his arms stretched out to blockade.

"Well..." I cough. Wipe blood from my lips with a limp wrist. "At least now I know someplace nice and romantic to take your little Emily when she grows up."

The stars are beautiful. My blood arcs across them. Base of the skull hits a rock. I try to get up, puke into the dust cloud. How can that meat tank be so fast? A white blur above me, about to finish it. I close my eyes and savor this. At least I tried.

Nothing.

I sit up.

Jay has Boil on his back. He's sitting on Boil's chest, pinning his arms down.

"LUKE! STOP."

"Fuck you, spic! You heard what he said," Boil growls. He spits. "Talking that shit about *my daughter!* You heard him!"

Julio raises his fist, pauses, then slams it into Boil's nose. A sick crack, like wet twigs snapping.

Jay stands over him. "I heard what you said, too."

Boil remains on the ground, shell shocked, staring at his own blood in his palm.

Bernard's got his arm around me, helping me to my feet.

"Jesus, Tim," he says. "Damn, I didn't think you had that in you. I mean, you didn't exactly win, but... Were you gonna kill him? You wouldn't really..." The look on his face says it all. He can see the answer. "Seriously?"

"Am I wrong?" I ask with a throat feeling like a caved-in chimney.

"What?"

He's stunned, letting me snatch Kitsune up from the ground. I still feel it. I lost. But I feel the Curse inside me. A weapon. I am the Devil Ray, stinger ready to strike. I look back at him and repeat the question, feeling a wrong relief, and more distant than ever.

"Burn, am I wrong?"

He just stares back.

Depth Perception

Breathe. Stop shaking. Ease up on the sword. Take inventory.

Back of head feels hot and wet, swollen. Skull throbbing like a stomped nutsack. New cuts singing, a hot sticky mess in my hair. Mouth dry like clay, tastes of past vomit. Ears ringing, blood rushing through my face. Weak, shaking hands. Little scrapes and bruises, tears in my Hawaiian shirt, shoes splitting apart, dirt on her pants. A walking toilet. Eventually the ringing stops. Fades into a swarm of gnats, gnawing at my eardrums. A night of beatings.

Julio is squatting in front of Boil, pressing a beer against his face. "It's not broken, Luke. Man up!"

"I swear, the next time you cheap shot me—"

"Yeah, yeah. You're lucky I pulled my punch, bitch."

I fall forward, catching myself on the sheathed sword like a cane. Bernard has his arm around me again, leading me away in awkward stumbling steps. We cross over the dunes. The dirt fades into soft white sand. The only true treasure of Sponge Island. We top the ridge and a beautiful full moon smiles down, bathing us in pure half-light. Dark waves lap the shore. I can breathe. My lunar soul is pleased.

"Holy-moly, Boil is one son of a bitch," Burn said.

"You're just figuring that out?" My voice feels like I've sung Norwegian death-metal for decades.

"Not for nothing, I'm glad you clocked him."

"All the good that did…"

"Nah man, for real. You won by losing. Like, symbolically and stuff. Someone had to do it."

"Yeah, Julio."

"But you struck the spark!" Bernard slapped my back.

Burn and I stand on the empty beach, chalk white and blue glows, with that whole ugly scene behind us, over the dunes. A sand rampart to separate us from the group. Just two old friends, standing beneath an impartial sky. Bonfires twinkling far, far to the West. The slap of waves on sand. We spoke calmly over the howling wind, natives born into this shore's wicked solace.

"How are those two friends?" I asked. I sat down in the sand, letting the perfect cold cool off my ass. "This night is gross. Everything should be so simple and easy and it's all wrong. It feels like I don't even know Jay anymore. There's that Sergio guy, and Boil, and now he's skipping town! You know, if I didn't randomly show up at his house... Do you think he'd have left? Without even saying goodbye?"

"Honestly, Tim, I don't know." Bernard squatted down beside me. He rubbed my shoulders. "Want to hear something funny?"

"No." I shrugged him off.

"Barry told me one time, like maybe a few years ago, that he caught Boil snooping around in the bushes, looking up at Tracy's window." He spoke as if each word hid a laugh ready to pop.

"Are you a moron, too?" I moaned. "Please, Burn. I don't want to hear any of this shit right now."

"No, no, wait. Let me finish, it's funny," he said. He leaned back on his elbows and looked up at the moon. "So you know how Barry is. He goes running out there ready to knock this creep out, even though he wouldn't stand a chance."

"Sounds familiar," I snort, sucking some snot back in. Wipe a bit of blood from the corner of my mouth. So aware of the veins and nerves, now that they're swelled up shouting their pain. Lip feels like pregnant worms. And the tingle of survival. I like it at this level. This is good pain, physically. "Fine, what happened?"

"Julio happens to show up. He was gonna smoke a joint with Barry or something, I don't know. Fast forward, and they're all stoned, and I'm sure Barry is kind of paranoid and wary about having Boil in his house, or Tracy catching them, but they smokum peace pipe or what have you, and it turns out she isn't home anyway. Probably out on an adventure with you!"

"Great."

"One thing leads to another, and they figure, shit, you know how Barry's mom is. What with what happened with her husband, and Tracy acting out more and more. Helena's got to be on *something*. So they start going through her stuff. Looking for painkillers or more weed. I'm sure it was more Boil's idea, but Barry was stuck. I'm sure he didn't want to do it, but didn't want to antagonize them, either, right? Probably thought it'd all turn out fine or he'd outsmart them. You know how he is."

"I don't like where this is going."

He laughed. "Let me finish, dude. To make a long story short, they find some weird shit. Things you don't wanna find in your mom's bedroom. Handcuffs with leopard print fur around them, and other toys. So of course, Julio and Boil handcuff Barry to his mom's bed, and then... Oh god..."

"What?"

Burn gagged on laughter, tearing up, then caught himself and held it down before he finished. "They took his mom's dildo and rubbed it all over his face. Tried to push it in his mouth."

"In all of hell's names." I shook my head. "Madness."

"That ain't the end of it. They just left him there!"

"You can't be serious! Poor Barry. So then what happened?"

"I don't know. I asked Barry about it a while later, but he just turned red and walked away. You know how fire-bush babies are."

"That's terrible. That's absolutely..." It took a moment, but the whole ugly scene finally sank in. My laugh rose up, shaking off the tingling stress, letting friend-born empathy wash over my burning skin. It's horrible, I feel so wrong laughing, but I need it so bad. Perhaps the only reason to bear life is a chance to laugh.

"Yeah man, that's cruel, huh?" Bernard asked.

"Sometimes I forget how cruel Jay can be. Even if he thinks it's all a jape," I said. "But whether I like it or not, those two *do* have something in common." I lay down, settling into the sand, that fluid earth that always conforms for us. "Julio's rough around the edges, for sure. But he's still a great guy. The good doesn't wash out the bad, nor the bad the good, right? We've been there for each other so many times. He's always been there when I needed someone with true grit at my back. Like just now, for instance."

"True. Although if he let Boil break you apart, you could've got a free ambulance ride to Hawkhouse."

"But I still can't imagine that he's such good friends with that fucking creep! All those years, he was hanging out with him behind my back? How?"

"I wouldn't say they're all *that* close," Bernard said. "I'm a little surprised too. I mean, I don't know a hundred percent, but you know how Julio is. He's a hustler. There must be some kind of profit in being around Boil. Maybe they never really did anything together before all this, ya know? Lots of weird coincidences all threaded up, and their dynamic is... uh... you know?"

Bernard is pitching some real rough truth bombs at me, hypothetical or not. The ocean smells fresh. I blink and see the stars imprinted within my eyes, not at peace, just patching up the pieces.

"Take heart, Tim. Seems the great survivor Don Julio sees some profit with Boil tonight. They got something going on, that's for sure. And I'm sure if Boil wasn't vital, he wouldn't be here at all."

"Yeah, so why am I here then?"

"Duh. Jay wants a friend with him, too."

"For what?"

"For whatever's going down."

"Ah, Burn, sometimes you almost make sense."

"Better than never." He slapped me on the back, making me cough up something small and brown. Did it just burrow into the sand? Parasites, a fantastic addition to my sack of guts and bones.

"Going down? Well, all I know is that Boil's got endangered Iraqi lizards. They claim to be selling them to someone out here," I said, pinching my brow. "Those poor beasts are probably all starved or suffocated by now. But Boil said something before, something about Julio paying him to do this… I guess he's taking a cut? Something still doesn't add up."

I dug my heels into the sand, letting it fill my shoes, slip into my pockets, lay back so it gets my hair.

Burn yawned and stretched into a coffin pose. "I don't know that. Shit is weirder than weird, you know? I know you know. Think about it."

"Well…"

"Look, I wouldn't say this if you weren't my best friend…"

"Oh crap," I sat up. Squeezed my temples until it hurt. "Burn, I already have a cosmic migraine."

"I'm just saying, don't put all your eggs in one basket. We both know Julio is all about the profit."

"So?" What is he getting at?

"I know you guys are really tight. But he's no fucking saint."

"Burn… I'm raw. Just spit it out."

Bernard glanced over his shoulder. "Well, where do you think Tracy got those pills?"

A knife in the nuts would've felt the same. My new tattoo seared. Burned across my ankle, shooting up my leg into my neck. Sand inside the bandage. Pain. Infection. Infection spreads, one wound can kill the whole. "Bernard. What are you saying?"

"Don't make me spell it out."

"You're telling me Julio is the reason Tracy's dead."

"No, no, no! He didn't *kill* her. You gotta be straight on this, man. She bought that shit, she took them and pounded those bottles alone. It was her choice. I'm just saying, she had to buy them from someone, and we both know that Julio—Whoa!"

He rolled away just in time as I blew chunks all over the pristine sand. These mountains crushed into grain over unfathomable time, now painted with my steaming waste. I push it down into the sand, then brush the stuck granules from my palms. I hate when other people talk about it. It's not theirs. I push her room from my mind. Haven't eaten in so long, where is all this puke coming from? Pure stomach acid? Bile? Beer puke. Beer shits. Filth. I'm shaking and Bernard is saying something but all I can do is concentrate on standing up.

Damn it all, he's right. Who else would she trust when looking to score? How have I never even given it a thought? I stand. Perfectly still, solidly balanced. Start marching up the dune, back to their cars.

"Tim! Wait, I didn't mean to—"

"Enough," I said. Teeth grinding.

"I just don't want you to put all your faith in... Hey, we all got secrets, bro!" Burn's voice is ragged. He's jogging to catch up. "How do you think Barry would feel if he knew you about you and Tracy, huh? Hold on a sec, man! Relax! What are you going to do?"

I reach the dune's apex. I spin, glaring down at his skeleton shadow. Bernard is mortified by the tears creeping down my cheek. Seems I never run out of tears. Mourning is as inevitable as morning. These ones are like acid, though. No pressure released.

"Come on, Tim, stop! What are you going to do?"

"What am I going to do, Burn? Excellent fucking question. What am I going to do?"

"Tim, I'm sorry, I just..." He stops. Standing there like a shamed dog.

"Come on, friend. What am I going to do? Huh? Got any ideas?"

Again he stares, blank, sad.

They're all watching as I come marching back over the dunes. Star of the show. The scarecrow on display for a murder of crows. Boil is pissed, but his shoulders are relaxed. Julio... he just looks like... just some guy.

"You okay, man?" he shouts up to me.

"I'm fine." I march down to the group. Julio puts his arm on my shoulder as I walk past. I brush it off. "I said I'm fine."

Standing alone in the circle of headlights, I hear Julio's boots crunching as he approaches from behind.

"You need anything? Bro?"

"Look at that pussy. He's still crying," Boil said.

Julio snapped back at him. "Shut up. You're not looking so hot right now either."

"I need something," I mumbled. "Pain. What you got? No weird experimental shit this time."

"Uh, I have some vikes," Julio said. He looked down as he rifled through his pockets. "Couple of snorelazen. Beers. Coke. Still half a blunt left. Oh, here. These things are strong. Oxycollin. Expensive. Shit'll do you up right."

"Yeah, right. Sure. Give me them."

"One? Two?"

"All of them," I still haven't faced him.

"All of them? These are wicked strong, bro. You might over—"

"Did I stutter?"

My back still turned, I hear him rummaging around in his cargo pockets. His hand sneaks around me, holding six pink oval poisons. Hell's angels. I take them from his hand. For a heartbeat, my closed fist lays in his calloused palm. He still has a bit of Boil's blood on it. He looks me in the eye, confused, on guard. I turn my back on him.

"Jay, we're blood brothers, right?"

"What?" he walks around to my front. "Hell yeah. No doubt."

"And my business is mine. And yours is yours. Right?"

"Yeah... Right."

I squeeze my fist. The pills don't crush. I drop them in the dirt, stomp my foot on them. Grind. Feel them cracking apart, mixing into rocks and earth.

"Yo, what the fuck?"

Boil cuts in with his usual tactful care. "Yo, let's get moving, you loco homos! We can't be fucking late!"

I look over at Sergio's convertible, humming red and rumbling in the moonlight. Sergio is by the entrance to the trail, with the Brazilian. He's talking to her, shoulders slumped, palms outstretched. Her arms are still wrapped around her tits like a vice, her neck craned up and away from him. I can't hear them, but it's clear enough when she gives him the finger and spits in the dirt. He grabs her arm, and she spins like a puma, whipping out a sharp strike. The slap, I can hear. She shouts something, points at the rest of us, and then walks into the darkness. Sergio cups his cheek for a moment, watching her vanish into the reeds. He looks to us and shrugs.

I turn back to Julio. He's still watching me.

"You have really good perception," I said.

"What?"

"You know. For one eye and all. You see so perfectly, like you have no flaws at all. Nothing to hide."

"What are you talking about?"

"Nice punch, that's all. I'm rattled. Think I'll ride with Sergio and Burn for now."

"Yeah, maybe that's a good idea," Julio said, eyeing me sideways as he got into his Jeep. "You still want to go see Barry, right?"

I shrug. "You're my ride. You gave me your word."

He nodded slowly.

Bernard comes over the ridge. He stands atop the dunes, a completely pale shadow before the moon. I stare up at him, full of cold anger. The kind that doesn't explode. That real bad anger, that frozen fuse, settled into your core. Not an explosive rage. A nuke. Looking at him, Boil, Sergio, then Julio... I stare down at my own hands, raw. I'm just not sure who the hatred is for.

Recursion

We're back on the motel strip, cruising along the outskirts of Tomahok with only the occasional stop and start from a crossing herd of the walking brain-dead, stumbling from the public party to the beach and back. The moon pools perfectly. Julio's Jeep leads the way, swerving at the occasional drunken troupe, tossing an empty beer can at the passing heads. He and Boil lean out of the Jeep and yell insults, laughing as the partiers scatter.

For once I get to sit up front. The convertible's leather seats and legit seatbelts are a welcome reprieve. Bernard always prefers the back seat anyway so he can stretch out, as well as keep look out for cops and thieves. He's more paranoid and observant than he wants to let on. I have my feet up on the dashboard, my legs awkwardly hunched, my knees stuffed together. Not exactly the prominent knee position, but it will have to do. I cradle Kitsune against my right arm, the hilt jutting up next to my face.

"Tom, you weren't really going to stab that boy?" Sergio asked without looking.

"Tom? Probably not, but me? I don't think so. Maybe. I was just feeling more than thinking."

"Good thing Jay jumped in," Bernard chimed in.

I don't answer. Sergio guns the engine.

Sergio's ride is far more luxurious than Julio's Jeep, that steel and lizard-flesh prison. Now I get to ride with a smooth white leather interior. Large, thin steering wheel. Chrome fins and all that. A relic, well maintained, proud to cut through the swath of bloated SUVs and decadent repurposed weekend warrior gas guzzlers. The kind of car that looks like good old fashioned 1950s sex. The kind I used to shoot with paintballs.

"Would you like a cigarette?" Sergio asked.

Haven't smoked in years. Promised.

"Sure, why not."

"In the dashboard, son."

Cigarettes burn in abundance. I have two in my mouth. Every breath acrid and bitter. Thick tar breath. Screw it. Need to feel something dirty, something decadent. Need to see the smoke rising from my face. Make my mouth taste like my soul. Cough a lot, but not as much as I expected to. Ribs shake. It tingles and burns. Good self abuse.

"Pass 'em back, bro!" Bernard is stretched out in the back seat, sipping an Imperialisto Especial from the case by his feet. Even the beers are fancy here.

I blindly toss the pack over my shoulder. Burn curses.

"Crap!" I slapped my forehead. "I'm such an idiot."

"I could have told you that," Bernard mumbled while he lit his cigarette as if we're in a black and white film.

"Don't be so hard on yourself," Sergio said to no one in particular.

"I left my briefcase in their Jeep. With Barry's stupid fucking books."

"Right," Burn said. "Yeah, I thought that looked familiar. He used it instead of a backpack in college. Remember?"

"Yes, I was there. Stupid idea. All show, no functionality."

"Right. Like your time there? Fat lot of good that did you, huh?"

"I meant the briefcase."

"Oh. Well, I mean, the loans still suck, huh? How are you gonna pay them, now that you quit the only place in town that hasn't already fired you?"

I'll simply default for now. Just push it away, push it all away and deal with it some other day.

"Every day is someday, one day," Sergio said.

Weirdo. He was staring straight ahead at Julio's Jeep as he drove with one hand hanging from the bottom of the wheel, the other holding his cigar at the ready.

"Don't worry. Julio isn't going to steal it," Burn said.

"Yes, yes. Keep your wits about you, my boy. What did you major in?"

"Political science. Dropped out though."

"Yeah, he totally did it for this girl that—"

"Then I went back to a career in fast food." Did he get so damn stoned that he forgot what a secret is already? "I know it's safe with Jay. I just can't believe that I actually forgot about it."

After everything I went through for the blasted thing. Bugging out, brawling, seeing her, then tomb-raiding in her room. Dealing with Boil, letting them keep their lizard mystery a mystery.

"You're having a rough night, kid," Sergio said.

"No shit, Sherlock. So you're not just a lawyer, you're a detective as well?"

"What I am, young man, is calm and collected."

"Serge is one with the universe! Like a lawyer-monk. The jewel." Burn sounds like he's about to pass out.

"Right. You're you, and you're also me, and I'm you too, and we're both Burn and Jay and Boil, right? That's what you were saying at my house? You're quite the philosopher, as well."

Bernard coughed. Sergio glanced at him through the mirror.

"You could say that," Sergio said. He took a good long puff on his cigar. "I like questions. Especially those with multiple answers. I've done my share of traveling. Had many vision quests. I've learned a great deal in the last fifty years, sometimes contradictory truths, pretty lies, and sometimes at great personal cost."

"Sorry," I said. This guy isn't so bad. He's just being nice. I feel like a kid again, eyes glued to floor. I only noticed my ankle had ached and throbbed for so long once the tattoo settled down. "Thanks for the ride, Sergio. Don't get me wrong, I love Jay. But man oh man, once in a while, he can get me fired up. And Boil is throwing gasoline all over us."

"No problem, my boy, no problem at all."

"Please stop calling me that." I slid further down in the seat, my knees now nearly overhead. "I'm creeping toward thirty."

"You got two years," Burn burped.

"Yes, quite young."

"Well, I'm the oldest I've ever been." I fidgeted with Kitsune's false ivory hilt.

"Clever boy. Listen, Tom—"

"Tim."

"That guy, Lucas. He was lying to you. Trust me, I'm a lawyer. I know when people are lying."

"Of course. Veteran or not, he's still a proven degenerate. Hasn't changed since childhood. So what do you think he's lying about?" I asked.

"Everything."

"Okay. Speaking of everything, it seems like they let you in on their secret. So spill it." Maybe he'll spill the beans, who knows with this guy.

Burn lazily spoke from his hovering dream state. "He's cool, Tim. Trust him. He's awesome at poker."

"That's exactly how we met. Bernard and I happened to be at a bar down at the docks. We shared some drinks—"

"Which I'm sure you paid for."

"Yes, I did. Quite worth it, though. One thing led to another, good conversation, and then we were invited to play some games in the back room. Bernard did surprisingly well. The boy's got a knack for reading people. And an eye for bad luck."

"Damn straight," Burn said. I could feel him smiling behind me. "With Sergio backing me, I can double our money on a slow night."

"Well, Sergio, I'm a bit of an expert on bad luck as well. I was cursed once."

"Really? How so?"

"To violate. To poison and kill everyone I love."

"Good God, what ever did you do to deserve *that*?"

"Nothing."

"Nothing? The universe is cruel, but surely it holds no gods that cruel."

"Well it is. And it wasn't exactly nothing."

"Nothing is nothing, dear boy."

"Oh, give me a break. Look, I saw something I thought was beautiful and was deceived," I said. And at that moment Boil's taunting words ripped through my mind, and I saw Tracy's face beside his and felt sick. Distracting myself, I said, "This thing, this animal was so pretty when I looked down on it, but when I held it up and tried to feed it, I saw its other side. It was ugly on the other side. Wrinkled and gasping with gills and weird holes, pale unlike its sleek back. I freaked out, and I wanted to hurt it for scaring me. Just a child's stupid reaction to fear. But I didn't actually do anything."

"And the difference is?"

Burn burst in. "You said the old guy smacked you around before you could."

Truth.

"So you're guilty of intent," Sergio waved his cigar at me. "I'd appeal the sentence, though." Sergio shook his head as if he truly lamented, and thus validated, the existence of the Curse. "What were his exact words?"

"You have violated an innocent creature of our Mother Ocean. And so you are cursed to violate, to poison all that you love and watch them die, to swim the barren seas alone." The words came out monotone, robotic.

"Remember it word for word, eh? Sounds like you took it quite seriously."

"Quite." I've been forced to. But this new guy doesn't need to hear about them, or her. Distract tactics and get the info I want from him instead. "So, Sergio, you have some kind of history with Julio."

"Indeed I do. A long one."

"How so?"

He jammed the brakes, nearly fender bending Julio, who was swearing at another stumbling throng ahead. Boil threw a bottle at somebody. Orange street lights cast us eerie, the night sky purple, the dunes blue and yellow.

"Well, it started when I represented him on a few of his cases, back when he was a minor. Breaking and entering, possession with intent to distribute, et cetera." He took a huge puff from his cigar. Not once did he take his eyes off the road.

"How the hell did Jay afford a lawyer?"

"He didn't," Sergio said. "After his parents split up, Miranda—"

"His *mother*?"

"Yes, Miranda Corazon and I dated for a while. Only while I was out on the island, mind you. I had other engagements back in the city. That's my bread and butter. Out here, it was a nice vacation for jelly and jam."

Gross.

"DAMN, Sergio! You didn't tell me you banged Julio's mom!" Bernard shouted. He propped up between us with his hands on the seat. "You are one brave motherfucker, my man!"

"I wouldn't put it in those terms, but yes. We had an arrangement. It was a long time ago."

"Wow," I said, staring at the Jeep ahead. "Wow. And Jay actually likes you?"

"He's like a nephew to me." Sergio swerved around a couple lying halfway in the road, blindly dry humping and begging to be speed bumps.

"That's crazy, man." Burn burped again in the back. The leather creaked beneath his shifting spread. "It's like, you and I meet, and we're friends, and then by coincidence you were doing my friend's mom, and then we run into him and Tim, on the road chasing the same prey. Hell's bells, guys! Small world, huh?"

"It only gets smaller," Sergio said. "We are all facets of the same jewel, one meta-mind linked by a morphogenetic field."

Sounds like he's been trading notes with Barry. I have to hand it to Bernard, he does dig up some strange ones, all on his own. Sergio continued waxing about the past.

"Our relationship worked for a time. We met after Julio's father, ah… left. So I handled all the Corazon family's legal affairs. I was court appointed, but the sparks of love turned my heart. It was all pro bono after that. Although young Julio did keep me quite busy. Still, haven't seen the boy in ages. Not since his mom passed. I sent the occasional care package over the years, but sadly, we slowly fell out of touch."

"Serge, do you know how she died?" Bernard asked.

"Yeah, do you?" He's pretty tight lipped about it.

"Ah, you know. She did things to put food on the table, keep the house off the market. Of course, this was back when keeping a house out here wasn't quite the sacrifice it is today. But her line of work had many risks. She got sick. Let's leave it at that, as it is his business after all."

"Tell me about it," I said, folding my arms. "We all come from broken homes. All of us. This whole troupe of miscreant tyrant wannabes."

"Oh, come now. It's the new American standard," Sergio said. "Trust me, you're perfectly normal." He blew a smoke ring, which instantly gaped wider to blow back across his face.

"What kind of law do you practice?" I asked.

"I dabble in the usual. Divorce, drugs, murder. A little real estate here and there, business, domestic violence. I like to stay loose and limber, take it as it comes. That's why I've kept this up for so long. Private practice all the way, yes sir."

"That's commendable, I guess. No gods, no masters," I said.

"As is your devil run," he answered.

I turned my back to the door, staring him down as he stared down at the road, and Burn stared at us both.

"Okay, what the hell are you talking about? This jewel stuff, this devil's run. What are you trying to tell me?"

"Reality is recursive," he said, as if telling me the sky was blue. "Recursive means—"

"A pattern that repeats itself indefinitely. Yes, I know."

"Reality is a what the fuck?" Burn asked.

I leaned my head back, trying to remind him. "Like when you hook a video camera up to a TV, turn them both on, and point them at each other."

"Oh yeah, that's hella weird," he said. Satisfied, he fell back into himself.

"Well, Tom, since you already realize that, you should know that all of existence exists within every tiny miniscule aspect of existence, yes? All of reality is in the tiniest corner of every molecule of every hair on your head."

"So fucking what? Does that mean they're all the same? That's your jewel? Sounds like it can't change then, or everything would. Instant cosmic chaos. So that means fate exists. There's no free will."

"Unless you're fated to have free will. You have an undeniable aura about you. You smell of... of ..."

"Farts and fear," Burn said. His voice floated up from nowhere. He'd somehow disappeared completely in the back seat. "And dead things."

"Fear. Yes, fear, but a fruitful kind. Yes, I can tell. You're on your own personal Devil's Run," he said. He tapped his cigar out the window. The car stopped as another drunken pack stumbled by, swaying and smiling. "We're all tiny reflections of light glinting off a great cosmic hologram. Our own brief flash blinds us to the whole, keeps us from seeing the connection between the singular oversoul. The soul is not within the body, you see, but rather the body is within the soul. Do you understand? But you are shining out from a fracture that will crack apart, provided you don't conquer this fear. And thus your vision quest is now become another infamous Devil's Run."

"What the fuck are you talking about? My quest, as you call it, is to run some books up to my friend and comfort him." I rolled my eyes. "Our lives are linked. We're just brief, brilliant blooms. And I'm broken. Hooray. No news there."

"Well, no, actually I meant that maybe you were broken. But what if you broke yourself? In the end it doesn't matter, because only you can fix yourself. Pull that off, and you start fixing those around you," Sergio said. "Instead of violation and poison."

"And the inverse, implying I break those around me as well."

He sighed. I lit another cigarette. We continued crawling through thumping bass, neon, streetlamps, yips and howls of youth without fear.

"When we die," he began, looking up to the stars, searching for the right words. "When we die, we're just gone forever. Except we're not. And I believe tonight certain strains of that field are pulling together, tightening up frayed bonds. Yes? You follow?"

Maybe if I was ten years younger and tripping balls. Is this guy for real? If Burn wasn't beside me, I'd swear this was the true hallucination. Is this what I'll sound like when I get old? *If* I get old, the way this night's going.

"I wouldn't be surprised," Sergio said.

Damn, still doing it... I lit another cigarette and hung my elbow over the car door. "You think tonight is special and meant to be. And that identity is an illusion. And I'm a demon running some kind of marathon to fix a crack in mankind's meta-soulsphere. Right? Got it."

"Yes. But it's a Devil's Run, not a demon's. Very different. Devil can be a condition, but demons are creatures, of a sort. Do *try* to be precise when speaking of the higher metaphysical forces."

Okay, I can agree with that for sure. Already know what happens when it goes wrong. Perhaps this man's vision quests have been cold and broken. One thing's for sure, he means well. "Fine. I'm on a Devil's Run."

"Perhaps. Or maybe you're with one who is running. Or perhaps it is all of us, in a sense. These things can be vague on purpose. The source is an ancient Manichaean poem, by the way. The Kalbaza-gehena-var."

"Timmy sure loves big words and poetry." Bernard waved at a passing tight-skirt on the sidewalk. She waved back.

"Not really," I said, watching the turquoise miniskirt fade into the crowd. "But please, do go on." He's going to anyway.

"I don't remember the exact words, but general idea of the Kalbaza-gehena-var is... less a poem and more of an elegy for men who are too broken to live and too angry to die." He paused long enough that I hoped he was done. Nope. "The Devil's Run, when broken hearts besiege men, when kisses kill once again, true love lies just once more, dead seas... dead seas..."

"Dead seas rise to blacken the sun," I cut him off. "Dear friends rot on your shore, stairs to what's lost, only fools pay the cost when the devils must run to their war."

"Ah, so you do know of it?"

"Yeah," I took a cinematically dramatic drag off my cigarette. "Look, I have no idea what your Kielbasa's-thing is, but I hate to break it to you. That's no ancient poem, Senior Antonio Sergio."

"Ah, and yet, pobrecito, you recite it perfectly for one who laughs at Kalbaza's songs." He finally looked directly at me. Lips curled like a smile, but eyes hidden. Even at night he's still wearing those aviators, making him look like a bug-eyed alien. Hell, for all I know, he is one. What if I pulled them off and found empty sockets? Dried out muscles and veins turned brown and dripping pus? Or would I see the Rinnengan Eyes, the Sage Who Saw All, fabled to have combined heaven and hell, to shape the moon into a keyhole above. Archon of Contradiction, the only logic I can effectively follow.

"Listen, I worship cats and the Caffeind, Antonio. And I could go for a couple cups right now. Let's cut this crap and—"

"Yo! Dudes! I've heard that devil shit before, too!" Burn said. "Didn't Barry like that a lot? He used to recite it all the time. His sister, too. They liked it a lot, but Barry would mumble it almost every time he got stoned."

"He *likes* it. *When* he's stoned," I said, angry and unsettled by Burn's use of the past tense. The poem, yes, it is the kind of thing Tracy and I would laugh about and memorize. Her version of a bedtime song. Nightmare terror lullabies for a little girl who thrived in the dark-light. Damn, she was so cool. The car's side mirror betrayed me. Despite not feeling it, I was smiling. "It's from some real old sci-fi show. We'd all watch reruns at their house while their parents were shooting up at orgies and gods knows what. Way back when. Just kids… When Jay still swung by. Back when… back when I was into that silly stuff."

Sergio jammed the brakes as a pack of dogs darted across the street. Pastel pasted preteens followed, whooping and hollering with sticks and pipes. Surprised I didn't see Claude's younger brother leading them.

"Verses from the The Kalbaza-gehena-var were on a science fiction program? Ha! Well, well, well. Just where do you think those writers got their ideas from? Trust me, son, those words are far older than any of us. Art is recycled from ancient times, when our brains had no bridge, when the oversoul was all. We're just repeating it in a new vein. Recursive. Everything's made of infinite aspects of itself. We are in a constant cycle, all incarnations of—"

"The jewel, yes," I cut him off. "You're the most cyclical thing I've heard all night." Antonio Sergio is not a lawyer. Not like any I've ever seen. He pulls on the cigar, his features flashing crimson, the shadows darker. But he's got a golden feel to his bones, and a good gray heart. "It doesn't exactly roll off the tongue, but I get it. Well, I don't know what aspect of your precious poem—"

The night swallows my words. Light seeps down from those tiny holes that we call stars, casting beams in a veil over me. The burning blue shine of the non-deities, idly biding their birth. And lo, the beating war drums in my heart, even the slurred bacchanal of Tomahok's streets, are drowned out by those words...

The Kalbaza-gehena-var...

The Devil's Run
When broken hearts besiege men,
When kisses kill once again,
True love lies just once more,
Dead seas rise to blacken the sun,
Dear friends rot on your shore,
Stairs to what's lost,
Only fools pay the cost,
When the devils must run to their war

"HELLO! EARTH TO TIM DUNE!" Burn was snapping and shouting right in my ear.

"Beautiful delivery there, Tommy." Sergio's tight lips didn't hide his smile.

What in all icy-hell's name was *that*? And there's five more verses! I shook my head free from the stars. Tried coughing into my fist, while calculating just how long I... No, no. Just switch tactics on the bastards. Derail them while they're already on their heels.

"Mr. Sergio, I need to level with you. The truth is, I was—I truly *am*—cursed."

"Oh?" Sergio arched his eyebrow, as if I'd simply said I was adopted.

"Honestly. I was only five. It's pretty bad, really. An atomic grade curse. All this talk of love dying and friendships burning and..." My voice wasn't a charade. Why is this so hard? Everyone I've ever met knows this. "Look, I'm cursed to kill everyone around me. And I've been bloody good at it. If anything, I'm the one burying mothers' sons on this stupid devil's run."

Sergio stared at me again. His face stone cracked clay, wrinkles frozen. Not even his ponytail swayed.

He hit the brakes again. Burn and I dip forward, but he does not.

Burn slips his face between us. "Yeah, Tim really believes that curse is real. He's super paranoid."

"As well he should be. You call it paranoid, but it's smarter and more prudent to respect these arcane mysteries, rather than blindly dismiss them wholesale."

True. Or worse, mock them.

"Everyone you see bears some curse, some weight, spoken or not. You are not the first to make a devil's run, nor the last. And rarely is it made alone. Perhaps it's not you I sense. It could be me, for all I know."

"So you're a gambling man. If one of us in this freakish tribe is on a creepy run, who do you put your money on?"

"You tell me," Sergio said.

"Easy. Jay and Boil." I leaned forward, watching the glowing taillights as Julio braked for another wasted crowd crossing. Sergio inched up closer to his Jeep. "The run is a blind charge, isn't it? Hubris. Dead seas rise. It's coming, I can feel it. It's all of us..."

"Sorry, Serge, Tim can be a real bummer sometimes," Bernard said, laughing and clapping me on the shoulder. "He wasn't always, though. Believe it or not, this sad sack used to be the life of the party. But then he lost... Well, that's um... that's his story."

"Thanks, buddy." But it's true. She said as much before.

Sergio laughed, pleased. "Ah. So no denial of your flaws, then? Good. Good start. You're naked, leading the blind. You're selfish. Unkind. But self aware, at the least."

Fuck this twat! So casual with the ego assaults! Still... straight talk is good talk. Keep it cool, Tim. We've already seen how well it goes when you give in to the demon. Took too big a drag, nearly coughed my tongue out. Recovered.

"Is that more ancient arcane wisdom, counselor?" I shot more smoke out. Took a deeper drag. "Yeah, I'm an asshole. And no offense, but I don't know anyone who isn't."

"There is always a light in the darkness, and a shadow from the light.

I prefer to dwell in the light as often as possible. Life's too long to squander on regrets and sorrow," Sergio said. Suddenly his postured changed. He slumped a bit, the skin around his mouth hung. His grip on the wheel slackened. Even his cigar dipped. "Boys, do it all while you can. And pass it on to the next in line. Because when we're gone, we're gone. Connected or not."

We're all lost. Eventually everyone who even vaguely remembered you will be gone, too. Like tears in the shower, blood in the gutter, ashes in the rain.

"Mmm, yes that's nice," Sergio said. "Did you come up with that on your own?"

"Come up with what?"

"No matter. Like I said, I prefer to live in the light, no matter how small it can feel."

"Yeah, my parents were like that too," I said. Lit another cigarette. How many is this already?

"Where are they?" he asked.

"They... gone." Smoke drifted through my teeth. Staring at the mirror, it gazed right back, my crackling red eyes. I flicked it out the window, then lit another immediately. Damn it, they do feel good.

"My boy, please, are you trying to waste of all of my cigarettes on purpose?"

"Sorry. I quit a long time ago. This girl, she didn't like to kiss me after I smoked. Can I ask you something?"

"Certainly."

"Will you turn this car around and drive me up island to the hospital? That's all I really want tonight. It's the only reason I'm here, and I feel like I'm going to have a heart attack at any moment."

"Julio told me that he gave you his word he'd get you there," Sergio said. "He's mentioned you before, quite a bit when he was little. Don't worry yourself, Tom. He won't let you down. Besides, the Devil's Run has just begun!"

"Oh god." I slid down as far as possible. "Yeah, maybe he will, after all is said and done. But if you're willing... I don't have anything to pay you with. I can offer karma, for what that's worth. You can suck my soul dry for all I care."

"Yo, you got shitty karma, bro. Ain't much soul left."

"Thank you once again, Bernard."

"All our karma cycles across the jewel, a shared wealth and penance," Sergio said. He bit down on his cigar. "So you'd have no problem bailing on your friend so quickly?"

"It's not like that," I said. "I don't want to be that guy anymore. Jay's just... he's got other priorities. I don't hold it against him. I got my own priorities, too. And right now, we're headed away from them."

"But Jay already said he's taking you there after he's done with his run," Bernard said.

I tried to whack him with Kitsune's sheath. He slid away like an eel. "You back there! Quiet! Fat lot of help you've been."

We slowed to a stop again. Three couples climbing over the dunes and walking right into the road. No doubt heady from sandy sex and veins pumping with whiskey. Unsaddled. This guy is talking about a marathon starting up and I'm already on full lactic-acid overload.

"Look guys, sorry I'm being... difficult. I'm not so sure about anything right now, and I've never actually been worried about that." I stared at the dashboard. Stared at my knees in the white pants, stared down at my dark Hawaiian shirt's tattered remains. Height of the season. Even the out of the way places are jammed in Tomahok. Except the haunted Tiburon Pier, of course. "You know, I was on my way to see Julio earlier. If you two hadn't ditched me so fast, we could have all got together before, sans drama and insanity and crashes and violence."

Sergio shrugged. "Well, drama bonds. And I had no reason to think you knew Julio. Bernard never mentioned it."

"We live down the road from him! And seriously, Burn, you never talk about me?" I asked. Then I remembered Julio's words preceding my fight. A short, sharp shock. "And Jay... he said he's leaving?"

"What does that signify? My poor date, Ella, already left. And I'm fine."

"What was her deal anyway?" Bernard shrugged.

"Back to wherever she was before I picked her up," Sergio said. "The night didn't go as she hoped, and, well, she's an independent woman. I suspect I'll see her again if I'm supposed to."

"I think you should drop us off and go get her," Burn said. "I mean, I'm down for whatever, but what the hell? You'd rather chill with us than her? She's smoking hot! Go hit that! You just said to live life while we can!"

"I don't think that's quite what he meant." I said.

I caught Sergio's smile in my peripheral vision.

"That's not exactly my primary objective," Sergio said. "You kids play it rough, I'll give you that. But that's youth. I'm on a bit of a Devil's Run myself. I didn't expect it to happen tonight, but with all of your coincidences, it must be a sign. Things have taken a rather abrupt turn, and she simply couldn't adapt. Why drag her along? It's not her war."

Smooth talker made me forget that he *knows* that Boil is lying.

"There's no devil heart war! Rewind time, Sergio." I slapped the dashboard. Lit another cigarette. He's a masterful distracter. Dangerous. Warlock? "Tell me what the fuck is going on! What is Boil lying about? Yeah, you go way back with Julio. Fantastic. That doesn't explain the secrets. I don't buy the whole 'selling lizards to an eccentric friend' bit at all. I hate to say it, but if Boil's lying, and they're working together, then—"

"Jay is lying too," Bernard finished. "Big deal. Everyone lies. Tim, you're like the biggest liar I know."

Everyone lies. Bernard lies to hide. Julio lies to survive. Boil lies for fun. Sergio lies to defend. Barry lies to enchant. Mom and Dad lied to protect me. Tracy lied to love me. I tossed my cigarette out the window. It nearly hit a blonde shadow, bouncing out of nowhere, following her breasts. I didn't notice, of course. She shouted something that I'm glad I didn't hear.

Get sarcastic. "Thanks, Bernard. So, Sergio, what's your sage advice?"

"I think you should just relax and trust Julio," he answered. "He's a wicked one, but he's got his head on straight. Damn smart kid. Possibly a genuine genius. He couldn't have survived on his own this long if he wasn't. His mom showed me an IQ test that he took when he was very, very young. Apparently, Julio's got a one hundred and fifty-four IQ. Or one hundred forty-five. I don't remember exactly. Either way, he's not just smarter than your average bear, he's a whole other species."

"But a bear nonetheless. Will wonders never cease?" I said.

Sergio sighed. "Tom, trust me. If you work for it, if you're willing to see your mission to the end, things will work out. Even if only in harsh, disgusting ways. It's the way of the world. Best to learn it sooner rather than later."

I have. And is it?

"I think so," he said.

"Listen, my name it *Timothy*. And you claim all this metaphysical motivation, and I dig it, yes, it's amusing." I flicked a cigarette at a chiseled swimsuit barbarian escorting unclad underage twins out of a beach bar. Missed. "But what's your real angle? What do you really stand to gain by standing with us? No offense, but I can't imagine how a lawyer could see anything profitable in trailing a bunch of young goons through Tomahok. Those guys we almost killed? Remember? Because I do. So Boil's lying, Jay is lying, and I think you're lying. Spill it."

"Well, I can't break client confidentiality. You know how it is."

"No, I don't know." I hunched my shoulders, hands tucked tightly in my armpits. "I really don't know."

"That's the spirit!" Sergio said. "That's a good start."

"Okay... So you've been around. You're cool, you're calm. For better or worse, you sound like you really believe what you say, I'll give you that."

"Thank you," Sergio said. He hit the brakes, then honked at the heaving mass of delirious idiots in front of us. It's taken twice as long to travel half the distance since we hit this circus sideshow town.

"So then, can I ask another question?"

"Certainly, my boy."

My turn. Distract tactics to pull the true info through his defense nets. But in all honesty, I want these answers. Double win. Note to self: Play more chess.

"You look like you're about the same age my parents were. Your generation fought. Youth actually caring, ideals taking form. You bled and saw change. And now look at us. The economy is going down, the Illuminati isn't even hiding. Precious animals are going extinct left and right. The moon drifts away, our food is plastic. War spreads but death hides. And we're silent. No one's thinking about the world their kids are going to inherit."

"An abrupt change of topic, Tim. But you did study political voodoo, yes?" Sergio puffed his cigar. His temper took a turn. Not angry, but uncorked. "Do you really think it was all that rosy and beautiful? What about segregation? Civil rights? The Cold War? Nixon! The draft. Kent State, and the others we never read about. Vietnam? It was an ugly, brutal time. And it got worse. Crack, AIDS, starvation, globalization. It's getting worse, no doubt about it. The economy, global warming, mass war, and extinctions. Noticing a pattern? A bit of recursion? Kid, every

315

generation thinks it's the one that will face the end of the world."

Scholars have labeled us the Doom Generation though. Amongst other things. The generations younger than me have it even worse, poor things. Mine is stuck in the middle: the old hate us, the new hate us. We hate us.

"Look, all I'm saying is, we're hopeless, and the blame lays upon us. Even our super technology is killing our ability to truly communicate. Splitting apart your vast hivemind, or what have you."

"Interesting," Sergio said. "I didn't use that word."

"Yeah, Serge, Tim and I don't have cell phones." Bernard popped his head up front. "But he won't admit that it's just 'cause we're poor. We're not so noble."

"Just being practical. Be a lawyer. Look at the facts on paper. Either way, we lose. If we stood up again, what are we saving? A half-doomed world, ripe to boil away for the next wave?"

"I admit, it does seem that way," Sergio said as we watched Julio and Boil whipping around like monkeys on meth up ahead. Please, Jay, don't hit anyone. Sergio pointed his cigar inches from my eye. "So stand up."

"I'm too busy on this epic run, remember? What would my slogan be? All hail the Kingdom of Fear! Bow before the Bloodfields! I just... I can't—"

"Bernard is right. You are a bit of a bummer," Sergio said. "Life is tough. Children are born and do nothing but suffer, starve, and die. Slavery exists. Torture is paid for. People lose. People win. What's your point? What do you want to hear?"

My parents saying everything will be okay. That I'm not a selfish loser. That Tracy and I could have had a beautiful child and raised it right.

"Forget it," I said. "Look, I'm just saying, how the hell could I ever bring a kid into this world?"

"Ah, so there's the rub of it. A fine question, my boy. Now there is a noble problem to grapple with. The start of all conflicts, one might say. Are you thinking about having children?"

"Not anymore. Well, once I thought that... No. No, I can't."

Bernard coughed.

Sergio tapped his ash onto the road. "So kill yourself."

"Excuse me?"

"You clearly have a bleak outlook and act as if the world conspires against you. That life owes you something. So why not jump ship?" Sergio said. "As a lawyer, on paper, it's the most logical conclusion."

"Yo dude, don't kill yourself!" Bernard clutched my shoulder. "Serge, this guy's a lot tougher than he looks. He can handle it."

So she's not the only one.

"Sergio, do you have any kids?" I asked.

Sergio pounded the brakes. The abruptness thwapped my head off the dashboard. A girl with curly hair and braces fell before of us. Two shirtless studs rushed out, dodging her retched puking, then pulled her up. She fell to the side, head on one guy's shoulder, the other guy holding her ass. Sergio watched the trio fade toward Main Street. The Jeep was getting further up ahead. Burn tapped him on the shoulder. He hit the gas.

"You don't, do you? You wouldn't be out here doing whatever it is we're doing if you did."

"I tried, once," Sergio said.

"Tried?"

He turned to me, one hand draped over the wheel. Even through his stupid aviators, I felt his eyes, very cold, very small and dried. "You doubt that you're a good man." He swallowed. "My boy, you're not alone."

We caught up to Julio's Jeep again.

"Well, you seem all right to me. For a lawyer."

"Thank you," Sergio said. "Listen, kid, I think you're going be just fine."

"Even when friends die and true love lies?" I gripped Kitsune tighter. Twisting my torn palms around the hilt, ruining the white hilt.

He didn't answer. Bernard flopped back into his spot and cracked another beer. I haven't talked to an adult, a real adult, in a long time. Not since Dad paddled away and Mom fell down the porch. Free of the Jeep. No monsters up front, no horny, flesh hungry lizards in the back. I looked down at my cigarette, pondering the crackling flame. Agent of Cancers. They're playing a fool of me again. I tossed it out the window.

"Dude, at this rate you'll start a fire," Burn said. "Why don't you actually finish one instead of wasting them?"

Because I want the pain when it starts, just can't see it to the end. Silence settled. Even through that overly calm exterior, Sergio seems desperate to help. Perhaps atone?

"All right, Sergio, level with me," I said. "I saw you and those two freaks working out a deal. I'm here, I'm in the car, I'm a part of this. I'm asking one more time, and if you don't give me an answer, so help me god, I'll make sure you're remembered as nothing but a terrible person."

Took him a moment of poise before he grinned.

"Client confidentiality," Sergio said again. He smirked.

"Consider me a client."

"Terrible threats from one so young and doomed," Sergio mused, calm, but I can smell the intrigue and, yes, trepidation in his sweat.

"Next crowd that crosses, I'll smash your wheel with my sword and chop down on your knee. Manslaughter. Children. Your car, your fingerprints."

"I don't think you'd ever do such a thing, Tom. I'm sorry, you talk tough, but even on a Devil's Run, you have to cross the finish line first. The last thing you want is more innocent blood on your hands."

Blasted lawyers. Lit another one of his cigarettes.

"Oh, ease up, Serge," Bernard said slapping him on the back.

I jumped back in. "Come on! Spill it! What do you stand to gain in selling some guy a bunch of lizards?"

"Very well. Why not? I used to have a lot more clients out here," Sergio said. "I actually met my most lucrative client through Julio more than a decade ago. A dealer named Henry Poole."

My stomach twisted into a new, compressed shape.

"He always needed representation. Kept me on a nice retainer. For a time," Sergio said. "But he turned out to be a rat. Things went sour. Very sour. As they often do with men of his persuasion. Words were exchanged, but money was not. Outside parties were consulted. Things got ugly. In the end, I decided it was more prudent to just walk away from it all. He kept to himself and I did the same."

I know this story, with different actors. Jay... Bernard exploded into the space between the seats, eyes lit up like he was standing before an oracle.

"Serge, are you telling us Savage Jefe put a hit on you?"

"In a manner of speaking."

"This dude's a walking legend, man. Holy shit!" Burn squealed.

"When exactly was this?" I asked as sweat crept down my temple.

"Oh, a few years ago," Sergio said. "Anyway, it didn't work. I had other clients. Real hard asses, from the old world. They sorted things out in their own way. Just another occupational hazard. But, I have to admit… it just never sat right with me. All these years, knowing that Henry was still right here, getting richer, fatter. He could have paid me at any time, or at the very least apologized. Fat old Henry, still safe, getting away with what he tried to do to me. Every drug shipped in and spread through this region goes through him first. So why couldn't he pay me? It was not economics, it was a matter of respect and honor. He's an aspect of our collective being that I'd call a scumbag. Something to chip at until it's polished clean."

"He's a shit stain on your big cosmic hippie jewel, huh?" Bernard joked. "You defend scumbags all the time."

"Not always," Sergio said. He tossed his cigar stump into the street. "That's more of the downside to defending the innocent. I suppose everyone sees me differently. I'm a good guy and bad guy, at the same time. But back to tonight, I recognized those thugs earlier, and it just got me thinking about old Henry Poole. I wanted to see where they were going, see if I could catch them in some kind of act that I could pass on to the police. Start a little chain reaction to screw with Mr. Poole."

"Everyone calls him Savage Jefe now," I said, thinking of Julio's eye. Was chewing into an eye like biting into lychee? A slimy, salty gelatin? A chewy seed in the center? Then it pops and blood and white muscle and raw nerves coat your throat?

"But you must have enough dirt to bury him by now," Bernard said.

"Well, there's a thing called statute of limitations. Plus, it wouldn't do well with my… reputation… to betray trust like that, even if he does deserve it. Certain matters are handled in certain ways. But something new, something I'm not privy to as his—"

"Okay, okay, fast forward," I said. The bugs in my stomach were waging full on war, tearing up my insides. My eyelid twitched.

"It really was no coincidence, running into you guys. Almost literally," Sergio said. He laughed. It was an odd sound, like a fat dog barking. "My specific talents can be very helpful for Julio and Lucas. I can clear up a lot of tape, make sure things go smooth so long as they pull it off."

"Pull what off?"

Sergio laughed again. "You really don't know?"

"No."

"The lizards, they're just a ruse to get Lucas inside. They don't know him at all. Yes, the lizards really are for sale, that's no lie, but it's all a show to throw them off guard. For Julio!"

"Throw who off where? So Jay can do what? Who is he robbing this time?"

Sergio smiled again. Something inside him was coming alive. The father figure façade blew away. Seeing his core now. How he's lived dealing with himself. "He's not robbing anybody, my dear boy. Julio and Lucas, how do I put this? Their goal, which the three of us, in this car, *have absolutely no prior knowledge of...* is to lay Henry Poole to rest."

Like a bullet in the brain, my neck snaps slack, head falling on the headrest.

Boil had told me the truth.

Jay is going try to kill Savage Jefe.

Their Jeep was stopped up ahead while another gang of kids were stomping on something. We pulled up inches behind them. Julio was banging on the mangled dashboard, honking the horn, and screaming at the kids. Boil was chucking empty bottles at them.

You've got to be kidding me. He's leaving... He's throwing everything away after all these years? Is this it? I've Cursed him too? Which devil runs now? Bastard, how could he just give up like this?

I stood up on the front seat. Sergio looked up at me with concern.

"Hey there son, watch the leather!"

Fuck you, Julio.

I put my foot up on the top of the windshield, feeling the ridge press into my foot's arch. A strong flex of the quadriceps and a burst through the left calf, and I'm vaulting onto the hood. It buckles a bit, echoes as I take two quick steps, then leap.

Slam into the back of the Jeep. Ribs jam against the steel crates, lizards screaming, my shoes slipping on the bumper. The crates tumble, threatening to dump onto the road. I grab the roll bar and swing myself into the back seat, landed in a squat. Julio and Boil spin around, eyes gleaming with shock and reflexive bloodrage. I spring to the front of the Jeep, hunched on the middle console with my ass in Boil's face. I grab Julio by his pink tank top. Pull. Merely stretches the cloth.

"Yo Tim, you flippin', man! What—"

"HAVE YOU COMPLETELY LOST YOUR FUCKING MIND?"

"What? Get the fuck off me!" Julio grabs my wrists, gently, but his words slip between grinding, yellowed shark-teeth.

"Julio, get out!"

"Tim! Sit down, you crazy bitch!"

"Huh," Boil says behind us. "I like this version of him."

"Pull over and get out! Right now!" I try shaking Jay, to no avail.

"All right boys, cut the shit!" Boil shouts. I feel his nasty hands reaching to pull me down. I spin around and push his face to the side, forcing him against the door. Spin back to Julio, shoving his left deltoid so that his back shifts into view. I shoot my other hand down and grab the .44 from his waistline. I wave it around between us, not exactly aiming at anyone.

"Jay, get out of the fucking car or I'll blow your windshield out."

"Uh, Tim, chill out. You've never—"

"Look at you, you little faggot. You can barely lift that cannon," Boil said. "Come on. Let's see you do it, tough guy."

"Chill, son," Julio said, leaning away from me, but I still grip his clothes while he presses against the door. "Both of you. Y'all dickheads need to chill the fuck out."

I followed his gaze. The people in the road. They'd been kicking the crap out of someone. Not too bad. He managed to crawl a few feet toward the curb. His attackers are now deer in our one headlight. I wave the gun at them. "Go on! Gutter rats! Get the hell out of here, you punks!"

They do. I turn back to Julio, still standing awkwardly above him. If he hits the gas, I'll fly right out of the Jeep into a heap of fractured ribs and snapped femurs. But he won't. And he will get out.

"OUT!"

"Tim... Stop fucking around, bro. You ain't gonna shoot my car. What's your deal?"

I pulled on his shirt for balance. I point the gun behind me. Stared him in the eye.

BOOM.

Wham!

I missed the windshield entirely. Praise Saint Calibur, our Ballistic Arch Friend, because thankfully I missed *everything*. The kickback sent me flying face first into the back seat. Didn't even break my neck, though my body is shaped like a U and feels like bad yoga. Slowly, Julio and Boil's heads crept around the seats, timid, bug-eyed seals. The Magnum was still in my hand, which felt like someone smashed it with a golf club. Smoke wafted from the barrel.

"Shiiiiiit. I didn't think he'd do it," Boil whispered.

"Get out," I said to the seat cushion. I scrambled around to face them. "Let's go, Jay. It's time to settle this."

Boil's grin looks like a smiley face with stitched lips all split. Julio is confused, reflexively enraged, yet still letting years of our blood bond smother his violence.

"Settle what? Tim, you punta loco son of a bitch. Who do you think you are?"

"Thought I was your brother. Now get out, *amigo*. We need to talk."

The Jester Duels His King

Julio sat back in his seat, arms folded, refusing to look at me. "Okay. We'll talk. Now hand me my fucking gun." His Jeep rumbles. The lizards shriek. Restrained rage glows in his right eye. His lips twitch, desperately wanting to pull back and bite. His fingers dig into the seat, nearly splitting it. Blue veins rising on red skin. Right now, one of my best friends hates me. Perhaps we're jinchuurike, unwitting demon wombs who will one day split apart, ribcages cracking open, spewing geysers of blood, veins whipping like tentacles as we give birth to the first children of the Torturelands. Every lie, every betrayal makes these stupid ideas more plausible. This journey. This Devil's Run. Night of blood, eyes of fire, hearts are smoke. "Tim! I ain't gonna ask again."

I try to flip the .44 around so that the barrel lands in my palm, handle toward him, you know, like in the movies. Except I fumble. It clunks onto the Jeep's floor, and we all flinch away. It's fine. Boil sighs and slams the back of his head into the seat. Julio picks the Magnum up and slips it under the front seat, far from my reach.

"Aight. Now that you just popped a fucking cap right in the middle town," Julio said, slow, monotone, as if he were facing those hicks on the highway again, "let's go somewhere a little more discreet. And then I'll pull over. And then we'll talk. Okay, honeybuns? Can you sit still and wait that long?"

"Yes."

"Not too long." Boil tapped his cellphone slowly.

Bernard shouts behind us. "Tim, you're fucking whacked, man!"

"He's snapped!" Sergio shouts. "Watch yourself, Julio! The boy's aura is engulfed in azure flames!"

Julio whipped his head back, pointing his finger like a tired father. "Everything's cool. Just keep following us. Apparently we gotta go have a *talk*."

The tires squeal. Zipping around the edge of Tomahok, we approach the center, where Lakeside Drive cuts through the black heart of town. We pass the crowds, weaving erratically through traffic. Soon we're on the outskirts, about to be dead center in Tomahok.

Lakeside Drive is bordered on both sides by Lake Sheol, but it's really more of a pond. The Lakeside is so thin that there's no shoulder. Many drunk drivers become drunk divers here. There's a thin strip where the land gets a little more girth on the west side. There are only two small houses. We fly past, lit only by the moon. There is a long, waterside street, just before Lakeside curves around to loop back on the town proper. Industrial Road. A dead end. Like Lakeside, its name is larger than life, for life has no appropriate size.

He's picked a good place. Industrial Road is naught but pothole, gravel and crumbled cement, bordered by the Atlantic Ocean. Transistor towers form an arch over the road. Its west side is covered in barbed wire fences, pipes rising, rusted and tangled like vines, twisted telephone poles and their frayed lines sagging down. On the east side, jagged rocks, remnants of abandoned rowboats, mounds of shattered glass, and fields of cigarette butts.

Spiraling metal transformers hum in the darkness. Rusted fences vibrate. Only one streetlamp casts its pallid light at the corner, where the road hits a dead end. One wrong step could end in 10,000 volts of enlightenment or a jagged, watery grave. A crumbling, rusted maze of techno-industrial disdain and debris-laden shore. No one comes down to this polluted peninsula for anything of merit. Good place to dump a body.

We drive to the end. The farthest tip of Tomahok peeks around from the east, across the black water. The northern prong. The lighthouse sits at that tip, rhythmically pumping its life light across the sound.

We've reached the dead end. Just jungle brush and trees ahead. The trail, invisible to all but the trained, is embraced by fresher foliage. But our trained eyes still see the path. Julio guns the engine, as if to tear into the end itself, then slams the brakes, making us slip and slide until we stop, perfectly lined up to the camouflaged trail. He kills the engine, kicks the door open, spins around, then slams it shut.

"Everyone wait here!" He turns his back to us and starts marching toward the evergreen border. He whips back to me. "Let's go. Amigo."

I stumble behind him like a leper. We hit the trees, then start pushing our way through. Thick branches tear at us, thorns sticking our skin and hair. Damn prickers have taken over here, too. Julio stumbles over an empty oilcan. He pushes branches out of the way, letting them snap back at me. I duck. Trip over a tire. Crunch empty junk food bags and old condoms. Bottles so old the labels are just pale yellow. No one bothers with Industrial Road anymore. A place that cartographers choose to ignore. We are alone in one of Earth's many beating dark hearts.

A minute later, the pulsing brightness from the lighthouse washes over the tree line, and we emerge onto a small strip of rocky beach. Another crescent dead end. Scythe styled strip of rocky shore. Boulders twice my height jut into the air. The water laps slowly to the rhythm of a melting home. Every minute or so, the lighthouse beam arcs over us, then leaves us once more to the moon's glow. Truly alone in a dark crater bordered by wild trees and jagged rocks. A small space, a fine place to die.

Julio stands at the shore, his back to me. Water laps at his boots. "Well? Fuck's up with you?"

I let him get impatient, standing silently behind him. His fuse burns out, he turns, and I strike. My slap lands dead on his stubbled face. I may as well have struck a stone statue. He licks his lip and just stares, emotionless.

"That it? You feel better now, you maniac?"

My hand fell limp at my side, just long enough for me to think the slight would go unpunished. Yet he is kind, merely shoving me off my feet, letting the wicked damp rocks cushion my spine. He waits while I groan and squirm. He extends his hand, still like a gun hammer, cocked but not wanting to fire. I grasp it, and he lifts me to my feet.

"Sorry," I said.

"Bound to happen. Is that it?"

"No, I… Well, this isn't the most romantic spot. But good call. This is for real, Jay. Just you and me."

"You gonna hit me again?"

My hand stings, singing in protest. "No. And for what it's worth, it was just a slap."

"Exactly. If you're gonna hit a man, hit him."

Noted. No slapping. He folded his arms and stood at my side, both of us looking at the lighthouse across the water. I didn't know how to begin. Luckily, he did.

"First off. Don't ever pull any shit like that on me again, bro." He puts his hands on his hips and surveys the ragged strip of sand shore and rock. This is a lonely crop of land, where milkfish gather to gossip. A mermaid sanctuary. "So what the fuck's going on in that crazy dome of yours? Spill it, 'cause there ain't much time. And I actually do… I do give a shit. For now at least."

"So you and Sergio have a history, huh?"

"Everyone's got a history," he says, still facing the distant lighthouse. When the beam hits, he's just a solid shadow flickering before the placid lap of purple tides.

"Look, Jay, I'm sorry about all that, but I had to—"

"Second, don't ever apologize for nothing." He faces me. His body still rigid, but his face, his eyes, they aren't aflame. Rare. He's upset, but is he… sad?

"I ain't sad. And don't you dare apologize for hitting Boil neither."

"What? There's no way I'd ever take that back. I'm still sorry I almost blew out your windshield. Got lucky… Wait, I mean, I'm not sorry. Right?"

"Word. Well, I guess I bring that kind of shit on myself," he said. He rubbed his chin. "Honestly, I'm surprised it took you this long to snap. I mean, you handle some crazy shit, but ah… Yeah, tonight's been tense."

I picked up a smooth, flat stone. Perfect black, glistening in moonlight. I pitch out into the water. Two skips.

"So you're not pissed off?" I asked.

"Me? I thought you're the one who's all bent." He picked up a stone too, a small, jagged, heart-shaped pearl. Pitched it. Four skips.

I walked over to stand next to him.

"I am."

"So. Lay it on me. And not another slap. What the hell did I do?"

"I'm not pissed at you, exactly. Well, maybe I am pissed at you."

"Tim, spit it out. Be real. What's going on?"

"No, you tell me what's going on! You're running around shooting at people, you tell me you're leaving town, and now… I know what you're planning to do. But I want to hear it from you."

He crosses his arm and licks his lip angrily, darting. Bites on it. Bends down and slowly scans the rocks for the perfect find. Fingers running over wet curves. Finds a yellow arrowhead igneous. Pitches it into the living darkness. It cuts straight in, no splash, no skip.

"Jay? You're seriously not going to tell me? Me, of all people." I look down at him, folding my arms now. "This isn't a drug deal. You would have postponed that for me. You would have done it for Barry. I know what's up."

He exhaled loudly and turned toward the inlet. Then looked up at me. "Yeah?"

"You're going to kill Savage Jefe. That's why you're skipping town."

"If shit goes down right, yes. Took you longer to figure out than I thought."

Longer to believe. "So that's it. You've finally slipped off the deep end. You're going to full on murder someone?"

"Yup," he said. He brushed through the rocks, looking for another skipper. "You really so surprised? Are you gonna turn me in or something?"

"That's ugly," I said. "Don't say something like that. I'd never turn you in. You stupid beast. Besides, I'm kind of guilty by association now."

"So what's the deal, then? You know the big secret. Got your answer. You're in. So what's your beef with me?"

"Hey, stop and think about someone else for a change," I said. Did he just hide a laugh? He nodded to continue. "Well, what would have happened if I didn't show up at your door tonight? Were you really just going to leave without telling me?"

"It'd be safer for you," he said. "Cops come around asking questions, you could honestly cover your own ass." He pitched another stone. One skip.

"I'd rather dishonestly cover your ass. Shit, Jay, what do I have to lose?"

"Yeah, I bet you'd cover my ass," he says, chuckling. He finally smiles down at himself and then stands.

"I'm not—"

He spit. "I know you're not gay. I remember her. I remember everything. I know that's why you haven't torn up any pussy since then. You can't. It's cool. Kinda noble or romantic or some shit. Wish I had something like that to hold on to, know what I'm saying?"

No. I don't. You don't want this weight. This iron maiden called armor.

"Sick visual. Dude, don't get me wrong. I'm psyched you showed up. Seriously. A lot of weird shit like that's been happening, lately. You pop up right before we leave. Sergio drops in out of nowhere. And with Burn of all people! Shee-it, son. Everything's coming together. I'm sure of it now. It's like… uh, you know, divine intervention or something."

"Fate?"

"Yeah. Fate."

I sigh, looking down at the wet rocks. A nightcrab skitters past. Julio stomps at it with his boot. It escapes into the inky water. My heart is aching again. Feels like I've been running forever. Lungs burst. Too dried out to cry.

Shit.

All this armor I've built, and now it's pulling in tighter, the spikes piercing like slow meteors, burning into my flesh, no way to pass through and leave.

I don't want to do this.

But I do.

"Julio Sanchez Sin Corazon. Look at me."

He doesn't.

"Look. At. Me."

He does. Eye to eyes.

"You motherfucker. You sold Tracy those pills."

He turns his back to me again. We're hit by the lighthouse.

"So that's it, huh? Yup. I did. I sold her the pills. And I sold you pills, and weed, and booze and cigarettes. I slung to Barry, Burn, all y'all motherfuckers. Weed, coke, X, you name it. I've sold people you've never even met meth, heroin, coke... You know what I am. But I didn't stuff those pills down her throat. I didn't empty bottles of liquor into her. I didn't leave her alone! I didn't... I didn't."

His last words were too shaky for either of us to bear out.

"You could have told me."

"Really, Tim? I could have told you? Because Boil was probably just talking shit or his brain is out of whack, or you know what? Maybe he really did bang her. And I saw what you'd do. If I didn't put your ass down, you woulda done it. You'd slice him up. And it wasn't no surprise. You got a darkness in you. And I like it. But you said it yourself, you're getting worse. And that ain't no shock neither."

"He didn't fuck her."

"Maybe he did, maybe he didn't. Never asked."

"He. Did. Not."

"Man, for real. Think about it. If I told you she got the pills from me, that'd be it. Even if you didn't blame me to my face, you know you would. I don't care if you think I'm a beast, brute, hard-ass-motherfucker, scum, or—what'd you say once, a vampire? But I do give a shit if you think I'm—that I'd sell to her if I thought she was an addict. If I knew it was all for one bitch ass night. I never thought she was abusing the shit, or that she'd take it all at once. Alone. Did you? No. You didn't. So…"

"No. But I know why she did. But that doesn't matter now. You lied to me, Jay. We don't do that. And not a fucking lizard lie. A true lie!"

"If I didn't, you wouldn't be here now. You'd like… flip out and hit me in the ear, or try to cut my goddamn throat with that stupid fucking sword." He faced me now, shoulders hanging loose but fists clenched. Huge. A dark colossus. Bahamas. Mistakes.

"No. I would have done exactly what we're doing right now," I said. "I hate you for it, but you know what? I can't stand losing another friend. I just can't take it. These last years, just, everything, stripped away bit by bit."

"You so sure about that? If I told you she came to me for all that junk a couple years ago, you'd just want to have a talk with me? Or is it 'cause this is our last night and now you're too scared to turn your back on me? You think I'm proud? You think I haven't spent years fucking wondering when this would happen? That you'd bury me? You got enough dirt on me to lock me away forever. And shit, Tim, I wouldn't even blame you for it."

"I would never turn on you. It's just, why couldn't you be honest with me! Me, of all people!"

"I don't know what to say." He walked slowly along the shore, kicking rocks. Wet slapping, skidding as the lighthouse beam arcs around again. "I don't know what to tell you. I'm sorry, okay? For everything!"

"And now I find out you're friends with a guy that made my fucking life miserable! What the hell, man? How do you think it feels to go crawling to you for help, and find out you're running around with Lucas Boil! And *for this*? Murder? You don't trust me, but you trust *him*? Then you're going to disappear and leave me alone, just like everyone else does. How do you think that feels?"

Words rushing like an open artery. It's split now. Fine. Flow.

He glared at me.

"How do I think it feels? How do I think it feels? Knowing you killed your friend's sister? You think Barry doesn't know who sold to her? Shit, I know how much you loved her. How do you think it feels knowing I stole that from you? How do you think it feels to walk around every day knowing I killed her? That I ruined your life?"

"You didn't kill her. And you didn't ruin my life."

"So who did then? You? That stupid fucking curse? Oh, bullshit, man. Feeling guilty is one thing, but you didn't put the gun in her hand."

I stepped up and put my hand on his shoulder.

"I did. You have to trust me."

He shoved me back. Not hard, but the ground was slippery enough. I fell onto the rocks. Our eyes locked. I always try to look at the fake and real alike, no difference in the end. The light swings around. Blinding. Want to keep hiding in this humid dark. Pain womb. Agony shell. He walks over slowly and stretches out his hand. I take it.

"It's not like you have to try to sell drugs. They sell themselves. You know that. I didn't push them on her. She asked me. Can you just say that? Can you say that you... you know I didn't mean to... Ah, god fucking DAMN IT! Fuck this noise. Can you forgive me?"

Me? Forgive him? The king kneels before his clown?

"Dude, chill. I know. I know. I just wish that none of this..." I knelt down and squeezed my skull, hoping this time I'd crush it and all the gray spatters out, coating the seaweed, the rocks, gets pulled into the sea. Chest rattling. Each breath like a bar of iron rolling across my lungs. Don't cry, Tim. Not again. Not in front of him. Man up.

He shook his head. "Bitch, I don't care if you cry in front of me. Heh. Let it out. Just do it."

Again. I punched the ground. Felt my knuckles burn. Stupid. Knuckles split more. Salt water on raw skin. I can't look up at him. I shake my head at the dark, enveloped in the stink of low-tide.

"I can't forgive you."

Silence. He walks away. Hear a lighter click. Then boots come crunching back. He waits, god bless him.

"It's tough, Jay. Standing by your friends when you know they're set on a path to hell," I spoke to the black sand spying between the stones. Smells of salt and fish wafting into my face. Tears welling up. "I wish you didn't do it. It'd be easier to bear that than knowing the truth. I'm not an idiot. She did what she wanted to do. It's not your fault that she died. But I wish it was. I wish I could hate you. I wish I could have an enemy to crush. The only thing... It's your fault that you kept this a secret. You don't get a pass on that... but you didn't kill her. I don't buy that. Barry wouldn't either."

Julio sighed. He sat down on the rocks next to me. We're silent, watching the light beam leave us, then come back around, then leave us safe under night again.

"So we good, then?"

I stared up at the moon. So bright in all that darkness. Once heard it fills up with souls. When it's full, it carries them away. It's looking pretty full.

"Yeah. We're good."

"Aight," Julio said. He snorts. Looks away. "We never say this shit, but you know how I'm connected. I know a lot of people out here. Damn near everyone. Shit, I even got connections from cops, to kids, to the old dockworkers. Guys we grew up with. Hell, I even sell to some of *their* kids now! I got a whole high school of customers. And girls…"

"Yeah." I pitched another stone. Plop. "Sorry, but I don't care what you do with them."

"But I don't have a lot of friends."

"You have a million friends. Everyone loves you! Well, almost everyone."

"No man, I have a million customers. You're damn near the best friend I have."

I sit back in the damp bits of sand, my feet clattering on the rocks. Leaning back on my palms, my head falls back, limp. Snot drips down my throat. Cold slimy trail.

"So what do you think, Julio? Was Boil telling the truth? Did he fuck her?"

"I want to say no, but I'm not going to lie to you. Honestly, it's hard to say," Julio said. "I don't know Boil like the back of my hand. Same with Tracy. She was a hell kitten, you know that. It was pretty shocking that you two got together. I mean, it was great, but still… a surprise. You were like her guardian. Makes sense though. She was full of surprises. But there's no doubt in my mind you two were the best things that ever happened to each other, for real. But, you know… She was young. She made mistakes. Who doesn't?"

"Yes. Yes, she made some mistakes." We both let out a deep breath. "What about you?"

He leaned back into the darkest cove's shadow. "What about me?"

"Did you fuck her?"

He lit another cigarette. Immediately flicked away. Lit another. Great.

"We never had sex."

I waited. Each millisecond reminded me that my blood sugar was plummeting. I could pass out at any moment.

"We hooked up once, nothing serious, just some drunk night," he said. Quite slowly. "Way before you two did. She was like, fifteen? I know, it's screwed up, you don't gotta lay that on me. It's just like, shit like that kinda just happens. And after you told me what was up with you two, word is bond, never, ever again. Never even crossed my mind. And she *never* gave me another look. She was waiting for... Dude, she was crazy about you. And I was so psyched for y'all! Whether you had to hide it from her family or not. She was amazing. And you two together, it was like new people. I was sorta jealous. But never dreamed one morning it would all just... be over."

Held my tongue, for fear of my voice shaking and cracking. Every muscle in my face tightened like a fist. If he weren't him, I could drown him. Beat him with a rock. But he—I believe him. Can't hurt him, he's too raw, too real.

He stepped forward. Lighthouse flash. Ran his hand through his hair, looking up to something I'll never see. "Listen man, you gotta understand," he continued. "You said so yourself. She did what she did because she wanted to. Whether that was hanging around her shitty friends at school, or possibly Boil, or me, she always did what she wanted. And that includes you. And you were the end of it, man, for better or for worse. You remember how much she changed once you two were like, officially unofficial? Yeah she drank and partied, but you did too. But she ended that self destructive crap. Tracy was way ahead of her time. Maybe she was just nuts because she was sad. A lot of us are. Well, when you told me that you two were in love, you both changed, bro. You ever think maybe she died happy? That's the only thing that'd be your fault. She was happy."

"Oh god, I can't do this," I moaned. "My life is getting too fucked up."

"Life is fucked up! And it ain't *your* life, homes. It's just life!" He threw his arm out at the darkness. "We know this shit better than all those fucking cunts out there! Tracy's not the first sweet little girl to die too young! What about our parents, our other friends, man? Look, we ain't the first dudes to carry on in their wake. Shit is whack, Tim. What do you want?"

"I want her back," I whispered. "Did you love her, too?"

"Love?" He doesn't get hit with that word much. He looks away as the beam arcs back. He stares off at Tomahok's other prong. That end, sending out light. So far, close, yet so far. "Nah, man. I don't love no one. I thought she was cool, though. Mad cool."

Shit. He did. This weird thing I feel, this lukewarm worm twisting around my heart, this anaconda constricting me, but won't do it, it won't finish me off, this fucking Curse that won't take me, is this how Barry would feel? If he knew all this deception, mistakes, random bullshit, the lucky shot that shook apart our worlds?

"She had a hard life," Julio said. "That shit with her old man. That fucking scumbag. He deserved everything he got."

"It's like that family is cursed. But it's me. My Curse. Which means you're screwed, too." I leaned back on my palms again. "Man, Barry is really messed up. That car... I should have let him sit inside while I... just, like... How could I know?"

"Cursed, bro, yeah. Not just you, though. All of us," Julio said. "That was the thing you told me, right? About some crazy Bahama dude when you was little?"

"Yeah."

"Yo, maybe that shit is contagious."

"I've been thinking that myself."

He laughed. Such a strangely sad sound. Like the first laughs after a funeral.

"Dude, are you really wearing her pants?"

"Yes. I got cold and they were just sitting there... I mean, they're men's pants anyway."

"Ha, you are one twisted fuck."

"It's not like that, I just... I was in her room and it felt right."

"Be easy, I'm just playing. No wonder we get along. We really are like brothers. Sort of. I guess."

"Speaking of which. Julio, I've got to tell you something."

"Ah, son of a bitch! You *are* gay? Now I know why you snuck me out here."

"You goddamn freak, will you be serious for a second? This is important."

"I know, I know. It's just like, you're so floppy and wiggly. It's hard not to think you'd be a little flexible. Don't take this wrong, but I'd hit it."

I truly don't know what to say, but whatever way I'm looking at him, it's making him laugh all the harder. I'm about to make a distasteful joke about his father but luck strikes and he cuts me off.

"Ha! Aight, aight, I'm sorry. Didn't mean to get your hopes up. Heh. Go on, Tim, what's up?"

"I mentioned before, how I think I'm losing it." I took a deep breath. "Well... I think I saw Tracy's ghost."

He kicked his feet forward, slamming into the rocks like a mattress and the rounded Earth better get out of his way. Didn't even faze him. He lit a joint. "Word? Fuckin' intense. When was that?"

"Tonight. Dude, I didn't just see her ghost. I sat down and had a conversation with it. I mean her. Her."

"What did you talk about?" He passed the joint to me, but I waved it away.

"A lot of stuff. So that's it? You just believe me like that?"

"Of course, hombre."

"Wow. Because I'm not even sure if I believe me. I was all twisted on your stupid drugs and god knows what else. Or maybe I wasn't, you asshole. Maybe I had a mental breakdown. Like I hallucinated my idea of her and sat down and talked to it." I dropped my head into my hands. "Oh god, that sounds like schizophrenia. I really am going crazy."

"All right, drama queen, relax. Let me ask you one question. Did it make you feel better?"

Better than anything. Felt like falling backwards in time, back to when dreams of the future weren't so cold and dark. "Yeah, for the most part. While we were talking, I felt really good. Like when you can finally cry after your parents die? That kind. But after she was gone, I just felt so much worse, all over again."

"I wouldn't worry about it. The crazy part, I mean," Julio said. "I've seen some weird shit in my time."

"Weird as that? I'm telling you, Jay, it wasn't for a haunted second. We had a full-on undead date. So what kind of ethereal weirdness have you encountered?"

"Ghosts? Shit, I don't know. I can't explain it. Last year, I swear I saw my mother standing at the top of the steps. And I ran right up to her like an idiot. Almost cried, too. Except I ran right through her and slammed my head into the wall. Busted right through the plaster. Aye, mami."

"That's how that hole got there? Damn, what were you on?"

"Xanax, vicodin, ambien, tequila…"

"So why don't we see them when we're sober?"

"Fuck if I know. Maybe like… our brains open up? We can receive more signals."

Actually, yeah maybe. Pull back the curtain. Peek backstage.

"Well I'm never telling anyone else about this," I said. "Not even Bernard. And certainly not Barry."

"Shit, you self-absorbed prick," Julio said. He backhanded my hollow chest. "What makes you think Tracy didn't visit him too?"

"You sound like you really believe in ghosts."

"I believe in anything that makes life better."

I lay back and stared up at the stars. A dark sea of souls, each shining and fading into nothing, sending their last scream of light. Just to let us know they were there.

"We haven't talked like this in a while."

"Yeah. Don't tell no one, but I miss it. I guess we both been pretty busy."

Okay. Good. Let's pull the trigger. "So why now?"

"Why now what? Ghosts?"

"Why now, Savage Jefe? After all these years, why tonight?"

"Eh, it's not that easy. You think he hasn't been expecting it? I mean, the bastard chewed out my fucking eye. He's been waiting for me. I get older, and it ain't like he'd be blasting a kid anymore, ya know? I'm more of a target than ever. But tonight I can get close enough to do it," he said. He pulled out two cigarettes, lit them. Passed one to me, but I wave it away. He puts both in his mouth, a burning V. "Tonight. With my bare hands. Look him in the eye. Besides… I just thought like, I thought maybe things would get better. At some point, it wouldn't be worth it. But it hasn't. Dude, we're fuckin' adults now."

Really? Sorry, Julio. I disagree. Still waiting for Mommy and Daddy to point the way. Waiting without end. Fading.

"Nothing ever ends, Tim. You taught me that, remember? You were stoned out of your fuckin' mind, but I remember. Endless cycle, new mask? Nothin' ever ends."

"No. I was wrong. Some things end. Even if we have to force it."

"Damn straight, dude." Jay smiled, eyes shut, twin flaming cherries casting a red glow over his yellow shark teeth. "I'm gonna force it."

Tonight Always Happens

"We have to go," he said.

"How long have we been here?" I asked.

"Like ten minutes."

"Really? Wow, my concept of time truly is broken."

"Ah, fuck if I know. Twenty minutes? Who cares, let's just… relax before the shit storm. Those bitches can wait."

The oncoming storm. Just over that horizon, brewing behind the ocean, past the lighthouse's reach. Jay lay next to me, hands behind his head. Not too close. The smoke puffed up and danced in the swinging beam. The tidal rhythm washing over the rocks just below us. Tree tips framing the sky behind us.

"Adults. Ha. It's weird," he said, eyes still shut. "It's like we're the oldest we've ever been, but I still feel like I'm not, you know, older. Nothing's changed. So yeah, tonight. It's time to end shit. My way of growing up, I guess."

"You might be bringing a terrible hammer down upon yourself. The lords of Karma are fickle with their judgment. Every action has consequences," I said. "I almost killed a stupid animal because it scared me, and got I cursed forever. You kill Jefe, whatever happens next is on your head."

"I *am* the consequence of *his* actions." Julio punched his palm. His knuckles cracked like fireworks.

"So much for that," I said. I kicked the sand.

"Where'd you think you'd be at this point?"

I sat up, sifted through the rocks some more. Pitched a few, no skips. "Ah, I just took it for granted. Thought I'd stay with Tracy, and I'd help out you and Burn, and Barry would be making a name for himself too. And I thought my parents would be alive, and maybe we'd have kept the house. And maybe I'd be worth something and be a dad and…"

Shit. The silent tears. Note to self: We never run out of tears.

"Sounds good," Julio said. "I gotta say, if I ever wondered about you, that's about how I'd hope things would've turned out. But life sucks. Time is a motherfucker. Blah, blah, fucking blah."

"I don't know how you do it," I said. "You dropped out of high school before I even went to college, and yet here you are, still slinging your drugs and maintaining a fearsome rep. It's really amazing in a twisted, grotesque, way. I honestly thought you'd be dead or in jail by now."

"I might be tomorrow. Shit, Tim, I'm really going for broke here. You're right, I've hung on this long, made the right deals, been smart. Seriously though, a lot of it is luck, and it's gonna run out. I gotta do this before that. For real. I got no future. All I got is this weird feeling that if I do something this big, *something's* gonna happen. For better or worse. I gotta do something I can't walk away from. My whole life, it feels like always coming down after the best high. Just like always coming down. And I'm sick of it."

I know the feeling, brother. I patted his head. He laughed.

"Yeah, I bet you do. Seriously. Anything's better than this halfway shit, just scraping by day by day. But I got no fucking idea what I'm going to do after this. I'm going for revenge before he gets me. Gonna even out his karma. Then… I don't know. But you're right, I can pull tricks and bribe my way out of a lot, but probably not murder. Even a bastard like him. So I gotta go. I win and bounce out of town, or I lose and… die."

"So don't do it! Hire Boil as a mercenary or something. Let him do the wetwork! Leave it to him, and we'll go see Barry together. You, Burn, and me. We'll figure something out. We'll move to another town and get an apartment. Like Barry did."

"Oh, we're gonna go get us a little house to settle down in?" he laughed. It faded fast. His twin cigarettes bloomed as he pulled. "It doesn't work that way. No, I need to do this myself. Can't keep running. Tonight had to happen someday, so why not tonight?"

Why not, indeed? Face it down yourself, Julio. Can't argue with that. Smash the situation head-on. No running away. I wish I didn't hide in your shadow. Wish I could run beside you. Seems you're the devil on a run.

"All right, Jay. In some weird, twisted way, it almost makes sense. I'm scared for you, but I understand," I said. "But let me ask you this. What stake does Boil have in this? It's got to be more than just cash."

"Ask him yourself. It's stupid, but I feel where he's coming from. He's really screwed up, man. He might have done this for free. Maybe he gets some kind of high out of it? I still can't believe he actually got those lizards. I was sort of joking when I asked. I want to keep some.

And I know you hate him. I don't blame you. But he's the best backup I could hope for. This is a sick job, and I need a sick man to do it. Savage Jefe's gonna have protection. Local thugs and dumbasses. But it doesn't take superpowers to pull a trigger."

"Obviously."

"Boil's just a little bit more experienced in battle than you are, Timmy. And don't fucking tell him, but if I had to choose between you two getting caught in my crossfire…"

"Okay. Fine."

"Fine? That mean you're riding with me again?"

"Uh, no. I think I'll keep my distance until your work is done. But I'll stick it through. I still have your word. Need that ride to Barry."

Yeah. Yeah Tim, keep your distance and your Curse to yourself. Don't poison Julio too, if you haven't already. Everything will be all right, everything will be okay. There's no way this could go wrong.

"Fair enough. My business is mine, yours is yours."

"Yeah."

"Based on your little fight back there, you'd just get in the way, anyhow."

I laughed. Stood. He gave me a fist bump, then I helped him to his feet.

"Don't get me wrong, Julio. I'm not happy about this. Not at all. But hell, I'm not happy about anything. If this is what you have to do, then fine. It's your life. All I ask is that you do it right. Then get me to Hawkhouse and I'll do what I have to."

"Deal."

The trees shook as something ran away behind us. The light beam hit the tree line just in time. A reddish blue.

"Did you see that fox?"

"Ain't no more foxes, bro. That was just a deer or some shit."

"You believe in ghosts, but not foxes?"

"They're extinct, man. Everything is dying. I heard there's no more penguins anymore either, or some shit like that. And the pandas are gone! You're just seeing things, mi compadre loco."

"I'm definitely sober."

"Well, they're dead. And soon that fat fucker is too."

"Everyone dies," I said.

"Everyone poops!"

Rows of jagged teeth glowing in the moonlight. The surfer's terror staring up from the abyss. It's his creepy smile. Natural, unlike my practiced stare. I pity Julio's orthodontist. Well I would, if he ever actually saw one. I can see Jay, strapped in the chair, blood streaming out of the corners of his mouth, fist clenched so tight that the IV pops out, past my face, my knees on his chest, furiously hacking and smashing at his wisdom teeth, and his living eye, staring right into my own, tears pouring down his cheek, gurgling his horrible, bubbling laugh. Yellow as the sun. It's amazing they haven't fallen out yet.

"Well," I said, "let's get this over with. Thanks for... for this."

"I hear you. Yeah, um, thanks too. Do we have to hug now? Without hitting each other?"

"Only if you want to."

His true grin spread. Then he nodded, didn't hug me, and we started back.

The vines and thorns leached in once more, hungry for our sweaty flesh. Julio simply brushed them aside like a gorilla. Snapping, stomping, and pushing them away. I dipped and dodged in his wake before the branches snapped back in. I called out.

"Hey, am I really your best friend?"

"Yeah. You're god damned fucking weird, but you've stuck by me no matter what. Never judged me. You're the nicest motherfucker I know," he paused. "Ah, who am I kidding? Don't get all weepy on me now. It's game time."

"I'll stick to the bleachers."

He turned around, a beast with human eyes raising a palm full of thorn-laden vines. "You said some shit about standing by your friend on the road to Hell. Which one of us is it?"

Does it matter at this point?

"Sergio says we're on a Devil's Run." I was about to recite the lyrics but caught myself. No need to put that dark incantation into words. "We're doomed."

"Word. We're all doomed. For real, Tim, you're like my little brother. Hell, that means, you're—Tim, you're all I got. Like, uh, you're my..."

I waved at him to shut up. He smiled and turned back to clearing the brush. Damn it, Julio. Why do the best things still hurt so bad?

"What'd you say?"

Nothing.

BOOK THREE:
The Doom Generation

The Shark God Conspiracy

"So you're okay with being wanted for murder?"

"It's better than not being wanted at all!" Julio shouted back. Clever. Creepy. Calm. "You're already assuming we'll get caught."

The headlights push back at us through the black trees standing guard.

"And you're assuming nothing will go wrong. Everything will just go along with your perfect plan. You *do* have a plan, right?" I finally caught up to him. "The lords of karma are not always noble. Look at what they did to me just for thinking about hurting a stupid stingray. At the very least, make an offering to buy yourself some bad luck insurance. Bribe the toxic cosmos."

He turned to me. No more smile. Tapped his glass eye.

"Don't sweat it, Tim. We got a rock solid plan."

We. As in Boil and he. Not me. Oh no, not me. I already have blood on my hands, and I didn't ask for it like Jay is. He also hasn't asked for my help. A sign of respect, I suppose, or a sign of... No, he said it was to protect me. My, my, such a noble savage. Strangers see something wrong, "bad guys", the drug dealer and hired killer, with me, the betrayer and Cursed, self-absorbed coward. All the logic in the world can't change how I feel about him, just like it was with Tracy. You know how it looks to everyone else, but only you know how it truly feels. And nothing these days truly looks how it feels.

"Shut up and hurry, you faggots!" Boil stands on the Jeep's hood. The engine idles, shaking and rumbling. He yells more dumb things I pretend to not to hear.

"Yo, you get the fuck off my Jeep! So jealous, seriously."

Questions swarm my vision, gnawing their way behind my eyes, squeezing behind the sockets and burrowing straight for my brain. Scraping and unending, even as my body moves, I fall deeper inside. But I make sure to talk to our team, nonsense, anything, so long as it means my thoughts remain inside. Boil pounces beside me as I pass by. Somehow I don't even flinch. I'm lost in a sideways world, stunned, ready to just go. An inverted, invisible kingdom that overlaps ours, a world where they can all go, and just leave me. Just leave me so that I can finally let go …

"Finally! Let's go," Boil says behind me. "What were you doing?"

I turn around. Feel very… light. Relieved in the worst way. My voice feels different, slow and cold, when I tell Boil that:

"Sometimes adults talk things out. It's more productive than a fist fight."

"Yeah, if you can't win the fight," he snorts. Then glares at me, his smile all teeth.

"Anyway, it's a secret." I stare at his one real tattoo. Foxhound. Mine burns in response. "Your tattoo is stupid."

He must be responding, but only the back of my head hears it. Boil has likely killed dozens of people and been told it's okay. Even if some were pure and just, it's likely many were just "collateral damage". Tragic accidents. Statistics. No gods, no laws, just chaos and math. Of course I have no proof that he has, I'm just going on the same statistics as everyone else. Plus personal knowledge of the bastard and a dash of some pseudo-psychology. No matter, it happens, and if it's Boil this time, no one openly condemns him.

Yet Julio plans to kill only one evil man. I think Boil is worse. Easy choice. So I'm afraid for Jay, but I won't stop him. His business is his business. I'm not his master. Right? Or I just can't, or I'm afraid, or—the other option—I might not care. And I don't know which it is. Does murder really change the sum of who you are, or is this just revenge, a long delayed effect from Savage Jefe's first cause? Why do I loathe Boil as an evil killer and adore Jay as a potential murderer? Why do I feel increasingly numb? Too abstract? Will the smell of blood or a dilated eye sway my morality? Have I, desperate, stupid, and crazy, stumbled down an evil road? Is this how a Lucas Boil is made? Or how a Henry Poole becomes a Savage Jefe?

Perhaps Bernard is right. I'm not a good person. Now on the way to let a murder occur, my true self, indignant, selfish, and cold, is finally taking hold? And does anybody even care?

The three headlights. Glaring spots of red and green turn into darkness, change words into scenes. Concepts birth memory. Flashes of Barry hooked to bags and tubes and beeping cenobite machines. My father's bones entwined in coral and seaweed. Mom's ashes dancing off the cliff, dancing smoke above the ocean. Tracy as a porcelain doll blanketed in dirt. So I stare ahead at this man, ready to kill, and both of us either too brave or too stupid to be scared.

"Well! They look relieved," Bernard said.

"Indubitably, Bernard. They share a yellow aura now."

"Julio, you were the pitcher, right? Please tell me you were the pitcher," Boil said. He laughed. Nobody else did.

"Boil, shut up with the homophobe shit, aight?" Julio grabbed the driver's door and leapt right over into the seat.

"Yeah, you already know his dad is gay, you jerkoff. Did you just assume he hates him, or have you bothered to ask?" I snatched Barry's briefcase from the Jeep and head back for the convertible, feeling ten-feet tall.

Bernard gives me a quick shoulder rub when I'm back in shotgun. He smells musky, and I'm afraid his unique scent is permeating the Hawaiian shirt he borrowed. As a rule, Bernard is clean enough to be healthy, but dirty enough to be happy. Though more often than not, he chooses happy. He'd kill me if I told anyone, but Burn's secret pleasure is that when showering at a girl's place, he can't resist trying out all their foofy-poofy funny smelling lathers, scrubs, shampoos, and creams.

"Feeling better, buddy?" he asked.

"Yeah. Everything's cool. Better, actually."

"Excellent! All allies are aligned," Sergio said. He lit a new cigar. He threw the car in reverse and began snaking his way back down Industrial Road.

So we're back on track. Julio leads us around the rim of Tomahok. Avoiding the crowds and cops. We're headed for the docks. Tiburon Pier. The real docks, not the luxury ports. A no-man's land where the fishermen pull in cod and tuna by day and coke and heroin by night. And nightfall on these docks is under the sole domain of Savage Jefe and his degenerate posse. It is at the southernmost point of Tomahok's lower fishtail fin, with the lighthouse paralleling the cold docks upon the northern tip.

We ride in silence. The cat is out of the bag, and we all take on our private battle meditations. I pray to my false gods, the ones I think sleep in the Earth's core, plaguing us with their cosmic nightmares. Cthulhu sleeping in forgotten cities in the ocean deep. The Nightmare Child still gestating. The Caffeind and the Great Sloam and the Nameless Ones, the Never Borns, and the Frozen Tear Bathed Archons of the Outworld's Church. The ancient ones, the island lords, the tired standard bearers. Even the Stingray King. Take an offering, you bastard. Free us of my Curse. I pray to anything I'd ever seen or read or thought up as I screamed alone at night looking for something else to take the blame.

Bernard scratches his stomach. Sergio puts on music. The song is beautiful. It's a cover of "The Battle Hymn of the Republic" by Herbie Mann. A soaring cacophony of flutes, rising bursting notes shrilling, tripping over one another in a manic expression of passion and hubris. The music coats the air, enveloping the car in a blue white cloud of good goodness as we speed toward the fourth circle of Hell. Or is it the ninth? Or a hybrid bastard abortion of the two? Still, the music. Yes. Without music, life is just a cold and hollow cough, crying hallelujah. Language without words, a sweet unwritten aria of sorrow I play in my head, watching another sunrise. She used to sing. Especially when we were hitting the high white notes. Sing lines from her favorite songs, her voice low and soft: *"Drugs aren't free, but neither are memories."* It's not so cute now.

"Yo, Serge, you got any Ninja Dog?"

"No Bernard, I don't have that album."

"I heard Alec got an album or something," Burn said to me. "You hear it? Is it good?"

"What? Yeah, yeah it's good." Barry. Voltaire speed lights crunching, splatters. I can't ever hear that prophet album again. Then I smell the sharks. Hospital smells. Sanitized death and happy fake lights to hide the hurt and… We're here already? Didn't think it'd really happen, but no, this is really happening.

Tiburon Pier.

It all rolls into view old school, movement unreal but undeniable, just like the ancient art called stop motion animation. Vast, a clay colored twilight realm, waiting just for us. A weed entangled parking lot where the road ends and loops back toward town, and beyond that, a maze of wet dock, sleeping boats, and one grimy, sketchy bar. A man stands at the door, just a little blob surrounded by old neon lights. No one comes around here after dark. Not unless you want hard drugs or to swallow your own teeth.

There is a place where the fish are cut and sold, but not at night. Never at night. This is a savage inverse land at night. We stop in the expansive, empty parking lot across from the dockyard. Both vehicles are out of sight from the bar, shrouded by dense brush and dumpsters.

We kill the engines, cut the lights. Everyone is silent. Drinking in the dark.

The parking lot is a rotted concrete corpse, weeds and grass snaking through its cracked bones, the paved skin rotting away and burned with toxic rubber and wind-flung fish scales. A few old streetlamps sigh above, their mute lights flickering down. The docks are at the other end. It's nothing and everything now. I crave insanity now more than ever, but disassociation is impossible.

Tim, this is really happening.

Boats rock and creak. Bells chime. Water licks wood. The air is thick with rot and sea-death. Bitter musk. The docks stretch broken, jagged fingers into the black water. Slime clings. During the day, this place bustles as the ships troll in load after load of fresh steamers, lobsters, skate, cod, and all the best. But at night, everyone packs up and gets the hell out when that bar opens up. Leaving the docks to be prowled by the poor drug addicts and hopeless users, slaves to Savage Jefe's ways. Eager to do his bidding for their next fix.

Dark things sway in the moonlight. Dead things. I try to focus on them. God, they smell like an elephant's guts. Eggs rotting in a gutter. Even from here. Moonlight glints just right, and I get a proper view. They hang around the docks, in every direction. The sharks. Yes, bloated, dead sharks. Their stomachs drop down between rows of jagged teeth, hanging from their mouths like blood swollen scrotums. Watching us in their inverted hell, upside down with their ocean above and only our dry hell to hang in. Watching with marbled eyes.

I forgot. It's that time of year.

This sea-world horror show displays the trophies of our annual Great Shark Hunt. A chance for local heroes to prove their grit. These poor lords of the deep. Hanging from their tails, their guts spilling, dripping down to stain the gravel brown. Blood caking the moist wood. Flies thrive. Crude graffiti, hot pink and neon green, scrawled across a few of the slaughtered sea beasts. Like the streets of Brooklyn. All crying muerto. Their hanging bodies slowly sway. A macabre dance. Welcoming us. With enough distance, you'd swear you're at the gallows and gag as you realize no one had cleaned the steaming piles of shit that collected under each dead bowel. Steamy air rises from their guts, splayed open and shameless before nature. Even in this cool shore-side wind, the air is thick and hot like microwaved seafood pasta.

I can't take my eyes from the hanging sharks, and their King. The Great One. Hanging from his tail, a sagging reaper, false idol, harbinger of doom. Although it's merely a ceramic true-to-life recreation of The Great One, the sheer size of it inspires unspoken fear, even with us almost half a football field away. Some say to even touch one of its plastic rows of meticulously recreated teeth is enough to bring a deep-sea curse upon you. I don't dare take on another.

The Great One is why its flesh and blood cousins are slaughtered and paraded about. To protect us. The surfers and swimmers and boaters and tourists. Twenty-two feet and two thousand pounds of monster flesh. A man eater. Devil spawn of the great shark engine. Its brethren spawn, hanging about in mock offering to the ceramic idol, are killed in the annual Great Shark Hunt, a festival birthed in commemoration of the day our own Captain Bob Buddy met this monster on the open sea, conquering it in the name of all mankind.

"This is truly disgusting," I said.

"Appalling," Sergio agreed.

"Fucking rad," Burn said. "Look at all of them, man! They're out there while we're surfing every day! Not anymore."

"Monsters or not, they're just being what they are. This is a massacre. A celebrated one. Not a battle," I said.

"Fuck that. You ever been on your board and see a shadow circle under you?" Burn snapped.

No, but the animal kingdom is rotting away just fine without our additional genocide. Most importantly there is a shrine, dead center in the concentric circle of unmitigated savagery and slaughter. The deep beasts hang lifeless, stripped of power and grace, the fear and respect they inspire siphoned into the decrepit one-story shack at the center of the docks.

The Cantina Tiburon. A bar front named for two evil deities: Patron Saint Beezelglug, Lord of the Bar Flies, and Leviathan, the First Beast and Lord of the Deep.

The Cantina Tiburon is Save Jefe's headquarters. Hiding in plain sight. Small enough to run an empire without castle walls. Two decades ago, he'd never dare be so brazen. And neither would Julio.

Suppose that's one thing that ended. Now it's a hive of monsters. Make no mistake, this bar is not haunted with honest, hardworking men. Those bars are farther up the road, ironically out of sight of the legit daytime dock work. No, this bar is home to the dregs of our society. Vicious scum, every last one of them. Rapists, pushers, serial ravagers. Flat out creeps. Human stains. Vermin named man.

There are only a few empty battered cars parked around the Tiburon. The front door opens. An indistinct man steps outside, lights a pipe. Crack? How has this place lasted so long? This infection. This cancerous sore on the ass of Sponge Island. Julio is small time. Yet he thrives in a small town that should've buried him behind the pool hall long ago. So what is Savage Jefe? Is he a genius or a blessed demon? I always heard stories that he ran everything from one small bar and its basement. But I still imagined that Savage Jefe would have a fortress, with armed thugs like Boil keeping watch. A yellow Jeep and red sports car could never park behind a wall of dunes and trash this close. I take this all in from Sergio's car, parked next to the Jeep, just behind the mound of dunes and debris that border the parking lot. This is happening, Tim. Wake up.

"You see that?" Boil said. He pointed into the distance.

"Yeah, that car," Julio said, squinting. "It's those shit fuckers from before."

Strange, that they'd bother to get it towed, and back here of all places. The tendrils of the underworld run tight and deep, even in such a remote land. And so we watch this scene, like actors waiting to take the stage. Waiting for the big performance. No understudies. No rehearsal.

"Seems my hunch was correct," Sergio said.

"How many you count?" Julio asked.

"There's the bouncer out front," Boil said. "Plus the two we met on the highway. We have to assume they're both there. That guy smoking. So that's five counting the big man himself. In that case, I'd like to assume there's at least three more inside, and a bodyguard. The one I made the deal with. Enough to keep it running smooth but not too many to spoil the operation. So I expect roughly ten men. Prepared for twenty."

"Sounds right. He never kept too many guys involved back in the day," Julio said. "He's a paranoid fuck. Likes to keep it small and intimate. And that was when he was vulnerable."

"Indeed," Sergio said.

Julio loaded the Magnum in his lap. Boil reached down, fumbled around the bottom of his leg, and then pulled out his .45 as well.

"You're hunting them," I said. "You're stalking these guys. These…

people. You're hunting them like animals."

"Like prey," Boil said. "The biggest game there is hunts back. I knew plenty of fuckers in Iraq, real hardcore dudes. You think I'm some kind of monster, don't you? You'd shit yourself if you met the real monsters, Timmy. Signed up just 'cause they knew they'd get a chance to open fire with a tank-mounted turret on sedans full of people. Boom. But even the best of us—once you survive—and know you're right... Hell. It's like sex and dope hitting at once. Believe me, brother, after the first shock, you'll always need more. Takes most of us about five before it ever gets fun."

He was visibly excited.

"Bullshit," I said.

Boil shrugged.

"Hardcore," Bernard said. He was leaning over the convertible seat, hands propped under his chin like a kid watching Saturday morning cartoons. "Soooo how does this go down?"

"I'm the only one who's made contact," Boil said. "They're expecting me. They'll think I'm stupid if show up alone. So I'm bringing a cousin. Means I'll need someone to drive up with me, help me unload the crates and bring them inside."

"Someone?" I raised my brow.

"Obviously, they'll know Julio," Boil continued. He was staring straight ahead. There was a conviction in his eye. No burning emotion. Icy cool, like he's contemplating a crucial chess move. "Maybe the goons won't pick up on it, but even after all these years, Jefe will. You don't take a man's eye and forget his face."

Julio spit. "Take a *kid's* eye. Plus they'll know Sergio, and my Jeep."

I leaned over to Bernard. "I can't believe we're doing this. This is fucking murder. And I don't even... I sort of don't care. I'm not stupidly amped up like you, no offense. But I have no urge to stop this. Shouldn't we?"

"I know, me too! Isn't it balls-out nuts? It's okay, Tim. Stop saying murder. This is justice! This is gonna be local history, and we get a front row seat!"

"Oh yes, boys, forget about it," Sergio said, grinning with his head half cocked. "Premeditated murder, conspiracy. They're looking at fifteen to life for each murder, minimum. And the three of us, just sitting here, Class B Felony, conspiracy, up to 25 years without even touching anyone."

"Jesus shit on your mom," I moaned. I cracked a beer and nearly drained it in one gulp. "Why the hell are you all so calm about this?"

"I've been around worse, dear boy. Believe you me," Sergio said, trailing off into the past. He turned to me, lowered his shades, and looked me dead in the eye. "And I did tell you before, Tom. I'm not a good person." He smiled, pulled on the cigar so the cherry flared up nice and bright, let the smoke waft up around his face. "Regardless, these are hardly men. At best, they are true scum. Who will cry over them?"

"Don't you defend people like them?" I slid deeper into the seat. There was an avalanche in my bowels. The second brain is panicking, and all that amounts to is a gut feeling that this is going to get much worse. Argh, it just never lets up! Sergio's still talking, but I hear nothing, nearly folding my legs into my own abdomen, gritting my teeth, because I've never had to shit so bad in my fucking life. Now, I know what you're thinking, but this is actually worse than when I literally lost it in front of Helena. Because now my bowels are empty. So this gut reaction to Sergio's fork-tongued honesty, it triggers the warning systems on a bio-ship that's rapidly going down. Like a thousand serrated blades sliding down my inner walls. It's sweat on my brow and the need to evacuate from every hatch, but gods help me, this pain is real, but it's only a phantom turd! An evil, intangible burn! My stomach lining must be curling up like slug-skin under salt, and there's still nothing to release!

"You okay, kid?"

"Perfect," I groaned. "Everything's just… Agh, shit! It's all perfect."

"I never said I was perfect," Sergio said.

Even with my eyes pinched shut, I could feel the cool beam of his stupid smile. As if admitting what you are makes it all okay.

"Tim, this is it, dude! This is the stuff that legends are made of!" Bernard shook my shoulders from behind me. "Aren't you stoked?"

I groaned. "Gosh, if *you're* so fucking excited, then why don't you go help out?"

Bernard froze, still gripping me in mid-shake. But whatever thought stumbled through is gone, and he snaps back to jelly-jams and smiles. "Hey man, I know you're like, stressed or something. But for real, just… just, uh, don't sweat it! The pros are gonna settle this while we praise Jah from the shadows. You'll see. Hell, I bet we'll be back home and playing Rock and Roll House Darts before dawn!"

Barry is expecting me long before dawn, and—wait, wait, wait! These idiots! "Hey, hold up! What about the most obvious—damn it, you jackoffs, what if there's innocent people in there?"

"No one in there is gonna be innocent," Julio said. He spoke with a dead tone I'd rarely heard.

"Jay, come on, you don't know that for sure! What if there are strippers? Whores? Fucking... hipsters? I know, who cares, but still, man, you're a beast, not a monster! Are you seriously going to kill them too?"

"No," Julio said.

Thing is, I know he's right. It's too early in the evening, especially out here, to start diving into the booze, drugs, and pussy. First the heavy cash and dark deals, *then* the wannabes can come burn their cash on PCP Torpedoes, crack-encrusted ganja, pirate ship old rum, other wannabes, pro-whores, greasy has-beens, and other such predators. And I think of Tracy turned to ice and let the cold come in. Julio's right. No one allowed in that fucking shit-pit is innocent.

"Now listen up, you little pansy assed lot-lizards!" Boil barked. He wasn't grilling Sergio or Jay. "One of you two scroats is gonna drive up there with me. We'll get in, I'll show 'em the merchandise. Play it cool. Once they ease up, I'll accidentally knock over a crate and let the reptiles go wild. In the confusion, Julio sneaks around the back, pops in, and we liquidate the bastards."

"*That's* the plan?" I asked. "Seriously? Distract them with lizards and then you two just shoot everyone? Just the two of you?"

"Pretty much," Jay said, smoking his cigarette rapidly. Like a heartbeat. Puff puff. Puff puff.

"That's stupid!"

"Exactly. No one would ever expect that." Puff puff.

"You got a better one?" Boil said.

"Uh... no, but... I mean—"

"Savage Jefe's a freak for anything with scales," Julio said. He was fishing around in his mysterious cargo pockets for something. "He doesn't know Boil, and he's going to be psyched to see all these rare creatres. Last thing on his mind will be *me* popping up out of nowhere and ghosting his ass." He found what he was looking for. It looked like brass knuckles, but with a rubber handle and buttons on each end. "I got this little baby especially for him. Smackdown. Nine thousand volts right in the fucking face!"

"Electric brass knuckles," Bernard whispered. "Holy shit, that's ill. That's ill as hell!"

"For real! That's what's about to break loose, Burny Boy. I been waiting to try these on flesh for a long time." Julio started shadow boxing.

"If there's no further objections, let's move. Transfer the cargo," Boil said.

We formed a grim assembly line, passing the hissing crates from the back of the Jeep to the back of the convertible. Barry, if you only knew what I'm doing to bring you some books…

I take a crate from Boil and say, "You're enjoying this."

"It's not the kinda job to do if you don't."

"We're just freelancing for the reaper, homie," Julio grunts from down the line.

"What do you get out of this? Why do you care if Julio kills Jefe?"

"Same reason I joined the Army, dipshit. I want to kill people. And I want to be told that I'm a hero for it. That a good enough reason for ya?"

"Seriously?"

"Seriously."

I squint and back away. I wanted to be a hero once, too…

"Now boys, who's it gonna be?" Boil grinned. "Who's got the balls to be my cousin? Which of you is ready to roll the worst dice on the biggest game, huh? C'mon, you bitches. Who's got nothing to lose?"

Bernard and I stood there, silent, the last two kids being drafted for dodgeball. Dodgeball with bullets. Bernard's not going to do it. And if he does, he's going to mess it up. He's too happy with his life. He'll hesitate. He'll get himself killed. Or Jay.

I have to ask the obvious. "What was the plan if we hadn't come along? What if you didn't run into Sergio and have his car to use? You know, guys, this hit wasn't actually planned all that well."

"I dunno. We would have gotten some moron trashed out of his mind and tricked him into it," Julio said. "Stole a car. Paid someone off. Went in alone. Improvisation is part of the plan. But all this did happen. Fate is fate, and this is fate."

Bernard had slunk behind the vehicles.

Boil tapped his foot and stared at the sky, hands on his hips. Jay cocked his head to the side and looked at me, trying to find a way, anything, so I could bow out. Fate. They did get some moron trashed out of his mind.

I swallowed. Tightened my fists.

"Yo, fuck it, not your business," Julio tried to sound cheerful. "It's cool. Come on, Luke. We'll just do this ourselves, no biggie."

No.

"I'll do it."

They stare at me. Don't see any gleaming admiration in their eyes.

"You? You'll do it?" Boil looks thrilled. "No shit? Now I get why Julio likes you. You really are crazy, aren't you! Ha!"

"You sure about this?" Julio asks. He puts his hand on my shoulder. Is he relieved?

What happens if I die? I get to see them all again. If I don't, I return to my precious little life. The biggest tragedy is Barry won't get his books. If I go down, it's trying to keep Julio's dumb ass alive. Barry would understand.

"I'm one hundred percent sure," I say, feeling the muscles running up my neck trying to choke. "I'll regret it forever if I don't."

"Aight," Julio walks around like a gorilla, arms outstretched. He slams them around me, nearly fracturing my ribs. My spine elongates. "Guess it's no longer my business is mine and yours is yours, huh, bro?"

"It never really was," I choke out.

He whispers, "I'm kinda nervous. Heh. Thanks, Tim."

"Keep in mind I'm cursed." I tried to shift and avoid fracture in his embrace. "I'll get you all killed for just being here."

"Not this time, hermano." Jay's smile fades. "Tim, last time. For real. You damned sure you're down for this?"

More sure than I even want to be.

"I said yes. Now let's get this over with."

"Well I sure as hell wasn't going," Bernard said.

He laughs alone.

History's Worst Erection

Boil steers the convertible out of our hiding spot. The crates in the back are ominously silent. Animals have a sixth sense. Smarter than us, in the old ways. They realize they're being offered up to something more terrible than themselves. Boil's got his .45 tucked away and Kitsune is tucked under my seat, safely hidden, too. Just like my freshly shriveled balls.

Well, Tracy? Think I can I handle this?

True love must lie just once more, dear friends rotting on the shore. Trusting in our love and lies on our stupid Devils' Run. Gets less cool every time, doesn't it? That damned lawyer put his crap-counsel in my already infested head. How can I keep cool when I taste new fevers all over my skin?

"Just be cool, Tim," Boil says. His voice is low and slow, just like our ride creeping up on the bar. "You act like my bitch cousin, we carry these inside, then you go back out and wait by the car. All part of the plan. You're just buying us time, okay? If the gunshots stop and we don't come out, just peel out and get the fuck out of here. Don't even look back."

"Right." Left leg is shaking up and down.

"Are you scared?"

Not enough. "Yes."

"Good."

"Good?"

"It means you're not stupid. Man, timid little Timmy Poon, what happened to you? You must really be in love with Julio."

"There's a difference between loving and being in love, you jackass."

"Yeah well, get it together, 'cause we're all on the same team now."

"Why are *you* so okay with this? Why do you trust me?"

He looks me in the eye. It's not as intimidating anymore, just awkward. I see it. He can be a soldier in uniform emptying M16 clips into a crowd, and he can be a father to a little girl named Emily at the same time.

"I trust Julio, and God knows why, he trusts you. But more than that, Timmy... you got the look. You got death-eyes. I know them when

I see them. Wish you could see yourself, you creepy little fucker."

I flipped the mirror down and took a look. Sure enough, I couldn't even see my eyelids. Pupils focused like crosshairs. Dark circles hanging under them as usual, but the exhaustion is tempered with something freakish and new. Not human eyes. Not even fox. Almost... reptilian. Christ.

"Okay. But I need you to know something, just in case we die," I said.

"Yeah? What's that?"

"I think you're a fucking worthless scumbag and that if it has to come down to you—"

"Yeah?"

"Well... I truly, really do hope for Emily that you don't get hurt. But if I have to choose, I'll protect Julio."

"Gonna take a bullet for him, are you?" Boil laughed. Then he actually smiled. With true warmth he told me, "Fuck you, you little faggot ass bitch. Don't choke."

I won't.

The bar's so close. Every detail sharp and painful. Neon signs out front, blue, orange, green, the shark head blinking through gas tubes, frames of animation, roaring out of the deep and submerging beside the words "The Cantina Tiburon". The dock behind, the bells ding in the wind, the howl of black water and taut rope, creaking against the swaying boats. The bar's yellow plaster walls, wood. Dead sharks hanging from hooks before the black oil sea, brown oil pools of drying blood below their gaping maws, permanent smiles form nightmare teeth. The lighthouse beam circling far in the distance. Okay, now I'm getting the fear. Was it adrenaline, depression, or idiocy that got me in this car? Too late now.

Here's the man at the front. The bouncer. The bodyguard. Enforcer. Likely a violent sociopath of some kind. He's tall, probably over six feet. Broad shouldered, well built. Ropey forearms. Patched leather jacket. Green eyes. Stubble. Square face. Black boots, ripped jeans. Probably late thirties or early forties.

Boil sidles the convertible up in front of him, nice and casual. Calm as pulling into a gas station.

"You Raul?" Boil calls out over the rumbling engine.

"Maybe. Who the fuck are you?"

"I'm Lucas. I brought the stuff." He thumbs toward the crates.

"You're late."

"Not your problem."

"Savage Jefe has an appreciation for punctuality. He cleared special time for you. The boss has other meetings tonight."

"Well then let's get this over with! Give me a hand and we'll get these inside."

We start opening the car doors, but the man puts his hand before my face.

"Who are you?"

"His c-c-cousin."

He stares at me. His rifle eyes don't acknowledge my death eyes. "You two don't look nothing alike."

I swallow. "That's because we're *cousins*, not brothers. Dumbass?"

"Huh. Whatever. You stay in the car. I'll help."

No arguments there…

He walks over to Boil, who's grabbing one of the crates.

"Hold it right there," the bouncer who might be Raul says. He motions for Boil to put his arms out to be crucified. Boil complies. The man pats him down, around the forearms, under the pits, the sides, the thighs. Obviously, he finds the .45. "What's this? You think you're funny?"

Boil smiles, his arms still out to the side. "I'm not an idiot."

"You are if you think you're bringing this inside."

"Never considered it. But this ain't my first run, son."

"Right, right."

I imagine Julio, creeping around somewhere out there in the darkness, bobbing and weaving through the stinking carcasses. Magnum in one hand, Smackdown strapped on the other. I sit here, my leg humping up and down incessantly as Boil and the bouncer heave the steel crates out one by one and go toward the front door.

"What's his deal?" the bouncer asks, nodding toward me.

"Just here to help." I shift about, now hating the creaky leather.

"Family, ya know? He's the smart one, good with calculations and plans, but not so good with the face to face, ya know what I'm saying? I couldn't have gotten these monsters without him." Boil nearly convinces me of the lie as he hefts one crate with the bouncer. Then confides to him, "But between you and me, he's kind of a pussy."

Raul laughs and kicks the bar door open. They enter. It shuts.

I'm alone. The engine idles. Rumbling me.

Wondering about Sergio and Bernard out there in the bushes beyond the empty lot. It takes forever to swallow. The door opens again and they head for the next crate. Smooth. Real smooth. All part of the plan. This cycle seems to repeat for eternity. I count each heartbeat, getting successively louder. As they're carrying the last crate in, Boil looks over his shoulder at me. I think he winked. The door shuts one last time. I try to stay in the car but peer through the windows. They clearly haven't been washed in years. Plus, there's enough signs and advertisements to keep the inner hell well hidden.

So. Game time.

I wait.

And wait.

And wait.

I almost faint when the bouncer comes back out. I was hoping he'd stay in there for the slaughter. Shit. How are they going to kill him if he's out here with me? Okay, try to make some small talk. Be cool, Tim. Be cool.

He leans against the door, arms crossed. Sacred keeper of the satanic church. He doesn't look like the talkative type. Maybe he'll just stay quiet.

"Yeah, you'd like that, huh?"

Shit.

"Sorry, sir. I have, um, I have issues? I don't mean to say things sometimes."

"Who the fuck are you? You really his cousin?"

Remember. When you're with dragons, pretend you breathe fire. He's already in my face. My ankle tat burns. But I can handle this. Go for it.

"What—? Of course I am! What's wrong with you? What kind of question is that? I help, I get a cut. How stupid are you?"

"Fuck you just say to me?"

I just stare at him, praying that I still have the murder eyes and that I don't black out before I piss myself.

"What's his last name, cuz?"

"Excuse me?"

"Your cousin. What's his last name?"

"Boil. What kind of question is that? You think I wouldn't know my own cousin's freaking name? Didn't Boil—didn't Luke tell you I was coming?"

"Hmph. Yeah."

The man grunts. He takes a nice, deep breath, letting his chest expand. God, he's huge. He could crush my skull like a grapefruit.

"Damn straight I could."

Oh god, Tim, shut up, shut up! Don't think anything at all. Talk, lie, weasel your way out of true feelings.

"So this Jefe guy, he's really got a thing for creepy crawlies, huh? 'Cause I tell you, it wasn't easy getting our hands on those bad boys."

"Yeah, the boss has got eccentric tastes. So to speak."

"Pets?"

"He eats them."

"What? He eats them?"

"You fucking deaf or something?"

"Come on, Raul, you have to admit, that's pretty weird." I said that as if this were real. That was too easy. Too weird.

Weird is not enough for this scene. I wish it were merely weird. I'm sitting here in this convertible, slouched down, staring up at a thug who's just straight grilling me to death now. And then I realize, pretty damn soon, he's going to die. This man I'm talking to, this might be the last conversation of his entire life. I may be hearing his last words at this very minute.

I feel something shift between my legs. Good lord, did one of the lizards get out? No, it's—oh my. This is pretty bad. I'm hard. This is disgusting. My erection makes me acknowledge the terrible truth of it all. I'm truly not scared enough. So I *am* stupid. This was a mistake. I try to hide the murder boner.

"What the fuck? You some kinda homo?" His arms are dropped at his sides, fists clenched.

"Huh? Oh, uh—no, I… I was thinking about… Why are you looking at my crotch, anyway? Homo?"

Now I'm getting the fear. All these tough guys are so afraid of gay men. And I start to laugh, I try to hold it in, but I can't. I'm about to burst out in panic fueled laughter. But an eruption from inside saves my life. A loud, metal clang. Followed by a roaring cacophony of shrill hisses, reptilian hell shrieks, men stamping around, tables knocking over.

A deep, guttural bark from inside. "Raul! Francois! Get your asses in here!"

Not Raul? Francois? Raul or Francois, it's no matter. He is going to die. The living dead man spins around and runs inside. I stare down at my excitement, and at Kitsune, and wonder what she'd think of me now. Face in hands, waiting for the horror, I'm relieved to go soft. Proudly heroic, wrapped in the return of my cowardice.

And It Was All Going So Well...

One blink later, and I'm not in the car. A tornado shreds my soul. All I see is Barry's briefcase, the books inside, floating in the sky. The Amorphous Council is passing judgment on my case as I stand on lights and lasers, the Earth below. Will they pity my Curse and let me ascend, or cast me back to our senile world?

I blink again.

I'm covered in blood.

I'm back, just like on the Old Highway. Twitching, eyes flicking in every direction, defragmenting the past few minutes, attempting to cling to sanity.

Wasn't I alone in Sergio's car? How? Blood. From my midsection down most of my white pants. On my shoes. It's hot, it's thick, like syrup. Not a red watery geyser like in all the samurai films. Piss leaks down my leg. My mind is spinning with fear and the energy killing adrenaline dump. How did this happen? I was just supposed to wait in the car...

Things unwind, and it all starts flashing before my eyes. Re-watching a movie you forgot. Oh. Right. The puzzles knits itself together, synapses and neurons forcing their way up front, not to torture me, but to act. Right. It's all coming back to me. Francois or Raul running inside. Someone is shouting at me. Sounds underwater. Slow motion. Blood. Fire. Darn. And it was all going so well...

Army of None

Defragmenting my memories is not so easy this time. Too heavy, too much.

It starts with me shrinking into a ball at the sound of gunfire. What, I wasn't expecting it? Stupid Tim. It doesn't sound like a movie. Some are weird soft pops, others are so loud that even outside, my ears scream. Raul—Francois—whoever he is—spins around to go inside, reaching into his shirt for a weapon. Clearly he's an idiot or I truly don't present the aura of any threat at all. Quite fine by me. I can handle anything. Anything. Okay…

This is anything. Now handle it.

The moment the door slams shut, I stretch my hand down to Kitsune. Hot damn, what am I thinking? I'm going to run in there and stab someone? Can this thing even cut through human skin, let alone bone? It's sharp, true, but… I could run. I could run across the dock with my tail between my legs, leave Julio to his fate. Hide in the dumpster. Hotwire the Jeep. Tell Sergio to gun it. Cutting nothing but our losses.

But no, I'm pressing my back against the wall, just to the right of the bar door. If Raul comes back out to finish me, I'm going to spin around and plunge this sword straight into his fucking heart.

Ha ha! Yeah right!

I couldn't even win a fistfight with Boil.

What the hell am I thinking? No, this isn't real. I'm already dead. Must have been me that died last week on the side of Sponge Island Highway, not Barry. Yes, I kicked it on the anniversary of her death, with good brother Barry cradling my lifeless husk. And now I'm just a character in one of his stupid made-up stories. So poetic, so cyclical, so… At least it makes sense. More sense than this. Right?

No. No… Senses lie, but not enough. This is as real as anything else, and the promise of pain and torment is as real as the sweat caking my back. Reeking of fresh cut grass and ammonia, seeping through my Hawaiian shirt to glue me against the wall. And the other smells… The mouth-pinching stink of shark flesh, half rotted from the sun. Like gourmet carcasses baked and ready for the maggots. Garbage bags full of tampons and used toilet paper and baby diapers… Hard to ignore that. And the sounds of a chaos storm rolling in across the sea. My chest heaving, my knuckles crunching around Kitsune's hilt.

Dead or alive, this is still happening. Slow my breathing, close my eyes to listen, even though I'm not sure if that actually helps. But I hear it. I can't NOT hear it.

Gun shots layered over gun shots. Screams of shock, pain, infantile rage, and fear. Manic cracks and curious pops. But through them all, I hear the short, punctuated roars of Julio's Magnum, barking its stern orders. Die! Die! DIE! Some half-screams turned to gurgles. And those lizards! Good god, those damnable things! Scaled pyschodemons, singing their torturous chorus. Takes all my will just to stay pinned to the wall outside. But still, my sword is drawn. Ready to strike.

As long as I still hear the Magnum, I know Jay is okay.

No more gunfire.

New sounds. Wet smacking. Fist on flesh. But no electric bursts. Someone else has the upper hand. Then another sound, around the eastern side of the bar. The sharp smack of a door slamming into a wall. Boots on gravel. To my left.

"Don't worry Jefe, I got this one!" Whiny mixed with granite. "Fucking little rat. Don't you know who you're fucking with? You and your friend are dead!"

I peer around. Two men in the shadows. One marching in front, hands held up casually, shoulder height. Behind him, a scruffy man with no chin and even less hair. The son of a bitch from before! From our altercation back on the Old! He's got a gun at the other person's back.

The front of the bar has strange neon pink lights. Lampposts cast orange hue around the gravel. But here, on the waterside, it is as dark as a true Saharan night. Columns of hanging sharks provide cover as I creep closer, their sandpaper skin on my cheeks.

The smell. Hold back a gag. Try to breathe through my mouth, but now my tongue feels heavy with slime. They're at the edge of the dock now. Yet again I am a secret witness to very bad things. Big darkness. Julio? Is he marching Julio out to be executed? My blood brother is about to be shot point blank, in the back of the skull. Dumped into the grimy sea. Another body etched inside my eyelids for however longer I live. Every muscle from calf to scalp tenses. I grip Kitsune's hilt. Release her slow and quiet.

"You don't deserve this, you fucktard. Wish I had knife to gut you instead. Payback's a bitch, huh?" the executioner shouts. Sounds like a kid having a temper tantrum. But a kid with a pistol. "Fucking Raul, man! And Francois! Jesus Christ!" His voice rises higher and higher, cracking the threshold. "I should make you *watch!* Jefe's gonna torture your friend to death. Gonna carve him up nice and slow! And I'm gonna cut your cousin's balls off and feed them to him! But not you, man. You're going down right now. Say goodbye, shitlips!"

His cousin? Eyes finally adjust to darkness, a divine gift from the feline lords. Yup. It's Boil who's about to die. I can still run away. Or watch. Let this scum wipe Boil off the earth. But... his daughter. And Julio. I need Boil to save Julio. I've cursed them both. It's all happening again.

I try to scream and dash around the sharks. Instead I yelp, but more than enough to startle our enemy. He spins around and squeezes off a few shots. I slip in blood and bile, slide beneath the thresher shark it dripped from, and slam into a wooden post. A mako rests against it. The wet smacks of pierced meat above my head. Skin shaking.

Chunks of shark rain down. Don't even hear the gunshots. Saved by the steaming innards of the deep beast. Chunks splinter off. Sulfur and cold flesh spitting around me. I rest my cheek against the shark's sandpaper skin and kiss it. A mako halo. Mahalo.

It's enough. Peeking around the thick post, scrunched behind the mako, I see that my job is done. Boil spins around. An arm that had been bent behind his head in fake submission now becomes a whirling dervish. The elbow cracks the enemy in the temple. His legs wobble, just as the other arm is engulfed, his gunshot angles off harmlessly into the night. Now the right forearm slips all the way around the enemy's neck. I see the sickly green faded tattoos all over Boil's forearm. Fuck. Fukt. Fuck da World.

There's no sound. No crack, no snap. Just a limp body, slumping down. Boil's breathing heavy, his chest and shoulders rising like waves. Looking me right in the eye. His face is bruised, one eye almost swollen shut.

I get up, covered in all sorts of vile fluids. I stare down at our adversary. A meatsack. Dull in the moonlight. No struggle. No life. No drama. Nothing. All facets of the same glittering jewel? If we're all one as Sergio preaches, then Boil just committed suicide instead of murder, right? No matter, here we are. The monstrous Boil and I, and the dead man at our feet.

"You killed him."

"No shit," Boil says. He picks the dead man's gun up. "Come on, we gotta help Julio."

"What happened?"

He grabs my shoulder, a fistful of my shirt in his mighty paw, and swings me around. My shoes slip in the shark slop, and I nearly tumble over the edge into darkness. More pops. Thuds.

Two more dead, lying in the side doorway. Boil really was in the army. He really does want to kill people. And right now, that's the best goddamn thing in the world. I stand in the doorway, taking in the carnage. It's all so odd and slow. Couldn't have been more than five minutes, yet everything is murky. Deep diving in the Blood Sea.

A stream of strange beasts come rushing over the bodies, like bugs hungry for the harvest. Pinks and greens and yellows, spikes, horns, rolling eyes. The lizards are free! The Great Iraqi Regal Horned Lizard freezes as we approach, shoots a jet of hot blood that splats Boil's chest. He winces, but he doesn't pause. He shoots it in the face. Poor thing bursts like a melon in a microwave. The rest scurry across the gravel, down the slick wood. Outside, fearsome titans hang lifeless above them. Panicked hostages in an alien world, set free to scurry and hide in the chaotic void of Tomahok's wilds. Can't take my eyes off the dead one. Limbs splayed out flat, tail limp. An inverted star, brown and red, no head.

Of course, I step on one's tail. An accident, I swear! Great—do I get another curse for this? I look down at the dead man's feet. It's stupid, but it really does look like he's sleeping, but with his neck at a really awkward bone aching angle. If anything is worth a curse, it's that. There's no logic to this game. There's also no more sounds from inside. No screams, no gunfire, no wet smacking of fist on flesh. Not a good sign. Boil dashes through the door, squats down, gun forward, his vision tunneled through the sights. Left, right, forward. Professional. Focused. Clear.

There's one gurgle in the corner, but no enemies left alive.

I take in the carnage. Never saw this bar before the aftermath. Looks like their plan had worked, to a point. And then something went wrong. The ceiling lamp swinging, casting the dead men's shadows across the bar. Dancing shadows. Two metal crates spilled over. One still sealed, the scratches, thumps, and shrieks of the lizard prisoners muffled by the sheer carnage. The bar itself is straight out of every western shootout. Shattered bottles still standing, liquor pouring in waterfalls. Two tables cracked right through the middle, sagging to the ground. Two bodies on the floor. One flat on his back, blond beard, purple tank top. Aviator glasses with one lens blown out, blood crowning his head, pooling into the cracks in the wooden floor. They all look like generic rejects from some mid-'90s old school 2D arcade game. The kind of goons we used to pump quarters against endlessly. A game. Just a game. But no, they are men. I must think of them as men. Dead men.

The ceiling rises to a point, with a great ceramic model of the king shark looming out over the lone pool table. Its passionless eye stands guard over the graveyard below, vindicated. Once man had dragged this regal beast from its horrid depths and splayed it upon our land. Now its effigy leers over the fall of men. I step lightly. Each step on shattered glass or blood. The smell—oh god, the smell. Shit and burning piss poured on fire, dead fish and boiled ham, rust, gasoline, sulfur, vodka.

The gurgling. A pipe clogged with oil. It's Raul, leaning on the wall by the staircase leading down to the cellar. Blood bubbling from his mouth, each gasp making a bubble that bursts across his lips. Or is he Francois? Or all of us? Regardless, his stomach leaking blood and... other colors. Green and brown. Convulsing with his eyes open, glistening, looking at us. He stares across the room into my eyes even as Boil's boots echo across the floor. Spittle dribbling from his lips. He won't blink. Boil squats in front of him. Boil grabs his .45 out of Raul's waistband. Then he grabs the collar of his jacket, pulling Raul's face up. He never took his eyes off me, though. Just stares at me as Boil puts the gun in his mouth. I hear the clack of metal against teeth.

"Boil—"

BANG.

His brain blooms against the wall.

I puke.

This room spins. This mausoleum of carnage and bad energy, this dark place. My new womb. The Tim who could get a hard-on from the thrill of danger is long gone. He didn't see this. He didn't help this.

"Snap out of it, dickhead!"

I thought it was too quiet, but Boil was right. I was frozen. Now I hear the sharp, drilling whine. A machine revving up. Small yet terrible. A power tool?

"They got Julio," Boil says, huffing out of breathe. Just a fact. Accurate. No emotion. He's looking down the steps. I peer over his shoulder, Kitsune still in my hands, hanging at my side, dragging across the floor. There, at the bottom of the steps. A steel door. I remember what the dead man said before Boil killed him. That's Julio's private hell.

Tires screech. Doors slam. Another wave of henchmen? This really is like a bad game. We're going to die. I spin around to face the door, bracing myself for the lead rain. That's how it happens, right? It just happens. No epic score, no showdown. Boil puts his elbow against my chest. Then a sharp thrust. I tumble backwards, each stone step cracking some vital part. I slam into the metal door, legs in the air. Useless, stunned, a shocked puppy about to get neutered. More sounds from upstairs. Doors slamming, shouting, and gunfire. Boil laughing. A gryphon wracked with evil orgasms.

I scramble to my feet. My sword held high, my hand on the door handle. Why didn't I grab one of the guns? Because that's what you do in a movie. You stay cool and calm and do everything by the book. The script does all the work. You just wear makeup and shoot blanks. Something warm dribbles down my leg.

It's only been a few seconds, far too long.

Expecting it to be locked, I nearly dislocate my shoulder by slamming the steel door open.

Oh. Oh no.

They all stare at me, sharing my shock.

I'm too late.

The Devil's Run. The Curse.

Oh god, Julio. I'm sorry.

I'm so, so sorry…

Icarus Kairos

It all happens so slow, more proof—

Time cannot exist.

Instead of facing it, I once again retreat within. Wander away to something else, some other arcane distraction to hide from all this. Because this scene before me is yet further proof that the Curse is real, that all those I love are poisoned and doomed by my mere presence.

They're all staring at me and I'm too late and it's just as slow and awful as seeing her on the bed and too cold to touch and soon, no matter how fake time truly is, to soon it will... No, this isn't happening.

These micro-moments of terror before me, time becomes the ultimate herald of cruelty. An illusion crafted by the human mind, which some say cannot survive in the wake of madness when the true nature of time unfolds, not linear, but in four dimensions. No cause. No effect. All sense of free will relegated to predetermined motions with no meaning at the end, for there is no end. All moments are equal, happening simultaneously. No past, present or future. Some say it's the spell of a demon meant to keep mankind enslaved in the Forgotten Kingdoms. Trapped from the knowledge waiting in the Invisible College. Standing in the Cantina Tiburon's basement doorway, I finally understand these things.

Because it all happens at once.

Too bad, Timmy. Defrag time is over.

My senses conspire to force me back into linear time. To face the cruel pentagram of our perception. First, the smell. Sweat, beer, mold, and musk. Lions mating in the desert. Children rotting in the dirt. Fear and anger, pheromones, the putrescent horrors. Then touch. Cold cement somehow passing through my shoes, right up to my mind. The sweat on my palms, making the sword hilt slippery. I clutch tighter as the taste takes hold, the bitter acid of sweat and fear, dry paper-cut tongue, sandpaper cheeks. Sound. Just an electric whine. Vision.

Three men in the room. The cellar itself is larger than upstairs yet is choked with crates of beer and liquor, ominous black safes, bags of pure china snow and brown heroin and god knows what else. But it feels like Dad's old garage. At the center of the room, a work-table. On it, a

Magnum. Julio's Anaconda. And his precious Smackdown. Useless toys. And an extension cord running like a hungry snake from the socket above the table, into a power drill, held in the hand of a little fat man with the face of Abaddon's pus filled sores.

Hello, Jefe.

He's not exactly the brimstone coated kingslayer, nor the spike covered flame blackened tooth-and-claw king, that I had imagined. Just a pockmarked face, balding head, gray strips of beard and a shitty goatee. Insipid ponytail lying on his hotdog neck. Small eyes. Short, pudgy limbs. A gut. Flannel sleeveless shirt. Sandals. And the power drill in his hand.

The second man in the corner is far bigger. Bathed in shadow. Boxed in by crates of drugs, cash, sin, and whatever. Yellow eyes and charred skin. Pink and yellow Hawaiian shirt. Bastard! Doesn't deserve to wear the camouflage of the tropical divine. In his hands, a head, bent back, pulled taught.

I see all these things at once, yet all I really see is Julio.

Strapped to a steel chair, leather belts and straps hastily cutting around his arms and legs. It's worked; he's bound, but no gag. Guess Jefe was savage enough to relish in the coming screams. Blood streams from Jay's mouth. Deep cuts on both his cheeks. Veins straining to release their nitroglycerin.

Jefe is frozen, the power drill inches from Jay's right eye, and all their eyes on me.

"Now who the fuck is *this*?" Savage Jefe spits at me. I don't twitch. He's still paused, spinning drill inches from Julio's eye, which is lasered in on me but oddly unafraid. "What are you, kid? Some kind of fucking ninja? Hold him down, Desmond. I'll deal with this moron."

Desmond, the shadowed man, grunts, pulls Julio's head back farther, and slips a finger into a cheek gash. Julio roars. Powerful, the tiger in the cage, consumed with bloodlust. His scream ignites my adrenaline. A tsunami crashes. The illusion of time spills away. I'm back in the human world, and I can move. The storm hits. All I see is Savage Jefe's hand reaching for Jay's Magnum. I feel the cold whisper of a hand wrapped around mine, and then Kitsune moves on her own.

THUNK.

She finally tastes flesh.

Savage Jefe is confused. His left hand still stretched out with the power drill, right hand on the bench, just inches from the gun. Four of his fingers rolling around like little blood sausages. My sword sunk into the table beside his new stumps. Blood splurting onto the nails, the saw blades, the oakwood table. Savage Jefe turns to me, manically twitching between shock and rage. He reaches out with the hand, now just a thumb and four little squirt guns. I flinch away from the blood. Get hit in the face, the shirt and pants. Can smell the iron in it.

Absolute silence fades into the drill's whining spin. Then the screaming. Too much of it. Jefe's savage pain, Julio's terrible, shrieking laugh, and the silent one, Desmond, staring in shock at his crippled master. I twist the sword out of the bench, then hold its razor point in front of Jefe's face. He lowers his hand and backs away, so consumed with shock and pain that he doesn't see how much my arm shakes.

"Let him go," I say. My voice cracks. Swallow. "Let him go. NOW."

Savage Jefe roars. "I'll kill you!"

That's it? Where's the super villain speech? Just 'I'll kill you'?

He tries to spin the power drill toward me, and reaches back to the table. We all realize that he's still in shock. Still thinks he can pick up the gun. The poor thing doesn't realize he's finished. Desmond is moving now, fish-hooking Julio's mouth to pull him back, raising his other hand to strike Jay in the throat. But Jay bites down hard, and Desmond hesitates just long enough for Jay to jerk back in the chair, kicking his horse legs out, cracking them into Jefe's shin. Jefe stumbles, and somehow I keep the sword right under his bulbous throat without slitting him open. Barely.

Jefe is cradling his mutilated hand, blood streaming between his arms like four shattered fountains of crimson overflow, power drill still held tight in his good hand. He snarls at Desmond, "Don't you dare untie him!"

I look at Desmond, cradling his bitten hand. "Desmond? You can walk away from this. Just… just go."

A twitch under Julio's glass eye enforces what we all know. Nobody's simply walking away from this. But the thug backs up, hands raised. He thumps into beer crates.

"Untie him." This is… kind of awesome. In the truest sense of the word.

But Savage Jefe has the primal fear. An animal now, he lunges at me, but Julio pinches Jefe's ankles with his feet, tripping him again. I can barely move the sword in time. He slams his jaw into the table. The power drill hangs impotently by its cord. My left hand snakes out, grabs the Magnum off the table. Jefe's index finger rolls off the table and plops onto the floor. Jefe touches it, like he thinks pressing the bloody remnants will make them stick back together.

I've been holding Kitsune at arm's length for a long time, careful not to actually cut anything vital. And damn, she's gotten heavy. Then Jefe looks up. In that moment I get the fear and the fear flows into anger and I protect us. It's just one more cut, this one across his right deltoid. His flesh slides open like a zipper. That's all. Just two cuts. And where the hell is Boil?

"I said untie him." I hear myself say in a voice I'll never be able to repeat.

Sword in right hand, gun in left, both pointed at Savage Jefe. It's funny—right now, I'm the most powerful person in the room. Yet I still don't feel secure.

Julio's mouth is free now, so he spits blood on the back of Jefe's head.

"FUCK YEAH! This is sick!" Julio shouts. He's almost bouncing out of his restraints with pure glee. "Goddamn! Tim, I TOLD YOU! Fate! Man, I love you!"

I move the sword under Jefe's throat. His head inches up and away. Desmond begins untying Julio, no doubt banking on his compliance squeezing a drop of mercy from us.

Julio rises like Adonis, stretches his arms, then abruptly spins, dropping a right hook into Desmond's nose. Cartilage caves in.

Jefe's eyes are wide, realization pouring through his greasy pores and down his face. But it's in his nature to survive. To chew out a child's eye. He tries.

"You think you're gonna get away with this?" Jefe screams. "I *own* this town. I'll hunt you down. I'll kill you! I'll kill your family! I'll skullfuck your mother and make you watch! When I choke the fucking life out of you, your last fucking words will be—"

"With one hand?" Julio laughed.

Julio walks over to the workbench, paying no mind to Jefe, who's now curling up on the floor, getting the shakes, even as he reflexively threatens. Julio grabs Smackdown and returns to Desmond. It sounds like a whip cracking. Every hit makes Desmond twitch. I can't see over the crates, but the shadows flash against the cement wall. I hear the sledgehammer taser crushing his face. Like a four-hundred pound moth hitting a bug zapper. I wince and shrug away, lowering Kitsune, but making sure the gun is trained on Jefe. I want to stop him each time the electric crack follows the wet smack of flesh. It starts to smell like burnt sausage. Desmond's face must be fried paste by now.

It finally ends.

Julio walks over to us, looking down at his enemy. Julio turns to Jefe. I can't look at his face as he descends on his prey. I hear him rip the power drill from the socket. He flings it into the crates. Things break. He turns to look at me, then finally lets out a deep breath. He pulls two cigarettes from his pocket. Lights them together, sticks his chin out as he puffs. Eyeing me.

His face is death. And just like that, boom, he laughs. And I can't help but blink and smile. I accept a cigarette.

"Damn son, look at you," Julio says. "All grown up."

Julio presses his cigarette into the back of Jefe's neck. Jefe screams, Julio snags the ponytail and jerks him to his feet. Then Jay slams Smackdown into the small of Jefe's back. He shrieks like a bat.

"Look at me!" Jay is a beast again. A wounded, angry, tiger. "I said *look at me*. Good. Now, sit down, Henry. We need to talk."

He shoves Jefe, savage no more, into the steel chair. I keep the sword's point right under his chin as Julio fastens the straps around him. Julio puts Smackdown on the table. I hand him the Anaconda Magnum. We hear a gurgling shuffle, and Julio spins around and fires. Jesus, Desmond! No more gurgles. I'm sorry, Desmond. I don't know why, but I'm so, so sorry. I don't even really mean it, either, I just feel like I'm supposed to. I have to feel something. God, why don't I feel something?

"What's good upstairs?" Julio's glistening with sweat, every muscle twitching with electric life, one corner of his mouth in a permanent grin despite the hideous cuts.

"Uh… Boil seems to have things under control."

"Sweet." He turns back to Jefe. Henry. Whatever.

"So Jay, um…"

"It's been a while since we danced, eh?" Julio says as he leans down in front of Jefe's face. Blood trickles from the gashes on his cheeks. "Look at this, Tim. Poor *Savage* Jefe is *crying*."

Jay slaps him.

"Jay, could you, uh, hurry up? This is kind of fucked up."

Jefe manages to choke out more threats. "You think you're gonna walk away from this? My gang will get you. I'll have the fucking *cops* get you. Everyone you've ever loved will die slow and painful! They'll beg to turn you in. I'll rape—"

"Bitch, shut up." Julio uses his .44 Anaconda to crack Jefe on the back of the head. "If this guy's down here, then Boil is alive, which means *no one's coming to save you.*"

Julio looks at me. I nod and confirm Boil's health. He's looking at the bench, at the tools. His hand brushes over a wrench. Then a screwdriver. It hovers over a pair of pliers. Then a hammer. "You don't have no gang left, Henry."

"I don't need a gang to wipe shit like you off my ass. I should have finished you off when you were a little spic brat."

"Yeah, well, missed opportunities," Julio says as he calmly scoops Jefe's three other fingers up from the table. Then stuffs them into Jefe's mouth.

Okay, I'm starting to feel something.

"Tim, you wanna bounce?" Jay switches gears so fast. What an image, him stuffing a man's severed digits into his mouth while he stares at me like a concerned father.

"No... No. If this is part of you, then I need to see it."

He nods, shrugs, and turns back to the bloody blob that is Henry Poole, the Savage Jefe.

"There you go. Shush, shush. You got soft, Jefe. Too comfortable. Look at you, you fat piece of shit. Can't believe I lost a brawl to you. You must be asking yourself, why now? It's been so long. So many years for him to knife me in the back. Why tonight?" Julio bent down and poked Savage Jefe's chest. "Well? *Answer me!* Why tonight?"

Jefe gurgled. Chewing against his own flesh for spite, vying to retain his menace. Defiant to the end. Shattered mirrors. Julio spun on his heels, hands behind his back. He paced in small circles as he continued to talk, occasionally touching the fresh wounds on his cheeks, kneading them, spreading his own blood like red war paint. Curiously contemplating his new scars, like shark gills, the last legacy of his former master.

"You know, Henry, for the most part, you really *did* make me your bitch. For real, I know how lucky I got. You dropped it. Smart enough to let me live, pay for the damage. Cover your trail. But then again, you didn't really have no choice, huh? Tough to kill kids. But it ain't so hard to kill fat, old drug dealers. Still, I stayed out of your way."

Then Julio pointed to me, now leaning against the doorway, not feeling so tough, Kitsune hanging at my side, Jefe's blood sliding down her onto the floor.

"That guy over there, he's just about damn near the only person I know that's not afraid of me. You know what I'm saying, Henry?" He pinched Henry's cheeks together with one hand. He shook his jowls, sloshing around like severed fat in a bowl of spew. "So you let me live? Did you think I'd be afraid forever? Or did you secretly hope I'd come back? You do realize *why* this is finally happening, right?"

I guess Jay gives the super villain speech...

Julio turned his back again, then spun around and planted his foot square in Jefe's gut. Fingers and blood burst out. Coated his stomach. Okay, yes, I'm feeling more than numb now. Just... must remember that this guy blinded Jay. He was about to kill him. He deserves this.

Jefe could still scream, through fits of bloody coughs and gags. He snarled, "I didn't kill you 'cause I'm no fucking child killer! I'm not a monster! You got greedy! You betrayed me! You deserve everything you got! I let you live with your shame! Your fucking shame! Oh, pobrecito, did your mami ever tell you that I—"

The punch hit so hard even I felt an aftershock.

"You *are* a monster," Julio said. "And we all knew that's what I'd end up being. I mean, shit, I've practically been your apprentice all these years. I was just kinda hoping I'd find my own way. Started buggin' out, thinking my fate was set, gonna grow up to be you if things didn't get better. But shit got worse. Too bad, for both of us. All I got now is hatred. I fought it. I coulda snuck up, popped you with rubbed off serial digits like some punk ass bitch. But nah, that wouldn't do our last throw down justice. See, to kill you, it has to be close and intimate, ya know? I need to look you in the eye. See, isn't this all just so... so..."

Poetic.

Julio paused. He looked down and rubbed his sweating forehead with his thumb and forefinger. The arc of his outline, from base of skull down thick, bent neck, over his deltoids and down his back, it was like a gargoyle, perched atop the icy tower of Gorgaroth itself.

"So many nights, all blunted up," he muttered. "Trying to convince myself I could let it go. Impressing everyone with how I *hadn't* gone after you… but still rehearsing this moment. What I'd say to you. It's always perfect in my head." Julio looked up at me. He smiled and laughed. "Yo Tim, can you think of anything badass to say?"

Me? I shook my head. Teeth wired shut to keep them from chattering with my increasing uneasiness. Started feeling like I'm in the window, watching him fuck.

Julio threw his arms up, as if in taking a bow. "Ah, fuck it! Who am I kidding? I just want to torture you! Let's start with the face."

"Oh!" I jumped. "An eye for an eye!"

"Thank you, Tim. Very good idea. Mad props, son!" Julio bent down and gently kissed Jefe on the brow. Then he whipped back, screamed and tore everything off the workbench, cutting his arms on various tools that spilled down near Desmond's corpse. "HENRY? YOU FUCKING GET IT YET? Why tonight? This ain't gonna be the night Tomahok's fearsome Savage Jefe got snuffed. Nah, don't you worry. I'll make sure everyone just remembers that it's Friday."

Savage Jefe stopped writhing. That's what finally got the bastard. Realized he's not Savage, he's just Jefe now. Not even. Just Henry. He's about to taste his own self-imposed curse. Sorry, Henry. I almost empathize. But you earned your fate. And that blood and sweat dripping down Jay's face, the barely hidden tear in his right eye… No, no I can't feel bad for you. When I sliced you down, I was just saving my friend.

But I didn't kill you.

"Hey! Yo, snap out of it. You okay, Tim? You're looking pale." Julio's boot was planted in Jefe's stomach, and the blood on his hands, his face… and the fingers and that Desmond guy cooked dead in the corner like something on a grill and—

"I've had enough." My voice is weak. Need fresh air. "Unless you need me, I'm going to go… uh… leave you two alone."

Jefe groaned. The room began to stink of old beer, mold, piss, stale blood, and shit.

"No worries, dude, it's all good. I got this."

"I'm going to wait upstairs."

"No problem. I'll be up in a minute." Voice changes on a dime. Like he's doing his laundry.

I turn my back on this fat little monster who blinded my brother and is about to die at his hand. I take each step to the surface slowly, shoes filled with iron and veins drained past empty. Head spinning and sagging like I drank the place clean. Coming down from the adrenaline. A numb zombie. My blood brother, the Cyclops. A beast. My limp arm lets Kitsune clank against each step.

Tink. Tink. Tink.

Boil's on his way down and slams right through me.

"What happened?"

"It's cool. Julio's fine. I guess. We won."

"Tim saved my damn life!" Julio called out from the cellar. "Rolled right over these bastards like a mother fucking ninja! I'm telling you, the dude's my hero!"

"No shit?" Boil squeezes my shoulder and smiles. "Seems like you're a natural born killer. Timmy Poon, the hero!"

Although I want to, I just can't smile back. Halfway up the stairs, I fall against the wall, eyes watering. The concrete is ice on my neck. Ha. Aha, ha. I thought being it would feel so different.

No Fade to Black?

Boil kicks the cellar door shut. The adrenaline dump is thinning out. But the smell is still here. I look at the bodies. Aren't we supposed to fade to black now? Resume when everything is over and safe?

"Well, let's clean up," Boil said.

"Clean up?"

"We gotta get rid of the bodies. Ditch the weapons, erase our traces. Take care of whatever Sergio can't get us out of."

"How?"

"Uh, how do you think, dipshit? There's a ton of boats and a whole ocean out back."

"We don't have a boat."

"Jefe does."

"Jefe did."

Boil laughs. I wish I could take that back. Then the weight hits. I drop to my knees. The sword clatters to the floor. I can't cup my face. My hands are sticky with blood. Already I feel myself becoming an eldritch slave. This is the true Curse. They're fattening up my soul with evil karma and extra Cursed deaths. My afterlife is either slave or feast for the Witch King, waiting high up on his Corpse Throne in Angor. I'll never see Tracy again.

"Holy shit," I said. "I'm a killer."

"What?" Boil smacked the back of my head. "Get up. You're no killer. Who the fuck did you kill?"

Tracy, Mom, Dad. More. Namu amida butsu—oh shit, I'm as guilty for everyone in this bar as I am for them. Certainly Henry Poole. I literally have his blood on my hands.

"Fuck Henry Poole. He got what he deserved. And you did save your precious friend. You didn't kill no one, so shut up and help me."

"You're right. I'm not a killer. But—"

"Well, what *did* you do down there?"

"I sort of cut Jefe's hand off…"

"Wow," Boiled grunted. "You're a criminal now, brother. That's for damn sure. First-class felon. Now get up and help me."

So what do you think, Tracy? Seems you were right. That certainly was 'something', and I handled it. But it's not even close to over. Boil walks over to the shattered bar. He picks around, finds a bottle that isn't burst. Pours a shot. Hands it to me. We clink. I haven't blinked. My eyelids feel like sandpaper. I look at Boil, who's actually waiting for me. I nod and take the shot. It slides down like water. Stomach so cold that there's no burn.

As I stand up, I realize something quite extraordinary. There's actually not that much blood on Tracy's pants. So I was wrong or hallucinated. Right now I'm kind of okay with either. Even though my Hawaiian shirt looks like a tie-dye of gore. I kick my shoes off. Using just the tips of my thumb and forefingers, I start stripping her pants off.

"What the... what the fuck are you doing?"

"I don't know. I just can't soil these. Can't get more blood on them."

"You really are one strange little bitch," Boil said.

He hands me another shot. I decline. His hand stays out. I take it.

"Hey Boil, that guy said something about Jefe having another meeting. What are we gonna do if they show up?"

Boil nods at the two new men, lying dead in the doorway, their bodies folded over wrong, acting as doorstops. They're young. Blond hair and a jersey. Black hair shaved down and... No, enough. Their car idles outside next to Sergio's.

"Don't worry about it," Boil says, then slugs back another shot.

"Can't we roll to credits now?"

"Fuck you talking about?"

Boil lines up a row of shot glasses, grabs whiskey, and sloshes it down the line. He waves at the bar, as if there were no fresh cadavers expelling bodily fluids behind us. No bullet holes splintered around us. No fat, dead lizard. No new dawn hours away.

He takes a shot. So do I. The cycle continues. His smile grows. If I'm smiling, I don't feel it. Don't know when I will again. Hear something downstairs, like a tree splitting apart in a firestorm. Take another shot.

If you'd have told me all those years ago, when I turned my back on Boil and did nothing to stop him as he watched those cats claw each other to death, that I'd end up struggling to carry damp, sagging bodies with him out to a drug dealer's boat in the dead of night just a couple of decades later...

"Oh yeah, the cats," Boil said. He slapped his hands together and stood up. "You used to be such a pussy. Ha! Get it?"

Yes, I get it.

A one-hundred-and-eighty-pound man feels like three hundred when he's just a limp, empty shell. Boil does need my help. He always takes the wrists. I twitch each time I grasp the ankles. Don't like looking at the faces. We shuffle like crabs toward the boat.

It didn't take long to find, being docked right behind The Cantina Tiburon, and "Jefe" painted across it in bright orange. He really did feel invincible. The vessel was a sort of an oblong triangle, double decked, with a hot tub in the back. A grand vestibule for coke orgies, unprotected ass sex with minors on the high seas. An obnoxious false whale, floating arrogantly between good old fashioned wood and steel fishing vessels.

It rocks back and forth, now master-less, now with eleven or so bodies slumped about its deck like it's any lazy, freaky afternoon. They look like blacked out drunks. I tiptoe around them. Boil just stomps right over them. We make our way to the edge of the boat and sit on the bow. We're still tied to the dock, watching the bar through the tangle of dead sharks, waiting for one more body. Oh, right. Desmond. Two more. Always hated math. That's not gonna change.

"Fuck math," Boil said. "Let's go back in."

We do, and we take more shots. The place is still streaked with red trails like giant, wounded snails crawled through. And nests of bullet holes, broken glass and dead dreams.

"How much longer is he going to take?" I asked.

"I'm sure he's savoring it," Boil said. He lit a cigarette.

"I just can't believe it all worked out," I said.

"It ain't over yet," Boil said. "We still have to get away with it."

"Yeah, but you guys… you must have a plan. You know how to get away with it, right?"

Boil laughed. "Ease up, Dune. We're gonna be fine. Unless you think Bernard is gonna flip on us?"

"No way." I shake my head. "No way Burn will rat us out. Besides, he's an accessory or whatever."

"Okay, then."

Really? Huh. Okay. Good.

"This is… this is more fucked up than I… I read a lot. Saw so many movies," I began, still staring out the back door at the bodies piled on Jefe's boat. Moon corpse pyramid. "Inextricable. We're inextricable now."

"What?" He pours two more shots.

I throw it back easy, but at least now my throat's starting to burn.

"We're all stuck with each other. Forever. No matter where we go, we're threaded by all this. We'll never be free. Sergio was right."

"Okay, Tim, look," Boil started. His shoulders were slumped. He stared out the back door as he spoke. "You never saw this before. I get it. I've felt it man, I've been there. And as god damned shocked as I am, you really came through for us. Not just Julio. You saved me, too. Ha, fuck, think about that. Never would've guessed that in a million years."

"That makes two of us."

Two more shots. He raises a toast. I meet it. Eyes. Clink. Slam.

"There's this bond you can only get when you're in battle with someone. Side by side. When your life is in someone else's hands. You become something more than friends. You're—what'd you say? Inextricable. Whatever. Bonded. For life."

"So what, are you saying that we're friends now?"

"Hell no," Boil said. He slapped the table and laughed. "But. Shit. Thanks."

"Okay," I said. I looked down at my hands, fingers knotted around one another. "But you should know, I still don't like you."

"That's fine."

"You really surprised me as well," I said. "I always pegged you for a violent piece of shit, but damn. I mean, you really just went to town in here. So this is my tax dollars at work, huh?"

"Nah."

"No? I saw you in action. You've clearly killed before. It didn't even faze you."

"Nope, never killed anyone," Boil said. Another shot.

"But you were in Iraq! You're a vet! You're going back!"

"I just drove around in a Humvee most of the time," Boil said. He put his hands on the bar and stood up.

"Bullshit, you just killed like a million people!"

"Your math's a little off for a guy who thinks he's so smart."

"But—"

"I did a lot in Iraq. Leave it at that. You gonna put your pants back on or what?"

Oh, yeah. I hopped out onto the dock and picked the neatly folded pair of blessed white up. You're not going to fool me, you murderous prick. He snapped the guy's neck like I snap these buttons. He's bullshitting me again, and… Who cares? Let him.

"Hold on. Neither of you even wore bulletproof vests. That's just basic logic. Why not?"

He looks over his shoulder at me, and I see the single father, not the soldier.

"You wanted to die. Both of you?"

"Figured it'd feel right if we let things play out with higher stakes."

I can buy that. I don't want to. But I certainly can.

"So the whole night, you knew you were going to do this. You actually told me the truth back at the gas station. And you didn't care that I came?"

"I did at first. Thought you were gonna screw things up. And you're fucking annoying. But it made Julio more relaxed, so that's good enough for me. I wanted a wild ride, and I got it."

Jay was nervous? I'd pay to see that. Oh, I did. Not used to this new life.

"You're like an addict, aren't you? You caught some crazy, horrible high in the war. You're trying to get a fix."

Boil shrugged. He walked outside and flicked his cigarette into the water. I stayed in the doorframe. "What's your excuse, Dune?"

Don't have one. I didn't wear any armor either.

"So what's next?" I asked.

"We drive this boat out to sea, dump the bodies, and sink it."

Of course, so simple.

"And then you guys drive me up island."

"Oh yeah, you gotta see what's-his-name. Man, you're a good friend. You might even make a half decent soldier. After you put some muscle on those bones. And grow a pair."

God, no. No, I'm nothing like you.

"You're not?"

"Uh, anyway, his name is Barry. You know him, remember? You stuck his mom's dildo in his mouth."

Boil stared at me, dumbfounded. Then he doubled over laughing.

"That's right! Shit, how could I forget that?"

I squared up on him. No bugs in my stomach.

"Those things you said earlier. About Tracy. You were just fucking with me. You were trying to hurt me."

"If I wanted to hurt you, I could have done a lot worse," Boil said.

No, you couldn't.

"Listen, Lucas. I saved your life. You owe me this. One honest answer."

Boil sighed and then spit on Jefe's boat. He watched the black ocean roiling before him, the lighthouse bathing us every few beats. Arms folded, guns in hand, he hung his head. My bowels churned as I waited for his answer. The seconds folding into tremors.

"Listen. I've been through a lot. Killing, explosions, thinking I'm going to die every time a kid ran up to us. You ever honestly believe a little boy would have a grenade in hands? Watching my friends drag themselves across the desert, not knowing their legs are twenty feet behind. So... so maybe I get mixed up. Maybe I... You know, I get confused. Can't control it. Only thing you can control in this life is yourself, and how you act. And maybe I lost some of that. Any stupid bullshit you feel, any pain, any regret, that's yours. I'm not gonna change that, Julio's not gonna change that. It's on you."

I lay Kitsune on my shoulder, wiping the grease from my hair.

"So you were just confused."

"Sure. She was a crazy hot and a girl about town. I probably just jacked off thinking about her. Right? That's what happened."

That's what happened. I paced across the bar, looking at Sergio's convertible and the new sedan beside. Burn and Serge were still hiding somewhere out there. Boil spoke behind me. So damn silent, lit up all my nerves.

"Shit is weird, isn't it, Timmy?"

"Yes, Boil. Shit is indeed weird. Very, very weird."

He slips the guns into his belt line. Deep in thought. Taps his foot. Then stands beside me. Strange. He looks tired. Worn. Acting out a role that he got sick of long ago.

"Since we're on the subject, just to be clear, we're cool," he said. "But if you ever mention my daughter again, I'll kill you."

"Hey, you want to be cool, that's fine. But the same goes for Tracy. Disrespect her in front me again, mistaken or not, I'll kill you. I'm serious."

He cocks his head, eyebrow raised in amusement. Head down, I glare into his eyes. His amusement fades. The practiced stare works, because this one is as real as I'll ever get.

"Understood." He spits on the ground and looks back up, without malice.

Then the Anaconda booms beneath us, the wooden floorboards shake, tossing dust with glass and termites. We wait. The door creaks open and boots clomp up the stairs at a steady, relaxed rhythm. Jay stands before us, spattered in blood. A canvas of the newvoid wave of art gore. Arms held high, forearms a dull crimson from fist to elbow, smoking gun, jagged rips in his face, and smiling like the sun. Those yellow teeth glinting under the broken lamps. The fan whirs overhead, broken but still doing its job. Well?

"The king is dead!"

Boil gives him a high five.

I am quite comfortable doing nothing at all.

Close my eyes. Come on. Come on. Fade to black.

Funny

Funny. After all that, the last thing I expected was a fight with Bernard. Standing there, my shirt covered in blood, and him in *my* blue and orange deluxe Hawaiian shirt, clean from head to soul. We were by the cars out front, Sergio's red convertible, and the black sedan that those other hooligans rolled up to their funeral in. Its engine was still running, waiting for its masters to return. I felt strangely sorry for the flashy car, with its shiny, spinning rims and erotic purple lights, glowing enticingly under the body. Made me think of my own twisted wreck, being fondled in a dungeon up island until I came up with enough cash to rescue it from the mechanics.

"Burn, don't make me mad. I've just been through hell and back," I said. "Give me my fucking shirt!"

"But what am I going to wear?"

"I don't know! There's plenty of bodies back there that don't need clothes. Look, it's my shirt. I'm the one who just chopped up a dude and piled carcasses and... What the hell did *you* do? I can't believe we're even having this argument! Burn. Give. It. Back."

Bernard grunted and muttered under his breath as he slipped my shirt off his back. Its silky smooth interior caressed my weary skin as I clasped the coconut buttons together.

"Ah. I feel like a new man," I said. Kitsune, now sheathed, acted as a cane to prop me up as I leaned confidently. I kept the stained shirt balled in my fist. Soiled or not, I'd worn it for too long to just abandon now. Tied it around my neck like a cape. But it will need to be baptized in the sea.

"I bet you do," Bernard said. "Come on man, spill the details. What did it feel like? Were you scared? We could hear some of it. I was a little worried. Just a little."

"Ah, walk with me, talk with me, friend," I said. I felt like an aristocrat of doom as I walked away from the others, waving for Bernard to follow. "Barry's briefcase is still safe, right?"

"Yeah, don't worry, it's safe and sound."

"Good."

Julio, Sergio, and Boil were off by Jefe's boat, working out the details. Though deep in debate, they remained calm and level headed. A trio of destruction and hunger, brains, brawn, and primal urge. Jefe's bloated corpse lay atop the pile of his servants and slaves. Well, what was left of him. I looked away as Julio dragged him up the stairs, but I heard the thunks, slips, sloshing, and cracks. His death was Jay's work of art, one that I could not appraise without giving up even more than I'd already sacrificed. They should just set fire to the damned boat and set it adrift. A Viking funeral to signal the end of Savage Jefe's era. A pyre of sin. And they're forgetting.

"I don't mean to interrupt, fellas," I said. "But they said something kind of important. About Savage Jefe having other meetings tonight. What are we going to do if more of his friends show up?"

"Friends? Silly lad. Henry Poole didn't have any friends," Sergio said. "Clients, that's all. Clients and goons. I imagine it will be some illicit business transaction or another. And in that case…"

"In that case, they'll still deal with Savage Jefe," Julio said. He crossed his arms.

"You mean…?" Bernard started.

"Yeah boys, take a good look. There's a new boss in town!"

"No shit," I said. "How are you going to pull that off?"

"Hell, ain't like I'm unqualified for the job," Julio said. "Boil and I were just talking about it. It was just a gang of assholes who'd been mean and dirty enough to sink their teeth in to a sad little hood. I can bribe the same cops he did, I can push the same dope he did. The infrastructure's already there, son. Just needs a new hard ass motherfucker to step up."

"Always the entrepreneur," I said. "So you'll be sticking around then?"

"We'll see," Julio said.

Sweet.

"More showing up?" Burn's voice had just a tint of concern.

"Stop worrying about it," Boil said. Boil lifted a duffle bag and unzipped it. Cash. Lots of cash. "Look, it was probably the turd munchers who showed up in that car. I iced them already. It's over."

"Ooh," Burn said, now swinging back to optimism.

"Sergio, what do you think of all this?" I asked.

"I think this opens new and potentially lucrative doors for personal business," Sergio said. He was smiling ear-to-ear, eyes still hidden behind his aviators, a fat, fresh cigar pinched between his teeth. Where does he keep getting them?

"Boil?"

"Whatever. I don't give a shit."

"Right," I said. "So uh... I don't want to rush you, but you still have to bring me out to the hospital. What are you going to do about...?"

I thumbed toward the floating caravan of soulless husks.

"We're going to pick out the fastest, quietest boat on this dock and hotwire it," Julio said. "Then we go way off shore with both. Then sink that bitch."

"Hoo-rah!" Boil said, pumping his fist in the air.

"Okay," I said.

"Ya'll dudes mind waiting here?" Julio asked.

"Not at all," I said. "I've had my fill. But what if Boil's wrong? What if there are more thugs on their way?"

"Just tell them we had an organizational shake up," Julio said. "Or hide. I'll deal with them, aight? Relax, bro."

Sergio nodded.

Bernard strolled over to the edge of the dock, naked arms wrapped around his torso. He craned his neck and examined our vile pile of triumph.

"They all got holes in the shirts," Bernard said. "Everything's so gross! I can't wear any of this."

"We'll be back within the hour," Sergio said.

"An hour! Cripes, this is taking forever," I said.

Julio patted me on the shoulder. "Fuck it, the worst is over. We'll crack some brews, cruise up to see Barry. It's all good."

"It's all good," I repeated. I wanted to believe him. But something bubbled like tar in my core. Something itching and clawing at this shell of euphoria and accomplishment.

"Hey, I still need a shirt!"

"Shut up! It's summer," Boil said. "It's warm! Fuckin' Christ."

"If it's so warm, then give me yours!"

"Fuck off."

Burn stuck his tongue out at him. Ha, man, he's damn good at what he does, whatever that is.

"In the meantime, why don't you fine boys make yourselves useful and pull my car around back to the Jeep," Sergio said. "And dispose of that other vehicle as well."

Sergio pointed at the sedan that arrived during the carnage carnival. "How?" I asked.

"Drive it off the dock," Boil said. "Here, hang onto this till we get back. Just in case."

Boil handed his .45 to me.

"Tim's more of a hands-on kind of guy," Julio said. He grinned ear to ear as he began to dance out a mock ninja sword fight, complete with stereotypical high-pitched Bruce Lee shrieks.

I stood for a moment, holding the gun, feeling the heft in my dry palm. Then looked at my friends. Julio, covered in blood. Some his own, some not. I wanted to hate him. Deep gashes on his cheeks under each eye. Accept that he is a monster. But he's not. He's... I'm not fit to judge him. If someone had killed Tracy, I'd have exacted a far worse vengeance than he has. Then Boil, eye starting to bruise and purple, blood on his hands, caked around his lips. Sergio clean. Physically. Bernard half naked, shivering for no reason.

Julio found a boat he could hotwire. A white cruiser with elite rods and antennae sprouting in every direction. An ivory water bug. I smile, because he didn't even seem to consider the practical local boats. Wouldn't steal anything that looked like it fed a family instead of an ego. Good on him.

Jay and Boil drove Jefe's corpse-laden boat toward its murky grave. Sergio piloted the hotwired one behind them. No lights on. Stealthy risk. Necessary on the open seas.

"Peace out!" Jay shouted.

They coasted into darkness.

Bernard and I walked back to the cars, the sound of gravel crunching with each step, the pale lamplights mingling with the moon and lighting our way.

"Boy, does it stink out here," Burn said, pointing at all the sharks.

Wasn't until then that I noticed that I no longer noticed the smell. We hopped into Sergio's convertible and started pulling out. We returned to the dead gang's car, still rumbling with contempt. Bernard nodded at my new gun.

"You really going to use that if someone else shows up?"

"I don't think anyone will," I said. "Why, would you rather have it?" He stared blankly. "Didn't think so."

"You've never even shot a gun," Bernard said.

"Inaccurate, pal. I shot Julio's tonight."

"Yeah, but you didn't shoot it at a person."

"But it was a big fucking gun." I stabbed Kitsune into the ground, still caked in Jefe's blood. Left the sheath on the ground. Thought of all the bodies I'd carried, growing cold and heavy and the stink of it all etched forever in my skin. "Relax, Burn. I can handle it."

"So are we really going to drive this into the ocean?"

"I think we're dumping enough trash in our mother tonight," I said. "I mean, what are we going to do anyway, drive it at the dock and then jump out? It would be found tomorrow anyway."

I pulled Kitsune from the ground, the sound echoing like the sharp thunk of wood and flesh. Sheathed her. Kept the gun in my hand. But I put the safety on. I'm not that dumb, I've seen enough movies to check if it's off, even in the slight chance more miscreants did show up. But knowing my luck, if I'm not extra careful I'll cap this wonderful escapade off by blowing off my dick.

Bernard hopped into the dead man's driver's seat and motioned for me to follow. The interior felt like a hearse. We drove around to the edge of the docks, where the sandy shore over takes the aged wood and the natural beach rises up to meet the jetty. The bar was just a black rectangle from here. The sharks just hanging blobs. Perfect dark. Bernard cut the motor and we got out.

We jumped on the hood, savoring its warmth. It felt great, everything considered. The pavement cracked and crumbled before us, tumbling into thick bunches of sand and seaweed. The lighthouse was out of sight, the northern prong of Tomahok obscured by the island's curve. Just cool, icy, perfect blue moonlight. Clean light. Jellyfish glowed near the shore. Bioluminescence answering the stars' call.

"So," Bernard said. He spit into the water. "Turned out to be quite a night."

"Indeed."

"Stop acting so cool, man," Bernard said. He shoved me like we were still children. "I know you were scared shitless the whole time." He pulled a cigar out of his pants pocket and chewed off the end. He started lighting it as I watched incredulously.

"Where'd you get that?"

"Sergio."

"That's just a real cigar? Not a blunt?"

He puffed on it, letting thick white smoke billow out around his lips. Blew a smoke ring. "Yeah. What's the problem?"

"No problem," I said. I took a deep lungful of moonfresh air. Rolled my head around on my stiff neck. Crack, crack, crack. Synaptic electricity shot up my spine. I kicked my legs against the car's grille. "This is definitely the weirdest night of my life. There's no denying that. But even with all this, it's still not the worst. But it is one of those nights. The kind that defines everything thereafter."

"Mmmhmm," Bernard mumbled. "There's no going back. Shitty, epic, horrific. Like the night Tracy died."

"Yes, that's what I was hinting at. But also, those other nights. Like when our parents died."

"And the night Julio's mom died," Bernard said. "And the night his pops vanished. And the night Barry got smoked."

"Barry's not dead. He's fucked up, but we'll help him heal. I'll get those books and sit by his side," I said. And I'll come clean. Came so close to death tonight, just chaos and math and maybe fate. No, before I lose the chance, he has to know. I have to come clean. His sister died with my child in her. It's a start.

"Wait, what?"

"Oh, uh… Yeah, I think she was…"

"It's okay," Bernard sighed, staring at the sea, where the night stars reflect off an indigo sea and the boundaries aren't clean. "A lot of bad nights, huh? But there's been more good than bad, right?"

"I guess so. Statistically," I said. "Sure doesn't feel that way though, does it? Two car accidents, cancer, deportation, nearly killing her dad… her overdose. What does that say about us? What kind of people are we for all our kin to meet such ends?"

"Hey, I'm still here. And Julio. All those dudes in the bar are dead, not us. Maybe you finally passed your curse on? You're like a walking toxic cloud. Dude, you're the new incarnation of the god of death! That's so fucking rad!"

He meant well.

"Ha. Maybe that's exactly why I was cursed. Preparation. Maybe time isn't such a straight line. Destiny. Fate. A big loop. Cursed at five because of a crime at twenty-eight. Stranger things have happened."

Burn kept looking away for a long time. When he looked back at me, I got chills.

"No man, you're not cursed. Forget that shit and just take responsibility for your own actions. People die. It's just life. It sucks. The best we can do is say fuck off by being happy. Still… it is weird. Everyone around us, not one good old fashioned death in bed," Bernard said. He shook his head. "Maybe we're all just freaks. That feels right. So what exactly does tonight define, anyway? Besides our collective descent into evil. And you joining the psycho brigade."

"I'm not sure yet," I said. "These things are hard to judge without proper time to reflect and defrag. I'm not entirely comfortable with that word. Evil."

"What word then?"

"Justice?"

"Boil and Jay say you're a hero." Burn passed the cigar.

My cough melts into smirk. Blood tear eyes.

"Burn. I miss her so much."

"I know," he said. Then he actually put his arm around me. "I know."

And this time I did choke back the tears, staring down at the sand spattered earth. The crumbled stone, smashed jetties, and splintered piers behind the Tiburon.

"Hey, Tim. You ever think, like, if Tracy hadn't died, there's so many reasons you wouldn't have been here tonight. And tonight was always gonna happen someday. So in a way, she—you—uh, both of you, saved Julio's life."

"I can't process that kind of thought." I passed the cigar back.

Burn did what he does best. Switching gears.

"So which one of us you think'll kick it first? At this rate, I'd say you're next."

I lay Kitsune across my thighs and took the cigar from him. The tip was wet from his mouth. I wiped it on my shirt. The smoke burned. I tried blowing a ring. Failed.

"If I keep this shit up, me, for sure."

"I have a feeling tonight was a fluke," Bernard said. "Or I hope so. You're not gonna make a habit out of going on killing sprees with these guys, right? Or are you a hitman now? A wandering samurai cutting down dope lords?"

"Nope. I don't see a future in assassination."

"Let's hope not." He tapped his fingers on the hood. "Man, I feel like we should be listening to Journey or something. Don't stop believing! I mean, hey, we won!"

"We? Remind me again, what exactly did you do?"

"Moral support." He sat up straight, smiling ear to ear. "I'm the center these social circles spiral, dude. Besides, if you bit it, I'd have to bring Barry his books. See?"

"Sure. Man, it's not often you know that you'll wake up tomorrow as a different person," I said. "Kinda feels like you're right. Everything up to now was just leading to this."

"Yeah, that kind of transformative shit is usually subtle," Bernard said. "Except that one night in high school I woke up and was like six feet taller."

"You said it felt like being on a torture rack getting stretched out," I laughed.

"Yup," Bernard said. He looked away. "You don't have to wait until tomorrow. You're already different. Dude, the second you decided to leave with Boil, you were different. But damn, when you guys came back... No, dude. The Tim Dune I know is already dead and gone. Sayonara, amigo."

What?

"Really? Is that how you really feel?"

"Totally, bro. When you came back, you were like them."

He categorizes me with Julio Sanchez Sin Corazon and Lucas Boil? Good gods, it happens so fast.

"Yeah man. You went there. The edge. Look at you! You're not even nervous about getting caught. We're sitting in the open, and cops or killers or who knows what could come down that long empty road any minute. We should be stealing that Jeep and getting the fuck out of here!"

"I guess. What's stopping you?"

"No, for real. I don't think it's sunk in yet. But it will. Soon. It's kinda like... I don't smell any fear on you. Not anymore."

"Well, thank the gods for that." I sniffed my armpits. "I still smell pretty rank though. Blood, shark guts, piss and puke."

"Well, don't get a big head. It'll throw that skinny body off balance."

I laughed and hopped off the car hood. I grabbed Kitsune and walked off the crumbling pavement to the rocky shore. Held her sheath in one hand, her in the other. Marveled at the dried blood coating her silver body. Bernard joined me. A dozen boats nodded against the docks to our right, gently slapping and creaking in the wind. The light ding of bells continues. I sheathed Kitsune.

"I think it's time to let her go," I said. Before I could decide otherwise, I hurled Kitsune like a javelin, straight into the dark embrace of the sea.

"Uh, you know the tide is just gonna wash that back," Burn said. "Seriously, you just threw evidence into the ocean right next to the crime scene."

Oh. Yeah, he's right. Again.

"Of course I am," Burn said.

Still doing that, huh? No matter now. We stood there, two friends, silent by the sea.

"You're kind of freaking me out," he said.

"Why?"

"Well, I don't want you to take this the wrong way, but I can tell that you're happy."

"Happy?"

"It's been years since I've seen it. Shit man, I kind of forgot what it looks like."

I faked a laugh and turned away, feeling wrong.

"Man, this place is dead," I said, hoping to change the subject. "You're right. Jefe really had his turf staked out. Not one siren, not one curious witness."

"Yeah, well, this place'll be jammed with hungry tourists and fishermen at dawn. It's going to be a real shitstorm when someone goes into the Tiburon tomorrow."

"Yes. That's still a huge problem. I've been wondering what they're going to do about that. I don't feel so confident in their planning anymore. It's pretty much rolling dice with hand grenades."

"Do you think Julio will really take over?"

"I guess so. Symbolically, at least," I said. "Logically, there is a gap to fill. People will want their little illicit chemical escapes, regardless of who pushes it. He already had the small time racket in Thornwood locked down. Don't see why he can't run the whole thing now. And then... he'll stick around. I like that."

"Remember that summer he stole a brick of opium from that mansion? We spent like every freaking night laying on the beach, burning that shit and getting all whacky. Barry got so fucked up he passed out naked on the golf course. Almost got arrested the next day. Ha!"

"Ha, yeah I remember when we finally ran out. And then spending two weeks feeling like I had the flu, and almost losing my job."

"Boy, those were the days."

"Right," I said. "Doing drugs and breaking the law. Real fun being idiots."

Bernard pushed the cigar on me again. He blew a perfect smoke ring, then tried to blow another through it, but a sharp breeze banished them both. "Yo, so... when I was looking at all those dead guys, and—"

"Did you recognize one?" I interrupted. Fear flooding my veins.

"Yes... I think so. But he was a dirtbag, and, uh... it's not worth, you know. Whatever."

"Okay."

"Anyway, listen, I saw that Savage Jefe guy's pants were *soaked* in blood. I mean completely drenched. And his mouth looked like it was stuffed. Did you see what the hell Julio did down there?"

I surveyed the landscape. A parking lot on the moon. Our own legend sewn in this boneyard. No one can ever know. New legends. "Well, right when I busted in there, he and this guy Desmond the Demon had Julio tied up. They were about to drill his eye out."

"Yeah?"

"So I just bust in there and wham! Slice Jefe's hand right off."

"The whole thing? Like Vader?"

"Uh, yeah kinda. Then I cut Julio free, and without a moment's hesitation, jammed my sword right into the other guy's gut."

"No shit? Damn, Tim, you missed your calling. You really should be a samurai vigilante. So why didn't Jefe just put a bullet in his head or a slit throat?"

"Well, you know what Jefe did to Julio, right?"

"Carved his eye out when he was a kid."

"No, Burn. He ate his eye. And then spit it back in Julio's mouth."

"Oh my god. That's so... savage." He cocked his brow.

"No shit. So me and Julio tie the bastard up. First Julio made him eat his own hand, then... Jeez, Burn, I don't want to relive this. It's too soon!"

He shoved me. "Come on, bro. Don't leave me hanging."

I swallowed, turned my back dramatically. Then I whispered, "Julio tore Jefe's cock off with his bare hands."

Burn leaned back, aghast.

"And then chewed it up. And spit in his face."

"Oh, fuck you!"

I laughed, long and hard. Like a rare lizard escaping a steel prison, delirious with relief and awe. Little tears squeezing out the corners of my eyes. Bernard waited patiently.

"Okay, Burn, I might be embellishing. Just a bit."

"Impossible!"

"Hey, I was in the murder storm tonight. I need to joke around a little. Give me that. I saw four with my own eyes."

"Three and a half. You didn't actually see Jefe die, right? Tim, your math is terrible."

Good. I like it that way. Chaos and pain unexplained.

Then we heard the puttering hum of a boat engine, gliding by in the darkness. Those nuts. No risk too mundane, I suppose. We ran back up to the docks to greet them by the bar, leaving the enemy's car abandoned.

Only one boat, the one they'd commandeered. Punk pirates. The boat slammed into the dock with a distinct lack of grace. It looked completely empty. We held our breath until Sergio's head peeked around the steering console, pale with fear. Even his shades were off.

"Tom! Bernard! Come here!" he hissed.

We dashed to the side of the dock, apprehension clawing at the nape of my neck. I nearly tripped on a life preserver.

"Where's Jay?"

"Hush, listen! The Marine Patrol was out there! They saw us light Jefe's boat up, and before we knew it, the Coast Guard had us in the floodlights with choppers flying in. Boys, you have to understand. Please believe me, I didn't have a choice. I had to do it!"

"Had to what?" I shouted. There it is, the sting of salt water, the Cursed barren sea creeping up while my guard was down.

"God forgive me, those noble boys were on the boat as I sped away," Sergio said. He hung his head. "Oh gracious, I'm sorry. It was still burning as I fled."

Dice and Hand Grenades

"You left them to die on the fucking boat!" I screamed. I lifted Boil's gun and clicked the safety off.

"Well, hold on now, I'd wager the fuzz picked them up before that!" Sergio ducked down.

Bernard has his head back, hands on face, elbows pointed at the heavens. He stumbled around in circles. "Oh my god, oh my god, oh my god. We're doomed. We're going away forever. We have to get out of here!"

"You rotten son of a bitch!" I screamed. "No good lousy rat bastard! You abandoned my best friend!" I kept the gun trained on the bow, even though I wasn't sure how to use the sights. "Give me one good reason I shouldn't hop up there and blow your fucking head off!"

And then the heavens cackle. A high pitched, giddy shriek, mocking my misfortune. The Curse.

"Damn, give this kid one taste of blood and look out! Killer instinct. Got ourselves a real fiend here!"

Boil...

I stood paralyzed as both Julio and Boil leapt out from opposite sides of the console, arms spread like goofy eagles. They fell back in gulping fits of laughter. My arms shook with rage and relief. I lowered the gun and screamed, "Fuck your mothers, you motherfuckers!"

They high-fived, climbed off the boat and began tying it up. Julio was still holding his sides as he spoke. "Damn, son! You got some bloodlust in you now, huh? So, anyone show up? Get to let out more anger?"

"No," I said, still feeling a raw mix of rage and relief. Pizza and raw meat.

"You ditch that car yet?" Boil asked.

"It's at the end of the dock," Bernard said.

"Good, good. I got to thinking maybe we could sell it or something," Boil said.

"Or just leave it alone. Let it be part of the mystery," Bernard said.

"We got so much money out of there anyway," Julio said. "We're set for a good minute."

"Set five ways?" Burn asked, a hint of timidity in his voice.

Everyone stared at him.

Boil was the first to speak. "Fuck do you mean *five* ways?"

"Yes, five ways," I told Boil. Then to Jay, "You brought me. You brought him. Sergio is going to cover our asses pro bono, right?"

We all walked back toward the bar. Stood around at the entrance in various states of bloody, sweat-stained, dirt-encrusted, beer-battered, tender disarray. Well, not Sergio or Bernard. But I'm sure there must've been some sort of psychic damage left on them... at least I hope. Maybe not the lawyer, but my buddy at least has a human heart.

"This is fucked up," he said, arms crossed. Brilliant deduction, Burn.

"He's right," I said. "Shit is going to hit the fan tomorrow morning. Come dawn, this isn't going to be Savage Jefe's personal little No Man's Land. It's going to be a crime scene with our prints all over it. Not even these police can overlook something this big."

"It's never going to be Jefe's nothing no more," Julio said. "And there ain't gonna be shit here by dawn."

Dawn. Just a few hours away. A few more hours, and this whole wicked night will be just another wretched memory etched onto our karmic wheels.

"Well, you can't keep away all the tourists and shark hunters." Burn thumbed towards the bar and docks. "You all are getting caught. No matter what, your prints *are* all over that place."

"Shit," Julio said. He rubbed his scruffy chin.

"I got an idea," Boil said, nudging Julio. "I didn't use it all on Jefe's boat."

"Use all of what?" I asked.

"Oh, no doubt! Hell yeah, son!" Julio fist bumped Boil.

"Hold up," Boil said. He walked off toward our hidden vehicles.

"What are you degenerates planning now?"

"Yo, we degenerates actually did think most of this through. We got it on lockdown. Sort of. Follow me."

"It was a pretty stupid plan from the start," I said, leading the parade behind him. "I can't believe I just hopped onto a..."

Suicide mission.

Julio pushed open the door to the shattered bar. We followed him in.

"Grab the metal crates and come downstairs. We'll stuff as much coke, pills, and cash as possible into them."

"These ones never got out," I said, kicking the sealed lizard crate.

"So let 'em out."

"Julio, what's Boil getting?" I asked as he singlehandedly swung an empty crate into my arms. I dropped the gun as it slammed into my arms. It went off. The floor splintered.

"Jesus Christ, Tim!" Jay shouted. "Don't you put the fucking safety on?"

Nearly threw my back out putting the crate down slowly. We surveyed the carnage. Bullet holes in the pool table, the shattered bottles, broken stools. One room, one silent vortex of violence. Then Jay got that crazy grin again, all teeth and no eyes. He's waiting for me to get it. Oh. The border boulder. The junk car. The possible concussion. Of course.

"Don't tell me you're going to—"

"Shit, homeboy, we already sank a boat," Jay said. He slapped my arm. "Why'd you think we were doing those tests in my yard?"

They had C-4 and guns and smuggled reptiles and drugs in the Jeep the whole time. But they were smoking and drinking with C-fucking-4 under the seats! Granted, I don't really know how it works, but still. Come on!

Yet, this truly is bigger than big.

But… well, it *is* a very small building. A known den of vice that will go un-mourned. But haven't we pushed it enough? They're going to blow up the entire bar? Then I see my hands, the maze of concentric lines slipping around the undersides that are all over god knows what in here, and I think: *Yes, yes, anything, burn it to the ground, blow it to the sky!* Burn it all down… just don't kill the pier.

We've certainly fallen before the Warped Old Ones by now. Khorne the Bloodless God, Tzeentch the Changer, Nurgle the Vizier of Decay, and Slaanesh the Princess of Excess. Why not just go for broke and let the greatest Chaos Deity gorge at our hands? That one, some simply call God.

Jay has pulled a boat fuel hose in through the back. Splashing the place with gasoline. He nearly douses Boil as the vet strategically places his putty white destruction. He shapes some mounds into little deadly dicks. I drag the final lizard prison out into the parking lot.

They're done prepping their fire show as I kick the crate on its side and order Burn to unlatch it. Acid freak lizards spill out into the ecosystem, skittering and scattering in every direction like prisoners set loose on a foreign moon. I'm certain that I've just spread another plague upon Sponge Island with all these kidnapped illegal aliens. We'll see how the fauna fares next year.

"Okay, boys and girls!" Boil ordered. "We're going to have to get the fuck out of here pretty quick!"

"I'll get the cars ready," Sergio said. He slipped away like an eel.

We stood there, the four of us, next to the Jeep and convertible, engines idling, hearts beating, a pretty damn good distance away. I assume. Silently waiting for Boil to detonate the blasting caps and ignite this sacrosanct temple to Tomahok's decadence. Boil's thumb over the button, but frozen with the rest of us, all knowing this brief moment of peace and respite would end in clouds of fire.

So this is it?

He clicks a button and that's the end? We just drive away? Drive to Barry. Lucky bastards. Their devil run is over. Fair's fair. I've seen so many angels fall from blinding heights. At this point... Yeah, at this point, screw it.

Burn the Sky

Boil grinned.

"Fire in the hole."

Click.

The explosion was magnificent.

Our shadows spasmed across the dock as the flames tried their damnedest to lick the sky. Movies taught me that cool guys don't look at explosions, they just walk away in slow motion. But real people run the fuck away as fast as they can.

And run we did, sliding into fetal curls behind the cars.

Debris rains down.

Wood.

Hunks of twisted metal.

Charred shark flesh.

Dried fish and glass.

Ash and stone and metal nails mixed with frying blood.

Damned miracle that nothing lit up the docks.

We danced and dodged as the lightest bits got thrown our way, landing in the bushes and dirt. Gravel stung like shrapnel, eating into our hunched backs as we spun about, arms overhead. The last bits of singed debris clattered to the docks, making light splashes in the water. A dry rain. The bar was now a crater, twisted black pillars of foundation and wood collapsing in on angry bits of fire. The smoke wafted up like a great formless god, a tornado burst from the planet's core. A black skeleton blown apart, falling in on itself. A fiery—

"Why didn't you boys just blow it up in the first place?" Sergio asked.

"Had to make sure Jefe was in there," Boil said.

"Needed to do this eye-to-eye," Julio said. Completely monotone again. No smile. Even his shoulders were still visibly tensed up.

"We're going to hell for this," Bernard said. "There is no way we're not going to hell for this. If you knew you were gonna blow this place up, why bother dumping the bodies at sea?"

"Well, now it looks like they just disappeared," Sergio said. "Although it's quite clear the gang was murdered, there's no physical evidence of them laying around here. All it takes is a few fingers, some clothing, or teeth. In the end… specifics aside, the operation makes sense."

"Fuck yeah, hombres!" Julio folded his arms and bit another cigarette. "You think there's a CSI: Sponge Island or something? No one gives a shit out here. They'll probably be glad there's a few less criminals to deal with."

"Fewer," Sergio said to no one in particular.

"You're all so sure this is going to work? We're not going to be in jail by Monday?" I asked.

"Think about it," Boil said. "A known drug dealer's den goes up in flames. He and his men are gone, without a trace. Including his boat. *Of course* the cops are gonna know something went down, but the bodies are going to be little chunks at the bottom of the sea by the time divers go looking, if they do at all."

"You'd better be right."

"Hey, bright eyes, you got anything new to add, now's the fucking time," he said.

Nope.

"No, this is your field. I just deliver books to hospitals."

"And make last-minute rescues!" Julio slapped me on the back. "The hell with it, man. Guys, I. Am. Fucking. *Tired.*" He rubbed his hand through his hair, smoothing the greasy locks back against his thick neck.

Sergio was already behind the wheel, ready to spin the tires. His smile was infectious. You could literally see how young he felt. Bernard leapt into shotgun. Julio and Boil were heading for his Jeep. I put my hand on his shoulder.

"Jay, look, I know it's been a long night," I said. "I won't hold it against you if you wanna cut out early. But you gave me your word. I know it sounds stupid, but I seriously need to see Barry. Right now. Just as bad as you needed this. I'm sorry, but you gave me your—"

"Hey, hey. I know. I gave you my word," he said, but his slightly shaking, bloodshot eye said enough. His cheeks were already scabbing over. We all were beat up and tired. Christ, when was the last time any of us ate something other than pills or booze?

"Oh, make no mistake, dear Julio. I am going." I tried the creepy head down stare again. No good. No matter. "I gave him my word, too."

He laughed. "Really?"

"Well, no, not formally, but all the same…"

"No doubt, I hear you. Yo, the thing is, you're right. But it's been a looooong, epic night. Assassination is hard work," he said. He rubbed his craning chin. "Honestly, I thought maybe I'd get smoked, and you'd just take my Jeep and run. Wouldn't blame ya. I mean, I said I'd drive you out there, and I could, but... I ain't in the mood to see Barry all hurt up after all this. I ain't in the mood for nothing right now. I don't know *what* to feel. And there's no way I can stick around long enough to drive you all the way there and back without bursting my heart on more uppers, so..." Julio dangled his keys before my face. "Get her back in one piece?"

"Just remember, *you* destroyed the radio," I said. I took the keys and smiled. Really, I did.

Julio waved at Boil. "Come on, Private Boil. We'll ride back with Sergio."

Boil shrugged. "Whatever. I don't need to visit that loser anyway."

"Wait, wait, wait," I said. "I'm not going all the way up to the hospital with a load of coke and god knows what else you have hidden in there. Shit, you were firing guns while Boil had explosives sitting under us the whole time! Clean that shit out!"

"Fuck, I'm not leaving anything with you!" Julio said. "Except this." He pulled out a wad of cash and stuffed it into my pocket. Neither of us knew how much. But it was a very thick wad. They'd cleaned that place out. Looked like he stuck a damned softball into the front of my pants.

"Well, that's a start."

"Fuck you, Yojimbo," Julio smiled, then mimed an epic sword swing. He started dancing around, miming a samurai duel.

"Okay, someday that has to stop." I tried not to smile again. Pulled out the cash and thumbed through it, trying to ignore the others, but stopped counting when I realized it was ALL hundreds and there were still many, many, bills to go. "Wow. It's a start..."

So all the crates were full of drugs and money now. Jay heaved one into the back of Sergio's convertible. Boil swung another in with one arm. When the Jeep was clear, clean, and pure, the only precious cargo left was Barry's briefcase of books. I tossed it into the passenger seat.

"I'll ride with you?" Bernard asked.

"Nice of you to finally show some damned interest."

He looked down and scrunched his lips. "Well, I just... you know I think..."

"Actually Burn, if it's cool, I need do this alone," I said. "No offense. And… well, you know why."

He grinned. It was kind of sad. "No prob, dude. It's cool. Hell, I'm beat anyway." He yawned, arms wide as they could go, then turned back to our cohorts. "What say we all head back to my place and roll a fat one?"

Your place? OUR place had better clean when… Ah, it's never clean.

Julio turned back to me and gave a short, sharp wave. "Be cool. Tell Barry I said what's up. And, uh, maybe don't tell him about all this… At least until he gets better? Don't want to stress him. You know how writers are."

Oh, I do. He'll create all sorts of crazy new stories once he's digested the reality of this. But plenty of time for that. My mission's not complete. There's enough to worry about right now.

"No worries!" I shouted. I stared at them, felt some strange twinge in my chest. That sense of a shared secret, the weird bond you'll relive on drunk Sundays, but keep close to the vest until the end of days. "Seriously, I don't plan on talking about this horrible debacle. Ever. To anyone."

"Good soldier." Boil saluted me, but then promptly flipped me off. He almost smiled. "Try not to suck his dick too hard. Poor guy's probably got a catheter stuck up it."

"Seems the Devil's Run is good and done," Sergio said to no one in particular. He cocked his head at me, about to say something else.

Suddenly Julio ran over, grabbed me by the hair, and gave me just enough time to open the door before he lifted me out for another beastly hug.

"Yo, Tim. For real, bro. You came through. Epic."

"For once. Ease up, you're going to fracture my ribs."

"Go finish your mission. Send Barry my love. No homo."

I had to laugh at his sarcastic return to our childhood vernacular. I gave him a fist bump. "Word, son. Mad crazy homo." Then it's gone. "Damn. Jay, are you sure got this?"

"Call me if you make it back."

"You know I don't have a phone."

"Well fuckin' go BUY one. Get a burner! We're hella rich now, dog!"

We sort of laughed, and he pulled more cash out and just tossed it at me. I snatched every single bill up. They were mostly ones. "Thanks…

Wait, what do you mean if?"

He smiled, evil and warm, but just walked back to the others. But then he looked over his shoulder, ever so slightly. "Bro. For real, I think she'd be…"

I looked away. Clenched my teeth and sat down. Then watched them pull away, drifting into the darkness of Tomahok, a red blur growing ever fainter. Every muscle in my body began to sag. So dry. Scratchy throat. The empty, smoking docks, scene of slaughter and celebration, now felt defiled and dangerous. Without that combined karmic charm of my companions, I felt terribly vulnerable. Alone.

I got back in Julio's Jeep, feeling the large depression he'd worn into the seat. Turned the key. Haven't driven since that Brooklyn night. My hand doesn't shake as it grips the wheel. Instead I savor the scratchy old leather cover. Pat Barry's briefcase.

Finally.

Hold on, Barry.

I'm finally coming. And I'm coming clean.

Deus Necros

Jay's Jeep shakes as I speed west on the empty morning highway, the wind over the vehicle slapping me in the face and cleansing the car of devil karma. Perhaps even my Curse. Why not, I've been damned lucky this far.

This night, now burning into dawn, is a pillar to strange and terrible business. But I don't feel anything. This kind of thing, the heating planet, the poverty, the crime and corruption and violence, has spread across the world like a virus. And all the way out here, there's something about a borderland that attracts more of the people, these hooligans getting high off danger and paint fumes. Normally, I don't want any part of it. And yet some lonely nights, I burn for it like a savage thirsting for water. But I can't even listen to loud music anymore, and I'm still pretty young. People my age are the ones who make that loud music, for Christ's sake.

Tonight, however, I got a taste. Tonight I had business, both strange and terrible. And now the morning comes to wash me clean. This is the time for rambling thoughts, as the miles melt away and the sun races around to creep up behind me yet again. Good night, glorious moon, whose cold face lights our darkest hours. Yet even with its stoic grace, the lunar lords merely reflect the light of Father-Mother-Sun. Yes, our sexless Sun god, send your red-orange rays of warmth to light my way! A trillion atom bombs exploding simultaneously every second, reaching me on this tiny water covered rock, as I speed down the highway that crippled Barry last week. I'm worn and ragged, yet burning with pride. I did right by one of my closest allies, and I'm about to do right by the closest of all.

I'm a freaking hero! It's going to be ridiculously hard not to tell Barry. Well, no, I'm the asshole who knocked up his little sister. I'm no hero. The night defrags and flashes across my inner eye, from the fox tattoo that still burns to the red flames licking the sky and my friends driving away. Did we balance the karmic spire, or are we yet to be balanced?

Screw it. Screw it all. Despite the satiated ego, my head nods and dips. My eyelids struggle to balance atop my bloodshot eyes. Need fuel, and have suspicions. I lean over and pop the glove compartment open. Sure enough, a little white vial. I pop the top, stuff it under my nose, take a deep whiff. The burn. Cold slimy throat. Brain's lighting up. The Caffeind takes hold, happy to dig his claws into his old slave. Not a big fan of hard drugs anymore, but after everything else, it's the least vice on my mind.

I speed past the places that have tormented me. Around Tomahok town, down the New Highway, around Thornwood proper, then the assorted high-class villas that blight the farmland before splitting off onto the Sponge Island Highway.

Velocitor's blessings propel me. Sheesh, to think I went through all that, just for this ride, this simple, simple thing. Struggled to just be somewhere else. I can't help but think of Julio's idea of fate, and whether or not that necessarily means things work out for the best.

So much pain and suffering stuffed into this sphere. And tonight, I have become the Genesis, or at the very least its slave. Grotesque cosmos, chaos void beyond my heart. I have done bad, bad things, yet I've rarely felt this good. Something happened tonight. Whatever it was, after three years of wet sand, foggy beaches, and gray skies, at least *something* happened. Some new life yawns before me, a hungry void to feed. Please, you've already devoured my past loves. Now nourish my future. Fill the hole the forest ghost left in me. Anything will do. We're all sustenance to one thing or another. Give and take. Ebb and flow of the great tide, the spinning moon dimpled disc around long-dead solar eyes. And I'm finally yearning to embrace all the lonely tomorrows to come.

So much suffering, yes. But I am blessed, to be selfish. To only feel my own hurt. Being numb to the terrible screaming they call silence. No, I can't be cursed. I am not worth a deity's lone attention. I am not poison. I don't destroy those I love. I'm not alone. Silly little shellfish, selfish hubris. The barren sea cannot exist. There are too many good souls lost. They must be somewhere. Curse or no, there isn't room in the universe for me to have a private, barren, water hell. Even if Barry ends up hating me, I'm still not alone.

No, if the Curse was real, then why did all those with me live through this wicked night? If I'd poisoned and killed all those before, why not Jay and Burn, or even Boil and Sergio? No, we won. All part of the plan.

Now my reward. To kneel at Barry's bedside and confess. Beg forgiveness. Accept his judgment. Whatever it may be.

Time passes. The Earth spins and warms. Miles melt into memories.

No music, only wind, and the early morning sounds of peace and tranquil half-sleep. The exit for the hospital draws near. Blue square, white H. This is it. Temple of healing, squealing, hope, and numbing pain.

Hawkhouse Hospital.

Park in the dew-tipped lot. Sunlight feels shameful without sleep. Saunter into the lobby with Barry's briefcase, looking like I showered in the ocean (head and arms at least) and smelling worse. It's time to burn and mutilate my past like Saint Julio has. To coat my skin in the ashes and rise like a one-winged phoenix. Don't worry, Tracy. You were always right. I can handle this. I won't let either of you down.

The receptionist is not pleased with my early arrival. Her coffee isn't even steaming. Bags under her eyes, blonde hair pulled back tight. She looks up from her forms for the barest moment.

"Sir, it's not visiting hours yet," she says, voice clipped and curt.

"What time is it?"

"Sir, are you serious? It's five in the morning."

"Okay. I'll just read in the waiting room until it's okay to go in. If that's okay. That's okay, right?" I asked. "I've traveled a great distance to be here. Surmounted many obstacles. Can't turn back."

She sighs, either ending or starting her day with my bullshit. "Your name, sir?"

"Timothy Gordon Dune."

"Which patient are you here to see?"

"Barry Cameron."

She looks for his name. Tapping at the keyboard, computer glow reflected in her glasses. I tap my foot and ignore that. People in blue pajamas and white coats roll withered bodies about. There is a slow eeriness to the day-lit lobby. As if everyone was gearing up for another day of emergencies, lost causes, and horror. But what about the good they do? Is that their fuel? Poor bastards, this place is dripping with nightmare fuel, smelling of pain and burnt skin, decay and sterility, lemons and piss, moans and drips, beeps and silent denials that either pray or deny that it's finally time. Makes flipping burgers look goddamned glamorous.

"Excuse me, Mr. Dune? You said Barry Cameron?" Her eyes roll back up to my awkward, frozen smile. "Visiting hours for the ICU begin at ten, but…" She bites her lip and cocks her head to the side. She squints at the chart. "Hold on for a second, please."

"ICU? No, he's not in the ICU. When I left, he was…"

She pages a Dr. Cardoso.

Cardoso comes down the hall, his white coat flying out like angel wings. He's a good guy. I recognize him from the night we rushed Barry in. The doctor that assured me Barry would recover in time. He's an ivory bat sweeping in from a rainforest of tubes and chemical saviors. Yet I suddenly feel like a big, juicy beetle with no shell. Scalp starts tingling. Bowels clench. An empty ocean roars within my skull.

He puts his hand out. I touch it, shaking like a ghost.

"Mr. Dune? You're here for Barry Cameron?"

"Yes, sir."

"Are you a family member?"

"Uhhhh, yes. Yes, I'm Barry's half-brother."

"Right, I remember you. You came in with Ms. Cameron. Listen, I'm glad you're here. We didn't have your number on record. How were you contacted?"

"Contacted? No, I don't have a phone, I just… He's expecting me. I think someone got confused, she just told me Barry was in the ICU now."

He looked down.

"We've been trying to reach someone since last night," he says. "No answer at his house."

"Yeah, he's mother's line is down. She's way out in the woods, no reception, so there's no cell service, no one else to—why?"

He sighs. Slips the clipboard into his armpit and puts his hands on my shoulders.

"I'm sorry, sir. Please, you may want to sit down."

The Idiot King

TODAY: Sunset

Back home, and done. Done with dreaming of that night with Tracy, done with Julio and Boil and Jefe. Done with... just waiting on Bernard for that coffee, because without it I'm sure to collapse over dead at any moment. A sludge pumping heart.

Out back on the beach once more, our garage shelter behind me. Wet sand. Foggy beach. The sky is gray. A truly bitter air for a summer day. But summer's dying. Crawling back down beneath the brittle brown leaves to slumber with cicadas and maggots.

I go back one last pathetic time and relive that first night with Tracy's kiss. Wake up to find a stale coffee cooled beside me. Sorry, Bernard. I sip it, determined not to let him down again. If he comes back.

Still haven't slept since last night. It's all been an illusion of the long night, one life. I ditched the clean shirt that Burn first borrowed, then tried to set fire to my worn out one, the black and white Hawaiian I'd worn for most of my life. Terribly ravaged, covered in blood and ghosts. It did not burn so easily. Eventually I resigned to tossing it into the waves and letting the tide take over. Unwrapped my tattoo. Blurry, red, but clear enough. Not infected yet. Still kind of looks like a fox face. Need to clean it soon.

All these rituals to push away the truth. I am a monster. Drinking the lifeblood of the Cameron line most of all. I think of Barry's crazy theories about souls, as I stand here, gripping his briefcase still full of his favorite books. Stories. His joy, his purpose. His gift. His life.

The beach is slowly eroding. Every year the shoreline is just a little closer. Waves rise and crash, and for the first time, they're mocking me. Swelling with promise, churning into frothy white water, reaching their peak, crashing under their own momentum. Scattering into nothing, diffused into the great salty sea. A tire floats by. A tire! A buoy cut free, red and white bobbing past. A fin briefly rises into view. The sun slowly dips.

I hope to god that there was some truth in all that crazy shit Barry said, about Byron J. Brick's soul filtering into him. Influencing his work.

The kindred spirit factor of the Great Magnet. One facet of the jewel reflecting upon another. There's a strange tendency among writers to think of themselves as visionaries, as judges, or of possessing some extrasensory faculty that makes them special. But all it boils down to is a stubborn retention of the newborn's fearful wonder at everything it sees. They are the child always asking "Why?" Stripped of the essential, precious human filter that lets us not be afraid of colors and cars and other things. Awkward vagabonds of the mindscape, both watchers and chroniclers, wishing to join the tribal games we celebrate.

I couldn't face Helena. Couldn't tell her the news. I don't even know if she knows yet. She must. She will. Here I go again, being a selfish prick. Thinking I'm the sole keeper of the secret knowledge of what's rightfully hers. I keep telling myself that her phone line will be fixed soon. On the way out, I told the hospital to keep trying. That I lied, that I'm just an old friend and have no contact with the family at all.

Family. Another word I don't like now.

We are strange beasts. We are not as our parents were, and our children will not be like us. Life is change. So is loss. But I'm not convinced that life is loss. They wouldn't want me living that way. No more. If Sergio keeps us free and I survive this, I will heed her words. I did not die with her, nor any of the others. Yet I fear I'll never quit waiting for that glint of moonlight, those strange sullen faces in the darkness. But now I've got nothing to lose.

It is not so liberating.

I look down. The briefcase. Knuckles white around the handle. It's getting dark. Too early. Well. Whatever. Here we are.

It's time.

So I dig my right heel into the sand, lift my left foot a bit, and begin the cosmic cartwheel. Spinning around, feeling the centrifugal force tugging, rising, higher and higher.

I let go.

The briefcase spins through the air. Farther than I ever imagined. A mighty hammer toss, worthy of our ancient origins. Once more there is no time. An infinite cascade of moments where Barry's world is suspended before the sun, before the gray fog overtakes us, before the ash-choked sea can swallow it whole.

I don't hear Bernard approach. He stands next to me, silent. Puts a cup of coffee in my hands. He went and made more after I'd slipped away from him into the past.

"I'm sorry," Burn says. "It's not your fault."

"Bullshit," I said. "Don't start with that. Yesterday you said it was all my fault, and you were right. Don't placate me."

"Sorry."

"Don't worry. I can handle it."

I never look at him, the purple rimmed ocean shooting up to envelop the blazing volcano core sun. The briefcase taking on water, gradually sinking, bobbing like a pleasant little seal. Wave goodbye. Still, in the end, here I stand, staring out to nothing at all.

"You know what, Burn? You were right. I am kind of happy."

"What?" He nearly spills his coffee.

"It is my fault, but now I know for sure. There's no room for doubt. I am indeed Cursed. No question. And I finally believe with all my heart that I truly deserve it."

Burn sighs. "So I guess I'm next then?"

"How's Jay?"

"Passed out. I didn't tell him yet. It can wait. Boil is still over at his place. He seems a little paranoid, keeps talking about someone named Emily. But mostly okay. I'm surprised you even give a shit."

"Doing my best."

"Said he's leaving for another tour soon. And Sergio took off, promising he'd be in touch after he's sure he's covered our tracks. Didn't seem fazed one bit. Asked me to remind you that—"

I must have made some kind of sound because Burn abruptly stopped.

"Are you going to say something stupid, like I'm not Cursed?"

"No." He sips his coffee again. "Belief is a powerful thing, ya know? If you think it's real, it's real, so maybe—"

I spun around at him and nearly screamed. "Do I need to point out the fucking evidence? Do I need to drag you to every grave?"

There were so many responses in his pocket. We could fight all night. He just looked away. I returned to the sea. That was uncalled for. Then again, I'm no hero.

"So."

Burn is silent, watching the briefcase bob in the tide. He points.

"You know that's just going wash right back," he says.

"Jesus Christ, Burn. I hope so." I spit at the sea. "They kicked me out when I started to freak. I couldn't even watch. Alone in the end, just like she was."

Bernard sips his coffee again. I just hold mine limply by the lid. Neither of us look at the other. My eyes are extremely dry. Can feel the veins cracking across them.

"Hey, I'd have freaked too. Tim, when you're ready to talk—"

"I'm ready." My words are dry and sharp.

"Okay," he sighed. Scared. "Was it quick?"

"It was... abrupt. There was no countdown. It just happened."

"If you think about it—"

"It was quick."

"No, I mean..." he stutters. "Well, I just mean, you did it. You made it in time."

"I guess."

The humid fog. Like ghosts floating down to our clammy skin, sinking in. I rub my eyes and cough. Bernard shuffles his feet down under the sand.

"So, tell me what happened."

Disintegration

I'm escorted to the Intensive Care Unit. Fluorescent, private tomb. The room's smell turns my stomach. A heady disinfectant air to cover the sick and broken. Damn it, Barry. Why'd you go and let your condition get worse while I was out treading hell and high water to bring you these... to come to you.

He's alone. One other empty bed in the room. And he's a mess. A carefully manicured and controlled heap of life and pain. A shock of red hair, bleary eyes, and pale freckles smiling up from a bionic grip of wires and tubes. No mincing words here. That accident has fractured and twisted him. I thought you get better in hospitals. Barry. Sitting here for a week, morphine drip, drip, drip, all alone. His distant, disturbed mother, dead sister... and me, his lousy excuse for a spirit brother, away on his own private painscape.

We're left alone.

Tubes in his nose make me listen to him breathe. No rhythm. Bags drip human nectar into his withered arms. He wasn't this skinny before. I sit down next to him and place the briefcase on the floor between us. The loud clack against the tile wakes him.

Sometimes protection hurts. Right, babe?

"You made it," Barry said. His voice is like parchment, softly disintegrating in the wind. Eyes half open.

"Good god, man, look at you," I said. "You look like shit."

His brittle laugh tumbles into coughs. Eyes fully open now.

"And you smell like shit," Barry said. "Oh, I think I'm going to throw up."

"Come on, Barry, you can do better than that. I smell like shit? Really now, describe my offensively pungent odor."

He really did throw up. Somehow I knew which metallic bowl beside the bed to stick beneath his chin. He sighed, looked up at the ceiling, blew some more air out.

He stared at the ceiling for a long time.

"Okay, Tim. But you literally smell like shit. And raw meat. Sweat.

Chicken soup. Rotten fish. Dead skunk? Like you just crawled out of a grave."

"That's more like it." I leaned back. "Jay and Burn say hello. They'd have come with me, but... it was kind of a hectic night, and they planned to come another—uh, hey! I got your books! Your mom nearly took my head off in the process. She still hates me."

"No she doesn't. She just doesn't like you," he said. Always smiling. Glassy eyes. "What'd you bring me?"

"Only the best," I said. I put the briefcase on my lap and unclasped it. I fumbled through the random selection, pausing to read each title. "I got, um... *Maze of Alien Intrigue*, *Splintermind*, and uh... some others."

"Those are good," Barry said. "All they have here are stupid tabloid magazines and reality TV."

"No Paradox Layers in here yet, huh?"

"Nah."

"They'll regret it after you blow up." I smile and he doesn't. "How do you feel?"

"Tired. Blood hurts."

"Ha. Yeah, sometimes I feel like all my cells are made out of sand."

"Yeah. What did you do tonight? Or last night. Whatever..."

"Holy shit, Barry. It's one king hell of a story. But I don't want to wear you out with it right now. I still need time to decompress it anyway. Let's just say Julio fulfilled a long-foretold prophecy. And the Tomahok ecosystem is about to be ravaged by an avalanche of endangered Iraqi lizards."

Got some emotion out of him on that one. He's sitting up a little, turned toward me now.

"Wow. Assuming you're not lying as usual, that's intense. Well, I have the time."

He doesn't know. Or he does. Or he doesn't believe. Fuck.

"Sorry man, I just can't right now. It's a really long story. You'll laugh when you hear it. I got beat up pretty bad, drugged, and crapped my pants."

His laugh collapsed into another round of coughing.

"So a night worthy of fiction? Think I can get a good story out of it?"

"Yeah, maybe. If you wrote it. It doesn't make enough sense. Heck, I even saw Lucas Boil."

"Oh lord… Why?"

"Yeah, it was… interesting. We actually hung out for a bit. He's not all bad, you know. He's a father."

"Really?"

"Yeah man, full-on. Little girl named Emily. Who'd have thought? Anyway, he sends his regards." I swallow. He's still staring at me with that dopey grin. "How many meds are you on now?"

"Enough," he said. He stared back. Eye to eye, I watched the brightness fading. "Tim, you seem different."

"It's the drugs."

"No really, something about you… Your face is better. You're… ugh…"

"What's wrong?"

"I'm fine."

I took a breath and folded my arms. I stared at the floor as I began.

"The hell with all that. We got other shit to talk about."

He looks at me, so still, curious, no hint of malice or suspicion. Just waits. Need to do this carefully, with eloquence. Yeah, Tim. Fake it. Right. Okay.

"Barry, I'm sorry," I say, looking at the floor, at the curtains, the IV needle, the hanging bags, the tubes, anything but him. "I never should have told you to get out of my car."

"Ah, don't even think about it, Tim. You can't… you can't live with that kind of attitude."

"No. Shut up and say it. You wouldn't be here if it wasn't for me."

His smile faded. He still faced me, but his eyes shifted to the wall.

"Okay. I wish you'd let me stay in the car. I don't know why you thought I could even help. You know I'm no good with cars."

"Good. Good. Okay, look. I don't even know how to preface this. I'm just going to say it. Okay? I'm just going for it."

His eyes shifted back. I bite my lip and a bit of blood pops up on my dried out lips. He's still waiting. The beeps on his monitors remind me that there is nothing that's actually silent.

"Barry, I…" I'm terrified. Jefe and his gang were nothing compared to these next few words. And… here we go. "Barry, I was in love with Tracy. Not was, am. I'm still in love with Tracy. And she loved me, too."

He blinked so slow.

"And… and… I'm so sorry I wasn't there to stop her that night. I

414

was supposed to protect her. We never did drugs like that. We'd read and—"

"Tim…"

"And she was my first. I swear to god. The other girls I told you about, at school, those were all lies. Tracy was my first and only. That's why I didn't go to her funeral. I couldn't take seeing her face like that, all stone and ice. That's the last way I remember my mom. It overshadows every memory. I can't think of my mom without seeing her there like a doll. And I imagine my dad out there, drowning and… I just couldn't take that again, and I—"

"Tim…"

"And god help me, everyone kept saying it, and I wouldn't listen, but I know she really was pregnant. And you have to trust me. I know it was mine."

"Tim, please…"

"And your mother really does hate me, and I don't blame her. And I'd give anything, *anything*, to have her back. God help me, man, I'm *still* in love with her. I can't let it go. I'd rather have her back than my m-m-mom and d-dad—"

"Tim!"

I finally looked up at him.

"Tim, I know," he said. A soldier's smile. "Come on, man, how stupid do you think I am?"

I laughed. The kind of weird hiccupping laugh that threatens to collapse into a sob.

"Oh shit, there's more," I moaned. I wiped snot away. "I fucking hate you. I love you and I hate you. I'm so jealous of you. How you move on. Your talent. You always were, all of you, always were my family. All of us, Burn, Jay, like… it was nice. I wanted to be a part of everything so bad. I had all these plans, and it's all just slipping away. And now look at what I've done to you! You're—"

"Is that it?" Barry asked. "Is this what's been killing you all these years? Why were you so afraid to tell me?"

I stood up, if only to collapse properly. I fell forward, catching myself on his bed's guardrails.

"Because I'm such an asshole. Look at this! This situation *right now*. You're on the brink of… of… and it's my fault. It's my fault, and don't you dare pretend it's not. And yet somehow I've still made this all about me. You're the one suffering, and I've somehow made this whole damn thing about me." I shot up, turned my back to him and walked to the window. "You know, I almost didn't come here because it was too much of an inconvenience? What the hell was I thinking? What am I doing that's more important than being by your side? And what's more, the real reason Julio and Burn aren't here is because I didn't want them to be. I wanted this moment all to myself so I could come clean with you, instead of thinking about what you wanted."

Barry coughed. "I bet you're thinking about asking for some of my morphine too?"

I turned around and saw through his eyes. My dirty, red, streaked face. The muscles finally relaxing after all these years. The start of wrinkles. Some gray hair.

"That'd be nice," I said.

"Go ahead, just slip this IV into your arm," he joked, limply lifting his arm toward me. "Hey, are those Tracy's old pants?"

"No. Yes. No. Yes, yes they are." I returned to the seat by his side. "Barry, I've known you my entire life. You're the best friend I could have ever asked for, and I've treated you like dirt. I put you here. You let me into your life like a brother, and I fucked your sister and knocked her up behind your back, and didn't ever have the balls to—please, just… react."

"What do you want me to say?"

"That you hate me. Say, 'Tim, you're a liar and scumbag! You've betrayed my trust and lied to my face. You don't deserve my friendship!'"

He turned his head away. Each second slipped into dry infinity, waiting for him to speak.

"I don't hate you. I couldn't be happier for you. I'm sure if Tracy had lived… I couldn't be more proud that my sister saw all the goodness in you that I do. I'm… Tim, I'm relieved to finally know what I always hoped. You were the father. Because you would have helped each other do the right thing. Love, friendship, it's a two-way street, man. You haven't just taken, you know? And you're right, we are family."

"You really don't hate me? Not even a little, tiny bit?"

"Reality is subjective to perception," he said.

"Uh…"

"Okay, how about… Things are not what they appear to be, nor are they otherwise."

"That's better. What is it?"

"Surangama Sutra."

The sunlight spits through the window, cracking off my eye. "That other thing you said, in the car. About a grain of sand and rocks…"

"Yeah? Pretty sure it's some old Buddhist thing."

"It helps. Crazy. Crazy enough for me. This guy Sergio talked about—fuck it. Yeah, crazy. I've been going crazy. The littlest things stress me out so bad. I'm freaking out twenty-four seven. No car, no phone. I'm broke. My parents are dead. Tracy's dead. You're—I keep having these racing thoughts and thinking they're just in my head, and then it turns out I'm saying them out loud. Terrible things, weird fucked up things. Some really awkward, embarrassing shit, only to find out I'm sitting there *actually* saying it. I can't feel my heart no more. Like I have tar and piss in my veins. I'm seeing *ghosts*, man. Ghosts."

"Parents?"

"No."

"Tracy."

"Yeah. But it could have been a hallucination. Still, I think I talked to her last night. At the old fire pit. She said she'd visited you too, because of course, I thought she'd only come to me." Barry looked away. "Did she?"

"I've noticed the talking thing," Barry said. "Tim, you've always been crazy. It's okay. Chill out. You'll probably only get worse as you get older."

"Older," I repeated. "How old are you?"

"What? Twenty-seven? What's your point?"

"Isn't it funny how each year we get closer to thirty, your age means less and less? It used to be the most important thing in the world. Until about twenty-one. Then BAM, straight downhill."

"Uh, it doesn't *have* to be," Barry said. "That's your problem, man. You're neurotically pessimistic. Legendary. But you're holding yourself back."

"By the way, you're actually twenty-eight. Your birthday is July 15th. But mine's in February, so I'm still older. Loser."

"Ha. Guys don't remember each other's birthdays, Tim. That's very touching," Barry said.

I wrung my hands together. Threw my head back. "How do you do it, man? How do you take all these hits and just lie there and smile? How the fuck do you keep adapting?"

"Morphine."

"Just say it, Barry! For fuck's sake, just *say it*. Tim, you ruined my life. Tim, you're a selfish piece of shit, and you've taken everything I ever had to give. Tim, I hate you!"

Veins popped out of my forearms, fingers clutching the armrests like desperate pythons. More wetness on my forehead now. Sweat stinging my eyes.

"If that's what you really want, I'll say it. But I hate lying."

"Okay then. Okay," I released the bedside and put my hand on top of his. It was too clammy, and the IV was in the way. "What do you want, Barry? Just tell me that. Please. Anything. I'll give it you."

For the first time I notice how much weight he's lost. A whole other chaos struck him while I ran and fought, bitched, cried, whined and soared. He looks so tired. Beyond pale. Translucent and far too sleepy. I've never watched disintegration. It's always been BOOM. Things are gone.

"Barry?"

I couldn't hear him the first time.

"I don't want to die."

"I'd trade places with you in a heartbeat if I could."

"No, you wouldn't." His pale cracked lips parted into a perfect smile.

"Ah, you know me too well," I said. "You're the only one."

He's quiet. Beep. Drip. Beep. Drip.

"Aria Dune," I said.

He closed his eyes and nodded. That smile took a lot of effort, but it was real. I wiped his one tear away. He kept his eyes closed as he spoke.

Wasn't afraid of that beeping until it started to slow. But I heard the practiced panic racing toward the room. Time slows, dies. I sat down again, close enough for him to whisper. He let me put my hand behind his neck. He let me. Talk, man. Talk! Keep him going.

"Barry, remember that time…"

"You know, it's funny," he coughed, each one fading lower. "It's kind of funny. A shitty night at the diner. And then a long ride back home with a real jerk-off. Stuff like that can actually be… be one of the best nights of your life."

"Seriously? Barry, that robbery, and the crash? All of… of *this?*"

"Yeah, Tim. That—that was a good night."

"How?"

"It didn't feel like an ending."

Victor Giannini is a 32-year old, naïve, hypocritical author. Rumored to live somewhere in New York, he's also a visual artist, quite short, and covered in scars. He's devoted his life to writing in all forms, striving to tell stories that show us:

"We live in a world where evil can be intelligible, but justice is still desired. Sorrow can be endured, and love remains possible."

Since 1998, his short stories, articles, novellas, non-fiction, illustrations, artwork, comics, skateboards, embarrassing fan-fiction, reviews, and even clothing designs have been featured in a large variety of venues, but most were published just this past decade. In 2012, he earned an MFA in Creative Writing and Literature from Stony Brook

Southampton. *Counselor* is his first major novel, and fourth publication with Silverthought Press. For a full bibliography, please visit his website.

Victor continues to hone his craft, hoping to honor all those he's learned from, assisted, and even worked with. Being quite proud and humbled by the extensive list of mentors, friends, and heroes who've tolerated him, Giannini is honestly too terrified to risk leaving even a single one out of any list...

Giannini also teaches creative writing, most recently for The Young Artist & Writer's Program, but he's also taught pre-school and various classes in circus-skills, skating, martial arts, graphic art & design, and after a mere 16 years, he managed to earn a Black Belt in Street Combat Ju-Jitsu. He's also a passionately awful skateboarder.

Victor's favorite color is sand, favorite food is the moon, and favorite music is good. He worships cats but fears insects. His spirit animal is a fox born from blue flames. Although Giannini insists he's too busy—and certainly not lonely—please feel free to email him at: Victor.Giannini@gmail.com.

Thank you!
Seriously.
Thank you.